THE EXPLODED HEART

BY JOHN SHIRLEY

NOVELS:

Transmaniacon
Dracula in Love
Three-Ring Psychus
City Come A-Walkin'
The Brigade
Cellars
In Darkness Waiting
Kamus of Kadizhar: The Black Hole of Carcosa
A Song Called Youth:
       Eclipse
       Eclipse Penumbra
       Eclipse Corona
A Splendid Chaos
Wetbones
City Come A-Walkin' *(revised)*
Silicon Embrace *(forthcoming from Mark V. Ziesing Books)*

SHORT STORY COLLECTIONS:

Heatseeker
New Noir
The Exploded Heart

PRODUCED SCREENPLAYS:

The Crow

John Shirley

THE EXPLODED HEART

with a foreword by
Bruce Sterling

SF eyeball
BOOKS

ASHEVILLE, NC

THE EXPLODED HEART

Foreword © 1996 by Bruce Sterling

Cover design by Rick Berry

Cover illustration © 1996 by Rick Berry

Book design and typography by S. Patrick Brown

Printed in the United States

*The stories in this book have been revised
from their original publication.*

"What He Wanted" © 1975 *Amazing Stories*
"Tricentennial" © 1976 *Portland Scribe*
"Shadow of a Snowstorm" © 1977 *Amazing Stories*
"Cold Feet" © 1975 *One Dollar Magazine*
"Fragments of an Exploded Heart" previously unpublished
"Seams" © 1982 John Shirley, from the record album *Obsession*
"Parakeet" © 1982 *New Pathways*
"The Incorporated" © 1985 *Asimov's Science Fiction*
"When Enter Came" © 1990 *Yellow Silk*
"The Prince" © 1991 *When the Music's Over,* edited by Lewis Shiner
"V, H, and You" © 1991 *Zyzzyva*
"Where It's Safe" © 1994 *The Earth Strikes Back,* edited by Richard T. Chizmar
"A Walk Through Beirut" © 1991 *Newer York,* edited by Lawrence Watt-Evans
"Epilogue to The Exploded Heart" previously unpublished
All song lyrics © 1996 John Shirley

PUBLISHED BY

Eyeball Books
P.O. Box 18539
Asheville, NC 28814

First printing June 1996

ISBN 0-9642505-0-0
Library of Congress Catalog Card Number: 96-84838

0 9 8 7 6 5 4 3 2 1

For my wife, Micky

CONTENTS

Foreword by Bruce Sterling   1

What He Wanted   11

Tricentennial   53

Shadow of a Snowstorm   65

Cold Feet   91

Fragments of an Exploded Heart   97

Seams   119

Parakeet   129

The Incorporated   155

When Enter Came   177

The Prince   197

V, H, and You   225

Where It's Safe   239

A Walk Through Beirut   261

Epilogue   291

Aftermath (Song Lyrics)   299

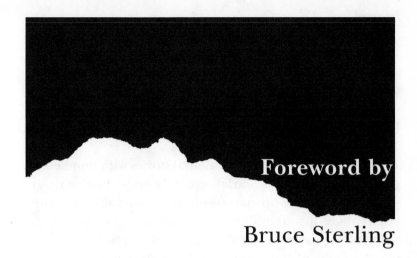

Foreword by

Bruce Sterling

I KNEW THIS GUY JOHN SHIRLEY when he was the first and only punk science fiction writer in the world.

Back in those days, William Gibson was a hobbyist teaching-assistant who was whiling away his youth, in his ivied, meditative fashion, in Canadian junk shops. I was an engineer's kid from a smoggy refinery town who had had my head utterly twisted by three years in India and was hanging out with cowboy-hatted interstellar longhairs deep in the heart of Texas. Rudy Rucker was futilely trying to pass for normal as a math professor somewhere in upstate New York. Lewis Shiner was enamored of hardboiled detective fiction and living in Dallas.

But John Shirley loomed on the horizon like some prescient comet. The rest of us paid a lot of attention to him. We were right to do this.

Most of the science fiction writers who later got called "cyberpunks" are and were, at heart, really nice middle-class white guys. They have some pretty strange ideas, but in their private lives they dress and act like industrial design professors. John Shirley was a total bottle-of-dirt screaming dogcollar yahoo.

1

There were still a few New Wave people around at the time earnestly writing stories with hippie protagonists. The people in John Shirley stories weren't hippies. They weren't progressive. They didn't mean well. People in John Shirley stories were canaille. They had no brakes. They didn't know what brakes were.

Other people wrote experimental stories with numbered paragraphs, but John Shirley wrote "stories" that were so profoundly fucked-up narratively that you could feel the guy's fingertips trembling spastically on the keyboard. Some of the more daring sf writers of the period were testing the limits of the genre. For John Shirley the limits of the genre were vague apparitions somewhere in his rearview mirror.

Science fiction is a genre by and for bright people who feel a tad ill at ease in bourgeois society, a tad under-socialized, but also a tad inventive. . . . Nice people, really. You get used to them, they have a lot to offer, these insect-eating Mensa-freak people who like making puns about neutrinos while they sip ginger ale in the con suite. John Shirley was never like that. John Shirley in his early days was the kind of guy who was visibly orthogonal to the human species.

I share certain deep and lasting commonalities with John Shirley. We're very near the same age and we've shared some crucial generational experiences. Harlan Ellison was a guru of mine and was kind enough to commission and publish my first novel. Harlan Ellison was utterly enraged with John Shirley and once publicly challenged him to a duel. I once angrily walked out on a bad panel at a science fiction convention. John Shirley liked to topple over the tables at science fiction conventions and wallow howling in the crushed ice where the fans had hidden the beer. I listened to a lot of punk music. John Shirley wrote, performed and recorded punk music.

I think that drugs are an intriguing social and tech-nomedical phenomenon. John Shirley had serious drug habits. I got married and had a kid. John Shirley has been married four or five times and has three kids by two different women. I've written nine books. John Shirley has written more books than I can count, a lot of them under pseudonyms. I once wrote a book with William Gibson. John Shirley is the guy who convinced William Gibson that writing science fiction was a good idea.

I'm kind of interested in military stuff. John Shirley was joined the Coast Guard. I took some martial arts classes. John Shirley had a beer bottle broken over his head in a bar brawl. I've moved house twice in the last seventeen years. John Shirley has moved about seventeen times in that same period. I travel in Europe quite a bit. John Shirley has lived in France.

The typical Bruce Sterling fan is a computer-science major in some midwestern technical university. "Stelarc" is a John Shirley fan. Stelarc is an Australian performance artist who has an artificial third hand, sometimes bounces lasers off his eyeballs, and used to suspend his naked body in midair by piercing his flesh with meathooks. I had lunch with Stelarc recently. I was surprised at how much I enjoyed Stelarc's company and how much he genuinely reminded me of John.

People are sometimes a bit intimidated by my fearsome cyberpunk-guru reputation, until they get to know me. John Shirley writes ghastly horror novels that scare the living crap out of people. A lot of people are pretty scared by John Shirley. When such people actually meet John face-to-face, they become more scared.

It may be that it all boils down to this: I am a professional science fiction writer who happened to get called a "cyberpunk." John Shirley is a uniquely authentic avatar of the weltanschauung.

John Shirley has written brief introductions to all these stories. Like the stories themselves, these introductions are abrupt, brutal and confrontational. You might get the impression from these disturbing introductions that the author must surely be a shattered wreck of a man, a moaning veteran of convulsive debaucheries whose wizened Dorian Gray portrait appears next to the term "karmic retribution" in the dictionary. Actually, John Shirley is in excellent condition. He's a lithe blond six-footer who could bite nails in half. He's as hard to kill as a cactus. I live a life of conspicuous cleanliness, and John Shirley could probably break my back like a twig.

These are weird stories. There aren't many jolly stories in this book. In point of fact, though, John Shirley is a very funny guy. He laughs a lot and easily, and never stands on ceremony. He feels things very deeply, a lot more deeply than I ever have, but there's no neurosis in him. Whatever it was that John was venting in these stories, it seems to have been good for him. John has never committed the serious literary crime of hiding his light under a bushel. Bushels placed upon John Shirley will explode into livid flames. He's had his share of troubles, but whatever troubles the world has given John have always been repaid immediately and in spades—and the world is a better place for it.

I could go on about my good friend John and these stories, but I've gone on enough. There's just one more matter. As it happens, this particular John Shirley book contains what is, to my mind, the ultimate John Shirley sentence. Here it is:

> Trying not to wonder where the crosshairs were centered, they climbed gratefully from the rancid, moldering underground into the sloppy heat of the summer night.

If you're the kind of perceptive reader who can fully savor the myriad virtues of this wonderful sentence, then this is the book for you. John Shirley can do things for you and to you that nobody else in the world has the nerve to do.

February 27, 1995
Austin, TX

Here comes Johnny Yen again
with the liquor and drugs
and the sex machine
he's gonna do another striptease . . .

—IGGY POP, "LUST FOR LIFE"

. . . I am now about to become a professional writer, yet having no
practice at all either in respect of all the established professional rules
and procedures or in respect of what is called the "bon ton literary
language," I am constrained to write not at all as ordinary "patented
writers do," to the form of whose writing you have in all probability
become as much accustomed as to your own smell. . . . Such a blessing
arose and now flourishes everywhere on earth thanks to that extraordinary new disease of which for the last twenty to thirty years . . .
the majority of those persons from among all the three sexes fall ill,
who sleep with half-open eyes and whose faces are in every respect
fertile soil for the growth of every kind of pimple. This strange disease
is manifested by this, that if the invalid is somewhat literate and his
rent is paid for three months in advance, he (she or it) unfailingly
begins to write either some "instructive article" or a whole book. . . .
I am in general not writing so as to make a career for myself, or so as
to plant myself, as it is said, "firm footedly," thanks to this profession,
which, I must add, in my opinion provides many openings to become a
candidate d-i-r-e-c-t for "Hell"—assuming of course that such people
can in general by their Being, perfect themselves even to that extent,
for the reason that knowing nothing whatsoever themselves, they write
all kinds of "claptrap" and thereby automatically acquiring authority,
they become almost one of the chief factors, the totality of which
steadily continues year by year, still further to diminish the, without
this, already diminished psyche of people.

—G.I. GURDJIEFF,
"ALL AND EVERYTHING: BEELZEBUB'S TALES TO HIS GRANDSON"

They say no one person can do it all
but you want to in your head
But you can't be Shakespeare
and you can't be Joyce
so what is left instead
You're stuck with yourself
and a rage that can hurt you
You have to start at the beginning again . . .
As you pass through fire as you pass through fire
try to remember its name

—LOU REED, "MAGIC AND LOSS"

The Exploded Heart

What He Wanted

I was nineteen, and I was naked, walking through a class of freshmen college students: a drawing class, where I was posing nude for $20. I couldn't understand (truly, I mean it, I *really couldn't*, back then) why the pupils all seemed so uncomfortable when, after I was allowed to break from my pose, I went to look at the drawings people made of me. Why they were bothered when I stood next to their desks, stark naked, my exposed, uncircumcised dick wagging as I bent to look, my scrotum brushing their arms, the stink of my proto-punk post-Zappa-freak body making their nostrils twitch. I honestly couldn't understand why the teacher was signalling me frantically to get away from the students . . .

I was pretty out of it. When I was nineteen, I was immunized against work. Which was just as well because I was so unsocialized I was unemployable anyway. I did some illegal things for money, and also sold blood, and got the art class gig, and collected social security for going to college which I never much showed up for (maybe went to three months worth of classes total); attending classes would have been (for me then) unspeakably bourgeois, philistine, square. I wanted, as John Lydon later sang, "to be anarchy."

I wrote the first draft of "What He Wanted" that same 1972; the final draft was published about 1975 in Ted White's version of

Amazing. The story makes it clear just how *outside* I felt. Only the circumstance of my going to the Clarion writer's workshop prevented my getting farther outside: Clarion gave me an alternative; it saved me from burglary, prostitution, further knifings, and probably prison.

A RECENT *IMAGE MAGAZINE* ARTICLE about the Rave Scene in San Francisco quoted one young patron of the underground clubs as follows: "The scene is a gathering of youth to engage in ritual dance and techno-shamanism for the dissolution of alienation . . . using the technology of the System . . ." Another kid said, "It's a shamanistic tribal religious experience." That's in 1992. In 1972, when I was nineteen, I wrote "What He Wanted." It took me a couple of years to get it into print. This is not surprising since the story's narrator, our "hero," is emotionally arrested (but so was I), hostile (so was I), a bit jejune (so was I), and generally just not likeable (me too, probably). It was hard to get a story published in the science fiction field if it didn't have a "sympathetic" hero. Damon Knight and others patiently tried to explain this to me. What reader wants to identify with a vicious S.O.B.?

Well. I was reading Artaud and Genet and Selby and William Burroughs and J.G. Ballard and Baudelaire and Celine, and not much Larry Niven or, I don't know, Heinlein say, so I just didn't get it. And I would have liked Dunbar fine, back then— I was a pretty twisted kid myself. But Aaron Dunbar wasn't so very atrocious, beneath the surface; he was tormented and all too vulnerable.

This story was most definitely a punk statement, before the official emergence of punk.

I was a rock fan, of course, because that was where the energy and the Attitude was, and, besides the Doors and the Stones and the Animals, I was very much into the harder bands like the Stooges, the Velvet Underground and MC5, and the more bizarre acts like Alice Cooper and Zappa and Beefheart, as well as some of the early metal bands. There was a bit of Zappa in Whistler, and a lot of Iggy Pop, Jim Morrison, and Arthur Brown, and some Alice and Ozzy (Osborne, not Nelson).

There are satirical elements to the story, as in most of my early stuff. The awkward term "agony rock" was supposed to be a joke, and of course there was the more obvious satire, e.g. the leather-clad Jeezus Freak gangs.

Aaron Dunbar's world was a kind of surrealistic, cruelly alien-ated variation of the Rave Scene. He—and I, a rock fan and an amateur anthropologist—understood shamanism instinctively. The story showed my age on some levels, but it began an exposi-tion that was important to me, and it was written in a delirium of inspiration. . . .

The story resonates with the first seeds of the protopunk crystallization at the end of 1972. "I'm a street walkin' cheetah with a heart fulla napalm . . ."

When the music's over, turn out the lights.
—JIM MORRISON

MOST PEOPLE NOTICED HIS EYES FIRST. His eyes were shad-owed and cateye green and they went through you like a searchlight through fog. Even when he wasn't deified on stage, people on the street would comment on "the funny look that guy gave me." His stare. The rest of his face was constantly animated while his eyes seemed to be fixed on *something* no one else ever saw. No one else except me.

His name was Samuel Whistler and when I met him at Eggman's party it was only by proxy; he was stamped into the grooves of a black vinyl disc. He was lead musician and composer for an agony rock band called *Whistler.* I had never seen him or heard his music until the first night. The first night of the Submerged Apocalypse. He was smeared all over the magazines, and TV, but I had given up reading newspapers and magazines after my parents, my dear father the publisher whose fingers are dirty with newsprint ink, canceled my subscriptions and stopped sending college money. I canceled my subscription to my old man and his drugged half-zombie third wife, that same day.

Tension churned the arabesques of smoke at Eggman's party. The party-goers were faceless blobs, but the smoke-patterns became leering faces as I came in the front door. A few people acknowledged my coming by leaving the room. The rest tried to ignore me. But a sneer curled around a red-eyed joint: "Oh fuck, Dunbar is here. We begin the downhill slide." Hearing that, I smiled.

I wore virgin-white leotards that night. I made sure they noticed me: I walked like a cop, with a painted-on blood-stain for a badge. Sleeping downer freaks, corners itching with couples or triples under blankets, dopers squatting in cathartic clusters doing unfunny imitations of professors they didn't like. Typical college crowd, 1998.

City traffic sounds honked from the record player. Conversation like a wasp trapped in a bottle.

And there was a telephone booth in the center of the Persian rug, six people smoking kif crammed into the booth with the door shut. Eggman had spent an evening with some friends stealing the booth from a park. I put a bicycle lock around the booth's doorhandles so that it couldn't be opened from the inside. A black light in the booth made the smoke luminous ectoplasm. Realizing they were locked into the booth, they began to rock it back and forth, screaming at me to let them out. The booth fell over onto one side, shattering glass panels. I thought I saw Lucy's face in the shattered glass on the floor. One of the girls in the booth was screaming at the top of her lungs, blood from a glass shard, her cheek secretly cut by Lucy's. I left the room fast.

I went to the party annex in Eggman's basement. Larry Eggman's bedroom-dungeon was decorated in heavy chains dangling from the black and red painted walls and ceiling, and with iron bars jutting at dangerous angles, dull blades protruding from corners. He knew the way through the maze reflexively without once brushing the iron bars only dimly seen in the dark room, so he was the only one really at ease there. I crawled under the waist-high lengths of thick black chains guarding the doorway, scuttling on all fours until I could sag into the worn colorless couch by the stereo.

The stereo was forging iron bands of rock with a group called Sore Throat. It sounded like electrified sandpaper. Nice. The song was a big hit, so popular it had been adapted by Muzak:

> . . . *Don't turn your back*
> *Don't turn your back*
> *the knife is behind you*
> *Don't take a chance*
> *Don't let them get*
> *behind you*

The song fit the resonance of the submerged apocalypse. I became aware of the submerged apocalypse as a ship learns about an erupting volcano miles beneath the ocean surface before its shockwave has arrived: Sonar. I sent out questing vibrations which bounced back with innuendoes. A storm was growing in the city's back alleys and tenements and bars and dormitories and discotheques. I could feel it coming.

The exorcism fad. I saw a fat lady scream in the middle of the street: "O Christ Jeezus help me, one of 'em has *got* me!" No one was surprised. Three or four people pulled small vessels of Holy Water from coat pockets and sprinkled it on her.

And four Safeways burned during the Housewife Riots. Then the Jeezus Freaks rioted and tore a dozen malls to shambles, calling them temples to the Babylon Whore. And

15

if I'd bought stock in electric fences and handguns three years ago I'd be a rich man now.

The newspapers were heavy with blunt headlines, my father's fingers grew blacker with editorial ink calling for reprisals against rioters, and the air grew oppressive.

I couldn't guess the outcome then, though Whistler's face was plastered all over town on posters advertising his Immersion Show.

I was harvesting all this from the snaking smoke and buzzing chatter in Eggman's black box when a head I hadn't met staggered over to me, sat down on the arm of the couch to my right, the overhead light making his bush of blonde hair into a corona.

"HeybloodI'mreallystoned," he intoned.

"I'm really interested," I replied. But he took me seriously.

"Wow, that's great. Nobody's ever interested. People should care about each other, *relate* to each other as indivi—" he had to pause for a rest and a breath between all those syllables in one word "—uals. . . ." A real relic. A neo-hippy. He'd babble in my ear all night if I didn't press the eject button. I saw Eggman on the other side of the room, his face caged in iron as if the smoke had suddenly solidified. Eggman was laughing at my irritation. He thought it was *funny*. I wanted to smash Eggman's face against the derelict hippy's, like cymbals. But Zoë came in.

She was always good for some spine-twists. She was shaking, as usual. Little heart palpitating. She was pale, her eyes sunken deeply, hiding insects. She walked in tiny, mincing steps, ludicrously birdlike under her spindly legs. She spotted me, and her nervousness visibly increased.

"Hey Zoë!" I yelled so that everyone would hear. "Don't cut yourself or the *worms* will get out!"

"What?" Her face screwed itself up as if it were trying to

retreat into her eyesockets.

"I said that you have *worms* in your veins now. They fit in perfectly, slide real cute right through just like little subways. Slimy though. You probably have to clean out your arteries with a toothbrush." Zoë put a finger between her lips and bit. "Don't bite your fingers," I said, making my words slither from my mouth like worms. I had heard that she was pregnant and I guessed she thought she could feel something crawling around in her uterus. "Don't bite your fingers or they'll get out for sure and leave little slimy trails on your skin and—"

And on. I asked myself why. But I went on.

Zoë stuttered but couldn't spit a word out whole. Her eyes said she wanted to say something that would hurt me, but she was afraid that I would turn it back against her. She backed off and ran, tripped over a chain, fell against another chain, her sobbing sharing a resonance with Lucy's.

"There, the worms have you!" I shouted doggedly, and turned away. You couldn't hear her cry much over the noise of the record player.

I slumped down next to Eggman. "You've gathered a menagerie," I remarked, leaning back, not looking at him. My eyesockets fixed in luminous brotherhood on the lightsockets. The wires in the house were so old and dilapidated the lights cut and flickered, on and off, the record player speeding up and slowing down with the vacillation in power. When Eggman didn't reply, I looked up.

Lucy was standing there, just looking at me. I smiled at her, wanting to run.

Eggman sensed my discomfort. "What's wrong, Dunbar? The *worms* getting to you?"

The lights flickered, the record player droned faster/slower like an old man on the verge of death, indecisive.

Lucy was wearing a wraparound sari about her hips, her tight conical breasts bare above it. Her shoulders and neck were painted in black glitter; her long black hair was pinned into a bun behind her head. The fey light that usually flared in her small, faun features was extinguished in her black eyes.

I still loved her, I told myself, trying to make it wholesome. She didn't waste words. "Aaron, I don't want the abortion. My mind is made up. I want to keep the baby."

I looked away, pretending to study the torn posters hanging from the walls like loose bandaids. I shook my head. "No, your mind is *pinned* up. A kid would pin you down even more."

"You mean it would hold *you* down, don't you?"

I hate being caught without a comeback.

She moved like a breezed willow, sat down next to me on the edge of the couch. Her head not even reaching my shoulders.

"Aaron, the kid means something to me. I thought we registered an Alliance? Well Christ, what *comes* from an Alliance? The proof of the pudding, the product of my thesis and your antithesis . . . the kid is our synthesis."

"Cut it *out*. The Alliance was enough. We survived in it." Why was Eggman still sitting there, listening? I put an arm around her. She shrugged it off. Not angry, but stiff, withdrawn. She had given up on me before coming here. My retaliation: "Maybe you're just afraid of the operating table, afraid to have that hose—"

"Shit, come off it, Aaron," Eggman spat in, rolling his eyes heavenward. "You get cornier by the hour."

"Butt out, Eggman." Pain painted itself into a corner of Lucy's face.

He snickered. I turned to Lucy but she was already getting up.

"Wait, Lucy—" We were in free fall and she was drifting away, tugged into another orbit. . . . "People want children as an ego-thing, that's all, actually. They see their kids as extensions of themselves and they live vicariously through them." I felt degraded: She was forcing *me* to appeal to *her.* She turned her back, hesitated. "Oh, all right then, do it that way," I said, hoping I was well hidden under the disdain. Lucy—all I had left now that my parents had canceled me—left without replying, gracefully negotiating Eggman's iron maze. The lights flickered, the record player sank, sound submerged, emerged.

"Shut up, Eggman," I said, though Eggman hadn't uttered a sound. But he was grinning from ear to ear, near where his throat should have been slit. Eggman thought it was *funny.* He changed the subject.

"Are you going to the Whistler concert?"

"What the fuck are you talking about?"

"Aaron boy, I didn't think I cared much for agony rock. I think most of it is redundant and unoriginal. But Whistler bypasses all boundaries. He's really *new* but it's still rock. You know? It's hard to explain. It evolves backwards, sucks you in."

Just then Dreyfus came through the room, dodging chains and bars haphazardly, chasing his little brother with a lit cigarette. Dreyfus tripped on a chain and fell against an iron rod, catching it full in his ample gut. He slid to the floor, choking. Eggman grinned, wiry lips pulled over jutting teeth, blotchy gums.

"Hey, I've got one of Whistler's albums here," he said.

He got up to put it on.

I didn't want to listen to it with him around because he'd sit too close to me and tell me to listen, then continuously interrupt my listening with, "Did you hear *that*? Did you?" I was prepared for Eggman, but not for Whistler.

Whistler made the first move.

He let the bass begin with lugubrious coughs. He tacked the bass up loosely with the rhythm guitar, steadied them with drums, and wove them with an impatient guitar lead. Then his keening violin burst through the propped fabric like a circus panther leaping through a paper hoop. An electric violin is sharper, more piercing than an acoustic. And the honed, razored bow stung shrill, like tin foil on a tooth filling.

Whistler's violin could grit its teeth and make a face and spit juices. Most good musicians play their instruments as extensions of themselves. Whistler was an outgrowth of his violin. He was stuck there, bound by talismans: His eyes, his violin, his violence. The violin rose and fell in quivering extremes, my feet and hands trembled apart from me; rhythms bandied like a hand winding an alarm clock. He fenced with the lead guitar, feinted, bluffed past and thrust.

I began to see pictures.

Images formed right from the music. There was only one song on the album with lyrics, but everywhere was rhetoric expressed musically. Whistler, in the hot railroad track framework of rock, emphasized the distance between the notes as much as their arrangement. He used emptiness. I was engulfed in his spaces and floating there I saw: The pictures. Another world. The Plaid Forest, ribboned hues of its terraced trees cross-hatching green indigo amber red. A crazy quilt labyrinthine forest. There was no sun anywhere in this world, and the sky was blueblack above the hovering Lamps. The Lamps were the source of daylight; glowing ovoids of luminosity hanging unsupported at regular intervals thirty feet above the soft forest humus. I was riding a zebra, Whistler straddled his own zebra to my right on the narrow, shady trail. Whistler was of medium height, with red-brown bushy hair, green eyes, round pug face barren of sympathy, broad chest, forthright posture. His face was ringed in beard, thin lips clamped. He wore a long black robe; mail armor glinted at the neck and loose sleeves. A cool breeze tantalized my conspicuously beardless cheeks, heralding the Season of Reason. Here, the fall season is called Season of Reason; winter is Season of Treason; spring is Season of Passion and summer is the Season of Fashion.

The Lamps cast a homogenous light over the Plaid Forest. Between the Lamps a speckling of black dots seemed to congeal and reproduce itself, becoming a swarming dark mass. Noting the swarm, Whistler unfolded a rainslick from a saddle pouch, put it over himself and tossed another to me. The mist collected into clouds. The lumpy clouds went from grey to flat black, seemed to appear from nowhere in the space between the Lamps. Tentacles of mist reached toward one another until the clouds were joined between the Lamps in a dark network jeweled with islands of light. A rumble, and the clouds let go sheets of heavy rain. Falling in intersecting sheets, the cloudburst was refracting the lamplight into an orchard of myriad rainbows. Keeping a mournful cadence with the rhythm of whirring rainfall, Whistler began to sing:

. . . His body they staked and covered with pitch
and they set afire the red-maned witch
during the Season of Passion

They all agreed it was a fine deed
to burn clean the witch's bad seed
during the Season of Fashion

But later the Plague raised agonized cries
though the witch was burned,
blamed for giving it rise
during the Season of Reason

The Red-maned witch might have stopped the plague
But they'd drunk the cask to its dregs
And now it was the Season of Treason . . .

The rain and the song stopped simultaneously. The forest faded, vanished.

"Did you catch that lead? Amazing, eh?" Eggman reached to change the record. "I don't know if I like those lyrics about the 'red-maned witch,' but they're practically the only words he's ever written."

"Don't touch that disc," I said, dazed by what I'd seen. I had seen it so *clearly*, like a movie over my eyes.

Eggman waved me off impatiently and put his hand on the turntable—

I kicked him in the stomach. He doubled up, his thin face changing colors like the Plaid Forest. He wheezed. I felt a smile climbing my mouth but I pulled it down.

"That was childish," he gasped. "You're getting more unstable all the time."

"Just becoming more appreciative, bag-of-wind. I'm learning to respect art enough to defend it."

"Sure you are. Is that what you were doing, defending art, when you fucked with Zoë?" He sat up, his face a red stoplight. "You knew how gullible she is. She's always on the edge of a paranoid breakdown and you make it worse. Maybe it's because she's pregnant like Lucy?"

I kicked him in the ribs, asking myself *why*. He fell onto his side, yelling, his nasal voice like a honking bicycle horn. The others were staring but no one wanted to interfere. I had cultivated their mistrust. Carefully.

"You enjoy making me squirm, don't you?" Eggman asked, getting to his knees, one hand on his bruised side. "You string Lucy and the other women along till they get dependent on you, then you let them know they're obsolete. I think you start the Alliance in the first place so you can watch them squirm—"

"Straighten up, I didn't kick you that hard," I said.

But he had resurrected what I'd said to Lucy: Maybe you're just afraid of the operating table maybe you're just afraid of the operating table maybe you're afraid (the words in a repeating tapeloop in my head) maybe you're afraid . . .

On the stereo, the song ended.

The lights made the shadows into dark birds flickering on and off, good and evil, maybe you're just afraid of the operating table. . . . I realized that I'd been listening to Whistler while arguing with Eggman, the music providing a sort of martial cadence for our mutual anger.

Sulking, Eggman left the room clutching at his side.

I looked at the album cover. I had never seen a picture of Whistler, to my recollection.

But the man on the cover was unmistakably the man of my vision.

The next song began. Listening to Whistler, shaking in his grip, waiting for his fingers to close tight and crush me, I felt as if I had been casually riding through the House of Horrors at a carnival, unconcerned until I discovered that the tracks wouldn't bring me to an exit.

Pictures came again. A great throbbing grey brain toted in a wooden cart with six-foot wheels, harnessed to a team of six comedy channel comedians telling mass-produced jokes as they strained under the whip of the animated stone gargoyle perched on a frontal lobe. The brain procession rolled by an operating table and a girl with a swollen abdomen impaled on the prosthetic pincers of a whirring robot doctor. And in the smoky distance on the mountain top, Whistler with hair flaming, strapped to a wooden post that was propped in a heap of burning bones, a witch condemned to the stake. His face, haloed in greasy blue-grey smoke, was calm, almost timorous and apologetic. And there was an appeal in his eyes, an asking.

His music rose from the flickering flames, spotlighting that dark place into and out of light like the unsteady lamps in Eggman's room—

I was hollowed-out. A ballbearing rolled around and around where my innards should be. I squeezed my eyes shut, banishing the vision. It faded but the feeling of *asking* lingered like a ringing telephone begging to be answered. The electric violin, shaking its treble, was a shrieking woman.

Sometimes during physics classes at school, or embalmed in the quiet of the library, I'd start to shriek. Simply for celebration. Or maybe contrition.

They kicked me out of my physics class when I stood up and screamed at the top of my lungs: *"I'm proud to live in the country that invented the atomic bomb!"*

And I wrote essays about screaming. I felt that it should be performed as an aesthetic exercise.

But Whistler had a screaming woman imprisoned in his violin.

Since Lucy left the room I had been repressing thoughts of her. A bullet needs compression before it can fire.

. . . *Lucy moving with me like light on the surface of an underground river* . . .

I stood up, trying to shed the memory with movement. But—

. . . *Lucy feeding her fish, feeding her cat, riding a horse, tossing bread to pigeons* . . .

I was a part of his music before he composed it. I wanted to scream, so the music screamed with me. Lucy might still be upstairs. Maybe I could—

. . . *Lucy holding the child, loving it like I never could* . . .

I saw Eggman come into the room. He glared at me from the doorway. I began to shriek with the woman hidden in Whistler's violin.

Alerted, startled, the others in Eggman's Black Hole of Calcutta looked at me, at my face shining like an iron in a forge.

Until they saw it was only me.

Eggman gave me a sour look and left the room.

II.

I eat with my eyes. I see with my ears.
—SAMUEL WHISTLER

I RESEARCHED WHISTLER'S PAST for my Psychology 101 term paper. His parents had been in show business, night club singers. His father died when he was nine and just learning to sing himself. His mother went through three more husbands before her son left her at eighteen to play first string violin in a Junior Symphonic Orchestra. After two years with the orchestra he joined a jazz band in New Orleans where he became addicted to heroin and a black woman who later left him for a big guy in the Bloods. Whistler left the band and moved to New York. He worked his way through several bands, first achieving notoriety with a band called Paper Lust which emphasized morbid rock theater in the tradition of Alice Cooper.

He became famous for his violin first, his singing second and eccentricities third. He funded psychic research to contact his dead father. A dozen mediums tried to fake him out before he dissolved the organization in 1995.

He was addicted to speed at thirty and temporarily dropped from the music scene, living off royalties until early 1997 when he broke his addiction and formed a band

25

like an oyster forms a black pearl. He was notorious for his ego, so no one was surprised when he named the comeback band Whistler.

He was avidly and overtly hated by every member of the band, who remained with him, according to rumor, because his was the highest paying show on the agony rock circuit.

III.

The motto of the artist is this: "I am willing to be used."
—SAMUEL WHISTLER

I RAN INTO MY PSYCHOLOGY CLASS ten minutes late and interrupted Mr. Cage's lecture.

"I've brought you my term paper, Mr. Cage!" I shouted, brandishing the typewritten sheets. I slapped the papers down in front of him on the silvery-flecked top of his fiberglass desk. "It's about a form of telepathy using a performer as—"

"What makes you think the class is interested, Dunbar?" Cage asked in his most brittle tone. The class consisted of twelve fatuous faces looking embarrassed about attending a psychology class as if they were afraid that someone would accuse them of being there for therapy. "Your constant self-centered interruptions are entertaining no one but yourself."

"You see there? You've proven my point. I said that telepathy is not limited to the communication of raw brainwaves but that since individual brains are only neurons of the collective worldbrain—" (I had rehearsed this little speech earlier) "—any image occurring simultaneously in two minds at one instant, for whatever reason—suggestion or otherwise—is a species of telepathy. Synchronicity is telepathy. Even if it comes from a conversational motivation. The only criterion is that it appear in both at once . . ."

"And how did I prove your point, Dunbar? I wish you'd get down to it because you're boring the hell out of us with all this."

"There is no need for you to lance my ego, Mr. Cage, my mind is not a boil, it does not fester and pustulate like yours, sir."

Mr. Cage's earlobes and wattles were bright red.

The old therapist allowed his emotions to show only on the perimeter; they worked their way in from there. There was a ring of red anger haloing his face when I said:

"And the reason you have illustrated my point? Because I knew that you would be pissed off and say something remarkably like 'What makes you think the class is interested—' and I realized that you would say it almost exactly at the same moment you realized you would say it. That is the sort of telepathy I'm talking about."

An impulse guided my hand to my manuscript and my legs to frogleap high in the air. I alighted noisily on Mr. Cage's desk. I began to read from my thesis dramatically, with many flourishes, to the nervously tittering class:

"Okay, this is from page three, fourth paragraph. '. . . researchers from Duke University took an interest in Whistler's agony rock performances due to the large degree of collective psychic manifestations reported to occur there. Collective telepathy, a phenomenon ordinarily classed with mass hysteria, had been noted at rock concerts for years, especially where the psychological tone was characterized by uniform uninhibited exuberance and unanimous elation. As far back as Woodstock, synchronization of mental images had been common at rock gatherings, especially in crowds steeped in hallucinogens—' "

Here I had to leap from my desk-perch to a nearby table

top because Cage was hysterical, cutting viciously at my leg with a wooden pointer. The class was throwing paper balls at me. But I read on with barely a hesitation and without stumbling, orating louder and louder to drown out Cage's whining protests.

" 'Evangelists use it, the technique substituting one identity as the surrogate for a mass of people! The audience focuses all of its attention on a single centralized hypnotic figure who links them into a chain which circles back upon itself as a closed system!' " I took a breath, dodged the pointer, uplifted the paper above Cage's snatching fingers and continued unabashed: " 'A team of federally funded researchers documented the levitation of a performer at a rock concert in 1994. The singer, who had his eyes closed, later said that he did not notice his elevation until he was fifteen feet above the stage. When he opened his eyes his surprise severed him—' "

"You can forget about graduating!" Cage shrieked.

To embroider the tapestry I injected irrelevant, off-the-top-of-my-head phrases like: "Box lunch for a tyrannosaur! Keeps a prayerbook in his underwear!"

" '—severed him from the rapport with the audience and he fell, breaking an ankle. Even when not so obviously demonstrated one can feel an overwhelming congregation of passions, an exchange of identities between concert-goers until there is no one independent activity. The moments when the degree of group passion needed to convey overt collective psychic phenomena are rarefied and usually last for a maximum of ten seconds. During those brief intervals the collective mind can be, in this highly unstable malleable state, remolded by the charismatic figure dominating the stage—' "

Cage had gone from the room, followed by half the class. I could glimpse him now through the open door

returning with a campus security guard. I concluded hastily, shrilling my voice:

"'—becoming what he wants!'"

I hopped off the table, causing the incoming Cage to
stagger backwards into the security guard. I laughed and
tossed the sheets in their red faces and dashed down the
hall, lost myself in the cafeteria crowds. The perimeter of
red had contracted to the dead center of Cage's round face
like the crimson center of a dartboard.

IV.

I'm sick of this stupid, infested planet.
—SAMUEL WHISTLER

I STRUTTED BUOYANTLY through Imaginary University.
Sliding through the cloying, spurious good will emanating
from the herding students, I was pleased as a tapeworm in
the bowels of a fat cow. *Cow* was not carrying the metaphor
too far, since I swung toward the financial aid office to milk
the school.

I was in a good mood, having left Cage staggering in a
poisonous wake of murmurs, and my good foot followed
my evil foot with insipid regularity. I was chanting aloud:
"Good! Evil! Good! Evil! Good, Evil, Good, Evil, Good, Evil,"
Slurring faster into, *"Godevil! Godevil! Godvl! Godvl! Godvl!
Godvl! Godvl! Gdvl, Gv, Gv, Give . . . Give!"* Perpetually and
loudly.

Chanting good/evil/god-devil/good/evil/give I tuned
in on the milquetoast frequency of the university, scooping
up vibrations soaking from floors and dripping from walls,
reverberations coded with an embryonic divination. The
sonar resonance good/evil struck the skulls racing past

(gaping mouths, furtive eyes), ringing blows like a xylophone's tintinnabulation.

Gold-panning from my good/evil sonar I began to construct an eidetic vision, picturing the dark hunching threat on the horizon, like a spider diminutive on a far wall, seeming from here only a dot, a vague blur that sharp focus discloses as an eight-legged hairy carnivore.

Whirlwinding good/evil, my chanting was timed by my mental replaying of Whistler's "Knife Life," a song that seemed to burst into full bloom—I could recall every note and nuance clearly!—when I felt again the concealed corpus of the submerged holocaust. The Indians say Death watches, waiting for its chance, from over your left shoulder, and if you turn around fast enough you'll see—

The submerged holocaust. I could see the submerged holocaust:

A) in the way the students all seemed to be leaning slightly to the left as they walked.

B) the undeniable fact that everyone was blinking their eyes in the same Morse code. The decoded Morse message was: *Danger, apocalypse.*

I decided to forego financial aid for the time being. I wasn't in the mood to pretend humility. Looking carefully about for the campus security guards, I retreated into the library, thinking calmly that many people would be killed when the holocaust was no longer submerged. And over all was the redolence of Whistler.

Lucy was sitting cross-legged ten yards outside the library window on a knoll of a small shady park usually thronged by lovers. There was a man sitting beside her. The man was bending over to kiss her, I couldn't see his face. He had bushy blonde hair and wore a red satin sash and an ancient tie-dyed shirt. I felt awful. I felt rotten. I couldn't look away.

He turned from her to mash out his cigarette in the trampled grass. There were as many cigarette butts as blades of grass. It was the derelict neohippy from Eggman's party. I almost felt better. Surely she wasn't taking *him* seriously. I went outside to make sure.

I stood a few feet from her, glaring, while the fossil rummaged in his leather bag for weed and rolling papers. He hadn't noticed me yet, he probably hadn't noticed anything unpleasant since the day marijuana and peyote had been legalized.

Lucy looked at me without speaking, only ashes in her eyes.

"Could I talk to you for just a second, miss?" I asked, petulant because she'd forced me to make the first move.

"No," she replied placidly, summing up. The hippy still hadn't noticed me, engrossed in his rolling. With one hand he fiddled with a portable radio.

"I just want to speak to you alone for a few minutes, Luce."

She shook her head emphatically.

Her companion looked up, phony affability melting from his eyes as he recognized me.

"What do you want, Dunbar?" he asked, his voice as monotonous as his face. I ignored him and looked at Lucy. "You coming over tonight?" I asked, trying to pretend nothing has gone wrong.

"No. Not anymore and not at all. I have a new Alliance."

I didn't look at her new amour. I knew he'd be smug. Just the type she wanted and needed. He'd be willing to take care of her baby, to show some responsibility.

A submerged holocaust cooked up inside me. I began to hear "Knife Life" in my head again. I turned and walked blindly away down a park path.

No, the song wasn't in my head. I was hearing "Knife

Life" on the derelict's FM radio.

The sunshine thickened, becoming so dense I had to plow laboriously through it, hearing the song dwindle behind me. Closing my eyes, I saw Whistler's world of lamps and Plaid forests again. In battle-gear, Whistler danced through a knife-and-armor stippled battlefield beneath the islands of light. He wore a helmet with antennas and mandibles and green-jeweled eyes, fashioned in the likeness of the head of a giant insect. He wore a black skirt, girded by a silver belt and scabbard. His bare chest bristled with wiry red hairs, shone with sweat. Each of his muscles was one in a crowd of rock-concert dancers. He wore a vest of barbed wire, points turned inward resting on but not raking his skin, though he moved in a thousand snaky contortions, his sword effortlessly flashing in and out of the white-garbed warriors who swung their pikes as ineptly at him as Cage had cut at me with his pointer.

V.

I'm the only ant in this ant-farm with a glass-cutter.
—SAMUEL WHISTLER

I CLIPPED THE TWO ARTICLES from the newspaper and laid them side-by-side on the grimy tabletop. I read them, re-read them, then stared out my apartment window at the clouds that seemed knotted, releasing late afternoon sunlight only reluctantly in pale shafts between grey tangles.

The first article related that Whistler's Alliance, Trash, had committed suicide. The woman, a mestizo, was the same color as his violin. Whistler had named her Trash. Trash had never spoken to anyone but Whistler. Two nights prior she had run on stage during a performance, shouldered in front of him and shot herself through the head with a small pistol. I was sure that Whistler's scheduled concerts would be canceled. But the radio announced that the show was still scheduled. Maybe Whistler could mourn only on stage. The story about Trash made me think bitterly of Lucy.

The second article quoted a parapsychologist who had been appointed to investigate mass psychic manifestations alleged to occur at Whistler's Immersion Show. ". . . Mr. Whistler gave us every cooperation, though he didn't seem much interested in our project. When I first met the man I got the impression he was mentally ill. I was told that mine was a common mistaken reaction. I didn't permit my unease to deter my investigation. However, I have been forced to give the entire project up completely. The whole thing. They can assign someone else if they like, but I doubt if they will stay with it for long, either. I'm a veteran of many rock concerts, but I couldn't remain in Mr. Whistler's company for more than an hour. I felt I'd be pulled apart. It was frightening. His music is engaging, certainly, but I don't think that's what gives him his marvelous control over them. It's his will. His willpower is frightening . . ."

I put the two articles in my Whistler scrapbook, right under the interview with Whistler's former drummer. The interview was characterized by this passage:

Q. Why exactly did you quit his band?
A. Like you said it, because it was *his* band, and no one else's. But there was another reason. I couldn't stand to be around him long. He just steals something from you. Maybe he's a kind of vampire. He's crazy, for sure. The guys still in the band with him would like to leave but they can't. I don't know. But I felt like in spite of his all-the-time ego-thing, he was always kind of pathetically asking me for something. But he wouldn't tell me what it was. . . .

Three-thirty P.M. Sitting alone in my room toying with grains of salt spilled on the greasy table. My room was a glove-box ten by twenty, with kitchenette and use of the bathroom down the hall. I was thinking about the interview and wondering where I was going to get the fifteen bucks for the concert. I stood up and kicked my way through the clumps of unwashed clothing and candy wrappers, tin cans, books on metaphysics and comic books, till I got to the stereo. For the fourth time that day I put on Whistler's second album, *Void Gnashing Its Teeth*. I went to the window to watch the crowds sweating through the hot July afternoon. I worried about being dead-broke, quailed at the thought of panhandling. I could either borrow money from my parents or panhandle, both degrading.

But when the record started I began to feel smug. I would get in somehow. He would take care of his own. The entree to the concert would come to me without invocation. I had four hours before the concert. Plenty of time for Whistler to arrange for me to get in. His way.

He told me personally. He let me know, while I wandered at his side through the Plaid Forest in the land of floating lamps.

VI.

Our music is the score for the real-life documentary movie about the end of the world. Music for Armageddon. Mood music.
—SAMUEL WHISTLER

AN HOUR BEFORE THE CONCERT, six thirty-two, I was wondering how Whistler would get me there. Sunset was behind me, someone pouring sour milk on the ulcerous tenements across from my flat. Through the crude faces traced in the grey film on my single window Eggman's face inflated as he loped up the steps three at a time. He burst through the door with a look that solicited gratitude.

"Okay Eggman, what am I supposed to thank you for that you haven't even told me about yet?"

"Be nice to me, smartass. I know how much you want to go to that concert. All you ever talk about anymore is Whistler. Anyway, I can get us in free."

I sneered and shook my head like I'd heard it all before.

"N'shit Aaron boy, my older brother showed me where. He's done it lots of times. I know the only way to get into the coliseum for free."

"All right then. That's it. That's how."

"How what?"

"Tell me, Eggo," I asked, leaning back in my wicker chair till its squawking made me smile. "Did you know that Whistler collects shaman paraphernalia and African witch-doctor's masks? He wears them on stage—"

"Very interesting. You told me that last week."

"They say that he never has to call anyone he wants to get in touch with. They call *him*. But I'll tell you some-thing, Eggman." I leaned forward and looked into Egg-man's shallow eyes; it wasn't far to the bottom where coins worth a wish apiece glimmered. Eggman was getting uncomfortable, he pretended to look at his watch. "Whistler can't be blamed for whatever happens." Some-how my voice was trembling but I clutched the arms of the chair and got a grip on myself. "He can't be blamed no matter what. Even if Trash's suicide was his fault, or even if he murdered her somehow." A throbbing, roaring shook my temples, my eyes were fixed on Eggman's. "Because this isn't his world and he has to make his own rules to get by. Our rules and laws make no sense to him. We're aliens. Because he isn't from *here*."

Eggman looked profoundly embarrassed.

I quieted the manic output and sat back, breathing deep. But I had to say it, "He's from another dimension of reality. And that other world is where his loyalty lies and rightly so. His presence here is sheer accident. I'll tell you something, *Ego*-man. He's going to take me back there with him, when he goes. To the land of floating lamps. Me and whoever I want to take with me." I wanted him to mistakenly conclude just what he said next:

"It's Lucy, isn't it? Do you really imagine all this pseudometaphysical bullshit is going to bring her back?" He lowered his voice patronizingly. "I understand exactly how you feel about, uh, alienation . . . we all have to deal with it, but . . ."

It was easy to plant suggestions in Eggman's chameleon mind. Let him think it was all an obsession with Lucy as long as he didn't take my slip of the tongue about the land of floating lamps seriously. *Things must be kept in hand until the right moment,* I thought.

"What are we sitting around here for?" I asked petulantly. "Show starts in forty-eight minutes."

Forty minutes later, in the steaming dusk, Eggman and I were breathing heavily on a ledge two stories above the ground.

"A goddamn drainpipe." I moaned. "You didn't tell me we'd have to climb a drainpipe."

"Shut up. You're here. We just go down the ledge about twenty feet, there's a window. Lock's broken. Just shove it open."

Fresh elation budded in me then as I followed Eggman on hands and knees, kneecaps painfully grinding against the concrete. I'd known that somehow a way would come to me; but actually being *there,* I could almost feel Whistler's hand on my shoulder. The submerged apocalypse roiled subtly beneath the buzzing conversation and catcalls of the crowd waiting for the gates to open, below us. I heard hoarse shouts as the five doors opened. The night air lapped humidly over us, smelling of dogbreath. I glanced down, nervous in the narrowness of the two-foot-wide ledge. The coliseum's exterior was a ribbed dome with great bent buttresses sheltering dope smokers and gang constituents, mostly Satanists, getting bombed, far beneath us.

Even Lucy is beneath me from up here, I thought.

"Hurry up," Eggman whispered urgently. "Don't let anyone see you or they'll all be up here and we'll never get to use this entrance again."

"We won't be able to use it if they see us but only because we'll be dead. They'll shoot us." A giddy wave of fear swept through me. I considered turning back. *Afraid of the operating table?* "Hurry up, go through the window. They have the legal right to shoot us because the crowds are so damned big and mean. They fixed the law so they can shoot us, after those four guards were wasted in Baltimore—"

But Eggman had already climbed through the window. I looked over my shoulder at the toothy city lights and wished I could see a mushroom cloud blossom over Imaginary City. Then I followed Eggman, expecting a club to connect with my skull as I climbed through. But I was met only by the scents of popcorn, dope, sweat, all glued together by cigarette smoke. We were at the topmost row in the mammoth auditorium, six rows above the highest filled seats. Eggman was already walking down the aisle. Someone large, greyclad and ominous was walking up towards us. A mercenary hired specially for this concert. He must have seen us from below as we came in. He walked straight at us, unhurried but purposeful.

The cop looked right at me. I sprinted, stumbling over

benches, to the left and down.

The cop angled into a run to cut me off and yelled something. I was running scared so I didn't look to see what became of Eggman. I saw another cop coming from my left.

My mouth bobbed open, my breath rasped. I stumbled, was almost trampled by the thickening crowd. Smoke stung my eyes.

The audience bellowed and stood, arms and heads like wheat in a windstorm.

A barbiturate freak blundered into the cop coming from my left and flailed mindlessly. The cop fell on his face and tried to extricate himself from the self-made moron.

I pumped down the stairs, caught a glimpse of Whistler picking up his violin, heard the accolade groan from the crowd.

Running around the perimeter of the wriggling masses under the stage, I tried to get close. A hard leather boot kicked into the hollows of my knees, I fell supine, rolled onto my stomach. A knee jabbed my spine, hands quick and hard pressed me sharply to the floor. I felt my nose get bloody. Other rough hands dragged my wrists painfully behind for handcuffs.

Magically, it ceased. The handcuffs never shut their jaws. I looked up at the stage. Whistler's tormented face was turned toward me, but his eyes were still fixed on the space over our heads. He gestured frantically at the hired police. He had seen me run. He spoke into the microphone.

"He's my guest. Let him be—let him stay." His voice was acid eating iron. I knew that this was going to be the last Whistler Immersion show. The submerged apocalypse tossed and turned in its uneasy sleep.

The pressure lifted from my back. I could breathe again. I coughed, tasting hot salty blood, hot like the growing expectancy of the audience.

The guards released me and Whistler locked me in.

The submerged apocalypse murmured in its sleep. Can a nightmare have a nightmare?

I looked around for Eggman, didn't see him. The painted faces around me wondered why I rated Whistler's intervention. They looked at me with respect but kept their distance. Many of them stood out in their imitation regal robes; the garb of royalty, costume jewelry crowns and rich ermine capes, was all the rage. Scattered in small constellations through the seething black pot of the coliseum's interior, multicolored electric lights sparkled. Eggman still had a minor scar where his own light had been surgically imbedded between his eyes. He had it removed because he said that the blue electric light, powered by current generated by the brain, was making him hallucinate.

I took some tissue from the carrybag on my belt and put it to my bleeding nose and Whistler put his violin to his shoulder.

The muscles in Whistler's face spasmed; his lips were always either clamped hard or baring teeth like an angry gorilla. His face was ringed in a scarlet poppy-circle beard. His eyes were trapped on the far side of his music. When he played he seemed to be aiming and elevating his violin like a statue I once saw of a huntsman about to send a falcon from his shoulder.

Whistler began alone, his violin croaked into a funeral procession. The backup band emerged by his command rather than pre-arranged timing. He would enunciate a stroke of the bow in a way that meant *drums now*. And he commanded the audience. We surrendered.

The auditorium was the largest on the west coast. Of course, from the back of the theater the performer was barely visible, except on TV screens mounted every thirteen rows. Seventy-five speakers were arranged so that sound was projected from every euphoniously possible angle, including from underneath, but channeled by sound-baffling screens hanging from the vast, clear-domed roof so that acoustics were crystalline lucid. Computers backstage measured the audience's vocal reactions and keyed the volume and pitch of the speakers to intensify excitement.

The light show was a vast holographic projection, fifty feet by one hundred, appearing in mid-air over the mandala-shaped stage. Computers formulated the writhing apparition of three-dimensional projections, moving the images in rhythm with the music's backbeat. *Any given musical structure has a mental image as its correlate.* And the holos illuminated the melody's concealed eidetic snapshot. And as our circuits clicked into contact, a jolt of electricity awakened the submerged apocalypse.

Men in black robes dispensed synthetic peyote, incense clamored in our throats. A blackrobed black man, the only light in him his glowing eyes, offered me three hits. I shook my head. I didn't need it. I didn't need dope or Eggman or Lucy. But Whistler needed me.

African-style masks were a tradition at Whistler's concerts and a fourth of the crowd sported their own cheap plastic witchdoctor's masks.

The holo was a billowing djinn whose body was storm-clouds, bloated and ponderous like the huge balloons of cartoon characters held by thin wires at parades. The music became whimsical, looney tune, and the holo *was* a huge balloon of a cartoon character. I began to get my bearings.

Dancing was perfunctory for the first few songs. The crowd was embarrassed, because Whistler hadn't spoken yet. But conversation died down and they began to watch the stage pensively even between numbers. There were the few inevitable pocket riots around the fringes, sections of the right hand balcony were set afire and instantly doused, stifling both flame and rioters, with automatic ceiling firehoses.

Whistler stopped playing, his band lost steam behind him, moaning into crackling stillness like an exhausted locomotive. Whistler didn't acknowledge the shouts and catcalls. His eyes were funnels for the palpable mass of our enthusiasm. We followed the path of least resistance into the land of floating lamps. The crowd fell oddly silent. You could hear the air conditioners hum.

Whistler's face twisted, revved up, then he jerked a long, toothy green-red-black African mask from behind an amplifier. Other than the amplifiers and instruments, and the few taciturn, robed musicians behind Whistler, the stage was empty, with none of the props common to agony-rock performers.

And when the last notes of his first song passed, the huge holo had vanished, shimmering slightly in its going exactly as the final note had wavered.

Now, the audience was all massive breathings like a sleeping dragon.

Whistler fitted the African mask over his head, the audience screamed, and he began "Broken Bottles, Open Wounds; Arthritic Hands." A holo appeared, a mammoth semi-transparent three-dee image of a withered old man coughing and shaking on his deathbed. The old man looked mournfully down at us.

The audience roared with laughter, throwing bottles through the old man's image. The energy level rose. The submerged apocalypse began to surface, preparing to lift its sea serpent head above turbulent waters.

The crowd moved closer to stage. I was pressed perhaps forty feet distant from Whistler himself. People at the very

41

front fainted from the pressure and lack of oxygen. The heat of the music melted the seated audience, trickling it down from the upper tiers. The swarming body on the dance-floor grew larger. The lights were very low so that the holos seemed more corporeal than the shadowy people around me.

The music was an uneasy sea with *something* darkening the surface as it rose from below. The holo shifted into a gigantic, thrashing plesiosaur plowing a green sea, its snaking neck dancing precisely to the music. The holo dinosaur quivered, its crusty fins rising and falling to the cadence of the bass. The energy level rose.

The crowd surged and collapsed into itself like a megalopolis traffic jam, kicking up a massive car wreck, eighty-car pileup. As the thought drove through me, *the holo itself became a traffic jam,* and then a massive car wreck. The melody and backbeat and supporting rhythms violently intersected, collided with each other, sounds of feedback like steel savagely twisted. The music panted and squealed and I thought: I had a woman once who squealed like that. And at that instant the holo was a woman arching her back and howling in orgasm.

We were afraid. Whistler cut into us, our fear bled into the air and mixed.

We were ecstatic. The music shook our groins and our groans fled and mixed.

We wanted to hide. Notes like hailstones pelted our names off of our foreheads and we mixed.

Abruptly, the song ended. We looked at one another, embarrassed by our naked immersion.

I was just one of the audience, now.

Whistler began "Homing Sin." Rampant power ascended in periodic pulses for the next fifty minutes. The energy level rose, fell a little, rose some more, fell a bit. We would begin to feel ragged and discouraged and used, as he loosened his grip on us minutely, allowing some play in the steering wheel. But he knew just when to tighten things up. He seemed to grow bigger and bigger until I thought the holos were pets playing affectionately at his feet, and the whole coliseum his dollhouse. He danced on stage because he had to, not because it was part of the show. Dancing like he was electrocuted, he was the fluttering neural impulse for the collective body of the crowd. The music was a mesh of wiring connecting us as transistors in an electric component. We were transistors receiving and amplifying the closed system, or capacitors discharging, electrocuting him. The music picked up, as he gradually turned up the amplifiers. The stage, the holo, the monolithic equipment, the performers, the crowd—all welded into a single solid state unit by the ubiquitous song. Through quivers, shaking upward from the floor and resounding, good/evil, from distant walls of our self-contained world, there soaked, peripherally, subliminally—Whistler's personality. It was conducted directly into our skeletons, radiating from bone outward into flesh, transmitted through dancing and Whistler made us dance because his was the first move. His loudspeakers were everywhere, saturating us, making us loose and pliable. I began to detect through the haze rising from the combustion of exhaustion (the kindling) with adrenalin (the flame), that everyone was dancing, each precisely like the other. Still wearing African masks which bobbed over their shoulders like berserker spirits guiding their steps, each dancer taken individually was anarchic fury; as a whole, regimental uniformity. I was fanatically aware of my every vein, capillary and pore, I felt my juices forced through rubbery pipes like liquid subways stuffed with drunken passengers. Blood, ideas, sweat and thought running into a common whirlpool. My feet wouldn't listen to reason when I felt them begin to painfully wobble under my ankles like poorly secured mannequin's limbs; they refused to slow their drumsticking roll. My arms were banners snapped wildly in a high wind. My chest heaved and I had to craftily pilfer breaths between leaps.

The holo was now two fencing swashbucklers from an Errol Flynn film. The image of the swordsmen leaping nimbly about the ethereal balcony was interspersed with shots of Whistler, seventy-five feet tall, writhing on stage under the violin's lash. The smaller but not realer Whistler on stage was dancing like a witchdoctor trying to cure us of inhibitions, his mask gleaming as if sweat were breaking out on the polished wood. The holo swordsman runs the evil prince through the side and the crowd, a great swarming body of parasites on the decaying corpse of a beached whale, stands and cheers. The holo picture preposterously runs backwards to the instant just prior to the stabbing and the rapier unstabs the evil prince until the film is run forward and he is gutted again, the hero stabbing with a motion of his arm remarkably like that of Whistler stroking the strings of his violin. A holo collaging above the crowd, the images distorted through braids of blue incense smoke. The stabbing swashbucklers, Whistler, the dying old man, a woman naked and wriggling in climax, whales mating in a lagoon, a beached seabird dying in an oilslick, two lesbians so interlocked in embrace that they are hardly distinguishable from one another, a flock of birds taking to the air in a misty swamp, a stabbing swordsman, Whistler, a beached whale choked with scavenging sea-gulls—

The frenzy was beginning to peak, the music from every side was a landslide, then it was pressure crushing an astronaut fighting his way from gravity's grip, we were shouting, choking from exhaustion, for a split-second I wondered what had become of the usual intermission, he was playing right through. ... My side ached, knees sagged, but the accelerated impregnation of what Whistler wanted grew inside me, overcoming weariness.

Whistler altered us, made us over in his own image. Released an aspect of him that had always been submerged in us. (As a child I witnessed the transfiguration of a random sprinkling of iron filings into a striking mandala pattern on a plate of plastic placed over a magnet. Whistler = Magnet. Audience = iron filings.)

Air burned in my lungs. I hallucinated sans drugs. The floor was tilting, seeming to rise and fall like the abdomen of a breathing animal: the Loch Ness monster about to make itself known.

The audience pressed closer, my dancing was compressed with their nearness and I spun, digging myself into the grain of the music like screw threads biting wood. The bass was uniform but hastening, the lead guitar wah-wahed like an infant crying for its mother in a storm, the woman, the infant's mother, screamed from Whistler's violin as her child was carried away in a hurricane gust.

Whistler removed his mask and tossed it contemptuously into the audience.

And for that lonely instant his face suddenly freed from the mask was the only reality. We looked at each other but saw Whistler, a gathering of seventy-five thousand separate and distinct Whistlers dancing side by side. I felt the violin in my hands, solid as the floor underneath, alive as the thousands of counterparts of myself thronging in red-headed turbulence wherever I turned. When Whistler on stage bent his right leg each of us bent ours. Whistlers in the audience snapped butts out behind and tilted shoulders forward precisely when Whistler on stage snapped and tilted. We jostled and bumped to get closer to the demon on stage, forgetting fear of touching. We shared one territorial imperative and raised the flag. The flag was death's-head, white on black.

The holo was a full-scale pirate ship flying a giggling jolly roger and its decks brightened with the uplifted blades of a squalid crew. Another ship, a fat Spanish galleon, sailed across the vast spaces over the audience; bass and organs merged into their lowest notes as the cannons belched smoke from the pirate raider. The mainmast of the galleon splintered, the captain's arm carried away by a cannonball. Whistler is on the bridge of the pirate ship, a woman beside him. At first, thinking the woman was Lucy, I wanted to stop dancing and run. *I was unable to stop.* But the woman was Trash. The holo collaged the ships with an image familiar to me: a wooden cart pulled by six laughing men, the cart holding a massive grey brain, the gargoyle capering and snapping the whip; a man—Whistler—tied to a stake, flames licking him like strains of the violin. The pirate ship above the cart rocked on the waves; on deck Whistler drew Trash near him like a violin, on stage Whistler hugged the violin closer like a woman.

Suddenly the music changed, became the sounds of bubbles popping and tumbling dice. Whistler on stage threw aside his black robe, his eyes glowing; under the robe he wore only a vest twined from barbwire, jags riding his naked skin but not ripping; a black belt and scabbard, sword. Seventy-five thousand mouths shouted: Seventy-five thousand hearts converged and became one organ, and there was a holo of a fifty foot human heart, pumping a river of blood through the coliseum.

Without warning, the music calmed, simmered down, gave us opportunity to recover, without relinquishing its grip. The synthesizer's long sheets of sighing sound, horizons for the landscapes rolling out of the violin and hills and valleys in the strumming of the guitar. The holo was a view from on high of the land of floating lamps. The Plaid

Forest splashed onto the flanks of a volcano streaming purple smoke. To its right, between a hulking sphinx-like plateau of obsidian and the low grey hills checkered by islands of light, two armies clash. One is an army of soldiers who look like the audience at the concert but carrying weapons. The other, pounding the first army back against the black mesa, are men on horseback, their faces hidden in insect-head helmets. Whistler is at the fore, his vest of barbed wire flaring silver in light reflected off of flashing blades. Huge ants, each one larger than a man's arm, swarm between boots to drag off the bodies of the fallen.

My eyes hurt and I looked away from the holo. For an instant the thousands of Whistlers around me became seventy-five thousand young people once more.

Suddenly, the music stopped. The band stopped precisely on the same note, leaving a ringing, startling silence. The crowd exhaled a massive sigh, as one.

But there was shouting near the rear of the coliseum, below the seats. I glimpsed a gangfight between the Jeezus Freaks and the Satanists. Knives flashed between the white robes of the Satanists and the polished black leather of the Jeezus Freaks. Whistler's voice hammered the ceiling over the tussle; everyone froze. Both gangs dropped their knives, as he said:

"Stop fighting, *now*. Dance instead."

There was no murmuring, no disgruntlement. The gangs parted quietly. I wondered where the rentacops were. But I realized that they were hiding.

Whistler made a hand signal, and his band drew their black robes close about them and put something half seen over their faces, hidden in hoods. They turned up their amps, and the music, gathering itself together between them, prepared to leap. When the chord came, it fell like a sledgehammer, all instruments converged in a single deep note.

"Murder it," And the euphoria made my limbs light again as the crowd became once more thousands of Whistlers. A hundred thousand thoughts were the same. *Murder it.* We heard it clearly, each one of us, though no one bothered to shout it aloud. *Murder it.*

The music hurried, built to a peak and abruptly cut once more into a silence filled with Whistler's scream:

"Jeezus Freaks told me I was demon possessed. There is no true difference between possessor and obsessed!"

A gong crashed and the cymbals simmered the song into locomotion. A webwork of shimmering bands of energy flashed between our waving heads. I looked at Whistler, the Whistler on stage, and he transferred his gaze from that *something,* to my direction. He was looking back.

I was summoned. I fell slightly out of time. The music became thick liquid, choking me, throwing me off balance with violent currents. Howling, barking of wild dogs. I could see that Whistler was scared. He had brought me here, he could feel me here, primed and ready. He looked at the violin as if it were a tarantula crawling on his arm. It was alien and he feared it. In his own world, the land of floating lamps, he didn't have to play an instrument other than the sword. Here, he was forced to play forever, no matter what. He went higher and higher on the scale. He looked at me, begging, appealing. At a snapped nod from Whistler the band members threw back the cowls of their black robes. They wore the rubber masks of Jimi Hendrix, Jim Morrison, and Keith Richards. Now all dead. Whistler's highest note keened and stuttered, careened and shuddered, like an over-tightened wire about to *snap.* Streamers of crepe paper fell in clouds from the ceiling, passing through the holo of a raging forest fire. A cop was striding nervously through the outskirts of the churning crowd. He could feel it too, though he wasn't directly involved. I ran to him from behind and snatched his gun from his holster. The cop was terrified but he looked at me without anger, all confusion. Nobody else noticed my taking the gun, all eyes were fixed on Whistler. I pointed the gun at the silver badge on the cop's blue chest and he backed away, swiping sweatsoaked hair out of his eyes with unsteady thick fingers. I caught a stray image from the cop, it wafted to me on the rising tide of the seventy-five thousand Whistlers chanting:

Murder it

The cop visualized our turning into an uncontrollable mob; he saw the mob turn on him to tear him to pieces. He bolted towards an exit, to call reinforcements.

It was unnaturally hot. A girl fainted and was trampled a few feet from me. I laughed, clutching the gun while the composition raged like a forest fire out of control, uniting us in ashes.

I felt Whistler asking me again. I glanced up at him, his eyes locked with mine. But I was afraid of the operating table. I admit it. I threw my head back to drink guidance from the holo. Lucy? No, that was Trash on stage with Whistler. It was too hot. I had trouble breathing. He wouldn't stop asking. The holographic Trash raised the gun to her temples. Again, Whistler asking; the shrieking woman in his violin implored. I vacillated. Maybe it wasn't the best thing. If he would first take me alone with him to the Plaid Forest to explain, in the harlequin shade of that calm place, between battles, why it had to be done. . . .

Through a split-second breach in the crowd I caught a glimpse of Lucy dancing with the derelict hippy. As the crowd swallowed them again my decision was made.

Trash, in gargantuan projection overhead, fired her pistol at the instant tailored for the music—at that same

49

instant I pulled the trigger.

I gave Whistler what his music asked me for, right between the eyes.

My hand seemed to explode like a wine glass shattered by the violin's highest note. The spaces between his notes swallowed me. Before I lost consciousness I saw a bright red bullet-hole on Whistler's forehead like a third eye.

Someone slapped me down. A thunderclap, a record skipped.

VII.

Consciousness is a disease.
—DOSTOYEVSKY

I WAS GONE, I CAME BACK. The floor was hard and cold. Its cold surface pushed me unwilling, upward to consciousness. I made the rendezvous with a grinding headache and a pain in my mouth, a pre-arranged business meeting. I stood up, shaking and dizzy, holding my head. A broken front tooth leaked blood onto my chin.

About eight thousand people were dead all around me. Eight thousand four hundred seventy-three, if we can believe the newspapers. The remainder of the audience was temporarily unconscious, prostrate like sycophants on the floor. Everyone within three hundred feet of the stage died instantly, when he did. Hemorrhages. Blood clots in their brains, right between each pair of eyes. The band was dead. There was a puddle of vomit and blood reaching fingers to the stage verge to drip onto the floor with hollow clicks. The place was empty aside from myself and an acre of bodies.

The most suggestible, eight thousand four hundred seventy-three, had for that split second peak, the concert's consummation, been extensions of Whistler himself as much as his arms and legs. An incomparable honor.

And when Whistler died, in that instant of perfect mental synchronization, they went with him. Why them and not me? Why do they deserve his favor? Hadn't I earned it? He took them, these ingrate Philistines, to the Plaid Forest in the land of floating lamps. The wind of his going sucked them along behind him. But why did he push me aside at the last instant? Maybe because what's left of him here needs an audience.

I came near him, blood sucking at my shoes, and I wasn't surprised to find his eyes closed, his face relaxed. The eyes of the audience's dead were open, staring at that *something*. They didn't look at all at peace or asleep.

Like a warehouse full of mannequins smashed flat and contents scattered by a hurricane: the gaping interior of the coliseum. Already flies buzzed over the corpses. Vaguely I wondered how the authorities would explain all this. Probably blame drugs.

I could reach out and touch him. I still held the gun in nerveless fingers. I ached, head thumping about the central node of pain between my eyes, my ears rang, and all this din of my wracked body seemed to blend together into a sneering voice, Eggman's voice, nagging me to turn the gun against myself. I raised it to my head. I pulled back the hammer. My roving eyes located Eggman's dead body, lying like a squashed spider near the stage. I threw the gun at Eggman's insipid face and laughed. I thought it was *funny*.

I searched for Lucy and the derelict, didn't discover them. Probably still alive on the edge of the unconscious horde and it's just as well. They don't deserve to be with Whistler. I do. But he needs me here, to take care of his castoff shell, to listen to him play.

The violin lay near him, intact. "Go ahead, Whistler," I

said, my words hoarse whispers, echoing vastly, merging with the distant rising song of police sirens. "Play now," I said.

I heard booted footsteps, glimpsed police coming out of the corner of my eyes.

The cops were coming for me, but they were a hundred yards away. There was still time. I leaned against the stage, crossed my arms on the platform and rested my chin on them. And waited for him to play again.

The police came. And took me. But I'm still waiting.

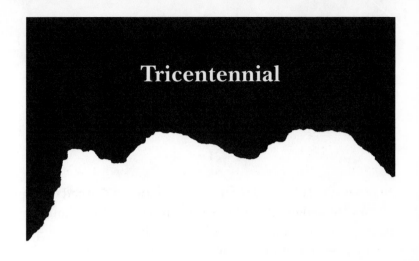

Tricentennial

ABOUT 1974 OR SO I LEFT OREGON for San Francisco, and lived there, more or less on the streets, with accommodating hookers and queens and with less accommodating people who attacked me, and at one point in a cardboard refrigerator box for two days. I didn't have a fucking *clue* how to survive, at first. I had first-hand impression of growing violence at the street level.

I WENT BACK TO PORTLAND, and two years later wrote this for an underground newspaper, as a reaction to all the plans in '76 to strut the nation's stuff for the Bicentennial. We, as a nation, were supposed to be wallowing in national pride, but I was seeing all the contradictions and a dark future; one I genuinely thought was coming—and it may well. This story was written before *Escape From New York* and *Mad Max* and *Robocop* and *Neuromancer* and *Judge Dredd* but it seems to have anticipated some of that imagery. . . .

At roughly this time in my life I was listening to Hendrix, the Stooges, the NY Dolls, Zappa and friends; not long after it would be the Ramones, Kiss (their first LP was intense and their act was then a novelty), and the Dictators.

If this story had been a film, its punk imagery—still before punk rock emerged per se—would have benefitted from a sound-track with music by, say, those bands and some bands soon to come down the pike: The Sex Pistols, Black Flag, the various Hard Core bands and my own punk bands Sado Nation and The Monitors. . . .

I.

"PRECISELY WHAT DO YOU SUGGEST *I* DO ABOUT IT?" asked Ollie.

"You're hedging. You know what has to be done. You got to go get one," said his sister Lem coldly.

"Look—we can make one for him out of cardboard—"

"No. He wouldn't fall for it, he has to have the real thing. Cloth. With the official Tricentennial medallion on the stick. He's not *that* far gone. And if we don't do it Pops won't sign the release and he'll die without turning over the stall to us and then we'll be out in the street. And *you* are the oldest, Ollie-boy. So you are elected."

"I don't know if I *want* to stay in this grimy cubey. I could be in the Angels. I got a Hell's Angels Officer's School commission and I see no reason why I shouldn't—"

"Because it would be *worse,* that's why. You don't believe all that stuff they tell you at the Angels recruiting office about the Cycle Corps, do you? They have it just as bad as the Army, except they've got the Rape Decree to back up anything they do. But big deal. You get your rocks off but do you get a decent place to sleep?"

"Okay. Okay, then. But—I ain't goin' alone. No way. If we're gonna get it for him, *you* are goin' with me, back-up. Because there's no way to go two big ones on 53rd alone without getting it in the back. . . . Look, are you sure we can't get one in Building Three?"

"I'm sure. I've called around. All the dispensaries are out of them except Eleven."

"Maybe we can roll the old man on the hundredth floor.

He's got one."

"He's got microwave barriers. We'd fry."

Ollie sighed. "Then let's go. And when we bring it back I hope to God the old sonuvabitch is happy with it. Because if he's not, Father or no Father—"

"Okay, don't get toxed. Let's go."

II.

AT FIRST, THE METAL STREETS seemed almost deserted. The frags and the joy-boy gangs and the hustlers and sliders were there, just out of sight, but Security was keeping them off the street for the Tricentennial Procession. Ollie'd heard the procession might traverse the 53rd Level but he'd assumed it would move through some less dilapidated end of the street. Maybe it all looked this way.

Crusted with grey-white scum from exhalations of methane engines and human pores, the kelp-fiber walls of the five stories visible on the 53rd Level bulged slightly outward with the weight of excess population—each stall cubey held at least five people more than regulations. Ollie cradled the Smith & Wesson .44 he'd received at age fourteen, on his Weaponing Day. He held it now, five years later, as another man might have clasped a crucifix, and he whispered to it piously, while his eyes swept the rust-pitted streets, sorting through the heaps of litter waiting for the dumper, the piles of garbage, the half-dozen corpses that were as much a part of any street as the fire hydrants. The streetlights extending from warped and peeling faces of the buildings were all functioning and the vents near the ceiling within the plasteel girder underpinnings of the 54th Level were all inhaling, judging from the thinness of the smogs wreathing the dark doorwells. There were only about twenty-five homeless or gangbugs on the street and no cars—nearly desolation, compared to any other time. Apparently the Procession was near.

Ollie and Lem, crouching just inside the doorway to their home-building, rechecked their weapons and scanned the sidewalk for booby-traps. "I don't see anything we can't handle," Lem said.

"We can't see into the alleys or doorways or that subway entrance. And—" Ollie was interrupted by the blast of a siren. A few ragged silhouettes shuffling the street scurried for doorways at the wailing from the cornice speakers. Others hardly looked up. "Looks like all that's left are dope-heads who don't know from shit. Christ, they so far gone they don't know the clear-streets when they hear it."

As the siren wound down Lem asked, "How long since you been on the street?"

"This first time in three years. Looks pretty much th' same. Only more dope-heads."

"Always more dope-heads. They don't get gutted much because they don't have any money."

"Well. Let's go, maybe we can dash the whole two blocks. I mean, since the streets are almost empty—"

"You haven't been on the streets in three years. You don't know—" Lem began.

"You're jimmy for venturing onto the streets when you don't need to. We've got everything we need on our floor, all the dispensaries and spas are there, and it's the same everywhere anyway and since you can't leave the Zone without a permit or unless you go with the troops, why bother?"

"We've got a half hour to get to Building Eleven. Let's do it."

Both of them were dressed in scum-grey clothing, camouflage, their faces smeared with gray ash so their pallor would blend, as much as possible, into the walls.

Lem, tall and thin, the fire in her curly red hair extinguished with ash, stood and checked her brace of throwing knives; inspected the uzi she'd got two years before on her Weaponing Day, and the cans of acid-bombs affixed to the two khaki belts criss-crossing her chest.

Ollie examined his own equipment, certified that the extra pistol he kept in his shoulder-holster was loaded and ready, the knives on springs lashed to his forearms primed. His .44 loaded and cocked.

Lem behind, walking backwards to cover the rear, they set off, looking like some odd two-headed predatory creature. The lineaments of the dour metal streets converged in a mesh of street-lamps, girders, stairways, and furtive figures, made tenebrously unreal by the smudged air and dim mucous-yellow lighting. The vista, shackled by metal ceiling and street merged in the distance, had all the elegance of a car crumpled into a cube by a hydraulic-press compactor. Ollie adjusted his infrared visors to see into the darker lairs. A frag, there to the right. The frag was a woman, left breast burned off to make room for a rifle-strap, a patch over her right eye. She waited, leaning back against the wall, her lower half hidden by a multiplex heap of refuse. Ollie hadn't been on the street in years, but the indications were ever the same: the suspect looked casual, relaxed—and that was bad. If she wasn't planning to attack them, she'd look tensed, in defense. So she was preparing to jump.

She was twenty feet off, on the low right, standing in the well of a barred basement doorway.

They carried $40 for their Old Man's toy. Frags could smell money. Even penniless, they'd be jumped for their clothes, guns, and on general principle.

The frag made as if to tie her bootlace. A signal. "Down!" Ollie cried.

Lem and Ollie went to a crouch as the woman who had

seen her accomplice's signal leapt from the doorway immediately to her right, and only her M-16's jamming saved them. Lem stepped in and with an underhand cut, gutted the frag and withdrew the stiletto before she could reach for another weapon. By this time the other frag was swinging her rifle round to take aim. Ollie had already leveled the .44.

He squeezed the trigger, the gun barked, the jolt from the recoil hurt his wrist. The one-eyed woman caught it in the gut, was thrown back, rebounded from the wall, and pitched forward to fall onto her face. Blood marked a Rorschach visage leering in red on the wall behind her.

He heard Lem firing at the other frags attracted by the gunshots. A young man fell, pistol clattering into the gutter. The others found cover.

"C'mon!" They sprinted, running low to the ground, gaining another forty feet, three quarters of the first block behind them. Another block-and-a-quarter, Ollie thought. Something lobbed in a wallowing tinny arc struck the sticky metal sidewalk and clattered past Ollie's right leg; he turned and grabbed Lem by the forearm, dragging her into the shelter of a doorway. The grenade exploded on the other side of the wall, fragments of the flimsy wall-fiber flew, laughter erupted from nearby frag-niches to echo from the distant ceiling, laughter as acid-drenched as the shrapnel that took out two dope-heads across the street. The blue smoke cleared.

A bullet struck the wall by Ollie's head, flying splinters stung his scalp. Swallowing fear—it had been three years— he crouched, panning his gunsight back and forth over the grey-black-engraved prospect. Sniper? From where? He looked up—that window, fourth floor. Glint off a barrel. He snatched free an acid cartridge and clipped it hastily on the launch spring welded to the underside of his pistol's barrel.

He cocked, squinted, and fired. The sniper's rifle went off at the same moment, another shot too high. Then the acid-bomb exploded in the sniper's apartment. A scream that began as a rumble, went higher and higher in pitch, finishing as a bubbling whine that merged perfectly with the returning off-streets-siren, a growing, piercing ululation. The sniper, slapping at his boiling skin, threw himself whimpering out the window and fell, writhing, three stories, striking the ground head first. Stripping the corpses of the sniper, joy-boys and the two dead women, the frags were momentarily distracted. So Ollie and Lem sprinted, zig-zagging to make poor targets.

Bolting across the intersection, they drew fire. Four strident *cracks*, four *pings*—four misses. They achieved the opposite corner. Crouched behind a conical heap of excrement and plastic cans, their left side protected by the extruding metal side-walls of a stairway. "Three-quarters of a block left," said Lem.

But frags were closing in from the right, at least a dozen piebald figures creeping hastily from shadow to shadow like scuttling cockroaches.

One of the frags caught another unawares and slipped him a blade. There was a bubbling cough and that was all.

"One less," said Lem. "But they'll cooperate to kill us before they turn on each other again."

A scratchy recorded fanfare announced the Tricentennial Procession.

The street was twenty yards from gutter to gutter. The Procession filled the street for half a block; two long, six-wheeled armored red-white-and-blue sedans surrounded by twelve Security Cycles. A recorded voice from the chrome fanged grill of the front sedan announced over and over:

REJOICE INDEPENDENCE DAY REJOICE INDEPENDENCE DAY REJOICE INDEPENDENCE DAY MAYOR WELCOMES ALL CITIZENS TO

SEYMOR COLISEUM FOUR PM FOR PUBLIC EXECUTIONS PARTY
REJOICE INDEPENDENCE DAY REJOICE REJOICE

Dimly, through the green-tinted window of the low, steel-plated limo, Ollie could make out the faces of the High Priest of the International Church of Sun Moon sitting beside the man he'd appointed as Mayor, whose name Ollie could not recall. A few token bullets bounced from the limo's windshield. The silhouettes within waved at the faces crowding the windows. A handful of excrement splattered the roof, cleaned away an instant later by tiny hoses in the windshield frame. One of the Security Cycles shot a microwave shell into the apartment from which the excrement had been thrown; there was a white flash and a scream, a thin wisp of smoke from the shattered window.

The Security Cycles were three-wheeled motorbikes, propelled, like the limousines, by methane engines fueled by gases extracted from human excrement. Issuing blue flatulence, they rolled slowly abreast of Ollie and Lem. The cops inside, figures of shiny black leather, heads completely encased in black-opaqued helmets, were protected by bells of transparent plasteel from which their various weapons projected cobra snouts. The cop nearest Ollie methodically snuffed dope-heads and careless frags with casual flares of his handle-bar-mounted microwave rifle. "Hey," Ollie breathed, "maybe they'll help us. If you call them they don't come but since they're right here, if we ask them for help getting to the corner they can't refuse, seeing as we're right in front of them and all. Hell, with the High Priest watching . . ."

"Ollie, don't be an asshole—"

But Ollie was already out in the street, waving his arms, shouting, "We need an escort, just a little farther, we are citizens, we have to go to Building Eleven to buy a—"

He threw himself flat and rolled, wincing as the invisible

microwave beam singed his back. The cop fired again but Lem had thrown a smoke-bomb, and Ollie took advantage of the thick yellow billowing to return to cover.

"Wish I could afford one of those microwave rifles," Lem remarked wistfully.

"Hey, Lem, maybe if we keep just back of the procession we can use it for cover and get the rest of the way."

Lem nodded and they were off.

Most of the frags were flattened to avoid the microwave beams; the cops ignored their shielded rear, so Ollie and Lem sprinted along behind, and Building Eleven loomed ahead. Ollie grinned. There! The stairs!

They were scrambling the two flights up the stairs when the doors to building eleven swung open and a pack of joy-boys, none of them over twelve years old, stampeded directly into Lem and Ollie's reflexive gunfire. But there were too many of them to spray dead at short range. Five went down, another ten were upon them—naked but for belts bristling with makeshift knives. Their gap-toothed mouths squalling, drooling like demented elves, they chattered and snarled gleefully. Their sallow, grimy faces—seen as blurs personifying aggression, now—were pock-marked, the eyes dope-wild. Swinging the gun-butt in his right hand, the spring-snapped knife in his left, Ollie slashed and battered at the small faces, faces like rotted jack-o-lanterns, and time slowed: fragments of skull and teeth flew, black-nailed hands clawed at his face, his own blood clouded his visors.

Ollie plowed forward, kicking, elbowing, feeling a twisted shard of metal bite deep into his thigh, another below his left shoulder-blade, another in his right pectorals. He was two feet from the door. He left his knife in someone's ribs. He glanced at Lem, three of them were on her back, clinging like chimp-children, clawing relentlessly at her head, gnawing her ears with ragged yellow teeth. He dragged them off of her with his left hand, wrenching viciously to keep them off his own back, and brained another who flailed wildly at his eyes—and then he and Lem were through the door.

It was cool and quiet inside.

A young man, a custodian chewing synthabetel and squinting at them, leaning on his mop, said, "You got some holes in you."

"Where—" Ollie had to catch his breath. He felt weak. Blood soaking his right leg—have to bind that before heading back, he thought, try again, ask: "Where we buy . . . flags?"

"Fifty-fourth level if he's got any left."

III.

LUCK WAS WITH THEM. They made it back with only two more wounds. A .22 slug in Lem's right arm, a zip gun pellet in Ollie's left calf.

Lem slumped outside the door to bind her wounds and rest. Ollie took the flag from her and staggered into their two-room apartment, stepped carefully over the children sleeping on the crowded floor, tried not to stagger. He was dizzy, nauseated. The tiny cubicle seemed to constrict and whirl, the stained yellow-white curtains over the alcove where his father lay dying on an army cot became malignant leprous arms reaching for him. He cursed, his right hand gripping the small, rolled-up flag. He felt he could not walk another step.

Ollie sank to a chink of clear floor-space. He shoved wearily at one of the sleeping children. Eight-year old Sandra. She woke, a pale, hollow-eyed child, nearly bald, a few strands of wispy flaxen hair. "You take this to Pops." He told her. "The flag. Tell him to sign the goddamn release."

Seeing the flag, the little girl's eyes flared. She snatched the bright banner away and ran out into the hall, ignoring Ollie's shouts.

She got three bucks for the flag from a man on the Hundredth Level.

A penny a year.

Shadow of a Snowstorm

THE CLARION WRITER'S WORKSHOP, 1972. Harlan Ellison was coming down the walk and I went to the window and howled to him in greeting—literally howled, doing my best wolf imitation. I was maybe twenty. Later, if I didn't hallucinate this (I was on acid some of the time at this workshop), I dropped out of a tree on his back, or just missed him. I entered the class by climbing up the outside of the building and leaping in through the window. I was a melodramatic little fuck. I remember Harlan standing outside my dorm room going "Whew! The *smell* from in there! Shirley don't you ever wash your clothes?! It smells like New York during the garbage strike!" Or something of the sort.

I wrote the first draft of this at Clarion. Though it was set in the future, this social satire was actually a fantasy. The arc of trajectory is clear. There are satiric allusions—as in "What He Wanted" and "Tricentennial" and, later, in the *Eclipse* books—to a power structure intertwined with catharsis for the masses.

Ostensibly it's a story about a future in which a Depression has become so widespread the government has had to create absurd jobs to keep the army of otherwise-unemployed harmlessly busy: for example the "profession" of humannequin and humannequin inspector. "Shadow of a Snowstorm" was consciously "absurdist." It wasn't supposed to be a "real" future. It was an experiment, again, in blurring inner and outer realities, in surrealism dedicated to social satire. It was my ingenuous attempt at a feminist statement, too; it was about the things we put women through. The neuroses we force on them; the expectation that they be perfect little Barbies for us during the day, perfect little Bunnies for us at night. And it was about the commercialization of our lives, our neurotic obsession with media image, with veneers; our using the trappings of the modern world as insulation against the heat of our inner beings.

(Remember, a few years ago, when "vogueing" was popular in the poseur-haunted discos of New York?)

When I wrote this story I was listening to glitter bands, hard rockers who wore makeup, like the Dolls and Mott the Hoople and friends. The identification with the Anima.

I would rather paint a man's eyes than a cathedral.
—VAN GOGH

SHE HAD NEVER SEEN A SNOWSTORM. But the snowstorm whirled through her head spinning flakes into drifts. She wanted to be a cloud of the snowstorm, and she tried to imagine its icy, pristine wind clinging to her in a second skin of white. She saw only a whirlpool of lacy white. The snowstorm would hurt at first. . . .

"YOU FLINCHED!" A sharp male voice. She brushed the snowstorm aside and flicked her eyes to the right without moving her head. It was the inspector. She blinked three times. That meant NO in the humannequin code.

"Yes, oh yes you did. Yes, you moved and you shivered too. You are simply breaking the pose."

She tried to keep from swallowing or showing other signs of nervousness. The inspector was watching so closely now that even swallowing would be considered an imposture. But his watching made her want to move. That's not fair, she thought. He does that deliberately. He wants me to get agitated. But if I do I'll lose the pose and lose my job. Relax . . . *Be poised on the edge.*

The humannequin inspector was a wrinkled little man with bulging eyes. He stared at her as a snake would, and for a moment she thought that when he blinked his eyelids came only from below. He shook his head and jowls. "Remember," he said, "you should be between motions. Like a diver on the end of the diving board. But *you* stand stiff as if you'd just finished a movement. You should be between motions, and *poised.* Do you think this store employs you solely because of the FBME? Hardly. Since you are new here—" He stopped speaking and rummaged through a large side-pocket in his orange checkered jacket.

This is it, she thought. The speech. I should have known I wouldn't get out of it.

The humannequin inspector cleared his throat and read from a small paisley-jacketed book. A crowd of customers gathered, hoping to see her break from pose. She was battered by their stares.

The inspector was reading: "'. . . in February of 1997 the Federal Bureau of Mandatory Employment, dedicated to finding constructive occupations for all Americans, decreed that department stores and any agencies or corporations using replicas of human beings shall replace them with those of the mass of the unemployed deemed suitable and trained by the bureau. HIP Stores, however, anticipated the need to create jobs in an overpopulated nation and was already in the process of preparing such a program when the regulation was instituted. HIP Stores has always been strongly aware of the needs of the American people and was more than happy to comply. But there is a purpose in the employment of humannequins, superseding mere legal conformity—'" The inspector paused and looked around meaningfully. But most of the crowd had fled from boredom, and the new humannequin seemed inattentive. He frowned but continued, " '. . . we use them because they're more realistic, more engaging to the eye than dummies. They alone can do justice to the high quality and carefully tailored standards of the fashions offered by HIP Stores.' " The Inspector stopped reading and glowered at her, searching out cracks in her photocopied calm. "I think you get the idea. I'll let your imposture go this time since you are a newcomer. But remember: You work here because your function is intended to be esthetically pleasing, not because of the law. There are more than enough applicants who would be delighted to have your job, and HIP Stores employ only humannequins who are artists, not people who have nothing to do but stand still for three hours."

Bullshit, she thought. You've got nothing to do but lecture me. They don't need a humannequin inspector. You're here because you had nothing to do. She ached to say it out loud. But she blinked: *Yes Sir.*

I can feel his eyes on my breasts, she thought. That's why he applied for that job. Because he can stare at female humannequins for as long as he likes. *Don't get angry,* she warned herself, or you'll break the pose and lose your first job ever.

Her first job, except for the teaching assistance at the Catholic school where she'd been raised after her parents were killed by the witch hunters at the annual Inquisition. Twelve years of maintaining her composure at the Catholic school had conveniently prepared her for humannequinism.

The inspector was still there, she realized. He hovered just out of sight behind her.

"You're breathing heavily," he said suddenly, in a whine like an overworked vacuum cleaner. "Remember, breathe only through the nose, take as long as possible for each breath so that your chest moves only fractionally. And for Heaven's sake, you're *sweating*. You should apply your anti-perspirant more thoroughly. Your makeup is smeared. And don't forget to join the humannequin guild. We make it a policy to employ only guild humannequins. As you perhaps recall, I hired you with the understanding that you would join the guild within a week after beginning work. Your week ends tomorrow. There is a guild meeting tonight." He stalked away.

When she was sure that he was gone she allowed herself a short sigh. Then she remembered the other humannequin up the aisle. She looked at him out of the corners of her eyes. Moving, her eyes felt like freely roving birds, perhaps building a nest in her skull. Their slight movement melted the racks of hosiery across from her into groves of trees. A man was standing there, amongst the trees, a black man clad in a white toga and silvery briefs. His pose was sharp and dramatic, captured in the swift movement of hands upraised as if about to catch a ball. His eyes were on something imaginary in the air and he wore an anticipatory grin.

Her vision of the imaginary forest vanished, leaving the black humannequin surrounded by racks of hosiery and togas.

His arms in the air! she mused, how difficult that must be to maintain. But he's muscular. The pose arbiter wouldn't assign a stance he was unprepared for.

A line from the humannequin handbook drifted past on the current of memory: . . . *any given pose has an emotional response corresponding to it in the model.* . . .

His pose would make me feel cheated, she thought, to be always waiting for the ball that never comes.

He should wear his eyes around his neck like pearls, she thought.

Don't think about that.

She rehearsed posture attitudes and exercises from the Humannequin Handbook:

1) Poised like a bird about to leap into flight.
2) Flying like a jet, everything stilled but the feeling of being airborne.
3) Not a sculpture, sculptures are frozen. You are the captured epitome of motion. A single frame from a motion picture filmstrip.
4) Hummingbird in a cage!
5) Say to yourself: I am a work of art. I am not a department store dummy. But I am a pose. I am the perfect image of every person's ideal self. It is my responsibility to the customers to be a picture of their happiness.

She reaffirmed her smile, hoping that no one noticed the adjustment.

She tried to picture her pose. As per Procedure she pictured first a woman conscious of her clothes as much as her body. Her feet were planted firmly but the left one was behind and slightly lifted at the heel as if just beginning another step. Her hands were swinging, frozen slightly upraised with the rhythm of an imaginary stride. Her smile was content and lively. But the eyes were the hard part. They revealed too much. When she struggled to exact their expression they seemed to draw apart from her like small animals crouching in the hollows of her cheekbones. She wore a genii-bikini with its transparent filmy blue top like the tinge of frozen skin. The thin panties, blue lace, were stylistically low-cut, disclosing a tuft of honeybrown pubic hair at their band.

The pose reminded her of a victim of smog asphyxiation she had once seen collapsed on the corner. The scantily clad young woman had fallen unconsciously into a loose genii-bikini pose where she lay on the grimy sidewalk.

The comparison almost made her grimace, but she caught herself. Tension was submerged in another fantasy. The snowstorm kissed her wetly.

A long time later one of the baser howls of the blizzard wind became the voice of her replacement.

"You can cut loose now Sandra, it's my turn." Sandra saw that the curtain over the dais was closed. She relaxed with a shudder.

"You didn't even notice when we put the curtain up," the woman said.

Sandra rotated her head to loosen stiff muscles in her neck and gazed gratefully at the enclosing black curtains. She wanted to sleep. She would go to sleep as soon as she got home, even if she had to take tranks to relax.

The Store covered the transition from one humannequin to another with black curtains, like sleep.

Weird, Sandra thought, that watching a humannequin change positions was thought perverse. If my mother were alive she'd declare that the dildo section on the fifth floor is dirty. She'd think the erotic photos adorning the sixth floor's Intimate Apparel were perverse.

Sandra stretched, wincing at the cramp in her right shoulder. As she stepped down from the platform her circulation caught up with the abrupt change in position. Hot flashes seared up her back. Her vision darkened and her eyes smarted.

The new humannequin took a deep breath as she took her place. Her expression softened, she became a woman walking gaily down the street—poised. There was no expression in her eyes other than the look that went with her posture. The woman blinking her eyes quickly four times for *open the curtains*.

Sandra walked behind the platform and drew on her coat, the corduroy fabric seeming abrasive against her bared skin. She opened the curtains with a pull cord and several shoppers, two of them fat old women spilling out of their own genii-bikinis went *ahh* as the curtains parted. An adolescent boy made a loud remark about the possibilities of satisfactory sex with the replacement model. Everyone laughed. The humannequin didn't alter her expression even slightly.

Poised.

On the edge.

Balanced on the high wire.

About to—

Not *quite*—

Just prior—

Poised.

Admiring the new humannequin, Sandra told herself: It *is* an art. Don't put it down because you can't do it right, because you have to be a nun among humannequins.

The thought of the guild made her curl her lips with disgust. They're not a guild, she thought, they're a cult. No choice. No sleep. No options. No sleep.

The numbness in her legs shattered like surf cascading over rocks as she walked away from the dais. She had never been to the sea but a tidal wave roared through her mind tossing black curtains of saltwater. Stacks of boxes and products on all sides resembled barnacled rocks; people surged between the rocks like otters. The otters surrounded her and urged her downward, safely under the roaring storm to where dark currents danced her back and forth—

EXIT

She blinked at the sign, then glanced quickly around her. Scurrying shoppers and a Security Smile. The Security Smile was a robot four feet high. It was controlled by an operator watching through its television eyes from a remote cubby in the building. The robot had a huge round yellow "happy face." Its face consisted of two oblong holes for eyes behind which twin cameras gleamed, and a painted arc of a smile.

The robot was watching her. Has the inspector told it to keep an eye on me? she wondered. But the robot made no move to come closer so she stepped onto the down escalator. She felt like running. She caught a glimpse of herself in a mirror. As she watched, her reflection sank, her features becoming fluid, draining down the mirror like water through a gutter grate. Her brown hair wreathing narrow shoulders, her amber eyes, small pointed nose, pink-edged lips too small, chin just weak enough so that she could never rate an Inner Stance beauty—she sank into the floor. She bit her lips and looked down at the lingerie products on the floor that rose to meet her. There was a humannequin modeling lace panties just to the right of the escalator as she stepped off. The same boy who had jeered at Sandra's upstairs replacement approached this humannequin and overtly pinched her right nipple. The model didn't react, but the nipple stiffened slightly. The boy grinned. A security robot whirred up behind him on silent rollers, extended a pincered limb from its chest-cavity and picked the boy up by the shirt collar. The boy yelped and whined:

"Hey cut it out!"

The Security Smile, its smooth stainless steel cylindrical body glistening a reflection of the dangling child on its chest in curved distortion, carried the offender away.

AT 8 P.M. WHEN SHE ARRIVED at the gold door of the humannequin guild hall she presented her HIP Stores card and was admitted after donning a black robe. The robe was floor length and made of the same material as the curtains that covered humannequin transferrals. The room was smaller than she had expected, with only about sixty black-robed humannequins, out of pose as much as they ever were, men and women sitting quietly. They were silent, watching a stage with curtains of the familiar black cloth. As she sat down in the back row the curtain rolled away to reveal two humannequins, a man and a woman, nude, in postures of people running away from one another. They were ornaments, adorning opposite sides of the stage. From a slit in another curtain behind them came a tall well-muscled man of the sort seen modeling men's underwear in catalogues. He wore a green suit and an engaging smile.

" 'Don't move,' " he said, according to ritual, " 'We are the bodies of the products, and it is our responsibility as products to remain stationary but poised, waiting for application. Let them stare. We are the mental cosmetic.' "

" *'We are the mental cosmetic,'* " came the audience's chorused litany.

Another man came from the wings at stage right. He was older, graying, but solid and sure of himself. Sandra recognized him as the guild president; he had never been a humannequin. "Well spoken," he rumbled, "A round of applause for Mr. Ackerman." There was sporadic clapping. "Mr. Ackerman has completed all the requirements and tonight will be purified so that he is fit to be a member of the Inner Stance of the guild." Applause. Ackerman bowed. "First we will make Mr. Ackerman complete by removing that portion of him which is a stumbling block to his total realization of the Inner Stance of the guild of humannequins." He gestured pontifically and two men all in white wheeled an operating table and a rack of complex chrome and plastic equipment onto the stage. The room became darker, a spotlight opaqued the goggles of the doctors and made their equipment shine like the involuted byways and freeways and towers of a city miniaturized by distance.

Ackerman removed his clothing, folded it in a neat pile, and laid himself on the table. One of the men in white injected him with an anesthetic. While waiting for the drug to take effect the guild president said: "Mr. Ackerman has exhibited total congruence with the products he represents, and at no time did he give indication of awareness of other than his posture and his product." Applause. "While we're waiting for Mr. Ackerman's preparation, I've brought along some pertinent diversion in the form of a newsreel . . ." The lights went dim and a screen whirred down in front of the operating table. The president left the stage as the film began and a voice said:

". . . Eric Lepzig, one of the seminal founding fathers of the neo-conceptualist movement in art—an approach advocating that anything in the artist's immediate environment becomes art when he declares it to be—has given up his manhole cover constructs to take conceptualism's minimalist mode to its ultimate extreme. His new work, which he says was inspired by the guild of humannequins, whom he openly admires, is himself. Lepzig signed papers authorizing an optimum lobotomy last Friday night. After the operation Sunday morning he was permanently placed in the Lepzig collection of the Museum of Modern Art. As he is now a human vegetable as well as the embodiment of Art, he must be fed and changed daily by a special detail assigned to the museum staff—"

The film showed Lepzig smiling and shaking hands as he signed papers. It cut to a shot of his lax face profiled against his famous bottlecap construct. He sits limply in a padded chair staring stupidly into space, one arm swinging loosely at his side, his mouth leaking drool. The voice explains that he has had a double lobotomy, completely imbecilizing—but the film is cut short and the lights flash on. The screen rolled itself into the ceiling and the presi-

75

dent returned, smiling enigmatically.

"We're ready," one of the surgeons said, standing by the prostrate Ackerman.

Sandra had not noticed the people beside her until she turned to the man seated at her right and asked, "Are they going to do it *here?*" She bit her lip when she saw that the man she was whispering at was the black guy who held the pose across from her on the third floor of HIP Store 34.

"Obviously," the black guy said. "Don't look so worried. They're not going to cut off his balls or anything. They'll mess about with some nerve ends and deaden a few. . . ." He appraised her with street-black eyes for many moments after he spoke. "But maybe you ought to forget about the guild, kid. I mean, if it's what you really want to do, but— The president is looking over here. Shhh."

The guild president was looking directly at Sandra. She pretended to be interested in the operation. The surgeons withdrew a shining silver needle from the incision in Ackerman's crotch. They sewed it up. Ackerman, eyes sleepy, was still smiling.

"Mr. Ackerman, after serving flawlessly in the guild of humannequins for four years, has achieved the Inner Stance." The president intoned. "Even when he is not in mannequin-pose he is always posing. He is always poised." There was applause and the two humannequins on the stage changed poses simultaneously and knelt, arms raised in symbolic supplication.

Now there was no sound in the audience. There were no whispers, no coughs, no clearing throats.

The surgeon wheeled Ackerman from the room and the posing humannequins returned to their original ornamentations.

"And now," the president said, "I believe we have a newcomer."

Everyone in the room turned and stared at Sandra. She wanted to cry out under the impact of so many stares, but she knew that would have marked her for failure as a humannequin. She stood, her hands seeking one another, clasped defensively over her belly.

"Your name is Sandra Newcombe, is it not?"

"Yes, yes it is."

"How long have you been working for HIP Stores?"

"About a week and a half."

"Have you ever worked for HIP Stores before or been a member of another chapter of a humannequin guild?"

"No. Never."

"Are you fully aware that being a humannequin is an *art?*"

"Yes. Certainly. Definitely."

"How long did you train before you started work at HIP number thirty-four?"

"About three months."

"Are you fully aware of the initiation exercises and examinations involved in becoming a guild member?"

"I . . . well, no, I don't know much about that part."

"You will be asked to undergo a series of postures in rapid succession before the attendant guild. You will also be asked to endure a test of resistance to outward stimulation of your sexual organs while in posture as a demonstration of your endurance and dedication to the humannequin ideal. Are you prepared?"

She hesitated and glanced down at the black man beside her. His face was as impassive as the rest. But when she looked into his eyes he turned away.

She felt as if each member of the silent audience awaiting her decision had a finger on her face, testing for any anomalous emotional twitch. She imagined the president pointing to portions of her face as if it were a television weather map. The TV weatherman was marking woodgrain patterns on the black outlines of states. The loops he drew across the map were the red marks the audience's fingers left on her skin, whorls of high-pressure, low-pressure, cold front, warm front: fingerprint marks from their gropings. The mapped nation suffered from a cold front coming from the south: her loins. The newscasters, as impersonal as humannequins, had fashionable hairdos, and mirror ties and triple-notched lapels on their suits, wire-rim glasses and shards in their eyes. She was brought rudely from the fancy by the president's impatient:

"Are you *with* us? Have you decided, Miss Newcombe?"

She could feel the eyes of the audience pulsing in their sockets, sucked close to their skulls by the vacuum inside. Their eyes rearranging her features like flowers in a vase.

She debated silently. If she didn't hold the job she'd either be stuck in the apartment which was clenched with too many people like the balled fingers of a fist, or she'd have to go to the Excess Zone, the haven for the surplus population with nothing to do. She'd spent days in the Excess Zone before the humannequin job, finding a hypnotic peace in milling from one level to another in the vast concrete and glass building. Here, at least humannequins are *given* a face.

"Go ahead," Sandra said to the president of the guild. He took a sheaf of papers from a side pocket and handed them to an aide who stepped briskly from the wings of the stage to carry them, with a pen, to where Sandra waited in the aisle.

"Sign these then. They release us from any legal responsibility should you harm yourself physically or emotionally while being tested."

She signed.

"Now. Come with me to the stage." She followed him, feeling the head of every person on the audience swivel to watch her.

If I don't get used to being stared at, she thought, I'll never be a humannequin. I'll be stuck in the Excess Zone.

She mounted the stage after the older man and looked at her feet, or pretended to examine her hands clasped in front of her, rather than face the constellation of staring eyes. The aide took the papers backstage.

"To begin, Larry!" The president barked. He stood at Sandra's right holding the papers she'd signed like Moses' tablets. One of the humannequins flanking the stage shed his pose, stretched quickly, then strutted to Sandra's side looking attentive. "Larry will give you your poses, Sandra. You'll have to imitate him as closely as possible."

"But he—" she started to protest, forgetting herself.

"Yes . . . he's a *man* isn't he? Very perceptive of you," interrupted the president, "But that is a deliberately imposed obstacle you are required to overcome. Do you possess a license for public nudity?"

"Yes, but—"

"Take off your clothes." Mutely she removed her robe, the yellow pantaloons and see-through blouse.

"Everything's set," the president said when she was naked. "Go ahead, Larry. 'Pose-don't-move.' "

Instantly Larry snapped into an exaggerated masculine bearing. He wore a neanderthal expression as he crouched low, like a football player about to spring for a tackle. His hands were outstretched, brutishly groping. Sandra followed suit, crouching, flexing back and shoulder muscles. She added a grimace. Unsteady, she slipped slightly from pose, then forced herself back. But her hands trembled. She realized that she must look absurd, and that they had intended it. Her eyes watered when the overhead lights grew brighter. Someone tilted a light toward her face. She flinched.

Larry suddenly shifted position. He was now in an Atlas-like stance, back bent and arms upraised as if supporting a heavy weight. Unused to shifting poses so quickly, Sandra's imitation was inexact . . . but she had looked at Larry too much already. The pose made her feel ancient, that it might be best to give up and find the nearest place to sleep, like a very old woman struggling to climb a hill.

"Your feet are wrong," the president admonished coolly. "Try another pose, Larry."

Larry melted from one aspect to another with alarming rapidity. He seemed to take no time at all to readjust. He became a stalwart pioneer figure, one hand shading his eyes, eyes sharply peering, back straight.

It looked easy. But in attempting the rapid move from the last posture to this she twisted muscles in her back. She drew her breath in sharply at the pain.

Desperately she strove to recall the mental posture exercises:

Poised like a bird . . .

—the bird exploded as it passed the muzzle of the hunter's gun. He shot it at close range and its head went flying one way, its wings the other.

Flying like a jet . . .

—the jet, just as it was about to touch down, ducked its snout and nosed into the ground, crumpling the entire forward section. The tail whiplashed off and flipped over the nose of the jet, crushing an airport fire engine.

Not a sculpture, sculptures are frozen . . .

—she was stiff, cold, aching with immobility. She wanted to move, to leave the pose but could not. Her muscles would not relax. A man with a chisel came at her. He split her down the middle. She screamed and fell to the floor.

Fainted.

The president helped her to stand, but even leaning

against him her knees were shaking. There was a stabbing pain in her legs. When she could stand without support she was again staggered by the audience. Every face was silent and expressionless. The president passed a small vial of amyl nitrate under her nose. Her eyes widened. She straightened as the pain passed from her head leaving a wake of chill. She laughed, suddenly elated.

"Let's have a hand for Sandra," the president said. Applause.

I can do it, Sandra thought. Or I can keep from doing the wrong thing. Or—

"Sandra," the older man said in a kindly tone. "Can you pose now?"

"Sure. 1 can do it."

"Then assume your pose assigned for work."

Sandra took a deep breath, relaxed, shifted, picturing the genii-bikini pose as vividly as she was able. She was surprised at the ease of the adjustment: she fell into the posture as easily as she would hang a coat on a hook.

"You're smiling a little too much. Pleased with yourself?" The president asked. She loosened the smile slightly. "Better. Now, Inspector."

The humannequin inspector for HIP Store 34 came from stage left. He held something in a hand but she couldn't make out just what it was without moving her head. "Don't break posture no matter what, Sandra." The guild president said. "Be poised, be nothing but your product's champion."

But Sandra was thinking of the stumpy humannequin inspector's pawing eyes. He has a face like a big navel, she thought. He's going to touch me and he's got white powder on his hands, I've seen it before, he smears it on everything he touches. It must be some kind of poison. . . .

But the humannequin inspector didn't touch her with

his hands. He came at her from the side, sidling up close enough so that she could feel his humid breath on her arm. She felt a cold and metallic nudge against her belly, just below the arch of her rib cage. The metal thing vibrated, gently but rapidly pummeling her skin like the inspector's thoughts about touching her. She felt the steel electric vibrator get warmer, as it moved back and forth over her waist like a spider on its web, spiraling up, circling her breasts, over her nipples. But as yet it was no more intrusive than the eyes watching her at work, hoping that she would break posture. Still, she held the pose as simply as water conforms to the shape of a pitcher. She pictured the pitcher, cold and smooth and brittle; the buzzing vibrator touched its glass and rattled, skipping over it, making sparks, scraping particles of silicon as it whined. Pain exploded from the strain of control. Pain just behind her eyes. *Now my eyes are trying to get out,* she thought, *to join the inspector's.*

The vibrator ran down her belly and shuddered on her pubic mound—she stiffened involuntarily. The humannequin inspector made a pleased noise like a rat squeaking in its sleep.

She winced. The glass was cracking.

Does he really think this is erotic? she wondered frantically. No, he knows I hate it. It feels like he's slapping me. The friction feels like it's tearing skin away. Is that supposed to arouse me? No, no. They're teaching the endurance that comes with humiliation.

She felt the metal press against her clitoris, producing sandpaper pain. The vibrator beat against her dully, like an insistent knocking on a door. *The knuckles that knocked grew raw and bloody as no one answered; after hours of knocking the white knuckle-bone poked through the ripped skin, chipped itself on the door.*

She felt the humannequin inspector's breath on her pubic mound. It made her skin crawl. Nausea welled up in her and tried to incite her stomach into vomiting. He pressed the vibrator brutally against the bone of her mons veneris. Her arms wavered and drooped as she fought the urge to tear the biting metal off.

"Okay inspector, that will do." the guild president's voice, soothing, "You can cut loose now, Sandra."

She moaned and bent over double holding her crotch. Her skin had a palpable blanket thickness, its outer layer encased her like a sarcophagus.

Her senses were wrapped in wax paper . . . from the Drygoods Department, first floor.

The unenthusiastic applause from the guild shook against her ears like the vibrator against her skin. She coughed, trying to keep from vomiting.

"Congrats and kudos," the inspector said. "You passed. Just barely."

Sandra's body seethed and burned and shone as if it had been covered in molten gold.

IT WAS ANOTHER MILE from the monorail station to HIP Store 34. She was eager to get to work, as if completing the final step of the ritual begun the night before.

She was to receive her certificate after work, as soon as the results of her electroencephalogram (given to her in a curtained black room after the meeting) were run through the computer. *A mere formality,* the president had assured her. Maybe, if she attained the higher pay of Inner Stance humannequin status, she might eventually have enough saved up to rent a *private room.* All to herself.

She hurried through the neon-glazed streets, proudly pushing through night-shift crowds. Arrogantly, she decided to pass unbeguiled by the cluster of FBME workers under the next corner's streetlight. But a tall, round shouldered man put one hand to an ear in the sign of the Mandatory Employment Worker and clipped off, "I'm the FBME Clothing Inspector for Sixty-eighth and Cranshaw. I've been assigned to—" Already he was stooping to examine her clothing.

"I've heard it before," she said, "but go ahead."

He smiled. Then, though he was standing in the conical gown of light from the corner lamp he shined a penlight over her clothing. "Whoops! There's one!" he chortled, taking a wrinkle compressor from his pocket. He replaced the penlight in a pocket stitched with *penlight 8;* his rows of pockets were numbered and labeled. He placed a teflon bulb over the minute wrinkle he'd spotted on her sweater's shoulder and pressed a button. The wrinkle had vanished when he lifted the bulb away. *"There.* Too bad it can't be done for skin!" He chuckled at his little joke. "If you want the rest of your clothing straightened out, this fellow over here," he stabbed a nicotine-yellowed finger at a squat, bald little man waiting eagerly at his side, "is a specialist at straightening buttons. . . ."

There were four other FBME workers behind the bald man. Probably shoe-lace cappers, shoe-polishers, cuff-reliners, collar-straighteners and spiritual comforters.

"That's okay," Sandra said, "I've had my clothes rearranged three times already tonight."

"Are you quite sure? It's free you know," piped the little man. "Public service."

"I know, I'm a humannequin. I work for FBME too."

Lowering their eyes respectfully they slipped out of her way.

Humannequins have a certain mystique these days, she thought.

Shouldering through the milling crowd, she glanced at

her watch. Seven-thirty. She had forty-five minutes before her shift. The night sky was sullen with smog, skyscraper apartment buildings zippering the skyline shut.

Most of the crowd here were FBME employees: Public works polishers rubbing down fire hydrants and gutter grates. Concrete maintenance men filling cracks in the sidewalk or chipping holes so that they would have holes to fill. Men holding up mirrors so that a pedestrian could easily see if his or her hair was mussed or teeth unbrushed. Sometimes a clothing straightener would rearrange public works polishers while looking at himself in a mirror held by an FBME employee listening to a comforter recite aphorisms. Sometimes these mutual Mandatory Employment interchanges became a chain many blocks long.

Sandra left the FBME cluster behind and passed thinner crowds until she came to a small bridge over a strip of inky river emerging briefly from the subterranean tunnels. The city had been compelled by lack of space to build housing that spanned the once impressive river. It moaned vastly from the dark, steel-barred mouth of the huge cistern. Reflected in the half-mile stretch of exposed river was the monolithic Excess Zone. Sandra looked up into the steel and glass face of the man-shaped building, remembering from the inside out. The structure was a seventy-seven story likeness of a man from the waist up, spacious features smooth and stylized so that he had hollows instead of eyes, his barrel chest and torso made of lateral strips of clear plasteel. Its insides were patrolled by cops on monowheels, keeping the surging crowds moving and amenable. The crowds sifted from the upper levels to the lower like tickets in a revolving sweepstakes basket, each one waiting for the unseen hand to single it out. Often Sandra had looked out of the parted lips of the Excess Zone building, wishing for some other place to go.

She left the river and hurried up the boulevard until she came to an alley that was her shortcut to HIP Store 34. She was halfway down the dark ravine of concrete when the way was blocked by a young man in a chain-mail jacket. A large battery powered knife chattered in his fist. His bald head was polychromatically painted. His eyes were dull, like the steely sockets of the Excess man.

"Lay down over there—" he stabbed a finger at a discarded, rotting mattress humped behind a row of garbage cans. "—*now.*"

Reacting with reflex and without really knowing why, she snapped into the genii-bikini pose.

The rapist gaped at her, shocked.

Sandra didn't move. There was no place else to go; and no looking back. There were a few hardened people watching from the sidewalk at the opening of the alley, but she knew she could expect no help from them. She had taken refuge.

The young man licked his lips and reached out to touch her. His fingers paused less than an inch from the soft skin of her throat. . . .

She didn't move. She knew that it had become part of her now, autonomous as breathing. She wouldn't move even if he cut her. She'd just stand there and bleed, she decided. The knife hummed loudly into her ear.

But the thug drew his hand back.

"Why don't you move?" he asked, a note of panic in his voice. She watched him out of the corner of one eye but remained frozen into the stance of the humannequin pose officially assigned to her by the arbiter.

"Come on," said the mouth behind the knife. "Cut it out or I'll cut it out. Move, cow. Move or something." A look of revulsion swam over his narrow features. He shook his head. Suddenly his hand darted and the sawing, serrated edge of the electric knife bit her upraised right arm. The pain was like an unexpected drop of rain.

She didn't flinch.

He drew the knife away. Blood chased after the edge and flowed down her arm.

She didn't move.

The boy shrieked. He threw the knife down and ran into the choking night. The knife, still turned on, chattered to itself on the sidewalk.

She remained in the pose until the tickling of blood threatened to stain her dress. Then she relaxed.

She took a tube of flesh-tone bandaid paste from her pocket and smeared it over the cut. She daubed the blood away with a handkerchief then smoothed out the fleshy paste with a makeup brush, so that nothing would be noticed while she was in pose.

HIP STORE 34 WAS ONE MILE LONG and three-quarters of a mile wide. It included groceries, drygoods, hardware, nutrient bars, car parts, chicken parts, drugs, clothes of every sort, imports, sensual accessories, souvenirs, furniture, and it trained and featured the "most dedicated humannequins available."

Sandra came to her modeling dais and closed the curtains around the humannequin who was already there. The humannequin got down immediately, stretched, did some quick exercises, pulled on her coat and left without amenities.

With the opening of the curtain Sandra was ready. Sandra would always be ready. But as the hours passed, tension built irrevocably in her.

Three middle-aged women came by, stopping to stare. Sandra felt their eyes crawling over her bare midriff, eyes hot and moist, jelly-orbs revolving in slick sockets. Out of the corner of her eyes she thought she saw the eyeballs crawl from the hollow sockets of the shoppers, to drop on strands of ectoplasm to the floor. Sandra's haunting tension called the eyeballs closer. They were followed by the tongues and fingers of the shoppers, detached and travelling freely, eyes, tongues and fingers rolling or creeping or slithering onto the platform and up her legs. She shivered, flexed her muscles as hard as she could without dropping the pose. The members fell away; the illusion left; the shoppers left.

But the inspector had come by to look at her.

Sandra became acutely aware of the soreness between her legs.

She wanted to tell him how much she'd like to tear his gaze away from her. She tried to listen to the background music played somewhere in the vast department store. But the muzak was slashed into distorted segments by the chatter of shoppers and the clatter of cash registers. Sandra was an illusion of stasis like a whirling electric fan, spinning blades that would cut off your fingers if you tried to touch the seemingly solid disk they made.

The inspector was still watching her.

She wanted to roll up into herself like the telescopic belts in section E or burn his eyes with the hot skin liniment from Drugs. She wanted to cover her face with hosiery to make it flat and ugly so he'd turn away.

The inspector was still watching every flickering nuance of her pose. His stare tried to pierce the spinning blades. . . . Tension tightened in her as she realized that she was being tested.

The inspector stared at her, his eyes gleamed like fruit asking to be picked.

She tried to think of the snowstorm but saw only its shadow.

The tension uncoiled and flew out along her arms.

She snapped out of posture and reached for the inspector's face.

AFTERIMAGE:

The manager of HIP Store 34 conversed with the coroner as he led him through the stockrooms to the door marked *Prop Storage.*

"I suppose we should have known. Even after the computer categorized her brainwaves as characteristic of psychosis we couldn't be sure it was the sort of, uh, derangement that would interfere with her work here. Sometimes that sort of, uh, excessive zeal is very helpful to the career of a humannequin. So we sent the inspector to examine her for—well, for the possibilities of *violence.* He was about to question her when it happened. . . . But this extraordinary physical reaction—"

"Well . . . aren't there cases of people changing their bodies psychosomatically? I mean, like those nuns who made their palms bleed with stigmata and women who make themselves look nine months pregnant just by believing in it? Couldn't it be that?" suggested the coroner.

"Maybe. But the room has been heated to ninety degrees and she still hasn't melted. And if she hypnotized herself into making her skin like that, it should go away after she's dead. *If* she's dead."

"But of course she's dead," the coroner said quickly. The store manager opened the door for him.

Inside were a number of actual dummies, plastic mannequins left over from before the Mandatory Employment Act. All were covered with dust but one. It wasn't plastic. It was a woman, frozen, iced solid and gleaming white; coated with a thin layer of fine snow. The woman was frozen into a typical humannequin pose. . . .

. . . Except that she clutched the humannequin inspector's eyes, one in each icy white fist.

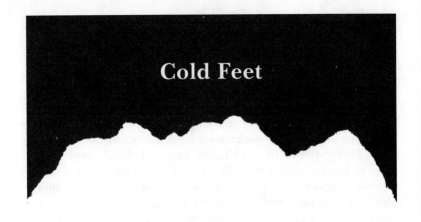

Cold Feet

MAYBE 1975. Sometimes I did something punk with reality itself. I was trying to use the Paranoid Critical Method of Dali at the time, to get complete objectivity from things around me, and it showed here and in later stories. . . . Surrealism (the true Surrealism of Duchamp and Ernst and Dali and Tanguy) was an influence. In other, punkier stories, I took the often rounded images of surrealism and sharpened them to barbs. . . .

An English teacher at an Ohio college, one Joe Sanders, wrote as follows for some encyclopedia of sf writers: "Shirley had already participated in the punk scene as a rock musician, and also had made a reputation as an unusually vivid, uncomfortable writer. He liked the idea of fusing high-tech concepts with the visceral images he had been using to attack reader's preconceptions. . . . Actually, Shirley's work has always been distinctive for its stern insistence that people need to open themselves to new possibilities, enlivened by stunning imaginative riffs. . . . Shirley says that he 'was trying to make the impossible seem possible and palpably real, to make it seem so concrete and visualizable, so cinematically striking, that the reader would end by questioning his or her own sanity. I wanted people to question reality, their assumptions, political, social, existential, everything. . . .' "

Maybe I was just trying to get them to see *my* world, out of sheer loneliness. I got married the first two times simply because

I was asked. I'd shrug and say, "If you want." I had no concept what marriage meant to people. I didn't know then that it was brutally inconsiderate of me to get married to be people I had no intention of being faithful to. I didn't understand monogamy. I wasn't just alienated—I was seriously out of it. I didn't know what insurance was; I barely understood bank accounts; I didn't know what "interest" was in banking or credit; I didn't understand taxes or tax forms and if I owed them I didn't pay them. I drove without a driver's license (a huge silver hearse I'd gotten somewhere . . . driving everywhere like I was in a chase scene from a cop movie . . .) till inevitably I got busted for it. I just didn't have a clue, in those days, and it wasn't really the sporadic use of drugs—I'd always been like that, even *before* drugs. A year or two later I impulsively joined the Coast Guard, where I lasted for six months. In the CG I was forcibly integrated among Real People— but they invariably said the same things. "Shirley—what the hell are you doing in the Coast Guard?" With a look of real bafflement on their faces. And, "Shirley—why is it you act like you're from fucking *Mars* all the time?"

I was listening to early David Bowie about then, and people like Charles Wuorinen and Penderecki (the latter two were introduced to me by my close friend Rob Hardin, who is now an accomplished poet, short story writer, composer and musician). Also, a very important influence, The Blue Öyster Cult: The most intricate, most sinister, most mysterious and artful of hard rock bands—the band that inspired Metallica and the other speed-metal bands. My first novel, *Transmaniacon,* was named after one of their songs. I have referenced the BÖC half dozen times in my fiction. And now, almost twenty years later (as I write they are getting a new record deal), I write lyrics for them, and they're friends of mine. One of my songs, which they now perform, is called "The Power Underneath Despair."

Trust me. It's there.

SHE DIDN'T LIKE THE LOOKS of the wheatfield beside the apple orchard. The wheatstalks looked stiff and uncompromising, and she suspected that they were actually sharp rods of yellow-painted steel which would impale her if she tried to lie down. But he had said to wait at the corner of the wheatfield. And her doctor had told her to start seeing men, escape her introversion. At least, this meeting with Clancy wouldn't be as boring as the usual drive-in dates. She tossed her red corduroy coat onto the wheat and lay down on it, wincing at the feel of crushing wheatstalks brittle underneath. She looked around nervously for insects, shading her eyes against the glare of the Indian Summer sun. Clancy was approaching through the apple orchard, taking bites from a bruised yellow apple. *Clancy couldn't be his real name,* she thought.

He stood over her, tossed aside the apple, his silhouette blotting the sun into a halo. He just stood there, watching, trying to seem confident. "I knew you'd come," he said in a measured monotone.

"Pretty sure of yourself?"

"I didn't come here just for myself, you know." He sat down close to her.

"Well," she said, in a conscious effort at unnerving him, "Let's dispense with all the game playing and get down to brass tacks. You didn't ask me to meet you in a secluded place for a discussion about psychology. The grass is high, and no one is around."

"You're kinda . . ." He cleared his throat. "Well, that's fine with me."

She removed, with ritualistic aplomb, her purple wool skirt and light pink blouse, leaving only pink see-through briefs. She laid her clothes in a neat pile and waited for him to remove his blue workshirt and dungarees. She closed her eyes and daydreamed:

A neatly furnished room, with couches, easy-chairs, coffee tables, doilies, and pre-Raphaelite prints. In one corner a very average-looking man of middle age in a dark business suit stood perfectly still. He was completely unmoving, unblinking, unbreathing. Another man—a chubby and cherubic butler in coat and tails—entered, humming to himself. He dusted all the furniture with a large feather duster. He then approached the immobile man as though he were a suit of ornamental armor and began to dust the right arm. There was no response from the frozen man. But strips of white were produced in the wake of the butler's brushing. The white was the shirt under the coat of the man being dusted. In a few minutes the coat and trousers had completely vanished, having been brushed away by the feather duster like paint darkening a wall. The butler continued matter-of-factly, breaching none of his outward calm as the shirt and underwear of the stationary man fell into dust at the lightest feather touch, heaping grey particles between his polished black shoes. The butler raised the cocktail duster to the stationary man's head and dusted away his hair and epidermis. Brushing in equanimous spirals, front to back, peeling him candy-stripe away, the butler left an oozing red surface on every inch of the frozen man (who still hadn't moved or changed expression). Whistling "It's a Long Way To Tipperary," the butler removed the second layer of flesh under the outer skin, leaving a filmy blue transparent membrane with the tendons and muscles clearly outlined underneath it. The butler dusted inexorably through tissues of crimson dampness down to fat and flesh. He exposed underlayers of veins and cartilage without inflicting damage on them when brushing the layer directly above. He chafed down to the muscles and glands, melting down to primary organs and veins which hung loosely from the skeleton like baubles on a Christmas tree. Though the heart was not beating nor the lungs filling, the organs seemed soft and fresh as if preserved in the amber of an instant's hiatus between beats of metabolism. The butler, still whistling and stepping carefully around the multicolored heaps of dust on the floor, said to himself, "Tsk, I should have put down some newspapers."

He brushed away layer after layer until only the skeleton remained. He took out a rag and applied furniture polish, shining the bones for some minutes.

The sunlight seemed to want to pierce her eyelids, insistently telling a story like light from a movie theater's projection booth. She opened her eyes and saw that Clancy still wore his pants. A peculiar expression danced on his thin nervous face.

She reached casual fingers to unzip his jeans. He arrested her fingers with his sweaty palm.

"What's wrong?" She asked irritably, "Getting cold feet?"

"No. I should tell you though, Clancy's not my real name. My real name is Avram. And I'm not here for dreams."

She reached back to brace herself against the ground; and gasped. She had stabbed her hand on a wheat stalk. Stiff and metallic, yellow paint was flecking from its wiry shaft.

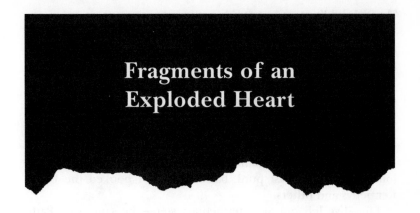

Fragments of an Exploded Heart

"WHO ARE THE SEX PISTOLS?" the magazine said.

Late 70s, I was visiting my Mom, and reading the sunday papers. Skimming through a sunday supplement for the hoi polloi, my attention was arrested—and my life changed—by these anomalous words in bold black letters "WHO ARE THE SEX PISTOLS?" I immediately wanted to know, myself. The article excoriated them, reviled them: this "so-called singing group" from England of snotty "punk rockers" who stood in angry opposition to everything in the world, spouted obscenities and spittle when it pleased them, dressed in tatters, chains, spikes and ugly boots, did unspeakable things to their hair (and their girlfriends) and made a hideous noise when they played . . . some of their songs banned from the radio. . . .

Well I'd heard enough. I was in love. (The irony, of course, is that the magazine was trying to warn people about the Pistols and their kind—and instead probably converted thousands of teens to punk.) I went down to the import record store *immediately* and ran in breathlessly, demanding, "Have you got the SEX PISTOLS?!"

"Hey Joe!" The guy yelled, laughing. "Another one for the Sex Pistols!"

They were sold out.

I soon found the Pistols, and the local punk rockers, and tried to become one. I was so astonishingly, well, *Martian,* that I even failed to become a cool punk. I never could master being a part of something—not even the punk scene. I had no concept of coolness, then.

But I had energy and I had lyrics and I had attitude and I did become the lead singer of several punk bands, including the first one in Portland, Terror Wrist. I learned to shout rhythmically, and I was off. I'm sure we sounded perfectly hideous. But we rocked.

I started the first Portland punk club, The Revenge, where various early West Coast punk bands played. I booked the Dead Kennedys and others.

Oh—I've left out an intermediary step—the same step Patti Smith went through: My earliest performing was actually at poetry readings. I did a kind of early rap thing, chanting lyrics and punky fantasy prose, then I got a guitarist to flail away with me. Just me and him. Then came Terror Wrist and other bands, like Sado Nation and the Monitors. I was invariably lead singer and "twitcher." I went into genuine, unalloyed, unaffected *frenzies* on stage, during the guitar solos, trying to be physically a literal interpretation of the music—trying to respond to every note, every KA-WANNNNNG, with maximum energy. I achieved some genuine states of shamanistic ecstasy. I was such a socially out-of-it lunkhead that I sabotaged my standing with the Scene offstage, made lots of enemies and tried to fuck everything with a pussy. This was uncool, at least in Portland—punks or not, there were social niceties, though in Punk Terms.

I was listening to the Buzzcocks, the Pistols, the Ramones, The Nuns, the early Clash, virtually all the punk bands. Also a bit of Howling Wolf and other blues masters. I gradually learned to do something like singing. (Later, I actually did sing and recorded on the Celluloid Label, in New York).

And about this time I wrote *The Exploded Heart*. Herewith is a portion of that unpublished novel. It seemed to baffle many editors, though they commented on its "impressive raw power. But . . ."

In this novel, Aaron Dunbar returns. Having been released from custody for the killing at the end of "What He Wanted" he himself becomes a rock star called Hustler.

In the novel *The Exploded Heart* Dunbar has been contacted by a figure from another of my novels, *Dracula in Love*, the character "Lucifer," who wants to use a combination of rock music and crowd-hypnosis to open a gate into another plane. There are dark figures in the background who want Dunbar to back down, as you'll see. One of the characters in *The Exploded Heart* was borrowed from another sf writer's books—by permission—and I'll let the aging hipsters out there recognize which character that was.

The story blends mysticism, pseudo-science, early cyberpunk, supernatural fiction, fantasy, and poetic imagery in a way that seemed perfectly normal to me at the time, but must have seemed a bizarre mix to editors. I was interested in finding ways to felicitously fuse incongruous genres and kept experimenting at it, with uneven success. I was influenced by certain film makers and by Zappa, e.g. his LP *Weasels Ripped My Flesh,* which juxtaposed seemingly disparate music types into one overall sonic experience. My reading in mysticism pervades this work and others, but ultimately my statement was protest, was punk repudiation of the status quo, was a celebration of dark glory. And as always, back then, I was drunk on words.

JERRY HAD TOLD HIM NEVER TO answer the door personally.

"Stupid of me," Dunbar said aloud.

"Yes," said the black man in the white suit, nodding to the angry jocks at his side. They moved into the room and seized Dunbar by the shoulders.

He glanced over his shoulder. No one there but Walker.

"Let's go," said one of the men, dragging Dunbar by the arm through the door of the suite, into the hall. After he was rabbit-punched in the kidneys, his resistance diminished notably. One of the men was a classic pug, replete with broken nose and scarred chin, football jersey and crewcut. The other was thick and short and smelled of curry; his skin was sallow, he giggled as he yanked Dunbar's left elbow, sending a hot wire of pain up his arm and into his shoulder.

"Hey this isn't necessary, I'll come, since you got me,

without—" Dunbar began.

"Shut up asshole. You love it. You're *agony* rock, right?" His laughter was cut short as Walker, wearing only jeans and running on her implanted horn-heels, cracked his spine with a kneejab. He yowled as his darker partner turned and lashed out, using a martial arts thrust to catch Walker on the jaw, sending her flying. She bounced from the hallway's wall, fell flat on her face.

Maybe her jaw's broken, Dunbar thought. *Maybe she's got a concussion. Maybe she's dead.*

The East Indian had let loose of his arm. Dunbar turned and swung hard at the bigger jock. The man stepped easily aside, the blow swung wide.

The black man in the white suit sapped Dunbar glancingly above the left ear. Dunbar gave a childlike cry and crumpled, still conscious but too stunned to resist when they dragged him into an elevator. Through a milky film over his vision he saw a chambermaid walk by, take in the scene, shrug, and walk on.

They didn't try to take him out through the lobby.

They'd rented a room for the occasion on the floor below.

It was a more modest chamber, a bedroom, living room, bathroom, all with typically mass-production-bland hotel furnishings. As they dragged him, his limp feet left faint trails in the rug.

They were towing him with a grip encircling his shoulders and armpits, his feet dragging behind him—to the bathroom.

He was beginning to feel almost normal again, his motor functions returning, when they bent him over the tub, twisting his arms behind him.

The black man, who wore blue smog goggles even indoors, sat on the toilet-seat, crossed his legs, leaned back and spoke low, soothingly, consolingly to Dunbar. As they beat him.

Dunbar stared into a porcelain infinity, waiting to turn into liquid and go down the drain, as the blows landed on his shoulders. They were beating him with something cold and jagged, and he could feel his skin tearing, bones chipping; felt the chill metal impart itself to his bones in a ringing that came with each *thud* and *thunk*.

I've got bells in me, he thought distantly. The blood began to run off his shoulders, into the tub, tick-ticking onto the porcelain like Whistler's blood running off the edge of the stage more than a year before—

"Not much more than a year ago," the black man was saying, "you did something for which you've never been properly punished. You got off easily because you had a smart lawyer that played you as a martyr, Aaron my boy. He made it seem as if you were caught up in the general madness and had no real self control and you were a victim of circumstance. We're giving you something of what you should have got, Aaron. Not nearly the punishment you're going to get once you've died. That's when you really start to pay. You can change, Aaron. You can save your soul, at least."

Dunbar fought to keep from throwing up, afraid he'd choke on it and strangle.

He watched the patterns made by the blood, his own blood.

The ringing of each blow seemed to prolong into the next until there was an endless clamor of bells ringing, a thundering pealing of pain.

"You can consider this therapeutic, Aaron . . ."

But Dunbar was remembering something he'd read. . . . About a scientific experiment, where they'd put electrodes on the skull of a man being executed, guillotined, measur-

ing his brain waves. The technician had observed significant brain activity for more than a minute after the man's
head had parted from his shoulders, as the brain used up
the last of its oxygen. The technician had been horrified,
thinking of dreams which had lasted only a minute in real
time but which had seemed to take hours, days, weeks in
the subjective time of dreaming. . . . So the guillotined man
might be experiencing his mutilation almost endlessly, the
minute in which he lay trapped in his own severed staring
head could seem to stretch on and on, each second becoming an hour. . . .

And that's how Dunbar felt. It was taking years. It was all
of the pain of adolescence crowded into a couple of minutes.

The jagged-ended pipes bit into his neck, shoulders,
back, striking his scalp only glancingly (they don't want to
kill me, he thought, Relief when they kill me. God grant
they kill me.)

". . . I don't think you'll be stupid enough to go on working for Whistler and Jerry and the gold-footed master. I
think you'll take the plane ticket and the three thousand
dollars we're leaving here, and I think you'll go away because you don't want to hurt anyone else. And you don't
want any more hurt yourself.

"Right, Aaron?" He finished. And the blows finished as
well.

Dunbar choked out, "Right. Right. Right."

"Here's the ticket and the money, my penitent friend." A
dark hand reached out, entering the field of his vision, carrying an envelope in its fingers. In Dunbar's distorted per-
spective, the hand seemed that of a giant, big as a house. The
hand reached down and rather delicately dipped the envelope in Dunbar's blood, laving one side of it. The hand
pressed the envelope to the tile wall; it held fast, sticking with
blood. A long drip trailed over a typed name: AARON DUNBAR.

There was a rasping sound, then something warm and wet splashed on his shoulders, stinging. Urine dripped off him to mix with the blood, diluting it to orange swirls like fingerpaints. As a child, he'd painted mostly in red, orange, yellow, and black.

"Stop it," said the black man. "We don't want to give him blood poisoning."

"Queer punk-rocker asshole," said the larger man, sounding, oddly, as if he were about to break into tears.

Dunbar scarcely felt it when the man kicked him in the ribs.

He hardly noticed when they left.

He watched the sticky filigree made by the blood in tub, tried to trace the black specks swimming before his eyes.

After a time, someone came into the room humming and there was the sound of a mop and bucket set onto tile. And then a woman's scream, and running footsteps.

He never quite made it to blacking out. Just a translucent grey.

But the greyness was almost good enough. It was everywhere.

HE LAY ON HIS STOMACH with his eyes closed, listening, pretending sleep. "Cracked scapula, wrenched cervical vertebrae, pernicious contusions, cracked ribs, bruises, and shock," said the woman doctor. "That's all we've found so far. Oh, and two contusions in his scalp, near the nape of his neck. Could have been worse."

The doctor left the room.

"Why didn't they kill him if they wanted to stop him?" asked Walker. She had modulated her voice to a monotone to seem emotionally detached. So, then: she cared.

"Perhaps they thought Jerry might find a replacement 'Hustler.' " Mills voice. "Better to distract us by making us try to find him. They've given him a plane ticket for New York. . . . Or perhaps killing him would be too direct an intervention, at this point. In terms of the cosmic balance."

"When is someone going to explain that stuff to me? What's this vibratory bridge bit you guys keep—"

"I think that Jerry feels you know as much as you need to, Ms. Walker," said Mills gently.

"Fuck *him*," said Walker. " My jaw hurts when I talk. Lips puffed."

Dunbar heard her leave the room.

"She's gone, Aaron. Do you want to talk?"

So Mills had known. "No," Dunbar mumbled into his pillow. "Walker's okay."

"She's only bruised. . . . I've arranged to remain here, as your bodyguard."

"How long—in the hospital?"

"It will be two days before Lucifer can get to you."

"What? What you mean about Lucifer?"

"I have said too much. Rest."

He closed his eyes. The first day in the hospital wasn't bad, really. He floated in and out of consciousness, drifting in heavy doses of anesthesia and lying on his stomach.

But the second day, when the anesthesia wore off (and they thought it unwise to give him more) was tedious, uncomfortable, pounding slowly with pain and fever. His back afire, it hurt to breath, and Walker didn't come to see him. They tilted his bed so he could watch TV. It nauseated him. Mills read the newspaper to him. It made him wince.

He wished more than once he'd been able to take the ticket and the money. And the plane. Out. *Get out.*

Sometimes he wished Walker would come, sometimes he was glad she didn't: she might sense his defeat. She might laugh at him for giving in, for being unable to go on to be Hustler.

The third day was worse than the second. He was going stir-crazy. He tried to practice singing, but it hurt to inhale deeply. It hurt when he moved at all. In his mind's eye he saw the smashed and torn topography of his body as a sort neon map, prettily glowing abstract tubes marking the coursings of the pain.

After the nurse had forced him to swallow about half his bland noon meal—she'd left him with the maddening calm, and Mills—Dunbar tried to get out of bed. He managed to sit. His muscles spasmed as he moved, his stomach quaked. He was dizzy when he sat up. He wanted to lie down again, but he couldn't face the stained pillow and the lumpy white paint of the wall.

He thought he was hallucinating when he saw the man outside the window.

"Mills, didn't you say we were on the seventh floor?"

"Yes, Aaron. Oh. I see why you asked."

"You see it too?"

"Yes."

In the glare from the window, the man was a silhouette against the blue sky. The outline looked familiar. It was Lucifer—Dunbar never thought of him as "Bill."

Mills went to open the window. It opened to the side. The man outside bobbed up a few feet, hooked a leg through and followed it in. In a moment, Lucifer stood over Dunbar, frowning down at him. Dunbar swallowed. and moved slowly to his former position on the bed, belly-down.

"That's better," Lucifer rumbled. "Dumbshit. Make it harder for me."

"Make—make what harder?" Dunbar asked despairingly, Thinking: *He's going to kill me, I've become a liability.*

"You waste your strength trying to get up too soon."

Dunbar's heart was climbing into his throat, He could hear it pounding, louder and louder.

He's going to beat me, Dunbar thought, *because he knows I was going to give up. He's going to punish me, to try to force me, to—*

Lucifer laid his hands on Dunbar's back.

Dunbar's back arched with pain.

But when he heard Lucifer laughing, he realized that the man (the man?) had touched him gently, and that the pain was in his expectation. He closed his eyes and relaxed.

The room began to heat up.

The window began to rattle. The springs on the bed vibrated sympathetically, shaking to the subtle fibrillation of the fibers of Being Itself. Dunbar twisted his neck to look over his shoulder; he could make out only Lucifer's left side. The air about Lucifer (who wore a cream-colored suit and white shoes, the hooves unmanifested) shimmered like heated air over a stove. Dunbar straightened his neck convulsively as his every muscle suddenly went rigid. And it passed. And then again something poured invisibly from Lucifer's hands, passed into Dunbar's back, entered his spine, stirred up the action of certain enzymes. And Dunbar went rigid, And again it ceased, And again it commenced—each time the current passed through him, Dunbar experienced an irreconcilable combination of ecstasy and sweet relief. It was an orgasm that hurt. Sweat beaded, formed puddles on his back, ran down his sides and between his buttocks. His feet moved from side to side on his ankles, his hands made abrupt patterns in the air, his arms shot straight out from his shoulders. His erection came and went. His brain felt like it was swelling, would crack his skull from inside as frozen egg yolk bursts its shell.

He could feel the blood start freshly from his wounds. His pulse pounded grandly in his ears. He gasped, between chattering teeth: "You're ki-kih-kuh-killing me-me!"

"Some rock star," Lucifer chuckled.

One more brilliant infusion (lighting up his nerve ends, he could see the neon map again in his mind's eye: this time it lit up his entire neural system, a man-shape sculpted of twigs and wire) and Lucifer took his hands away.

He dried them on a sheet.

Dunbar was wheezing, twitching now and then like a city in the aftershocks of a quake.

But there was no more pain in his back, only a warm glow. And for the first time in days, he was ravenously hungry.

"See that they bring him food when he wakes," said Lucifer. "He's going to need lots of protein, iron—see that he gets all he wants."

"Very good sir," said Mills.

Lucifer bent and blew in Dunbar's ear. And as if his conscious mind were a pilot light or a candle flame—it went out. Black out.

It was the twenty-third of December. Eleven p.m.

Jerry had moved headquarters to a split-level house in Sausalito. They were in the basement. The equipment was set up.

Jerry was just removing his bass guitar's neck from the automatic tuner. Walker had just arranged her drums. Ruskin's fingers were poised over the keyboards. Glasstop tootled impatiently on her alto.

Jimmy chuckled to himself and fingered his strings, waiting.

Dunbar plugged into his amp. He tested the mike, and tested it again. . . . He complained that it wasn't loud enough in the monitors. He couldn't hear himself. He glanced up. Golden eyes watched him from beside the crackling fireplace in the far end of the long cement basement. Lucifer stood by the hearth, the flameflicker streaking light at his feet was like a dim memory of some greater conflagration.

Dunbar swallowed and tested the mike again. "Okay," he said reluctantly.

He thought he saw a black man in a white suit out of the corner of his eye. He whirled, breathing heavily, wanting to cut and run. But there was only the high basement window onto the night, darkness between the white curtains flapping in the breeze. "Close that window," he breathed. Glasstop moved to the wall, reached up over her head and latched the window shut.

Walker walked a beat into the room, Jerry introduced the beat to a rhythm, Jimmy and Ruskin ushered in melodies and harmonies, Glasstop gave the whole thing a manic fringe and Dunbar bent to the microphone—

He forgot the words.

The musicians one by one realized that Dunbar had missed his cue. The music trailed off.

"Sorry," Dunbar said. Sweat stood out on his forehead. His shirt felt sticky. He welcomed an excuse to remove it. He felt he had to expose the scars on his back. He was healed, but scarred. They should remember that. They should respect him for it. He removed his shirt and tossed it at Walker. She caught it on a drum stick and flung it behind her.

The musicians chuckled. Lucifer waited grimly and silently by the fire.

"For Christ's Sake," said Glasstop. "Let's play. We gotta gig in a few days."

"Shut *up.*" Dunbar snapped. "You're working for me! You begin when I'm ready."

Glasstop shrugged and turned her back to him.

Dunbar took a deep breath.

"Okay," he said. "Let's do 'If God's Dead.' "

. . . With the third try, he remembered the words. His head pounded and he felt hollow, squeezed out. The excitement, the abandon—it was all gone.

He kept glancing toward the window.

They could shoot me through the window, he thought.

He made it through the set. When it was over, he felt that his bones had gone soft in him. He walked on wobbly legs to the couch, and sat down. He was cold, sitting at this end of the basement. But he was afraid to sit by the fire. Lucifer was there, with his penetrating golden eyes. Whistler seemed more distant than ever. Whistler was just a dream.

The others packed their instruments and, one by one, left the room. There was no chatter, no playful insult humor as after other practices. They felt let down. Dunbar felt their disappointment keenly. His singing had been mechanical, uninspired. He had generated nothing.

Lucifer had healed his back. But some things were too internalized for easy healing.

Later, Dunbar wrote in his journal:

. . . I've had the nightmare two nights running now. The black man in the white suit and Lucy have sex—while I'm tied to a chair and forced to watch. In the shadows beyond the bed are faces, people I don't recognize, thousands of them. I think if I could count them there would be eight-thousand-four-hundred-and-seventy-four. Exactly. . . . And I seem to see Jerry standing over me with some peculiar instrument in his hands. . . . And he saps the life from me somehow and leaves my clothes empty neatly folded on the floor. . . . The nightmare comes freshly to mind when I close my eyes—when we're practicing. The show is tonight. I think I'm going to fail. Jerry is a psycho, and the whole thing is going to fall through because of me, because I can't get it up to rock. And he's going to kill me. I swear to God I'm sure of it: if I can't become Hustler tonight, he's going to kill me. But I haven't sung as Hustler since I got out of the hospital. I'm just Aaron Dunbar, and that isn't enough. They scared the inspiration out of me. I haven't

had any dimensional-travel training sessions; I think Mills is afraid I'll botch it up and get lost or one of the Between Plane carnivores will get me and they'll be out a singer. But they're out a singer now. I'm no longer Hustler and if I can't become Hustler tonight, Jerry will kill me. I swear to God he will. Credit it. . . .

He and Walker slept together, embracing. They slept together, but he wasn't able to make love to her. He told her it was residual pain from the beating, which it was—in a way. She held him with surprising tenderness. She was careful not to tarnish her image—she never said anything tender outright. But she communicated her feelings nonverbally. And once he felt her tears on his neck.

The morning of the show, he couldn't eat. But he went periodically to the bathroom and drank a glass of water, so he'd have something to vomit.

It was a cold winter day in San Francisco.

JERRY HAD NOT STINTED on publicity. The show was sold out. "Curiosity will butcher this feline," Jerry said lightly, as he helped the roadies set up backstage.

The Mainliner Club held a thousand people. But there were fourteen hundred packed into the cavernous smoke-choked redlit hall.

Dunbar could hear them breathing.

He sat in the dressing room, his head in his hands. Every so often the stage manager would look in on him. "Half hour, Hustler," he said.

Dunbar shrugged.

But now there were two feelings in him. One was the familiar flaccidity, fear of failure. The other feeling was a strange tension, a kind of giddy revulsion that came on him in waves. It hit him whenever someone opened the dressing-room door, and he could hear the crowd.

It took him a while to recognize the tension. His spring

was coiling tight again. It was the exultation of anticipation.

The door opened again. The crowd catcalled, bellowed, whistled—

One feeling overcame the other.

Dunbar looked up into the dressing room mirror. Hustler looked back at him. "You need it," he said. "That's the secret."

The compulsion to perform had overcome the fear.

He heard the band begin to play. They were to play ten minutes before his entrance. He went and got into his costume.

Walker and the stage manager opened the door, both of them starting to egg him on—

"Hey Aaron—"

"Mr. Hustler, ten minutes till—"

"Get the fuck out till I'm ready, you pinhead slutters!" Dunbar shrieked. In fine voice.

The stage manager looked as dismayed as Walker looked delighted.

He was ready in ten minutes but he made them wait twelve.

He strolled onto the stage, wearing a black robe and cowl, mirror eye-covers (sans frames—they stuck with a gentle glue) and black stiletto shoes. He walked through a wall of music, emerged in a yammerwash of crowd noise. Much of the crowd noise was derision. *Let's get it moving—* they shrieked. And: *Who the fuck is this asshole?*

Singing through a filter of electricity crackling between his teeth, making them think he'd taken drugs because his movements were controlled as much by the music as by his own volition, he dragged them kicking and screaming through the first song.

The song ended, the room echoed for a moment with the final bass notes. They were to begin the second song.

There were peculiar expressions on the faces of the neo-punks/agonyrockers/stoners/computer-high-school students/streetcreeps/aging hipsters and journalists focusing their sense-receptors (they called them eyes and ears) on him through the smoke and dimness.

He was supposed to launch them into "If God's Dead" now. But he smiled and turned to Walker, signaled her to wait. "I wanta have a few words with these assholes," he said.

Dunbar . . .

Hustler . . . Hustler had to exert control, He had to take command.

A reckless megalomania sang through his veins. *Let them kill me,* he thought. *And I'll rule beside Whistler.*

He pointed a finger at the crowd. "Shut up and listen!"

They responded with paper cups, bottles, a firecracker. The mundane missiles hit the invisible force screen and bounced back into the audience.

"Chickenshit!" someone yelled.

"Turn off that field!" Dunbar shouted at Jerry.

Jerry glanced uncertainly at the audience. He shook his head.

"Turn it off or I don't play!" Hustler shrieked.

The audience roared in support.

Jerry shrugged, He said something to a roadie. A moment later a bottle whistled through the place where the screen had been, smashed on the stage, "Come *on!*" Hustler shouted. "More!"

Five minutes later, the stage was thoroughly littered in trash.

Hustler had a cut on his cheek from a broken wineglass. The blood dripped onto the black iron-cross upright atop the microphone.

Cheers from the crowd.

"Now I tell you gentle boys and girls a little story,"

Hustler bellowed. In his mind's eye, his words shot like disembodied fists into the sea of faces, churning it into the patterns he imposed. "Oh, it's a *sad* tale," his voice cold irony. "You see it seems that a decade back I read in a magazine about an experiment these Canadian scientists were doing. Yeah, see these monkeys were taken from their parents right after birth. Isolated in little metal cages. No contact with other monkeys thereafter and *no one* was allowed to touch the poor thing. They wanted to study the effect of isolation on primates, the need for touch. The monkey was fed and exercised—but not touched. So naturally it withered up and became, you know, catatonic. There was a sick photo of an utterly miserable little creature balled up in the corner of a cage. It made me ill. I was furious. Better they should vivisect it or something—at least that way it could go into shock. But Christ—they were fucking with whatever passed for a soul in that little bastard. The pukes. What were they proving, these jerks with their government research grants? You wanna know?" He paused, testing the air. They were quiet, listening. Hustler had emerged, the air crackled. Hustler's hands trembling out before him like transmitting antennas. "The lofty and studied conclusion of the experimenters was: if you isolate a monkey from birth, it will be unhappy and it will wither and die! Oh! What a revelation! Hey!"

Laughter from the audience.

"I mean these assholes are so fucking cold-hearted and detached from their world, apparently, that they had to perform an elaborate experiment taking months and lots of money to find out what any fool with common sense knows. It's a kind of spiritual asexuality, see. People either get more detached from everything, live through TV or scientific abstracts or something—or they become trank freaks or they join yet another idiotic cult. And others try

113

to buy everything electronic. But there's something else you can do. You can explode your heart. That means you can blow up your focus, stop seeing things localized, see things on the vast scale and recognize you're part of some vast symphony and you may as well play your melody sweetly. We can do it here tonight."

The hey-everybody-let's-harmonize-and-get-down-together approach was unfashionable because it no longer worked. The crowds recognized performer insincerity, they knew when they were being manipulated. But they also felt keenly when a man was telling the truth. They could see that Hustler was taking a chance, exposing his heart for them, holding it out—so they could explode it.

They heard him and believed, and Jerry looked on approvingly. The collective mind pattern was formed, in blueprint. The energy level was rising. The sound absorbers vibrated.

In another place, another world, a six-sided crystal affixed at the heart of a vast machine . . . began to quiver.

"Hustler's here to tell you," said Hustler. "Hustler gives it to you straight: the world, civilization, is half-electronic. You can't cope with that by running from it—but you can merge with it so totally you understand it, and then you got *control!*"

A roar of approval.

"You want *control* don't you? Then this is what you do: your body does its work electrically, right? The brain thinks with electrochemical reactions. Right? And everybody knows deep down inside that *sex—*"

Buzzword. They roared in reaction.

"Yeah, you know that *sexual union* at its heaviest is a form of telepathy, biologically generated—you following this?— Some people have never felt it. That's because they're afraid to explode their hearts. Afraid to surrender. Hey: sex isn't just *flesh*—any more than a tele*phone* is a telephone *message.* . . . Now, there's two ways—sometimes these two ways are one and the same—that this biological electricity is passed. Sex, and musical ecstasy. 'Specially, rock'n'roll."

He had them. Even the sizeable percentage not shouting support for him were appreciatively silent, listening.

Hustler radiated conviction. "Suppose we work out to perfection this electrical transfer of data from person to person. Suppose we learn to develop it as a person develops muscles. Maybe we'll learn to transmit it from person to person electronically. The governments regulate our world through computer technology. Right? Computers run on electricity, are programmed by electronic codification. My instruments here, man—they're all computer-mixed! The holos we're gonna have—they're computer-keyed! But *we* control those computers because they're attuned to our rock'n'roll and we make that rock'n'roll with our instruments and those instruments are our *guts on the outside!* Electronic rock'n'roll is the first step in the evolution of the new being! The new superman!"

He was shouting now. They rocked back from his voice. His electronically amplified voice.

"If you surrender to our music we'll pick up *your* electricity and translate it into music! We'll make music from our union with you and *you* will have—*control!"*

Hustler signaled Walker and Jerry and Jimmy, signing for the tune, "I am Electricity"—the first power chords opening the song commenced as Hustler screamed the word:

"—CONTROLLLLLL!"

And then the holograph came into play, making a strikingly realistic image of a bolt of lightning crashing into Hustler's microphone, crackling his body with electricity, defining his silhouette in shimmery blue. And his specially-treated black cloak burst into brief flames, falling into ashes, exposing him in white: toes to neck, skintight and pristine except for the bloodspot, like a sanguine explosion, over his heart.

He writhed to the music and the journalists in the audience justifiably drew the comparisons with Whistler.

He sang

Like strange flowers
flourishing in concrete,
Unearthly powers
Life in machinery
I—I am electricity
I—I am machinery
I am the fuel of urban living
I am the cyborg renaissance being
I am electricity
I am—all amplification
I am—your Satsang TV station
I am I am I am I am
Electricity—

The words were flashed on a screen overhead. Not for singing along, but for unconscious absorption. The holos shaped images of Hustler, split-second shots of Whistler, shining electrical arcs. . . .

"I'm talking about *you!*" Hustler shouted.

(In an Elsewhere, the crystal vibrated to alien musics.)

He could feel every eye on him. It was as if their gazes connected he-to-they physically, each stare producing a strand of ectoplasm that linked their eyes to his body so that as he whirled, jumped, twitched, the strands became more and more tangled, enmeshed, locking the crowd and Hustler in a webwork of psychic attentiveness. Jerry was almost smiling. Jimmy was grinning and amusing distant pagan deities with a melodic worship, the electric mantra split the hair (the antenna) of consciousness into a multitude of polychromatic slivers, making the mandala that superimposed its pattern on the seeming randomness of the audience (dancing, milling and rioting . . .).

Hustler had them; they generated the necessary power: the musical atunements and chord-patterns, designed by Jerry, caught that power and funneled it through space, between the currents of time, and—in the Elsewhere, the crystal . . .

Vibrated! (Hustler sang.) *She vibrated when I touched her!*
She was a woman but she was a thing of stone
She was a diamond, she was sweetly honed
And she Vi-i-ibrated
And she Vi-i-ibrated when I touched her—

"Hey, play it, Glasstop!"

Glasstop played her solo and each note of the electric sax Hustler interpreted in dance, making his body a needle for the soundwave graph, letting the music move him. The holos made psychologically-keyed imagery all around him, Hustler always at the focus.

He had them.

Forty-five minutes later they brought the nearly-exhausted audience to a climax. Left the stage, came back a minute later (invoked by the ritualistic pounding, whistling, shouting) and did their encore: "Thank God for the End of the World."

And Hustler—

At the climax of the climactic tune—

When everything was aligned perfectly and the crystal in the Otherwhere was keening in sympathetic shiver—

When Jerry threw a switch out of sight of the audience—

And Hustler vanished from the stage, seeming to explode in White Light, while the holograph framed him with a translucent beating heart. When the heart exploded, seeming to spray the stage with blood, Hustler was gone.

The audience assumed it was a stage trick. Illusion, prestidigitation.

But the groupies couldn't find Hustler after the show.

And Hustler?

He was gone, and he came back. He came back to his senses in Another Place. He woke into terror.

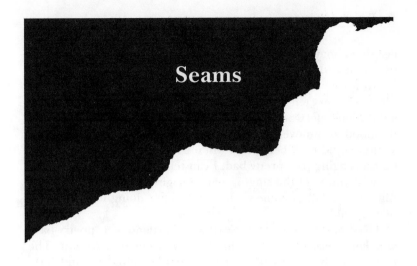

Seams

I WAS FRIENDS WITH SOME HOOKERS; I was part of that scene myself
in a sort of way. Not as a trick. Most tricks are a buncha fucking
pricks. Not all of them, but most. Someone once said the hookers
in San Francisco's Tenderloin are "thugs in miniskirts" and there's
some justice to that. But they're also women, and they are
women who weren't always like that. Lots of them are drug ad-
dicts or alcoholics or both, but not all of them. You can't gener-
alize too far about street people. I mean, up to a point, yeah. But
not too far.

Now this story is in poetry format because that's how I wrote it
and that's how I read it when it was performed. It was made for
performance. It's not supposed to be a short story as such, okay?
It's a story song. You're supposed to imagine music.

The "story" is romanticized, and the singing bartender is
hard to believe, and it gets kind of *Twilight Zone*. But it's all poetry, too. The fucking *Twilight Zone* show was poetry, written by
the unconscious.

When I recorded with my band, we never had quite enough
money to do it right. And the musicians always wanted to do hella
takes to get their parts right. Vocals were never a high priority
with these guys—maybe it had something to do with them being
my vocals. The vocals only got worse with multiple takes—or so
my guitar player assured me. So I ended up doing my vocal tracks

last thing, maybe four A.M. when we've got about ten minutes left in the studio and the engineer, who's been recording various bands for days and has run out of his crystal meth, is looking at his watch every ten seconds and has an expression on his face like a guy being electrocuted for a crime he didn't commit, and is in no mood to run overtime. I had *one take*. So they weren't as good as they could have been, and when I recorded "Seams" I fucked up the singing part pretty bad, I can tell you.

So if you read the singing part, imagine, say, Roy Orbison or Big Head Todd or some really swell singer doing it right, like I never could.

I first performed this in Northwest Portland at a "poetry bar," and later recorded it with my band playing background. The band was Obsession (Sync 66 aka Chris Cunningham and Jerry Agony aka Jerry Antonias and Jim Goodwin who later joined "The Call"); we recorded this for our self titled LP on Celluloid records. A British reviewer said the album was "surprisingly good." Thanks a lot, pal. Christ.

BOBBY WAS A BARTENDER, and Trina was a crazy bitch.
That's what he called her, anyway:
Crazy bitch,
he thought, when she came into the bar.
She always had a White Russian,
    vodka and kahlua and cream.
She always asked him to make up a song for her.
Crazy bitch:
he'd say it affectionately.
He never told her, but at night his heart
became a thing apart from him.
It'd tear itself from his chest and twine itself
around the little photobooth picture of her
    he'd framed on his cigarette-scarred bureau.
And he didn't mind that she was a hooker.
When she came into the bar
    he never said much more than

"Say whassup Trina, how's that crazy bitch today?"
He'd mix her a White Russian, she'd pay for the
first one, he'd slip her the second and third for free.
Ah, she wasn't a natural blonde,
but she'd done a good job at it—
a peroxide fall of foam fell way between
her creamy shoulders,
and the light would play on that hair
just the way it played
over the undulating hips
of the topless dancers to the left of the bar.
And when the dancer took a break,
and the music stopped,
Trina would beckon Bobby to a corner of the bar,
and she'd say,
"C'mon, make up a song for me, Chubs."
Everybody called him Chubs, because he was a little
overweight and his eyes popped a little and
his lips were a little too thick.
Oh, the way she said it,
between those soft, thin, flexible lips of hers . . .
ah, she always had 'em lipsticked pearly pink,
the color of
labia . . . he didn't mind. He'd shrug
and pretend to beg off.
He'd say, "Hell, I ain't sung in a band for ten years."
She'd say, "Aw, don't gimme that,
make up a *song* for Trina."
And she'd reach out and stroke his cheek. Just once.
That's what he'd been holding out for.
The chatter along the bar, the grousing
about prices and layoffs and bad husbands and bad lays,
you know, it all went to a
church-going murmur for a moment

as—pretending not to listen—
　　everybody listened to Bobby's
song, because Bobby used to sing
　　with the Soul Brothers. . . .

She got eyes like the shell of a robin's egg,
Her legs was turned on Heaven's lathe,
She got a shape that'd make the sailors recall hurricanes,
they think of her at night
and leave the bed sheets stained.

But she's a sweet-talkin' yalla-haired woman
　　talk ya oughta your bread,
You'd pay twice as much to shake her hand
　　as you'd pay another girl for bed.

She got lips that snap like a bullwhip to make you jump,
She got a smile that'd make a dyin' man's heart
　　bound and thump,
She got skin like the snow-battered mountain slopes,
You can get it up when you look at her,
But don't get up your hopes.

'Cause she's a sweet-talkin' yalla-haired woman
　　talk ya oughta your bread,
You'd pay twice as much to shake her hand
　　as you'd pay another girl for bed.

When he'd finish she'd clap and laugh
and she'd say,
"You old bullshitter, you don't make that stuff up
—not just for me."
And he'd say, "hey, it couldn't be anybody else."
She'd laugh and shake her head and ten minutes later

she'd be back out on the street saying,
"Hey, you wanna date? Hey, you wanna date?
 Hey, you wanna date? Hey, you wanna date?"
Bobby was saving up his money.
He knew he was no prettiness prize,
but he wanted to save enough scratch
so he could ask Trina to move in with him.
And maybe take her off the streets. Maybe.
But sometimes when she'd had half a dozen too many
White Russians,
she'd go into the sad drunk's endless
 tapeloop of complaints that come way too late.
She'd say, "Well, his name was Jimmy Rollins.
You know I woulda treated that man good,
but he ain't got eyes in his head,
 but fo' some other girl, and shit, it's been four years.
And it's not like I'm too old to get married,
but after four years I'm still thinkin' about him.
And that's the pits. You're s'posed to *forget* about 'em
after a few months and I just can't get interested
in nobody else.
And the longer I wait
the more it feels
like all the men in the world are just tricks.
I'm wastin' my time waitin' for another.
But I tell you he wasn't no trick.
You could say that about him.
He had *class*. And he *never* had to pay for it.
You know his name was Jimmy Rollins.
I woulda treated that man good,
but he ain't got eyes in his *head* but fo' some other girl,
and shit, it's been four years . . ."
And so forth.
Bobby would nod sympathetically and say,

"Wow. What a downer."
Trying to save up enough money,
Bobby got a second job in an adult bookstore,
surrounded by layers of pink intertwinings
and knotted human flesh
and inhibitions turned inside out
and tautology in genitalia.
Well Bobby hated the look of those rubber dolls
folded up in a plastic pack on the shelf,
    blow-up dolls supposed to look like women.
Not much like women,
unless you had a fuckin' retarded idea of women to start.
But the damn things sold.
Men took them home and stuffed them
    with themselves and kicked them around
and maybe used them for rubber rafts
in their swimming pools.
All the inflatable rubber girls had closed eyes
to root out all shadow of impertinence.
They had open, supplicating mouths and
breasts like rubber balls cut in half
and ugly wiry stuff glued on at the crotch.
Because all dreams have seams it seems.
Bobby looked at the rubber blow-up girls
    and he thought,
that must be how tricks see hookers when they pick them up.
They seem like the rubber dolls
    you prod and poke and bend,
the mouths always open, the legs always spread,
and the eyes always closed.
One night working the bar, tired from two jobs,
Bobby perked up a little,
    seeing Trina come in the door—
until he saw the look on her face.

She didn't respond to his whussup girl.
She said nothing.
She went to her usual bar stool—a fat Pakistani dude
was on it, she gave him a vicious kick
with her spike heels.
He wailed and fell off the stool
    and staggered out the door.
That's not like her, Bobby thought.
She ordered a drink, which wasn't necessary,
    and she called him "Bartender,"
like she didn't know him at all.
And she didn't order White Russians,
she wanted straight scotch.
She drank five of those without saying a word.
When the gears in her that had frozen
were oiled enough so she could talk again, she said,
in a whisper, staring into the cryptic overlay of initials
carved into the bar,
"Bobby, I . . . I saw him tonight. Jimmy Rollins.
I saw him and he didn't recognize me.
I wasn't hooking when he saw me last, I . . .
he didn't *recognize* me.
I guess I changed the color of my hair.
Bastard didn't recognize me.
He offered me *fifty bucks for a date!*"
She threw her glass against the wall
and walked out of the bar.
Bobby turned the bar over to his assistant.
He was afraid for Trina. He saw suicide in her eyes,
like the trail of smoke given off by a snuffed candlewick.
He followed her just to make sure.
    He knew where she lived.
He'd never been there,
but he knew she lived in a weekly rates hotel

run by East Indians.
A place with the constant smell of mold,
a bathroom down the hall and
syringes
discarded behind the toilet.
But she didn't go to the hotel.
She went to the factory district.
    She went towards the river.
He walked faster so he could be there to stop her
when she tried to jump.
He heard the sound of glass breaking
    and it was like a wire
snapped in his brain.
He ran, he turned against the door
and found she'd broken
the pane.
She'd left the door open behind her
like the jaws of a
skull.
He ran through, feet crunching glass, calling her name.
The factory was quiet. It smelled of rubber.
There were big vats of rubber simmering to one side
and machines for cutting sheets of rubber into shape.
All the sheets of rubber were pink,
the color of human flesh crossed with bubblegum.
He couldn't find her.
He called the cops and the cops came
    and they plumbed the
vats of rubber with poles and they looked in the guts
of every machine.
They told Bobby she must have gone out
some back way.
But the back doors were still locked,
and all the windows were locked.

Bobby felt like he had a brick for a heart.
He went home and he took four quaaludes.
A week passed and no sign of Trina.
He went back to work at the adult bookstore.
One night a young man with curly black hair came in.
The young man spent a long time
looking through the rubber girls.
He finally laughed kind of ugly,
and he brought a package with a folded uninflated
rubber girl dummy to the counter and he said,
"Hey, I'll take that one. Reminds me of a girl
I used to know."
Bobby looked down at the
    face flat under the plastic cover.
On this one the eyes were open.
    The eyes were robin's egg blue.
The mouth was open,
    but not wide enough like the others.
It looked as if it were about to say something.
It looked like it was saying, "Bobby!"
And the lips were lipstick pearly pink
    and the hair wasn't
natural blonde, but it fell in peroxide foam
to her creamy shoulders, and . . .
Now she was just a girl made out of rubber.
The young man tossed a credit card onto the counter
and the name on the card was Jimmy Rollins.
Bobby stared at the card
    and then at the rubber dummy.
The young man said,
    "Reminds me of a girl I seen hooking on
the street the other day. I'm, like,
pretending I don't know her. Man, she got pissed.
Hell, I wouldn't *pay* for that bimbo."

That's when Bobby tore open the package containing
the rubber dummy with Trina's face, and used its soft,
flexible polystyrene arms to strangle
Jimmy Rollins on the spot.
And handcuffed in the police car, on his way to jail,
Bobby sang this song:

Oh you can make your plans and laugh and clap your hands,
But then the joke's on some other man,
But there's worlds between men and women
     just makin' them blind,
When you think you've got ahead
     you know you left your heart behind,
She liked her drinks with vodka, kahlua and cream,
Because she knew that her dreams had seams it seems, it seems,
Because she knew that her dreams had seams it seems, it seems,
Because she knew that her dreams had seams it seems . . .

Parakeet

I GOT INTO A BATHTUB FULL OF ICE CUBES and beer bottles. I don't *think* I had taken off my pants, but I'm not sure. Someone came into the bathroom to get a beer and started yelling at me. I started kicking ice cubes around. They pulled me out of the tub, I got into a shoving match with them and they threw me out of the party. I had ice cubes in my pants. I went to the party next door. I was bored, see.

You have to understand, I was at a science fiction convention. That ought to explain it. I mean, *fuck,* but they're boring!

I was drinking a bit, but not drunk; I was not on drugs. I was trying to stay off drugs. It made me testy, staying off drugs; not through withdrawal, but because I was always fighting myself, fighting the psycho-compulsion—because at that time I hadn't found the support groups it takes to stay clean. So I'm afraid I took it out on any number of science fiction fans.

After *City Come A-Walkin'* I wrote other sorts of things—a suspense novel, *The Brigade,* with a punkish lead character, which was a thriller about vigilantism but also a parody of the robotic, redneck mentality that made the small Oregon town I was from feel like a police state. Avon published that book and my subsequent horror novel *Cellars,* which was about the selfishness I saw building up into the "Me Generation." The recoil from the 60s. About that time I started getting into shooting cocaine and heroin, especially cocaine, and it *really fucked me up.* I mean, I had some unspeakable experiences. (One of my favorite songs was Lou Reed's "How Do You think It Feels" off his brilliant *Berlin* LP, which is quite relevant . . . also listened to Richard Hell and the band Television). I nearly died a couple of times. I went psychotic on the stuff—but in binges. A day or two of it, then I'd swear coke off—then I'd go back on it when I had the dough, which luckily wasn't often. I fought the dope problem for years, and had years when I went without it, and only drank and took mushrooms and the like (occasionally) but "white-knuckled it" as they say in Narcotics Anonymous, till eventually I foundered, relapsed (triggered, as it happened, by a review from dear John Clute) back into heavy dope use, and nearly destroyed my life. I lived in Paris with a lovely French girl (we had children—I have decided not to talk about the kids here, it's too painful) for a couple of years too—and fucked that up also, behind dope. Both of us fucked it up. The drugs retarded my maturity, ate holes in my soul, and wasted lots of money and energy—but getting clean, which I did do, finally, forced me into self confrontation and a new maturity. Kicking drugs builds character. If you live long enough. Dope kills.

Somewhere in here I lived in the Lower East Side NY, played with my "futuristic funk" band Obsession at places like CBGB's and *nearly* got a deal with John Hammond Sr., on Columbia records—this is the guy who discovered Dylan and Springsteen and Stevie Ray Vaughan and a half a dozen other greats, but I didn't know who he was and I fucked it up. He offered. But he wanted me to get rid of my band and go with musicians he'd provide and like a jerk I said *no.* I kick myself for that once or twice a day. When I met him he was an old man and I had no idea who he was . . . he looked like Gary Moore with his bowtie and square gray haircut. But he was actually, unknown to me, one of the hippest guys in the world . . . I was shot down by my own arrogance, that time—not the first or last time.

I mentioned the conventions because about the time I wrote "Parakeet" I was occasionally attending science fiction cons. I was one kind of out-of-it-geek marveling at the other, fannish kind of out-of-it-geeks. I didn't belong there either, but who cared?

This was a story, first, a part of *Eclipse Penumbra* second. I wrote it before Lucius Shepard's story on similar themes, but not as well as he did his. It was also written before glasnost and before the dissolution of the Soviet Union. Still, the story for me is a meaningful protest against the dehumanization of man in modern wartime—in all wartime. I typically got as carried away with violent imagery as with rock imagery, and that shows here, and I know that seems hypocritical—a sense of celebrating war at the same time as denouncing it. But you'll see the same contradiction in Oliver Stone's *Platoon,* and sometimes contradiction is meaningful.

And, it has to do with how I feel about drugs—

I don't think there are any Russians
And there ain't no Yanks
Just corporate criminals
Playin' with tanks.
    —THE CALL

HIS NAME WAS RORY HAYES, he was a Sergeant in the United States Army, infantry, and on March 28, 2021 he was finally past being scared. Because it didn't seem to matter how he felt. And if he kept himself occupied, the medinject piranha left him alone.

So he took care of Parakeet. It was important to take care of Parakeet.

Parakeet: Pfc. Perry Katz, a wannabe comic, twenty-three, chirping his stand-up act at the other enlisted men in E Company as he handed out the new shipment of rations, taking it from a big green polymesh sack. All the rations were alike: dried fruit, freezedried soup, canned pseudomeat; but Parakeet was going on with, "Delveccio, here's your rat sandwich like you ordered with the tail stuffed in his cute little mouth—" Delveccio played tough guy a lot. "Pflug, here's your Soviet testicles on rye with mayo—" Pflug was gung-ho, a medinject spigot sucker.

"Becher, here's your Easter Basket—" Becher was religious, and it was almost Easter. "Carmody, here's Breck's undies, toasted, on a stick—" Carmody had a thing for their CO, Captain Patricia Breck. "Hayes, here's your mudpie with a side of sand." Because once, just once, Hayes had bitched he was sick of mud, why couldn't they get transferred to the North African front, get shot at in the desert where at least it's dry and you don't get trench foot.

Northern France wasn't so bad that clammy late afternoon: it hadn't rained in almost an hour. Mist hung in swatches of blur over the low hills to the north; it glistened on concertina wire, thickened over the gently rolling land to the east, cloaking the Soviet line. But here and there, in the unnaturally sedate No Man's Land, the slumped hulks of blasted autotanks blacked through.

Their position was lined in rock-hard insta. Hayes and Pflug had sprayed the insta down carefully when they'd dug in, but the mud tended to ooze over the camouflaged-colored lip of the "rockhole" anyway, or the men would track it in, so now it was up to their ankles. The mud was cold and slimy and persistent. It worked its way between your boot and your foot a hundred ways; you got it down your pants, and in your weapons so you had to field strip and clean them all the time.

Hayes crouched lower in the rockhole under the squat tripod of the tank killer, and winced at the tug from the medinject sunk into the meat of his left inner thigh. Breck'd send Shithead around with the new med-ups for the push north about dark, probably. The thought made his stomach contract. *Make yourself eat.* He opened two cans of pseudomeat. Parakeet called it sewermeat.

Parakeet hunkered down next to Hayes. Parakeet— Katz—was a stocky guy with wiry yellow hair teased up from being constantly pushed out of his eyes so it was like a bird's crest on his head; he had a narrow, bumpy, beaklike nose; small glittery blue eyes and slender hands; now and then he'd make a quick shrugging motion, maybe because of a nervous tic, maybe because his back hurt. Like most of them he wore a slicker over a flak jacket, plastic-mesh mud-caked boots, fatigues patched grey from dried muck.

Sexual frustration punctuated E Company's bantering with homophobic jibes; men who buddied up were ragged-on, even when there was nothing gay happening, so naturally tall, lean Hayes with his precise movements and quietness was "made in Gen Spec"* for stocky Parakeet with his nervous noise.

They ate their sewermeat gunk and chewed the rubbery fruit for dessert and gazed out over the green-brown, black-splashed terrain of spent farmland between their lines and the Soviets'.

Through mouthfuls of gummy food Parakeet sang a patri'pop tune. Only, he'd changed the words. They were supposed to go,

My Uncle Sam went for a walk down by his property line
Saw a big red bear bustin' down the No Trespassin' sign
He said, "Say Russian Bear you better back away!
And if you cross that line you better learn to pray!"

Parakeet's version, with an even worse meter, went,

My Uncle Sam ditched his wife and went to git some wine
Saw a hot-bod Commie bitch hanging out her Sex-for-Hire sign
He said, "Listen baby I got no money but I'll deal just the same
If you give me some nookie,
*   I'll trade you some fine American grain!"*

---

*GEN SPEC: Genetic Specialties, a black market lab—possibly mythical—which purportedly cloned lovers to specification for high-paying buyers willing to wait fifteen years for the clone's maturity.

Carmody laughed. He was a government ratkiller with a saggy face and droopy mouth. He laughed spasmodically at anything to do with sex. "Hey whatsa second verse, huh?"

But Hayes said, "Breck's sending med-ups over tonight, Parakeet. What you gonna do?" Katz had been refusing his meds.

Carmody said, "Hey let him sing—"

"Shut up, Carmody. What you gonna do, Katz? Take the meds or not?"

Parakeet said, "To BR* or not to BR, that's the question. Answer: no."

Delveccio came over to listen. Not to talk, just to listen. He was a sallow, ferret-faced guy who, the last few days, sat around watching, listening; twitching at little sounds, ignoring big ones; his eyes were deep-sunk in the sockets, his hands shaky. He was on the med-ups a lot, more than ordered, and sometimes he didn't sleep for days; or else he'd binge on sleep-meds, and doze out for twenty hours. Now he just sat there listening. Not saying a word, though sometimes his lips moved soundlessly.

"We got orders, Parakeet, and we're stuck with 'em," Hayes said. "You going to do the meds?"

Parakeet was humming the patri'pop tune, gazing blissfully west toward the brown humps of the CO's bivouac. After a moment he said, "No way."

Hayes could feel the place he kept quiet inside him twisting frantically, the piranha trying to break out. He needed Parakeet. He never laughed at Parakeet's jokes, but he needed to hear them. When he kept his mind on watching out for Parakeet, the dream piranha stayed away. Talking to Katz, and keeping him squared away . . . maybe the rela-

---

*__BR:__ Behavioral Robot. An expression describing someone conditioned, by drug therapy or other methods, to complete obedience.

tionship was *a place* he needed. Like a cupboard he could keep some hope in. It was the only one he had. And maybe he cared about Katz. Why it helped to care about people, he didn't know. "She'll put you on every patrol for a month, Parakeet. Edit you out, man."

"I m not gonna suck a spigot for her."

"You signed for it," Carmody said.

Parakeet shrugged. "They lied to us about what it really was till it was too goddamn late." He said something else but Hayes couldn't hear it because a squad of NATO Veetolls went booming over; the VTOL's—Vertical Take-Off and Landing fighterjets—rippling their furious noise over them all, a roar of anger that spoke for Parakeet so it didn't matter that Hayes couldn't hear him.

HAYES SAT IN HIS GREEN MYLAR TENT, taking the transparent tubes from the medinject pack he held in the palm of his hand. He inserted the tubes into his spigot.

The little plastic tubes snicked neatly into the medinject unit flesh-melded to Hayes' thigh. The tubes contained CRF in solution. The molecule CRF released ACTH, adrenocorticotrophic hormone, which stimulated the fight or flight response; but the CRF was cut with amphetamine and testosterone to make sure the response was fight and not flight. Turn the little release knob and you felt the stuff flow into your veins almost instantly. Your heart pumped faster, blood vessels supplying the skin contracted, and the skin went white. Carbohydrates stored in the liver were released as glucose for exertion energy. To supply the glucose with plenty of burning oxygen, the chest expanded, bronchial tubes widened, breathing deepened, sped up. Muscles tensed, pupils dilated, mouth went dry, body sweating to cool itself for the action. Your hair stood on end.

But not yet. He didn't touch the little knob. There was a

fourth tube for the fourth slot in the cardpack-sized med-inject "spigot." The P-tube, with Bromocriptine to stimulate the dorsal area in the hypothalamus: the pleasure center. And he had other tubes saved up in his sleeve-pocket, Vasopressin compounded with select neurotransmitters for alertness, vitamins, amino acids, additional amphetamine set up to dose out slowly, accumulating to a steady 70 mgs— at a low dose amphetamine makes you quick and euphoric, boorishly friendly; at a high dose it invariably makes you aggressive. *Mean*. . . . You synced the P-tube to the A-tube, the aggression tube just before battle; the P-tube didn't work without the ACTH and other secretions that came with combat. You fought, it gave you a jolt of pleasure. You fought a little more, it jolted you nicey-nice some more. You killed the enemy. But you lost touch with self-preservation. You tended to get killed, if you didn't get lucky.

Hayes dressed, went to find Parakeet. He was in the trench, with a lantern and a white paint-pen, painting graffiti onto the insta. *The Easter Bunny sucks tumors*, "My sentimental Easter message for Becher."

"I'll hold onto your tubes for you, Katz," Hayes said, skidding down into the trench. "In case you want 'em."

"Hold 'em, use 'em for suppositories, I don't care, man."

It was getting dark, and colder. The dark pooled in the trench like an oily liquid. The clouds turned to charcoal. Yellow at the horizon shifted toward orange; orange flirted with red. Distant *pock pock* of rifle fire. Thud of a mortar. Pflug kicked irritably at the mud, splashed it on the insta, started talking low to himself. Irritability, insularity, talking to yourself. Some of the spigot's side effects. Hallucinations was another.

"They're saying it's cowardice," Hayes said. That you're scared you'll get yourself killed."

"That what you think, Hayes?"

Hayes couldn't see Katz's face very well now. But he could feel Parakeet smiling. "No, Parakeet, damnit. You pulled Wiekowski out from under the Grinder, you blew up an Otto, you did more than enough—without spigots. You're not scared. But they'll lie, say you lost your nerve."

"Wiekowski. Jesus. Like draggin' an epileptic in a seizure back to camp. From spigots. You saw 'em too, Hayes. They were names and faces. Wiekowski, Potts, Depardieu, Tuttle, Shockley. Turned to BRs that laughed out loud or just grinned and ran into it and . . . it chewed 'em up. We could've taken this sector without they had to die, man. It's a sick game an' I ain't gonna play." He looked past Hayes beyond the second trench, to the insta-hardened bunkers of Command. Breck's safe little hidey-hole.

Hayes said, "I'll be back," as he climbed out of the trench.

"You coming back? Hey, I thought you was, like, going on a *Club Med* vacation."

CAPTAIN BRECK WAS IN THE Comm tent, sitting on a folding aluminum chair, frowning over her orders. She put the printout on the radio table and covered it with other papers when Hayes came in, blinking with the lamplight. She was standard female officer stuff. Hair cut so short you couldn't be sure of the color; warningly-cold grey eyes; her breasts neutralized by the baggy khaki jacket she never took off; a clip of medinject tubes—which she never really used—displayed in her sleeve-pocket. Pistol always on her hip. Her expression inquisitive but otherwise dispassionate; nothing feminine but nothing too aggressive either, wouldn't want to come across as an overcomper. "Sergeant Hayes. Been half expecting you. No orders for you yet on the offensive, and in fact it looks like I won't be—"

"I'm here about Katz. Write him a waiver."

"Just like that. Little boy doesn't want to take his medicine. He signed a contract. As part of the Army's pharmilitary experiment he gets double pay, he gets double furlough, he gets out sooner than—"

"He gets shot. He gets addicted to the sleep-agents they give us to cool out the aggression plateaus."

"Addiction? What makes you an expert on addiction, Hayes? I've got your personnel file on disc." Sarcastically, she ticked off facts on her fingers. "Says you were a foster child and you didn't like your foster parents; says you were a bounty hunter till you went into business cracking armored cars with a guy you were supposed to've brung in. Says you were an ex-con who got drafted from prison because the Army was short on men. Doesn't say a damn thing about you being a doctor. Or even a pharmacist. The meds aren't addictive."

"Bullshit. Half the men in E are strung out. They take the amphets out of boredom, cool out on the sleepers, wake up and do more amphets, and maybe once every four days they remember to eat. It isn't that way in my platoon. I keep it minimum. But the others. . . . And when we get into an offensive I lose control of my own guys."

"Experiment's got bugs to be worked out. In the meantime you have your orders. No waiver." She turned to the field computer on the light metal table beside the radio, snicked a disc into the playback for its TV monitor. New subject. "Going to be a show here in the supplies tent at 0900. Going to show the boys some of this." On the screen was a TV image of a battlefield, shot from overhead. American troops over-running Sovie positions. The Soviets in full rout, panicked, mowed down. Hayes felt an involuntary thrill. "For morale," Breck said. "Pentagon thinks they'll juice the men up with these, like juicing a football team—"

138

Feeling the thrill made Hayes burn with humiliation. And anger. "You pushed my buttons with that," he said, his voice breaking. "And they're probably not even real. Probably vid-animations. Using them like the drugs. Making BRs, conditioning us. Leaves no room for fighting for our country, for a cause, Captain. We're fighting because we're programmed. Don't it make you sick even a little?"

She looked at him blandly. "You don't usually talk much, but tonight you're babbling like the Grid. You really got a feather in your ass about it. Well listen: get used to it. That's an order. You been out here four months, it's gonna be another eight at least, if they don't start usin' nukes. If the antinuke treaty holds. And tomorrow we got a new med-up." She reached into a box, plucked out a pack of medinject tubes, and tossed them to him. Displaying her mastery of that difficult female officer's affectation: the paternal smile. As she said, "Free sample. Dismissed."

HE SAT CROSSLEGGED IN HIS TENT, looking at the new medinject pack with a flashlight. The label read: *Limbic TX4. Second sequence.*

Second sequence: it was to be released when the first surge of combat energy wore off. It was a second wind of aggression. He'd heard about it. It was said to be the biochemical distillation of pure rage. And there was scuttlebutt that a man using it in another Company had killed his entire platoon. His own people. His buddies.

There was shouting from the front trench, the scared kind. Hayes tucked the medinject pack into his first aid kit, grabbed his rifle and ran. He jumped into the rockhole feet first, splashing mud. "What we got?"

"Got us an Otto!" Becher yelled. An Otto, Autonomous assault vehicle, made in East Germany.

Hayes saw it hunching through the dimness, a black silhouette against the greybrown field, its camera eyes and gunsnouts reflecting orange from the setting sun. An unmanned thing, piloted by a computer, programmed to distinguish—if it didn't glitch—between Sovie troops, Sovie vehicles, and NATO. It was two hundred yards off and coming on strong.

The Otto might be just a probe, a stick to stir up the hornet's nest and see how well defended it was. Or it might be the point for a Soviet offensive.

He thought: Do I? Use the spigot?

Not now. Not unless he had to. And not with the P-tube. Never with the pleasure-tube. Because that was how they made you BR. With candy. A goodie for the dog that jumps through the flaming hoop.

Don't think about it. He checked the load on the tank killer, and took up his position at the firing post, looked through the infrared sight unit, its eyepiece cold against his skin. The Otto was a hunched shape of dull-red. He adjusted the crosshairs. Parakeet looked at the autotank through binoculars. "She's gettin' ready to open up on us, she's raising muzzle. Let's make a baby with her."

Hayes nodded and fired. The launch tube coughed its small missile; the infrared sensor in the tank killer's sight detected the flare in the tail of the missile, computer-calculated its flight path relative to the axis of the sight, and issued flight correction commands via microwave transmission.

The missile detonated. And a fat red flame was born. "She's havin' our baby!" Carmody cackled.

Hayes shook his head, seeing the tank advance through the smoke. "Uh-uh. Intercepted." The Otto had intercepted the missile with a laser, detonated it just before it struck. Parakeet had already reloaded the tank-killer. Hayes sighted in, fired. Nothing happened.

"Mud, oh Gridfriend it's the mud," Carmody whined. Mud jamming the weapon.

"LAC, Becher," Hayes shouted, while the Otto opened fire. A whine, the platoon ducked and—*thud*—the ground shook, spitting some of itself into the air. Gravel pattered down over them. The shell had come up short. Getting the range.

Becher was chattering into the radio for Light Artillery Cover, sneezing between coded sentences—he always seemed to have a cold—and the response came back almost immediately from Breck: *No can do, you're too close to the target.*

Lying bitch, Hayes thought. Tank's a good fifty yards off. She's trying to force Parakeet to use his spigot.

The autonomous tank plowed through an old stone wall, pulverizing lumps of stone big as a man's head; it snapped lengths of concertina wire, it splintered wooden posts, it came implacably on.

Pflug came sloshing up with the lantern. His grimy features—undershot jaw, eyes too close together, pug nose—lit up on one side as he said, "Come on, Katz, you and me."

Parakeet said, "Not procedure. We wait, we use a seismic grenade—"

"Cowards make excuses, Parakeet," Pflug said, the words coming in a rush, his lip curling. Hair bristling, his face vampirish. He'd turned on his spigot.

Hayes started toward Pflug, yelling, "Back off, that's an order!"

Parakeet put a hand on Hayes' shoulder, restrained him. "Pflug had a talk with The Missez, s'afternoon. She throws a stick, Pflug fetches." He looked at Pflug. "Come on, Pflug, let's bury your bone, if it's big enough to find. Show her something. Pflug with his med-ups, me without. See who kicks more butt."

"Katz, don't—" Hayes began.

But Parakeet was already out of the rockhole, running toward the Otto.

Hayes got up to go after him, climbing onto the insta lip—the Otto's cannon flashed, a shockwave hand slapped him contemptuously backwards into a pit where blurry forms of grey moved all slippery past one another. . . .

Not unconscious but stunned. Defenseless as the piranhas came from the underplace in his head; he saw himself underwater, saw the gembright wriggling mass of them swarming his face, chewing it away, swimming aside for a moment just to sadistically give him a good look at the bloody skull mask where his face had been . . . only it wasn't what he expected: it was Katz's face, revealed bloody, smiling sadly, under the shreds of Hayes's own features. . . .

His eyes focused, he saw he was in the rockhole. No sound but the ringing in his ears. Through a drizzling rain he saw a hemisphere of murky yellow lantern light around the stretcher, where Becher and the medic Tetscheim bent over Katz. . . . Parakeet crying—soundlessly but crying like a baby as they sprayed dressing over the gouting stump of his leg . . . he saw Hayes, and stopped crying. He gasped for air. Something went out of his face and it became an empty thing. And there was no sound but the ringing.

Tetscheim covered Parakeet's empty face with his rain slicker. Delveccio sat on his helmet, staring at Parakeet's covered body, snickering. Almost gone himself, another way. Tetscheim came to Hayes. "How you doing, Rory?" His voice sounded far away. Hayes was lying on his back in mud. Tetscheim wiped muck from his glasses to see Hayes better. "You don't seem to be bleeding. It hurt when you move?"

Mechanically, Hayes moved a little, shook his head. His ears were ringing. But he was alright.

Pflug appeared at the lip of the rockhole, grinning.

"Blew the sucker in half!" Blood running from his mouth. Eyes wild, chest heaving.

Hayes was up, pulling Pflug down, smashing his face into the mud, kicking him. Men pulled him off, held Pflug back. (Delveccio just watched. Sniggering.)

"It's Breck," Hayes said, to himself. "Not this spigsuck. Breck pushed Parakeet into it." He turned to look at the CO's bunkers. He closed his eyes. The piranha were swarming up, out of the hole that losing Katz had made in him. He had to do something for Katz—for Parakeet.

Tetscheim said, "Breck's gone. She went South to Rouen an hour ago. Transferred out. New CO's due in tonight."

Hayes decided. He opened his eyes, went limp so the others would let him go. They backed off, watching him warily. Hayes said, "Pflug's crazy from med-ups. Anyway Katz was right: Pflug does what Breck tells him. For P-tubes. So I won't kill him. But I'm going to kill Breck."

He slogged down the rockhole to ordnance and the others let him go. Delveccio sniggering. All of them thinking he'd give up when he realized she was sixty miles south, at least, and there was no way to get to her. There were sentries on the trucks, they'd never let him take one without authorization. He'd cool off, they thought. Let them think that.

He went through the weapons in the ordnance tent. Strapped an autonomous missile launcher to his back. Picked out a grenade launcher, a satchel of clips preloaded with SS-109 5.56 rifle cartridges and a NATO-issue Enfield autorifle equipped with a Laserscope. The Laserscope looked like an oversized telescopic sight atop the gun; the laser wasn't used as a weapon, directly—the problem of adequate power supply in hand-held killing lasers had never been solved. But the Laserscope aiming aid was lethal in its own electronically Taoist way. . . . He heard two men pass the quonset, talking, one of them claiming the Sovies were on the move again.

The hell with the Soviets. He wanted Breck.

MAYBE SHE'D KNOWN. Maybe it was cowardice, Hayes thought. She'd known the Sovies were going to push back, were trying to retake France down to the Rhone. She'd known they'd cut off E Company and the others from the rest of the division. Driving southwest between E's position and Rouen. Maybe she'd fled, getting through just ahead of the Reds. So it amounted to this: the Soviets were encamped between Hayes and Breck. Forty miles of them.

And he was AWOL, so there was NATO to deal with too. Once he thought he saw the silvery flutter of a drone surveillance bird overhead. Maybe they were tracking him. Might be either side. Them—or *them*. . . .

Hayes encountered the Soviet *them* an hour before midnight. The fulsome sky was drizzling, gusting. Hayes was slogging through a field, mud sucking at his boots, shades of grey and black delineating erosion-dulled furrows and the barbed wire fence he followed south; the hills at the horizon a frozen wave of darkness. He was chewing a particularly tough slab of dried fruit, and beginning to feel the aches in shoulders that suffered under the weight of the missile launcher strapped to his back; the gnawing aches were little piranhas burrowing into his flesh. The assault rifle in his arms had grown heavier; his throat was constricted with fatigue. But it wasn't time for the spigot yet. He had to hold off—

He bellied down in the mud. The hulk of a shack ahead, where the fence ended. A man-shape beside it, outlined in bluish light bleeding from the shack. Voices in Russian, or maybe Czech.

Hayes wormed through icy mud, getting it in his mouth,

down his shirt, shivering with it. But getting closer. Hearing
them laugh. Maybe they'd smuggled some vodka out to the
guard-post. The man-shape loomed up; the sentry spotted
Hayes, left half of Slavic face showing a scared blue eye.
Don't look them in the eyes.

Hayes wedged the butt of the stubby Enfield in the
mud, deciding he was too close to need the laser aiming
device, letting his instincts aim for him, firing a burst of
5.56 calibre rounds, splashing the frightened face apart.
Then Hayes was up, firing into the shack, raking it, hearing men inside scream. He stepped up to the door, finished the one who was crawling. After that, sticky with
mud, he continued south.

Forty yards over a low hill—a spread of lights. Men
shouting. They'd heard the shooting. Over there: tarps
over what was probably a fuel dump.

He caught the silvery fluttering, high up, out of the corner of his eye. No time to look. He was already unstrapping
the autonomous missile launcher, setting it up, looking
through the sights, forcing his cold-stiffened fingers to program it to fire its first two rounds into the fuel dump, the
rest in its eight-round drum at anything that moved, within
a certain scope—anything with a fan-spread of six meters
or more. Which might be a group of men and might be an
armored vehicle. Or a stray cow. He wedged the auto-
launcher's tripod in place on the hilltop—and ducked as
rifle fire unzipped the air by his head. They were coming
up the hill, firing from the south side. He rolled down the
north side, and began to circle round. Behind him he
heard the *shoompf! . . . click . . . shoompf!* as the autolaunch-
er let go two minimissiles at the fuel dump, then the *whirrrr*
as it tracked down to the men coming up the hill. . . .

Explosions splashed the sky red and rearranged the
other side of the hill. Hayes kept going (thinking: Maybe I

ought to switch on the spigot, go into overdrive. No. No, not unless I have to.) The enemy thought he was on the hilltop. They kept charging it, in bunches; the launcher kept flawlessly blowing them away. And Hayes kept circling the hill, coming around the flank, looking for a way through. Men loomed up in the darkness, limned with the background flames of the burning dump, forty yards off, looking like target silhouettes; he pressed the bladelike pressure switch attached to the forearm grip of the assault rifle. He held the gun at pectoral level; the laser lanced out, invisible now that it had stopped raining—invisible till it hit the chest of the first man running at him, making a red dot on his chest: a red dot harmless in itself, but telling Hayes he was sighted in. He squeezed the trigger, the man's chest erupted blood. A second man came at him, firing the latest in Russian Dragunovas, its burst making little geysers in the mud near Hayes feet, the guy screaming when Hayes pressed the trigger, sighting in effortlessly. He slapped in another clip, laid the red mark on them as they came, cut them down again and again. Once between clips he came on a man up close, had to gut him with a knife that he'd never used before except to open tin cans. Running. Exhaustion a weight on him. . . . More men up ahead.

He reached down and moved the cover off the medinject, turned the knob. The nighted landscape of the interior Hayes lit up with a flash of biochemical light and his heart started playing a drumroll and he laughed and found himself running and firing through a group of men, lining up the red dot, firing, lining up the red dot, the Laserscope aiming for him, firing. . . . Chewing the dried fruit like a kid happily chewing gum as he cuts a lawn. . . . Seeing clearly now the surveillance bird watching him overhead, not caring. . . . Caught up in the roaring delight of doing what he hated most.

*　　*　　*

Two A.M., AND HAYES WAS hunched under his slicker, in a cave of twisted, blackened metal: the overturned cab of a shattered truck. Hayes feeling like a mollusk in a sunken ship.

He sat shivering, dozing. He'd given himself an hour's rest. A film of rainwater curtained him from the roadside. Now and then he heard a *crump,* and a corner of the mercuric curtain lit up with a lightninglike flash from the shellings to the East. The rain sizzled and burbled on the metal overhead.

Another sound, growing. Rumble, metal gnashings, dronings. Vehicles coming, moving north to south. Going his way. . . .

He fitted a grenade launcher onto his Enfield, stood up, and stepped out into the rain. Felt chills and nausea and weakness sweep through him. Wanted to turn back, hide in his shelter. Felt an overwhelming self-disgust as he thought of the men he'd killed when he was hyped on the spigot; killing them in a biochemically induced frenzy was . . . sickening. But he thought about Parakeet. And Breck. He reached down, turned the knob on his medinject. Felt the spigot shooting him up. Flash: *Go.*

Two trucks, headlights rain-scratchy funnels of glare along the muddy road. He ran at the two trucks, seeing the red star on the side. Firing the grenade at the ground in front of the lead truck, his amphetamine-accelerated brain calculating the grenade's trajectory and the speed of the truck perfectly—so that the grenade went off directly under the truck's gas tank. He threw himself down: a ball of fire ate seven tons of metal and twenty shrieking men. Seeing the explosion he felt a neon-edged rush.

As if frightened by the explosion, the rain stopped.

The second truck pulled up short, and Hayes charged at it, the spigot-juice white-hot in him but giving him wicked razor-backed chills made of metal-flake colors and whiplash shapes. . . . There were muzzle flashes in the truck cab's window, and submachinegun rounds gnashed away part of his right thigh, two fingers on his left hand, a chunk of his left cheek. He felt the woundings as streaks of burn, and it inflamed him more, made him zig-zag, come around from outside their shooting angle, jump on the running board, shove the muzzle of the Enfield into the cab of the truck. Shoot the men in the cab neatly in their foreheads. . . . There were two others under a tarp between the rocket launchers in the back of the truck. He shot them with inhuman precision. They moved so slowly—it seemed to Hayes—it wasn't difficult, really, to kill them all.

Machines and dying men both steaming in the darkness.

Hayes sprayed sealant on his wounds. Then, too jacked up to feel pain, he prowled around the truck, dragging the limp bodies clear, checking out the intact truck in the shuddery light from the one that was burning. It was an enormous, eight-wheel, 22-ton ZIL-300 tokomak truck, camouflage-painted, broad and low to the ground, each of its wheels five feet high—and on its flatbed were two big BM-31 salvo rocket launchers, each with four rows of ten missile launching rails. Capable of firing forty 122mm rockets from each launcher. At once. Murderously concentrated firepower.

Hayes looked at the control equipment. Analogous to the NATO variety. He smiled.

IT WAS A CHECKPOINT. They looked up, bored, when they saw the truck coming, blued in dawn light, with its tired-eyed driver.

Hayes, wearing a Soviet overcoat, nodded to them and

started to drive through. One of them raised a hand to tell him to stop and, yawning, said something to him in Russian, probably asking for travel orders. When the sentry saw Hayes wasn't going to stop he raised his rifle—Hayes pointed a pistol through the window, and shot him. And his friend. He drove on.

Downshifting to go up a muddy hill, and before he got to the top saw a platoon of Russians outlined against the sky. One of the guys at the checkpoint hadn't been quite dead, must've accessed a radio. Because bullets were making crooked stars in the windshield, glass fragments stinging his cheek. He was already adjusting the salvo coordinates. The first rocket launcher behind the cab swiveled, tilted. He punched the *fire* button, and the truck shuddered. A noise like a razor strop magnified ten thousand times and then in multiple thunder the top of the hill—and the men on it—vanished into a fireball that heaved bloodied dirt and stone into the air.

Hayes swung to the right, off the road, circled the smoking, flame-flickered crown of the hill, and saw the camp laid out in front of him. More men coming at him.

Hayes lowered the first salvo launcher, raised the second, reset it for four ten-rocket salvos at four ranges. Fired.

Like instantaneously planting rows of autumned trees, trees with trunks of fire and roiling-smoke foliage. Kind of pretty.

The BM-31 Multiple Rocket Launching System could be reloaded once automatically—and then the reloaders would have to be restocked with rockets. He pulled the levers for reloading, waited nervously while machinery rattled and creaked to itself, and the fires diminished and the smoke tattered. Men picking themselves up, some of them literally, coming at him again. Bullets whining from the grill of the ZIL-300.

The machinery stopped creaking; a green light went on in front of him. He fired one salvo in four sets. Another grove of helltrees, the ground shaking, the sky echoing with artificial thunder.

He glimpsed a surveillance bird. There—and gone in the pall of smoke.

He drove on, through slow waves of fume and smolder. An armor penetrating round struck the ZIL's engine casing. The engine spouted steam from the bullet-hole, coughed. But kept turning over.

Once, in the smoke, he saw Parakeet; his limbs intact, his face shiny clean, standing out there in a new printout suit, microphone in his hand. He heard Parakeet's voice all mixed in with the clash of gears and the clank of the truck, fragments of his stand-up routine, "My buddy Hayes," Parakeet was saying, "He's my main man, the guy loves me—in a nice way, right?—but boy when Hayes gets irritable—he gets so irritable that—" Another rattle of gunfire from behind drowned out the punchline. The hallucination became smoke itself, swirled away. Hayes drove on.

Found a mostly-intact highway, and on it a sign said *Rouen 20 KM*. Exactly parallel to the sign, the engine died. Just as well, he was coming to NATO lines. He took off the overcoat and got out of the truck.

BY THE TIME HE GOT TO the first NATO checkpoint his nerves were frayed through and his wounds were beginning to hurt. It was like the piranhas were in them, burrowing. There were winter-stripped trees by the roadside, stark against the grey sky, and to Hayes they looked like his nerve-ends, exposed and creaking in the icy wind. His senses were sharpened till they cut him. He could feel his clothes rasping his skin, feel the sickening meatiness of his limbs, the clicking interaction of his joints, the soreness of his feet, feel it all too clearly and the sensations razzed him, nagged at him. He hated the feel of his own body. Hated the stink of it. Everything he looked at annoyed him. He knew it was drug fatigue but he couldn't help it, he hated the sight of the road, the strips of grass, that damn recon bird, the clouds, the abandoned farmhouses. Everything. And he was gagging from exhaustion.

A checkpoint. French soldiers on walkie talkies. They said something to him in French and he shrugged. He was prepared to kill them. To kill anyone who stood between him and Breck.

The guy with the walkie talkie got an order about Hayes. He spoke to the other man, who gestured for Hayes to come with him. Hayes decided to play along for awhile. They might just take him to Breck.

THEY DID. First they took him to an infirmary, got his wounds patched up. Then—contrary to the medic's orders—they took him to an old hotel that had been taken over by NATO, converted for military use. Turned him over to an MP who surprised Hayes by not trying to take his weapons away. The MP escorted Hayes upstairs and into a suite that contained a number of mismatched desks collected piecemeal from around town. Breck was there alone, sitting at a dented metal desk, drinking coffee and looking at a TV monitor on the desk top. He came to stand by the desk, a yard from her, the Enfield held casually in one hand. "Coffee, Hayes?" she asked, dismissing the MP with a wave.

"No." Kill her now? Just like that? It seemed anticlimactic. He'd know when the moment came.

"Why'd you go AWOL, Hayes?"

He just looked at her.

"You might have been shot for desertion. Except for

this." She turned the monitor around so it faced him.

He saw himself, filmed from above, running at the Russian troops, cutting down three men. Another shot showed the burning fuel dump. Another shot of Hayes, shooting the men in the truck. . . .

"It was just luck, of course," she said. "The drugs and the hormones helped, I'm sure. But with all those odds against you, you should've been killed half a dozen times. You had a streak of luck."

He nodded. She was right.

Breck leaned back in her chair, making it creak. "Still, Hayes—you're a hero. We need footage like this. We won't have to alter it much at all. And you can give some testimony, maybe some inspirational talks to the troops." Her voice dripped with cynicism. "It'll be cushy duty. . . . You okay, Hayes? You look like you're about to fall over."

He shrugged.

She nodded toward a door on her left. "General Moreland is in there, with Major Kessel. They're talking about the spigots, the pharmilitary experiment, the whole drug project—and about you. They were on the point of recommending that the project be canceled—but it seems your little performance here has convinced them the thing works after all." She smiled thinly, adding, her voice crackling dry, "Congratulations."

He felt like someone had kicked him in the belly.

She chuckled and lit a cigarette.

Bitch. "Maybe," he said, speaking with difficulty through a parched mouth, "I can change their minds."

He leaned over, pushed the muzzle of the Enfield against her cheek. "How many others are in there?"

"Hayes, what are you—"

"Shut up. No, don't shut up, answer my question."

"Half a dozen. And an MP."

"Good."

"What?"

He took the Limbic TX4 from his first aid kit. "Show me your spigot."

"I haven't got one." Saying it between clenched teeth. But there was more fear than anger in her eyes.

He set the TX4 on the desk, took a syringe from his first aid kit. Using one hand, keeping the gun on her with the other, he sucked the TX4 up into the syringe.

"Hayes—that's a full dose. If you put that into me it'll kill me."

"Probably not. But you won't know what you're doing, once the full dose hits you. The overdose. Anyone in your sights . . ." He jabbed it expertly into her arm, probed till he found the vein, saw her bite her lip with pain.

"Hayes—!"

He emptied the syringe in her—then hit her on the jaw with the riflebutt. She went over backwards. Bang and clatter as the chair fell—but no one came in. She lay there, dazed. He took her by the collar, dragged her to her feet, took her to the door that led into the room where General Moreland and Major Kessel and the others were. He put the Enfield into her hands, and held her firmly till he saw she was awake, saw the rage come into her face, saw the TX4 going to work. . . . Her face contorting, eyes dilating, foam showing at the corners of her mouth. . . .

He opened the door and shoved her into the room, told the startled faces, "Whoever survives, test her blood afterwards to see what she was on." Then he left the room, fast.

The shooting started almost immediately.

DOWN IN THE STREET, five blocks away, Hayes found an old French grocer who spoke English. The guy was willing to sell him some civilian clothes. Hayes changed into them, and then, running on sheer instinct, he went to look for a way out of town.

He'd need to move fast, he might have to kill some NATO sentries and a few MPs, and he was exhausted. So he had to use the spigot this last time, had to. He turned the knob on his medinject. Feeling as if fuses were burning out in his brain when the stuff hit him. Searing him, banging his heart like the hammer on a fire alarm bell.

He saw men materializing from shadowy doorways on either side of the narrow street. Russian soldiers, some of them missing portions of their skulls, their limbs, some of them with neat round holes in their chests, smiling at him with a sort of melancholy camaraderie. Parakeet, intact and in uniform, was leading them out into the street to Hayes. They surrounded him. But he didn't feel threatened. Didn't feel he had to fight. One of the Russian boys had an arm hanging by a shred of skin; the arm fell off, and Parakeet bent, smilingly picked up the arm, tucked it under the man's intact armpit. Then he turned to Hayes. "We have to get a move on, Rory, MPs'll come soon."

Hayes said, "I'm hallucinating you."

Parakeet nodded, happily. "Yes. You know these guys?"

"Yeah. They're the guys I killed coming here. So many. Katz—Tell 'em I'm sorry. I just wanted to get through."

"It's okay," Parakeet said. And the dead soldiers patted Hayes on the back to show him it was okay.

Then they all hurried down the street together. The dead Russians and Parakeet and Hayes, a crowd of friends. Parakeet staying close beside Hayes, telling jokes.

The Incorporated

"JOHN—YOU'RE FIRED."

I had but two or three actual jobs in my life. They only lasted about six months apiece. I tended to write at work; to play little jokes with the equipment; to practically sweat with the effort at staying at my desk when I wanted to run the hell out of there and be myself somewhere. . . . So inevitably I heard them say . . .

This story marked a new level of maturity in me as a writer, I think, and it was one of the more distinct early cyberpunk stories. It's about the moral struggle that tears you up when you ask yourself who you serve, the collective or the individual, your loved ones or the social unit. It was inspired by my reading on Japanese corporations . . . and was probably unconsciously influenced by Philip K. Dick.

I was listening to the new Bowie stuff, some German avant garde groups, and early Industrial stuff like SPK and Throbbing Gristle—roughly around then. Also Lou Reed solo stuff, always. Even *Metal Machine Music*.

KESSLER WAS WALKING EAST on Fourteenth Street, looking for something. He wasn't sure what he was looking for. He was walking through a twilight made raw by a mist-thin

November rain sharpening the edge of a cold wind. The wind slashed at his acrylic overcoat. The street was almost deserted. He was looking for something, something; the brutally colorless word *something* hung heavily in his mind like an empty picture frame.

What he thought he wanted was to get in, out of the weather; he felt a vague resentment to the city of New York for letting the weather modification system break down again. Walking in rain made you feel naked. And acid rain, he thought, could make you naked, if you wore the kind of synthreads that reacted with the acids.

Up ahead the eternal neon butterfly of a Budweiser sign glowed sultry orange-red and blue; the same design since sometime in the 20th century. He angled across the sidewalk, pitted concrete the color of dead skin, hurrying toward the sign, toward the haven of a bar. The rain was already beginning to burn. He closed his eyes against it, afraid it would burn his corneas.

He pushed through the smudged door into the bar. The bartender glanced up, nodded, and reached under the counter for a towel; he passed the towel across to Kessler. The towel was treated with acid-absorbents; it helped immediately.

"Get any in your eyes?" the bartender asked, with no great show of concern.

"No, I don't think so." He handed the towel back. "Thanks."

The tired-faced men drinking at the bar hardly glanced at Kessler. He was unremarkable: round-faced, with short black hair streaked bluewhite to denote his work in video-editing; large friendly brown eyes, soft red mouth pinched now with worry; a standard printout greyblue suit.

The bartender said something else, but it didn't register. Kessler was staring at the glowing green lozenge of a credit transferral kiosk in the back of the dim, old-fashioned bar. He crossed to it and stepped in; the door hissed shut behind him. The small TV screen on the front of the phone lit up, and its electronic letters asked him, DO YOU WANT CALL, OR ENTRY?

What did he want? Why had he come here? He wasn't sure. But it felt right. A wave of reassurance had come over him. . . . Ask it what your balance is, a soundless voice whispered to him. A soft, maternal mental whisper. Again a wave of reassurance. But he thought: something's out of place. . . . He knew his mind as a man knows his cluttered desk; he knows when someone has moved something on his desk. Or in his mind. And someone had.

He punched Entry and it asked him his PIN number. He punched the digits in, then told it he wanted to see his bank balance. It told him to wait. Numbers appeared on the screen.

$NB760,000.

He stared at it. He punched for error check and confirmation.

The bank's computer insisted that he had seven hundred and sixty thousand NewBux in his bank account. There should be only four thousand.

Something was missing from his memory; something had been added to his bank account.

They tampered with me, he thought, and then they paid me for it. Who?

He requested the name of the depositor. The screen told him: UNRECORDED.

Julie. Talk to Julie. There was just no one else he discussed his projects with till they were patented and online. No one. His wife had to know.

Julie. He could taste her name in his mouth. Her name tasted like bile.

*   *   *

JULIE HAD BEEN HOME only a few minutes, Kessler decided, as
he closed the door behind him. Her coat was draped over
the back of the couch, off-white on off-white. She liked
things off-white or battleship grey or powder blue.

She was bent down to the minifridge behind the breakfast bar. She stood up, a frosted bottle of Stolichnaya in her
hand. "Hi, Jimmy."

She almost never called him Jimmy.

Julie came out with a vodka straight up and a twist of
lime for each of them. He'd learned to like vodka because
she did. She padded across the powder-blue rug in bare
feet, small feet sexy in sheer hose; she was tall and slender
and long-necked. Her hair was the yellow of split pine, cut
short as a small boy's, and parted on the side. She was
English, and looked it, her eyes were immaculate blue crys-
tals. She wore her silklined, coarse-fiber, off-white dress
suit. The suit with no shoes. She looked more natural in
her suits than in anything else. She had "casuals" to wear at
home, but somehow she never wore them. Maybe because
that would be a concession to homelife, would almost be a
betrayal of the Corporation Family. Like having children.

What was it she said about having children? *If you don't
mind, I'll continue to resist the programming of my biological computer. When DNA talks, I don't listen. I don't like being pushed
into something by a molecule.*

He took off his coat, hung it up, and sat down beside her
on the couch. The vodka, chilled with no ice, waited for
him on the glass coffee table. He took a drink and said,
"There's seven hundred and sixty thousand NewBux in my
bank account." He looked at her. "What did they take?"

Her eyes went a little glassy. "Seven hundred and sixty
thousand? Computer error. Just accept it—that's incredibly

good luck. . . ."

"You know it's not." He took another sip. The Stoly was syrupy from being kept in the freezer. "What did you tell Worldtalk?"

"Are you accusing me of something?" She said it with her icy Vassar incredulousness then, like: I can't believe anyone could be so painfully unsophisticated.

"I'm accusing Worldtalk. You're theirs. They do as they like with you. If Worldtalk says it's not productive to have kids, if Worldtalk says it's not *teamplaying* to have kids, you don't have kids. Even when their disapproval is unnecessary: You wouldn't have had to take time from your job—I can understand you wanting to have a career. We could have had the kid in an artificial womb. I would've taken care of it during the day. If Worldtalk says listen for Usefuls, you listen. Even at home. They don't want employees, at Worldtalk, they want to *own you.*"

"It's pointless to go over and over this. Worldtalk has nothing to do with my decision not to have children. I worked eight years—"

"I know it by rote: You worked eight years to be assistant New York manager in the country's biggest PR and advertising outfit. You tell me *having children* is demeaning yourself! Eight years you browned your nose on Grimwald's ass! Going to Worldtalk's family sessions, letting them psych you up after work for hours at a time, letting them co-opt your instincts!"

She stood up, arms rigid at her sides. "Well, why not? Corporation families *last.*"

"It isn't a real family. They're using you. Look what they got you to do! To *me.*"

"You got some seven hundred thousand NB. That's more than you would ever have made on any of your harebrained schemes. If you worked for a corp you'd be making decent

money in the first place. You insist on being freelance so
you're left out in the cold, and you should be grateful for
what they—" she snipped the sentence in two with a brisk
sibilance, and turned away.

"So we've dropped the pretenses now. You're saying I
should be grateful for the money Worldtalk gave me.
Julie—*What did they take?*"

"I don't *know!* You didn't tell me what you were working
on—and anyway I don't believe they took anything. I—god
damn it."

She went to bathroom to pointedly take her Restem,
making a lot of noise opening the prescription bottle so
he'd hear and know it was his fault she had to take a tran-
quilizer.

BASCOMB WAS DRUNK AND DRUGGED. It seemed to Kessler that
the disorder of Bascomb's mind was splashed onto the
room around him: the dancers, the lights, the holograms
that made it look, in the smoky dimness, as if someone was
there dancing beside you who wasn't. A touristy couple on
the dance floor stopped and stared at another couple:
horned, half human, half reptile, she with her tongue darting from between rouged lips; he with baroque fillips of
fire flicking from his scaly nostrils. The touristy couple
laughed off their embarrassment when the deejay turned
off the enclosing holo and the demon couple vanished.

Bascomb chuckled and sucked some of his cocaine fizz
through a straw that lit up with miniature advertisements
when it was used; lettering flickering luminous green up
and down its length.

Sitting beside Bascomb, Kessler squirmed on his bar stool
and ordered another Scotch. He didn't like Bascomb like
this. Bascomb was young, tanned, and preppie; he wore a
Japanese Action Suit now, a kind of clinging, faintly irides-

cent jumpsuit. Kessler was used to seeing Bascomb in his office, a neat component of Featherstone, Pestlestein, and Bascomb, Attorneys at Law, friendly but not too friendly, intense but controlled. My own fault, Kessler told himself: chase the guy down when he's off work, hassle his wives till they tell me where he hangs out, find out things I don't want to know about the guy. Like the fact that he's bisexual and flirting with the waiter.

The bar was circular, rotating slowly through the club, leaving the dance floor behind now to arrive at the cruising rooms. As they talked it turned languidly past flesh-pink holographic porn squirmings and edged into the soft music lounge. Each room had its own idiosyncratic dark-ness, shot through with the abstracted glamour of the candy-apple red and hot pink and electric blue neon tubes running up the corners to zig-zag the ceiling like a time-lapse photo of night-time city traffic.

Bascomb turned on his stool to look at the porn and the live copulation; his mouth was open in a lax smile. Kessler looked over his shoulder. Again in the dimness the holos were nearly indistinguishable from the real article; a drunk-en swinger tried to fondle a woman with four breasts, only to walk through her. "Do we have to talk here?" Kessler asked, turning back to the bar.

Bascomb ignored the question. "The bottom line, Jim, is that you are a nobody. Now if you were, say, a Nobel-Prize-winning professor at Stanford, we might be able to get you your day in court, we might get a Grand Jury to investigate the people at Worldtalk. . . ." Talking without taking his eyes off the intermingled porn and people. "But as it is you're a mildly successful video editor who makes a hobby of working up a lot of media theories. Every day some crank looking for attention announces a Great Idea has been stolen from his brain, and ninety-nine percent of the time they turn out to be paranoid or a liar or both. I'm not saying you're a paranoid or a liar. I believe you. I'm just saying I'm probably the only one who will."

"But I have the seven hundred sixty thousand—"

"Did you request the name of the depositor?"

"Unrecorded."

"Then how are you going to prove a connection?"

"I don't know. But I know an idea was stolen from me. I want it back, Bascomb. And I can't work it up again on my own from scratch—I wouldn't know where to begin; it was all on a disc, and in paper files. Both are gone. They took all my notes, everything that could lead me back to it. I guess they figured I might have mentioned the work to someone else. So they gave me the money so I'd just accept the loss. But I *don't* accept it, Bascomb."

"Sucks," Bascomb said sympathetically. They had rotated into the lounge; people on couches watched videos and conversed softly. Sometimes they were talking to holos; you knew when you were talking to a holo because the holos said outrageous things. They were programmed that way to ease the choking boredom of lounge bar conversation. "I want it back, Bascomb," Kessler repeated, his knuckles white on the rim of the bar.

Bascomb shrugged and said, "You haven't been in this country long; maybe you don't know how it works. First off, you have to understand that . . ." he paused to sip from his cocaine fizz; he became more animated almost instantly, chattering, showing off: "you have to understand that you can't get it back the way it was taken. Whoever it was probably came in while you were asleep. Which adds credence to your theory that Julie was involved. She waits up or pretends to sleep, lets them in, they shoot you up with the receptivity drug. The beauty of the RD is that it works instantly and not only makes you cerebral-program receptive but keeps you sedated. They put the wires and tubes in through the sinuses, but they don't damage anything. They've got lots of microsurgicals in the big box they've brought with them, right? They look at the screen they've set up that translates your impulses into a code they can understand. They get some dream free-association maybe. But that tells them they're online in your brain. Then they put a request to the brain, fed into it in the form of neuro-humoral transmitter molecules they manufacture in their box—"

"How do you know so much about this?" Kessler asked, unable to keep the edge of suspicion out of his voice.

"We get a case like yours once or twice a year. I did a lot of research. The ACLU has a small library on the subject. It really gets their goat. We didn't win those cases, by the way; they're tough. . . ." He paused to sip his fizz, his eyes sparkling and dilated.

Kessler was annoyed by Bascomb's treating his case like a curiosity, a conversation piece. "Let's get back to what happened to me."

"Okay, uh—so they made a request to the biological computer we call a brain, right? They ask it what it knew about whatever they wanted to take from you, and your brain automatically begins to think about it, and sends signals to the cortex of the temporal lobes or to the hippocampus; they 'ride' the electrochemical signals back to the place where the information is stored. They use tracer molecules that attach themselves to the chemical signals. When they reach the hippocampus or the temporal lobes, the tracer molecules act as enzymes to command the brain to simply unravel that particular chemical code. They break it down on the molecular level. They extract some things connected to it, and the chain of ideas that led to it, but they don't take so much they make you an idiot because they probably want your wife to cooperate and to stay with Worldtalk. Anyway, the brain chemistry is such that you can ask the brain a question with neurohumoral transmitter molecules, but you can't imprint on the memory, in an orderly way. You can feed in experiences, things which seem to be happening now—you can even implant them so they crop up at a given stimulus—but you can't feed in ready made *memories*. Probably because memories are holographic, involving complexes of cell groups. Like you can pull a thread to unravel a coat fairly easily but you can't ravel it back up so easily. . . . Look at that exquisite creature over there. She's lovely, isn't she? Like to do some imprinting on her. I wonder if she's real. Uh, anyway . . . you can't put it back *in*. They take out, selectively, any memory of anything that might make you suspect they tampered with you, but lots of people begin to suspect anyway, because when they free associate over familiar pathways of the brain and then come to a gap—well, it's jarring. But they can't prove anything."

"Okay, so maybe it can't be put back by direct feed-in to the memory. But it could be relearned through ordinary induction. Reading."

"Yeah. I guess it would be better than nothing. But you still have to find out what it was and who took it. Even if it turns up as someone else's project—proves nothing. They could have come up with it same way you did. And you should ask yourself this: Why did they take it? Was it simply for profit or was it for another reason? From what we've been able to find out, about a third of the ideas that are stolen out of someone's brain are stolen for reasons of protection. The bigger corporations have a network of agents. Their sole job is to search out people with developing ideas that could be dangerous to the status quo. They try to extract the ideas before they are copyrighted or patented or published in papers or discussed in public. They take the idea from you, maybe plant some mental inhibitors to keep you from working your way back to it again. If you came up with an idea that was *really* dangerous to the Status Quo, Jimmy, they might go farther than a simple erasing next time. Because they play hardball. If you keep pushing to get it back, they just might arrange for you to turn up dead. . . ."

BUT RIDING THE ELEVATOR up to his apartment, thinking about what had happened, trying to come to terms with it, Kessler realized it wasn't death that scared him. What chilled him was thinking about his wife. Julie had waited till he'd slept. Had, perhaps, watched the clock on the bedside table. Had got out of bed at the appointed hour and padded to the door and ever-so-quietly opened it for the man carrying the black box. . . .

And she had done it because Worldtalk had asked her to. Worldtalk was her husband, her children, her parents. Perhaps most of all her dreadful parents.

And maybe in the long run, what had happened to him, Kessler thought, as the elevator reached his floor, was that the Dissolve Depression had done its work on him. For decades the social structures that created nuclear families, that kept families whole and together, had eroded, had finally broken down completely. Broken homes made broken homes made broken homes. The big corporations, meanwhile, consumed the little ones, and, becoming then unmanageably big, looked for ways to stabilize themselves. They chose the proven success of the Japanese system: the corporation as an extension of the family. You inculcate your workers with a fanatic sense of loyalty and belonging. You personalize everything. And they go along with that or they lose their jobs. So maybe it started with the Dissolve

Depression: five years earlier, a Moslem Jihad terrorist group had set off a controlled hydrogen bomb explosion in the upper atmosphere; the explosion was contained, directed outward; but the bomb's Electromagnetic Pulse—the EMP effect—swept over the continent. The defense systems were shielded. But not the banks. The pulse literally burnt up the computer memories of millions of bank accounts. Hundreds of banks collapsed, and the economy with them.

So now jobs were precious. Jobs were life. You embraced the new Corporation as home and family system. The breakdown of the traditional family structures reinforced the process. And you put your employer above your true family. You let its agents in to destroy your husband's new career. . . .

And here we are, he thought, as he walked into the apartment. There she is, making us both a drink, so we can once more become cordial strangers sharing a convenience apartment and a convenient sex life.

"Aren't you coming to bed?" she called from the bedroom.

He sat on the couch, holding his glass up beside his ear, shaking it just enough so he could listen to the tinkle of the ice cubes. The sound made him feel good and he wondered why. It made him visualize wind chimes of frosted glass. . . . His mother's wind chimes. His mother standing on the front porch, smiling absently, watching him play, and now and then she would reach up and tinkle the wind chimes with her finger. . . . He swallowed another tot of vodka to smear over the chalky scratch of loneliness.

"You really ought to get some sleep, Jimmy." A faint note of strain in her voice.

He was scared to go in there.

This is stupid, he thought. I don't know for sure it was her.

He forced himself to put the glass down, to stand, to walk to the bedroom, to do it all as if he weren't forcing himself through the membranes of his mistrust. He stood in the doorway and looked at her for a moment. She was wearing her silk lingerie. Her back to him. He could see her face reflected in the window to her left. Her eyes were open wide. In them he saw determination and self-disgust and he knew she had contacted them and the strangers were going to do it to him again. They would come and take out more this time, his conversation with Bascomb, his misgivings. They would take away the hush money they had paid him since he had shown he was unwilling to accept it without pushing to get back what he had lost. . . . They would take his argument with Julie . . .

Go along with it, he told himself.

That would be the intelligent solution. Let them do it. Sweet nepenthe. The pain and the fear and the anger would go with the memories. And he would have his relationship with his wife back. Such as it was.

He thought about it for a moment. She turned to look at him.

"No," he said finally. "No, we don't have enough between us to make it worthwhile. No. Tell them I said next they'll have to try and kill me."

She stared at him. Then she lay back, and looked at the ceiling.

He closed the bedroom door softly behind him, and went to the closet for his coat.

THEY HADN'T TAKEN THE MONEY YET. It was still there in his account. He had gone to an all night banking kiosk, sealed himself in, and now he looked at the figure, $NB760,000 and felt a kind of glow. He punched for the telephone, and called Charlie Chesterton.

The screen asked him, YOU WANT VISUAL? No, he told it, not yet.

"Sap?" came Charlie's voice. "Huzatunwushant?"

Wake Charlie out of a sound sleep, and he talked Technicki. He'd said, *What's happenin'? Who's that and what do you want?*

"Talk standard with me, Charlie. It's—"

"Hey, my man Kessler, what's happening, man! Hey how come no visual?"

"I didn't know what you were doing. I'm ever discreet." He punched for visual and a small TV image of Charlie appeared below the phone's keyboard. Charlie wore a triple mohawk, each fin a different color, each color significant; red in the middle for Technicki Radical Unionist; blue on the right for his profession, video tech; green on the left for his neighborhood: New Brooklyn. He grinned, showing front teeth imprinted with his initials in gold, another tacky technicki fad. And Charlie wore a picture T-shirt that showed a movie: Fritz Lang's *Metropolis,* now moving through the flood scene.

"You went to sleep wearing your movie T-shirt, you oughta turn it off, wear out the batteries."

"Recharges from sunlight," Charlie said. "You call me to talk about my sleeping habits?"

"Need your help. Right now, I need the contact numbers for that Shanghai bank that takes the transferrals under a code of anonymity. . . ."

"I told you man, that's like, the border of legality, and maybe over it. You understand that first, right?"

Kessler nodded.

"Okay. Set your screen to record . . ."

BASCOMB'S OFFICE WAS TOO WARM; Bascomb had a problem with his circulation. The walls were a milky yellow that seemed to quicken the heat somehow. Bascomb sat behind the blond-wood desk, wearing a stenciled-on three-piece suit, smiling a smile of polite bafflement. Kessler sat across from him, feeling he was on some kind of treadmill, because Bascomb just kept saying, "I really am quite sure no such meeting took place." He chuckled: "I know the club very well and I'm sure I'd remember if I'd been there that night. Haven't been there for a month."

"You weren't enthusiastic about the case, but you ended by telling me we'd take 'em on." But the words were ashes in Kessler's mouth. He knew what had happened because there was not even the faintest trace of duplicity or nervousness on Bascomb's face. Bascomb really didn't remember. "So you won't represent me on this," Kessler went on. Only half a question.

"We really have no experience with brain tampering—"

"I could get the court files to prove that you have. But they'd only . . ." He shook his head. Despair was something he could smell and taste and feel, like acid rain. "They'd tamper with you again. Just to make their point."

He walked out of the office, hurrying, thinking: They'll have the place under surveillance. But no one stopped him outside.

CHARLIE WAS OFF ON ONE OF HIS amateur analyses, and there was nothing Kessler could do, he had to listen, because Charlie was covering for him.

". . . I mean," Charlie was saying, "now your average Technicki speaks standard English like an infant, am I right, and can't read except command codes, and learned it all from vidteaching, and he's trained to do this and that and to fix this and that but he's, like, socially inhibited from rising in the ranks because the socio-economic elite speaks standard good and reads—"

"If they really want to, they can learn what they need, like you did," Kessler said irritably. He was standing at the window, looking out at the empty, glossy ceramic streets. The artificial island, a boro-annex of Brooklyn anchored in the harbor, was almost deserted at this hour; everyone had either gone into the city, or home to holo, or into a tavern. The floating boros were notoriously dull. The squat floboro housing, rounded off at the corners like a row of molars, stood in silence, a few windows glowing like radarscopes against the night.

But they could be watching me, Kessler thought. A hundred ways they could be watching me and I'd see nothing.

He turned, stepped away from the window. Charlie was pacing, arms clasped behind him, head bent, playing the part of the young, boldly theorizing leader of radical politicos.

The apartment was crowded with irregular shelves of books and boxes of software and cassettes and compact discs; Charlie had hung silk scarves in The Three Colors, blurring like multicolor smoke. "I mean," Charlie went on, "you can talk about our job security but it's a sham—"

A warning chill: and Kessler turned, looked out the window. Three stories down she was a powder-blue keyhole shape against the faint petroleum rainbow filminess of the street. She was looking at the numbers.

She might have guessed, he told himself. She met Charlie once. She might have looked Charlie's address up in ref disc.

She came to the front door. Charlie's bell chimed. Charlie went to the screen and looked. "It's your wife," he said. "You want me to tell her you went overseas? Japan?"

"Let her in."

"Are you kidding, man? You are, right? She was the one who—"

"Just let her in." She got it from the address list, he told himself. There was a cocktail of emotions in him. There was a relief at seeing her, shaken in with something that buzzed like a smoke alarm and it wasn't till she was at the door that he realized that the sensation was terror. And then Julie was standing in the doorway, against the light of the hallway. She looked beautiful. The light behind her abruptly cut—an energy saving device—suddenly she stood framed in darkness. The buzzing fizzed up, and overwhelmed the relief. His mouth was dry.

Looking disgustedly at Kessler, Charlie shut the door behind her.

Kessler stared at her. Her eyes flickered, her mouth opened, and shut, and she shook her head. She looked drained.

And Kessler knew.

"They sent you. They told you where to find me," he said.

"They—want the money back," she said. "They want you to come with me."

He shook his head. "Don't you get sick of being puppeted?"

She looked at the window. Her face was blank. "You don't understand."

"Do you know why they do it, why they train you in that Americanized Japanese job conditioning stuff? To save themselves money. Because it eliminates unions."

"They have their reasons, sure. Mostly efficiency."

"I know. What's the slogan? 'Efficiency is friendship.' "

She looked embarrassed. "That's not—" She shrugged. "A Corporate Family is just as valid as any other. It's something you couldn't understand. I—I'll lose my job, Jimmy. If you don't come." She said *lose my job* the way Kessler would have said, *lose my life*.

Kessler said, "I'll think about going with you if you tell me what it was . . . what it was they took."

"They—took it from me too."

"I don't believe that. I never believed it. I think they left it intact in you, so you could watch to see if I stumbled on it again. I think you really loved them trusting you. World-talk is Mommy and Daddy and Mommy and Daddy trusted you . . ."

Her mouth twisted. "You bastard. I can't—"

"Yeah, you can. You have to. Otherwise Charlie and I are going out the back way and we're going to cause endless trouble for Worldtalk. And I know you, Julie—I'd know if you were making it up. So tell me what it was, what it really was."

She sighed. "I only know what you told me. You pointed out that PR companies manipulate the media for their clients without the public knowing it most of the time. They use their connections and channels to plant information or disinformation in news-sheet articles, on newsvid, in movies, in political speeches. So . . . ?" She paused and went on wearily shrugging off her irritation. "So they're manipulating people, and the public gets a distorted view of what's going on because of special interests. You worked up an editing system that sensed probable examples of, uh I think the phrases you used were 'implanted information' or 'special interest distortion.' So they could be weeded out. You called it the Media Alarm System." She let out a long breath. "I didn't know they'd go so far—I thought they'd buy out your system. In a way they did. I *had* to mention it at Worldtalk. If I didn't I would've been . . . disloyal." She said *disloyal* wincing, knowing what he would think.

But it was Charlie who said it: "What about loyalty to Jim Kessler?"

Her hand fluttered a dismissal. "It doesn't matter at this

point whether it was wrong or right. It's too late. They *know*. . . . Jimmy, are you coming?"

Kessler was thinking about the Media Alarm System. It didn't sound familiar—but it sounded *right*. He said, slowly, "No. You can help me. What they did is illegal as hell. If you testify, we can beat them."

"Jimmy, if I thought they—no, no. I—" She broke off, staring at his waist. "Don't be stupid. That's not—" She took a step back, and put her hand in her purse.

Kessler and Charlie looked at each other, traded puzzlement. When Kessler looked back at Julie, she had a gun in her hand. It was a small blue-metal pistol, its barrel tiny as a pencil, and that tiny barrel meant it fired explosive bullets. *They* had given it to her.

"Do you know what that gun will do?" Charlie was saying. "Those little explosive bullets will splash him all over the wall." His voice shook. He took a step toward her.

She pressed back against the door and said, "Charlie, if you come closer to me I'll shoot him." Charlie stopped. The room seemed to keen ultrasonically with sheer imminence. She went on, the words coming out in a rush: "Why don't you ask him what that thing in his hand would do to me, Charlie. Shall we? Ask him that. Jimmy has the same kind of gun. With the same goddamn bullets." Her voice was too high; she was breathing fast. Her knuckles white on the gun.

Kessler's arms were hanging at his side, his hands empty.

"Lower the gun, Julie, and we can talk," Charlie said gently.

"I'll lower mine when he lowers his," she said hoarsely.

"He isn't holding a gun," Charlie said.

She was staring at a space about three feet in front of Kessler's chest. She was seeing the gun there. He wanted to say, *Julie, they tampered with you.* He could only croak, "Julie—"

She shouted, "Don't!" and raised the gun. And then everything was moving: Kessler threw himself down. Charlie jumped at her, and the wall behind Kessler jumped outward toward the street.

Two hot metal hands clapped Kessler's head between them and he shouted with pain and thought he was dead. But it was only a noise, the noise of the wall exploding outward. Chips of wall pattered down; smoke sucked out through the four foot hole into the winter night.

Kessler got up, shaky, his ears ringing. He looked around, and saw Charlie straddling Julie. He had the gun in his hand and she was face down, sobbing.

"Gogidoutere," Charlie said, lapsing into Technicki, his face white.

"Get off her," Kessler said. Charlie stood up beside her. "Julie, look at me," Kessler said softly. She tilted her head back, an expression of dignified defiance trembling precariously in her face. Then her eyes widened, and she looked at his hips. She was seeing him holding a gun there. "I don't have a gun, Julie. They put that into you. Now I'm going to *get* a gun. . . . Give me the gun, Charlie." Without taking his eyes off her, he put his hand out. Charlie hesitated, then laid the gun in Kessler's open palm. She blinked, then narrowed her eyes.

"So now you've got two guns." She shrugged.

He shook his head. "Get up." Moving stiffly, she stood up. "Now go over there to Charlie's bed. He's got black bedsheets. You see them? Take one off. Just pull it off and bring it over here." She started to say something, anger lines punctuating her mouth, and he said quickly, "Don't talk yet. Do it!" She went to the bed, pulled the black satin sheet off, and dragged it over to him. Charlie gaped, and muttered that the cops would come because of the explosion and would hold you for days and weeks till they were sure of what had happened, but Kessler had a kind of furious calm on him then, and he knew what he was going to do, and if it didn't work then he'd let the acid rain bleach his bones white as a warning to other travelers come to this poisoned well. This woman. He said, "Now tear up the sheet—sorry, man, I'll replace it—and make a blindfold. Good. Right. Now tie it over my eyes. Use the tape on the table to make the blindfold light-proof."

Moving in slow motion, she blindfolded him. Darkness whispered down around him. She taped it thoroughly in place. "Now am I still pointing two guns at you?"

"Yes." But there was uncertainty in her voice.

"Now take a step to one side. No, take several steps, very softly, move around a lot." The soft sounds of her movement. Her gasp. "Is the gun following you around the room?"

"Yes. Yes. One of them."

"But how is that possible? *I can't see you!* And why did I let you blindfold me if I'm ready and willing to shoot you?"

"You look weird like that, man. Ridiculous and scary," Charlie said.

"Shut up, Charlie, will you? Answer me, Julie! I can't see you! How can I follow you with the guns?"

"I don't know!" Her voice cracking.

"Take the guns from my hands! Shoot me! Do it!"

She made a short hissing sound, and took the gun from his hand and he braced to die. But she pulled the blindfold away and looked at him.

Looked into his eyes.

She let the gun drop to the floor. Kessler said, softly: "You see now? They did it to you. You, one of the 'family.' The corporate 'family' means just exactly nothing to them."

She looked at his hands. "No gun. No gun." Dreamily. "Gun's gone. Everything's different."

Siren warblings. Coming closer.

She sank to her knees. "Just exactly nothing to them," she said. "Just exactly nothing." Her face crumpled. She looked as if she'd fallen into herself, some inner scaffolding had been kicked out of place.

Sirens and lights outside. A chrome fluttering in the smoky gap where the wall had been blown outward; a police surveillance bird. It looked like a bird, hovering in place with its oversized aluminum hummingbird's wings; but instead of a head it had a small camera lens. A transmitted voice droned from a grid on its silvery belly: *"This is the police. You are now being observed and taped. Do not attempt to leave. The front door has been breached. Police officers will arrive in seconds to take your statements. Repeat—"*

"Oh, I heard you," Julie said, in a hollow voice. "I'll make a statement all right. I've got a lot to tell you. Oh yeah." She laughed sadly. "I'll make a statement . . ."

Kessler bent down, and touched her arm. "Hey . . . I—"

She drew back from him. "Don't touch me. Just don't! You love to be right. I'm going to tell them. Just don't touch me."

But he stayed with her. He and Charlie stood looking at the blue smoke drifting out the ragged hole in the wall; at the mechanical, camera-eyed bird looking back at them.

He stayed with her, as he always would, and they listened for the footsteps outside the door.

When Enter Came

I RAN OUT ON STAGE AT THE PUNK SHOW and put a garbage can over the lead singer's head.

That was in the late seventies, when I was in Sado Nation, playing in Seattle, and I was pissed off because some local band had insisted on going on when my band was supposed to go on, and they had clout with the organizer, so I acted out on it, I ran out there with the big metal garbage can . . .

During my set one of his friends smashed a bottle on my head. I bled all over but it looked cool so we finished the set.

Later his band jumped me backstage, held my arms while he pumped his fists into my gut. It was worth it.

But you can't do it forever (though Henry Rollins, a remarkable performer and lyricist, seems able to) and later on you find yourself sliding into the quicksand of the very life you were sneering at ten or so years earlier. The loss of your creative intensity (or the temporary suppression of it) is symbolized by a temporary dulling of the sexual energies. Hence this story, written in the late eighties.

This was an attempt to use surreal imagery (in a believable, real-life setting) to reconcile certain emotional problems I was having at the time, and to explore feelings and impressions I'd had in a lifetime of erotic experiences. The story is unabashedly erotic, unabashedly fantastic, and made a splash when it was unabashedly published in *Yellow Silk* magazine.

THERE WAS NO CONTACT. He was hard, or hard enough anyway, and he was inside her. He had his arms around her; their tongues worked expertly together. She groaned on cue, and thrust her hips to meet his. But there was no contact. The whole thing was a lifeless minuet performed by skilled dancers. It was sex for Buzz Garret and Elena Garret.

David Letterman was in the room. The TV was still on, in the background, but the sound was off. The only light in their bedroom was videolight, shape-shifting in pixel colors and shadow. Garret ejaculated, and thought of a line from a Lou Reed song: *Something flickered and was gone . . .*

Afterward, Elena went to the bathroom. He heard the faint plastic rattling that meant she was getting a prescription bottle. Taking a Xanax.

He thought: How did we get this way? Is it Elena? It's me as much as her. She's a bit more openly nasty sometimes, is all. She can't blame me for the career thing. She was in graduate school when we met; I was in a rock band, then. One that never made any money. She had the career momentum. I never asked her to give up her Physics R & D . . .

But somehow Garret became a booking agent, Elena became a housewife, set quantum physics aside for the glib comfort of astrology and mysticism; stays up late reading about the occult, never says a word to Garret about what she really believes. . . .

She came back to bed. "Elena?" he asked.

"Hm?"

"What do you really believe? I mean, about what we're here for, what the universe is—all the stuff you read about."

"What the hell kind of time is this to ask me, Buzz? It's almost one-thirty in the morning, Jenny's going to come prancing in here waking us up promptly at seven—"

"Okay forget it."

"I mean, I'm too tired to get into—"

"Okay, okay."

No contact.

THREE WEEKS and no further sex later.

"Come off it, Buzz, you love booking bands. It's the best job in the world except maybe astronaut, and that's quoting you," Elena said. He could tell she didn't like the direction of the conversation; she stared into the middle distance and used her weary, patronizing tone. "You're kind of young for a midlife crisis. Thirty-one. I mean, Christ."

It was all just her way of saying, Don't talk about it, it makes me nervous. Warning him that if he insisted on talking about it, there'd be a fight. They had a house to pay off, this was no time for a change in careers.

They were sitting in the back yard, in lawn chairs by the lawn table, on which the bones of T-bone steaks soaked grease through paper plates. The brick barbecue gave up a faint ghost of gray smoke. Elena and Garret: lounging in the soft California sunlight that went like an accessory with any Bay Area suburb, with this moderately pricey development in Walnut Creek. Elena was smoking a cigarette through one of those attachable filter-holders that strains the smoke to help you cut back. She chainsmoked to compensate.

He was tempted to point that out. But it would precipitate more snippiness. Pointless wrangling. He would be using it against her because he was angry. . . .

Around and around in his head. Thinking, no contact, no real contact. We could take X, maybe, like Barry recommended, the drug MDMA, supposed to get you closer to your spouse. But Garret was scared of drugs, after putting in a year in NA to get off cocaine. And he didn't know if he

wanted to get closer to Elena. She wasn't particularly interested in him, not really. She didn't even know why he was
nicknamed Buzz. She'd never asked, and probably thought
it was like Buzz Aldrin. But it was short for Buzzard. Because Garret had been in one of the first west coast punk
bands.

He looked around at his big yard, his barbecue, his two
story pastel-blue split level house, and thought, How did I
get from shrieking rhythmic obscenities under a mohawk,
to *this?*

He loved the house, in his way. It was like one big baby
crib for him and his kids. Being punk, by contrast, was like
being a flagpole sitter. It had a limited appeal. It was not a
career move. But it'd had one thing. It had contact, of
sorts.

He could never go back to it, of course. But maybe there
was some other kind of deep contact to be had. . . .

Louis and Birdy were over by the rose bushes playing
He-Man and She-Ra. They had the prop swords, bought at
Toys-R-Us. Louis was being She-Ra, which irritated Elena,
made her worry about the boy's sexual identity. "Oh He-
Man," four year old Louis was saying in a fluting voice,
"you're so strong, only you can stop Skeletor!"

Garret's seven year old daughter, in her best low voice,
said, "Don't worry, She-Ra! I'll help you!"

Louis stopped playing, like an actor on a stage startled
by the manager turning up the house lights. Looking
around. Distracted.

There was a rumble you couldn't hear. Elena frowned.

Garret felt a kind of indefinable dread, coming out of
the very bottom of his gut in slow, diffuse waves of anxiety.
Resonating with the unheard rumble in the air. A subsonic
shiver.

Garret said, "You feel . . . anything? kind of like something's out of whack or . . . ?"

Elena hugged herself, and pursed her lips, and said, "No." Lying through her teeth. Looking up at her workroom window.

The rumble, again. Felt but not heard. Rising again—and then gone. Garret saw Louis shiver, and look around. Then Louis shrugged, and raised his She-Ra sword. "He-Man—Skeletor's coming!"

And Garret thought, for no reason in particular. *Contact.* It sounded in his mind twice, in the voice of some mental phone operator. *Contact.*

"Skeletor is here!" Louis said. "But so is She-Ra and He-Man!"

IF YOU WRITE POETRY when you're a teenager, you probably write bad poetry. Especially if you were young in the late 70s, early 80s, with all the dour, gothic rock people around, and you were sensitive, a bit alienated, fairly smart. In that case, you wrote poetry that matched your clothes. Poetry dressed all in black, poetry with little silver skull ear-rings and kohl around its eyes and maybe a tattoo that said BORN TO DIE.

But bad poetry isn't meaningless. The day before Enter came, Garret was going through a box of press clippings in his office, looking for a nasty review of one of his own early bands—he was going to show it to one of the bands he was booking, to show them that arrogance was a perennial mistake. On top of a thin book of clippings, Garret found one of the high school notebooks he'd filled with bad poetry. Found himself reading some stuff he wrote one night after his parents came home drunk—they always came home drunk, and usually left home drunk. Drunk and snarling at one another.

He was the child of alcoholics, with all the attendant low

self esteem, fear of abandonment. The poetry, in conse-
quence, could have been cited in a psychological casebook,
with lines like:

> *Loneliness comes in concentric circles*
> *Like the circles in Dante's Hell*
> *And the innermost circle is the hardest to see.*

Pretty heavy-handed stuff, he thought. Garish. But now,
fifteen years later, it rang true, somehow. He was married,
had two kids, once had a lot of girlfriends; still had a lot of
friends. And he wasn't as lonely as it was when he was a
young misfit teenager, no. But he was still a circle away
from knowing anyone.

SHE CAME TO GARRET when he was trying not to masturbate.
He was working late in his office, upstairs in their house. He
had his feet up on the transparent plastic desk, next to the
PC he never used, a cup of espresso in one hand—from the
espresso machine on the file cabinet, a machine that he did
use a great deal. He was making phone calls that simply
seemed to breed more calls. He was trying to get the
TinTones on the same bill with Wind Window, despite the
irritating sound of the dual wordplay names, and at the
same time fighting the randiness that had plagued him all
week. He was tempted to slip into the upstairs bathroom,
run through one of his repertoire of sexual fantasies, discharge some of the sexual tension. Then get back to work.
But he knew it was a way to avoid sex with Elena. Sex they
were overdue for. Something she was getting bitter and sarcastic about. So he was trying to hold the randiness in for
her. . . .

It happened when he was absentmindedly changing a
light bulb. He was talking to Chalky, the Brit who was the

manager of the TinTones, telling him, "I just talked to Bill Graham, and if you can make a concession on the band's paycheck—Hey, Chalky, man, this gig is an important showcase for the Bay Area because the programmers will all be there, especially the guys from KROQ and KNET—" The walls hummed with a distant, almost unfelt rumble. And then, *phht*, the overhead light burnt out, leaving Garret in a darkness broken up by streetlight glow coming bluewhite through the blue curtains. It was like suddenly being put into photonegative. But he kept talking to Chalky on the speakerphone as he got a bulb out of a desk drawer, stood on a chair, tilted the fixture aside, unscrewed the dead bulb. Telling Chalky, "You do this one for me, pal, I'll do one for you—"

And then a thick, shining, violet fluid dripped out of the empty light socket.

Pop. The sound of the dead light bulb breaking on the floor. Slipped from his fingers as he stared.

The glowing fluid dripped in slow motion.

As Chalky rattled on about something, "The trouble is, luv, I've got more people to please than just my dear, dear mate Buzz Garret. There's the promoter, the record companies . . ."

A filmy ribbon of purple and violet plasma was issuing from the socket, swirling and dripping, fluid but gaseous too; like smoke, but it wasn't smoke. It crackled softly and flexed itself like an idea. Unevenly lighting the room in twisty neon.

Garret said, numbly, "Chalky, call you back." Hit the hangup button. Stared at the socket.

Some kind of electromagnetic peculiarity? Some kind of swamp gas sort of thing? A hallucination? Was he that stressed out?

The ribbon thickened and turned in the air, and took

shape as it torqued, like a figure emerging on a slow lathe. The shape . . .

He thought of certain paintings by Georgia O'Keefe. And others by Judy Chicago. He thought of women.

The shape was mercurial and full of promise. It reached octopally toward him—

He fell off the chair, onto his ass. One hand went into a patch of broken light bulb glass, cutting the heel of his thumb. His butt hurt from the fall. He hardly noticed any of this. He couldn't take his eyes off the shine, the shape growing, getting big. Big as Mindy Gretch. Mindy, the ebullient expanse of nude Mindy Gretch, his first sexual partner. She was a two hundred pound nineteen year old glitter rocker, into Bowie and Alice and the Dolls. Davie Garret, at sixteen, was mesmerized by the Niagran fullness of her breasts. Mindy put on a chilling tough-rocker-chick act, and though the young David Garret identified with her outsider status, he was kind of unnerved when she asked him to come over to sneak some of her parents' vodka. Maybe she'd get drunk and kick him around or something. But that night in her parents' basement she was tender and tentative. . . . Where was she now?

She was here, now. Standing there, nude, in his office. One of her eyes was smaller than the other; one of her breasts the size of an apple, the other enormous. She was listing to the side because one of her legs was six inches too short. Then the shape adjusted for parity, like a parade balloon inflating, and she was symmetrical. Her eyes and legs and bosoms equalized. The Venus of Willendorf with Mindy's face.

She was not quite there in the flesh. Her pink skin had a violet underglow, and there was a faint purple light in the very middle of her, shining like the filament in the new bulb he held in his right hand. The bulb, with no power source, for no damn good reason at all, was lit up in his hand. Glowing.

"Mindy?"

She'd died, and this was her ghost. It was the only thing he could think of.

He ought to be scared. Instead he was disoriented and—

And drunk. It came over him like a wave of drunkenness, as if he'd had grain alcohol intravenously. A rubberiness, a pliancy, rippling through him. The room rippling with it too; a rumbling wave of The Unseen that passed through everything around them. It emanated from that purple glow at the center of her.

The drunkenness that was more than drunkenness kept him from screaming when she closed in around him.

Pop. The other light bulb hitting the floor, as Mindy clamped home around him like the jaws of a gentle beartrap. A great soft pink and violet trap.

He was surrounded by Mindys. Six of them, all interconnected somehow, seamlessly joined at the hips and rolls of fat at her middle; six Mindys facing inward, a circular accordion of Mindys, pressing against him, naked and reeking deliriously of flesh and female lubrication, six pairs of enormous Mindy breasts . . .

His hard-on hurt him.

The drunkenness left him inhumanly loose, but didn't leave him flaccid or numb or tired the way booze did. This was being drunk on Mindy.

She peeled his clothes from him. He had enough rationality left to wonder what Elena would think if she came in, Would she even be able to see it? If Elena saw it would she scream?

Should I be screaming? he wondered, as he squirmed close to this Mindy apparition, felt her embrace on every part of him, all 'round. Closing in on him so he could barely breathe. Succulently warm.

Embraced by her at 360 degrees of the compass, the six interlocked Mindys around him, blended together at their hips and arms and legs; six faces, six pairs of breasts, six vaginas: six two hundred pound women symmetrically arrayed like fleshy petals, like the inner parts of a Claes Oldenberg flower, and for a moment he had a hideous, frightening vision of himself sucked into a venus flytrap made of this all-encompassing woman, sucked down into some sickening tube and slowly devoured. . . .

But then she reached down, under her hugely pliable belly, and two of her hands guided his cock into one of her vaginas. Smoking with sensation as he entered her. Drunk with euphoria, a wallowing in woman . . .

Contact. *Hello.*

His erect cock was a phoneline to her, and the phoneline was open.

All lines are open, she said. *Call our 800 number. . . .*

"What?" he asked. In a gasp, pumping into her. Into the purple shine at the mysterious heart of her.

Contact, she said, *You wanted contact.*

"Who . . . oh Christ . . ." Feeling like he could go on doing this forever. Standing here, making love to her. To all six of her. Hands exploring other orifices as his direct line to her jacked into the vagina directly in front of him. . . . Six tongues, all from one woman, lapping at him. . . . "Who? Are . . ."

Identity. You're asking about my identity. She didn't say it, and she didn't exactly think it at him. She formed concepts and he became aware of them, but it was as if they were occurring to him with a kind of cognitive synchronicity he shared with her. . . .

She answered his question, though he didn't know it for a while. She shifted. *Closer,* she said.

Picture a woman stretched like an image on silly putty, for one second; picture a strangely iridescent taffy in a transparent taffy-pulling machine, for about two seconds. Then the taffy loses its palpability, becomes a translucent matrix of light, for another incandescent second; then the light takes a shape in the air like an iris, a six petaled iris, each petal vaguely reminiscent of a woman, some undefined woman. The woman becoming less human but more palpable, more physical, as she flows over you. . . .

This time it was an effort not to scream. But he was afraid that if he screamed, he'd disrupt the rapport, break some fragile balance between them, and he wanted desperately for what was happening to go on. The contact was an unspeakable relief.

So he didn't scream when she enfolded him like a cocoon.

His eyes were open, when the cocoon closed completely over him, and what he saw was something like the patterns in peacock feathers, but made out of the faces of women, women he'd known and women he'd never known, overlapping, sliding one into another. Faces limned in knowledge and perception; a depth of feeling he'd only glimpsed before. He thought of making love to them—his erection was as rigid as a radio tower, and it was transmitting—and the women's lips blossomed, sucking, nibbling, kissing; an organ that was both a mouth and a vagina drew his erection into it. His hands skied the curves of waists, the fullness of hips and thighs, the roundness of arms; every epidermal inch of him coming into contact with her: with them. With the tautness of skin over collarbone, the exquisite silk stretched under a jawbone, a sweetly slithering chain of damp labia drawn past his shoulder, down his torso; a padded room of buttocks and breasts embracing him; a glittering panoply of eyes looking piercingly into his. A bouquet of mouths sweeping past his genitals. Everything was wet but nothing was uncomfortably sticky; was redolent of flesh, sweat and lubricant, and all those scents and effluents melted together into a symmetrical harmony in keeping with the kaleidoscoping visuals of her. She was an endlessly reproduced variant on pattern, like the ornate embellishments of the Sun King's palace decor, but none of it was simple decoration; it was *expression*. And none of it was fragmentary; it was all of a piece, symphonically articulated by a guiding mind.

She was around him like a great vagina, his body the penetrating organ, but the organ that enclosed him was charged with radiant intelligence, and was at the same time the electric piquancy of all sexuality. He moved peristaltically within her, his entire body pumping through her. When he thrust out his tongue, a tongue arose to meet it. When he squirmed away from one vagina and thrust his cock in another direction, another opened to receive him. Breasts filled the hollows of his body. He swam between them. He could breathe, he could move freely, and yet she was everywhere.

He writhed to escape and at the same time yearned to stay within her. And light and flesh began to intermix.

Light and flesh were one, was all around him (somewhere, the office phone was ringing, ludicrously ringing again and again, answered by the answering machine, Chalky yammering after the beep, wanting to try some stupid scam on him,), sliding against him, interpenetrating his own skin on the waves of some exotic electromagnetic field, stimulating each of his nerve ends so that he was sweetly feeling everything, not with sensory overload but with sensory renewal. His erogenous zones beaming like kleig lights.

The boundaries began to dissolve. He was no longer able to sense clearly where his own flesh ended and hers began. A shattering panic whistled through him—and then was absorbed into a long slow undulation of reassurance from her.

You will not be destroyed in me.

He believed her. He let go. Felt himself turn head over heels. Saw himself from the outside. . . .

And she shifted again. She was a specific someone, now. She was Jane Wasserstein. When was it? 1975? He was eighteen, she was seventeen, had jumped a grade. Jane, the girl he'd dated for five months before she'd broken down and . . .

And put out. What kind of expression was that, "put out?" It was both barbarically sexist and touchingly resonant of an adolescent boy's wistfulness. Put out: put it to the outside. Give, in a way that makes insiders of outsiders.

Here she was. Jane. Slender, curly blond, sylphlike Jane. A half-Jewish girl with asthma, who blinked rather often, as if her quick mind was taking in more frames per second than everyone else. Eyes like a blue-violet premonition of the underglow in this creature's skin. . . . "Just don't say 'Me David you Jane,'" she'd said, on their first date, a breathless half second before he *would* have said it. Second date she'd said, "You going to ask me to go to the drive-in or are we going to work up to that?" She was always a step ahead of him. He felt like he was playing chess with her. He'd make a pass and she'd snort, "oh *listen* to him!"

The undefined woman had shifted, now, in 1989, in the office of Buzz Garret and Black Glass Productions. Mindy had become the shifting cocoon which had become Jane, Jane all 'round him, Siamese sextuplets formed in a circle, but somehow all variations of one, and not a confined joining of many.

He knew this creature wasn't Mindy or Jane. But drove himself into the nearest Jane, and made contact. Hello again.

Jane's voice, coming on as if triggered by a mnemonic answering machine. Something she'd said to him, when they were both seniors in high school. *David you're a professional misfit, and you'll probably make big money at it like Alice Cooper or Frank Zappa. But you're not kidding me with this Rimbaud of rock act, all you really want is for everybody to love you, which is all every Joe Normal wants, too. . . .*

No, he told her, that's not all. I want them to love me as I am. No matter how I am. I want that much acceptance.

Now, in '89, his tongue brushing Jane's small, hard breasts, her nipples becoming stiff as little .22 bullets, the electric contact of his tongue on her was like a switch triggering more astrally recorded memories.

Buzzard Garret, punk romantic. Jane's words, riding on a sneer, as she broke up with him in their freshman year at UCB. Two weeks before he dropped out to focus on rock. *You always had a feel, David, for what women wanted to hear. They invariably thought it was endearing, too, that you were a punk romantic who could leave silver-spray-painted roses on a doorstep, quote morbidly romantic stuff from Verlaine in a letter, talk about psychic union in lovemaking, and still go out on stage and tell the world you hated it. That made you a tragic figure of romance, right? So why'd you do it, Buzz? Just to get laid? That was never enough. You insisted they had to fall in love with you. When I gave up the nookie, it wasn't enough. You had to make me say I loved you. You fucking pig.*

She'd gone right to the heart of him. He saw himself, through this Contact, as she had seen him: He needed them to be in love with him. He needed them to believe he was in love with them. But he couldn't be, not really. He could say all the right things and make the right moves. Could give them a good semblance of sexual passion. Surprise them with romantic gestures, call them funny pet names. Could even marry them. But he could never really, honestly love them. This way, he had them under his thumb. This way he controlled them, and this way he was safe from abandonment.

And all the time he thought these things, he kept plunging into Jane. Who was not Jane anymore. She was Sandy. Pleasantly plump, busty, spray of freckles across her cleavage. The same exact pattern of freckles reproduced on six linked manifestations of Sandy all around him.

Because if you don't want to have a baby, Sandy'd said, *you're not serious about living life. You're full of yourself and you'll never live that way.*

She'd wanted kids, and he hadn't, and they'd broken up over it. After that he'd dated sometimes three women a week for three years, and then he'd met Elena while he was booking a college where she was working in the student affairs office, he was blown away by the crystalline vastness of her intellect, the subtlety and intensity, alternating, when she made love. Her odd combination of spiritual emphasis and hard science. *The Tao of Physics* ruling their lives. She'd got pregnant and informed him she didn't believe in abortions.

So okay, babies and marriage. Their conjugal lovemaking was good up to a point till she realized he was holding back, holding back more than ever now that he felt trapped by marriage. Withdrawing more and more as the resentment in him quietly grew. Elena sensing it and withdrawing to protect herself.

Communication between them became businesslike or brittle with sarcasm and acrimony. They were caught up in the vicious circles of quietly angry marriage, endless reflections in a hall of mirrors—mirrors that were funhouse warped. . . .

And suddenly, now, standing up in his office, he found himself making love to his wife.

Six of her, at first. Then, the six Elenas collapsed into one woman. Like a string of paper dolls folding up into one.

He was making love to an Elena with a violet underglow to her translucent skin, and a purple orb shining at the center of her.

He wanted to run. But then he looked into her face, and saw none of the sophisticated hostility that Elena normally kept there like a falcon in a cage. He saw only the basic Elena, perceptive, vulnerable, curious, private and more emotionally complex than he'd ever guessed.

The impulse to run faded. He sank into her, more deeply yet. His fingers tracing the hollow of her back, her buttocks, finding them entirely new; and finding that his hands were dipping into her skin, shallowly sliding through her skin as if it were a fur of electrically charged flesh.

And then he struck gold.

He drove deeper into her vagina, and the electrode of his organ made contact with the electrical receiver of hers, some inner node of sheer receptivity. Contact.

Hello.

"You're not Elena," he said, ludicrously trying to identify her even as he feverishly pumped into her.

This time she spoke aloud. "Yes and no. Call me Enter. I need your help. I'm trapped in this otherness, trying to get to my husbandside. I'm trapped—" All the time both of them copulating deliriously, joyously, as she gasped into his ear: "Need your help getting through to the free level."

"What are you?"

"A consciousness; a body of different principles but similar essence. A woman. A connection to women, from your viewpoint."

"Where do you come from?"

"An otherness. Not this world; not this plane; not this universe. But with roots in it."

"How can I help?"

"Don't come."

"What?"

"You're about to have an orgasm. The electrical discharge that accompanies the reproductive discharge will come too soon. Don't come, David. Don't orgasm. Wait. Timing is crucial."

He saw it like a tidal wave on the horizon of his mind's eye. An orgasm rolling toward him with the inexorability of a force of nature.

He withdrew from her, just in time. The build of orgasm slowed, faded, stayed aching just on the brink of his groin . . .

He acted on intuition, or perhaps following some instruction she gave him through the secret connections they'd explored. He stepped *through* her, as if she were a door. Walked through Elena; through Enter, who became amorphous and plasmic. Feeling a shock that was almost a burn sear through him as he went. Coming out on the other side knowing that if he looked back, she wouldn't be there. But she *was* still here, unseeably, waiting for him to complete the favor.

He was standing nude in his office. Clothes heaped on the floor. Skin slippery with sweat and lubricant.

He walked to the door of his office, his erection wagging, transmitting, still, like a radio antenna. Opened the door, the doorknob crackling with sparks under his touch. Walked down the hall to Elena's studio. The room she kept for her hobbies. The door opened for him, before he got there. No one near to open it.

He stepped through. Saw Elena lying back on the rug, naked, her clothes heaped untidily about her. She was panting, glistening with sweat. Her legs apart.

Between Garret and his wife was a low metal table. On it was an intricate design of copper and silvery metal, some sort of occult ideogram made of metals, wired to the electrical socket overhead. Shimmering with violet glow.

With some strange combination of quantum physics and ancient female witchcraft, his wife had invoked Enter, drawn her from another world, channeled her through this one. And drawn someone else too. He could feel his presence. The husbandside. The male one. The one Enter was trying to rejoin. He'd been here, making love to his wife, even as Enter had been making love to Garret.

Like Enter, he was gone now, from the visible world; but he was here.

The wave of intuition that had brought Garret to this room filled in the blanks for him: Elena had been desperate for contact. Found herself unable to break through to him directly. Blocked. Neither of them could bear the humiliation of a marriage counselor. So Elena had tried something exotic and indirect, a quirky synthesis of physics and ancient magic, never expecting it to work. Some personal ritual, performed for psychological reasons, which had translated into objective reality.

Don't question it, Garret thought.

He went to Elena, lay down beside her. The true Elena. He lay beside her and then with her, entering her very soon after the embrace began. Feeling the first orgasm buck through him. Breaking down the barrier between worlds. Enter passing through her to him; Enter's male counterpart passing through Garret to her. Enter and Husbandside meeting and joining and passing on, freed now, into their own world. Having left Elena and Garret transformed behind them.

Garret had a glimpse of something, just before Enter and Husbandside passed on. That Enter and her lover were one creature, with two aspects; two sides of one coin, meeting here where dimensions intersected. And they had connections, interfacings with other consciousnesses—with Garret's, and Elena's. With all others.

Garret made love to his wife several times that night. And each time—

Contact.

The Prince

SOMEWHERE IN THE MID TO LATE 80s I was solicited by Jim Frenkel to write a trilogy for his shortlived Bluejay Books and I wanted to do something quintessentially cyberpunk, and the *Eclipse* books are what I had in my head. Raw, socially relevant cyberpunk, predicting a new rise of fascism and outright neonazism which—if you have been watching the news—you can now see coming about. Sometimes one would prefer not to have one's prophesies vindicated. The books came out eventually in Warner Questar editions.

Out of this dialectical milieu arose "The Prince" also. This was written for Lew Shiner's admirable (but puzzlingly titled, considering the theme) anthology *When the Music's Over,* which was an original antho about alternatives to war, alternatives to violence of any kind, methods for getting things done on a social level.

The story uses Jerome-X, a character who appeared also in "Wolves of the Plateau" and the *Eclipse* books. . . .

WHEN HIS ENEMIES LOCKED ONTO the autopilot of Haji's private jet, he was thinking about window glass. He was cruising along at six thousand feet, flying from San Diego to San Francisco, thinking about installing tint-adjustable glass in the picture window of his penthouse offices. He detested inappropriate lighting.

Why was the plane descending so sharply, here? They were still forty-five minutes from the Oakland airport.

He hit the intercom switch. "Carson! What gives?"

"I'm sorry, Mr. Haji, I can't seem to get the navigator to respond. The autopilot just up and engaged itself. Uh—we seem to be *landing*. Except there isn't an airport around here . . ."

"Carson, call the—the—" Who? "The authorities. Someone. The FAA. The FBI . . ." And he thought, Automated hijacking.

But the radio and the phone went out too. They descended smoothly, if rather steeply, whining down into the brown layer of smog and into the sun-cracked and mostly abandoned concrete hinterlands of Ventura County, Upper Los Angeles.

Haji and Carson were alone on the jet. There was room for twenty, but Haji didn't believe in an entourage. The cabin was decorated in soft brown leathers and yellow silk; the chair he sat in was an ergonomic recliner that massaged his lumbar, dispensed drinks, provided an intercom, sang softly to him or took dictation. It would soothe him all the way down. . . .

Radar will track us, Haji thought. They'll know we're not supposed to go down here.

But the air traffic controllers were overburdened. They tended to lose track of people. Anyway, it'd be too late. By the time the police showed up, the plane would be burning wreckage. Or the hijackers would have them. Hijackers? Kidnappers. Terrorists. Assassins. Lunatics of some kind.

He should fire Starger for not checking out the plane for this kind of vulnerability. Starger was head of security, but he couldn't even find a bodyguard Haji could tolerate—

now he'd left the navigational gear unshielded against cybernetic hijacking.

Fire him? Haji remembered "Duddy" Marchmain, president of Marchmain Synthetics, taken by terrorists, tortured, reduced to a shell that muttered slogans to a cheap camcorder. Found in a garbage sack on the steps of the Stock Exchange. They'd cut off his "greedy, grasping hands" and stuffed them down his throat.

And Haji was thinking about firing his security chief. A corpse doesn't send pink slips. Face it. You're tomorrow's headlines. And then they'll recycle the old newspapers, and you're gone. . . .

Carson came out of the pilot's cabin, shaking his head. He was a long-faced, tired-eyed, middle-aged man with beefy forearms, wearing a short-sleeve khaki shirt with the Crossworld Industries logo on the shoulder patch and a pilot's cap. "I tried everything, Mr. Haji."

The plane touched down on the disused, grass-thatched freeway, the wheels braying with the first bouncing contact, the plane shuddering. Then the plane trundled to a stop. Strangers with guns came out from under the crumbled overpass, and one of them spoke into something with an antenna. "Toss your weapons out the door, come out with your hands up." A casual male voice with a southern California slur to it, patched into the intercom.

Haji's stomach contracted around a chill ball of fear. Carson was already at the door. He took yellow UV-filter goggles from his shirt pocket and put them on.

"Maybe we should lock the doors, wait for help," Haji said. His own voice sounded small and far away.

"There's a guy carrying one of those slap-on bombs," Carson said. Anger was showing through in his tone, his pursed lips. He blamed Haji for this, somehow. "We get out or they . . ."

"I see." Haji stood just behind Carson as he swung the door open. The stairs automatically descended to the runway, humming. Heat and the smell of hot asphalt pushed in through the door, elbowing the air conditioning aside. "We haven't got any weapons!" Carson called out, as Haji put on his UV goggles and they descended the aluminum stairs.

"Good," said the big man in blue-tint sunglasses, grinning. He was Hispanic, but without an accent. "'Cause neither do we. Nothing's loaded." But they'd surrounded Haji and Carson by then. Most of them wearing tattered white sun-reflective shawls over their heads, and goggles. It gave them the look of some demented cult. Haji had seen footage of people who lived outside the shields, they all wore those things outdoors. A tanned, skinny young man, with goggles but without a shawl, greasy blond hair tied back in a knot, was already going up the stairs, carrying a battered red-vinyl briefcase—probably containing the microprocessors and transmitter he'd used to take over the plane.

Haji and Carson, surrounded by their kidnappers, were escorted across the heat-rippling tarmac to a break in the rusty chain link fence that bordered the freeway. Behind them, the stairs folded into the plane and it began to taxi toward the half-fallen underpass. Beyond the freeway was a barricade of junk cars and rusty girders and barbed wire, all of it sunken into rust-streaked concrete. Men and women, in goggles and shawls, crouched in the shade of crude shelters or patrolled wooden walkways near the top, carrying their guns prominently. Warningly. Others at the underpass were unrolling tarps camouflaged to blend with the underpass's sediment of debris and trash. Probably going to hide the jet under the overpass, cover it up.

Haji had never before felt genuine despair. He was surprised at how deep and resonant it was.

*   *   *

"NOW WE GOT YOU HERE," the big man said, "we want you to know that you're free to go."

Hope lived for about five seconds, and then Haji saw the expressions on their faces. Smug, secretive. "You wanted the jet?"

"No," the big man said. "Not particularly. We might think of a use for it, though."

They were indoors now, in a big, shadowy place, much cooler, and most of them had shed their goggles and shawls. Haji tried to imagine what they had planned. They'd let him and Carson run away through their turf, maybe, and the streetsiders would hit them with rocks and bottles and bricks and chase them down and beat them to death and the hijackers would laugh and say they just hadn't run fast enough.

"It doesn't matter who does it to us," Haji said. "Whether it's you or someone streetside. You'll be responsible."

"Who does *what* to you?" the big man asked. "You mean, someone here's going to hurt you? No. Anybody hurts you it'll be your own people. Our guns were a bluff. We won't let you take the jet—we still own your autopilot. But taking your plane is all the force to be used against you. Unless it's by your own employees."

The man didn't make sense, but he didn't seem dangerous. He had put aside the gun; there was nothing threatening about him. Haji took a deep breath and shuddered and found he could look around now. They were on the lowest floor, in the middle of what had once been an underground shopping mall, standing beside a fountain filled with dull, motionless water. Obviously an enormous squatter's haven. Vast squares of sunlight flooded in through the tinted, translucent roof, set off by deep shad-

ows in the old shops. The smashed storefronts were retrofitted to new functions: a dress boutique had become a
machine shop; an erstwhile Hansen's Juice Bar was home
to an old Chinese couple; the racks in a shoe store were
hung with oily used car parts; an imported leather-goods
store had become a day-care center brimming with children; an artificial fur boutique had become a home for two
families of Chicanos; an old Radio Shack was evidently a
storage room for junked appliances, electronic odds and
ends, and spare parts. The logos for the shops, in swathes
of cutsey cursive, were mostly intact, dust muting their
gaudy plastic colors. Each shop had a single naked electric
bulb, flickeringly lit by pirated electricity.

Haji stood amid fifteen men and seven women, from
young to middle aged. He saw no insignia, no paramilitary
gear. Just the rifles; some of which, he saw now, were
detailed toys or just plain broken; none carried with any
ease or expertise.

They stood in a loose circle around him, staring. Some
of them smirking, pleased as hell with themselves, several
of them distinctly unfriendly, but no one looking really hostile. Still, they aren't wearing masks, Haji thought. That was
supposed to be a bad sign, wasn't it? If they let you see their
faces, they meant to kill you.

Suddenly overwhelmed by disorientation, Haji asked,
"Anyone want to tell me what the point of forcing me down
was?"

"You are," This from a stocky, spike-haired boy—maybe
a teenager, maybe in his early twenties. His face was blurred
by a number of small scars, and a broken nose. "You're the
point."

"This is Jerome-X, Mr. Haji," the big man said. "My name
is Pastor Navarro. Or you can call me Dana. I can introduce
you to the others, if you like. Jerome's the one you need to

meet, though. He's going to be your guide, tell you what you need to know."

Haji turned to Jerome-X. Haji was thirty-two, about the boy's height but much slimmer and darker and in every other way a contrast. Haji wore a London-tailored linen suit with a powder blue tie; every hair in place, his nails manicured. The boy wore shiny denim and rotting sneakers. He wasn't carrying a gun, but there was an army surplus knife on his hip. He was missing a couple of teeth and his nails were black as the dark sliver on a gibbous moon. There was an odd earring in his left ear: a silver miniature of the Arc de Triomphe. "So this is about me?" Haji said. "You people know nothing about me."

Jerome-X grinned. He stared off into space and read from an invisible text: "Haji, Andrew Mahat, born December nineteen, 1988, Islamabad, Pakistan. Father: Ali Muhammed Haji. Mother: Olivia Bentworthy, a former British subject who became a citizen of Pakistan in 1987 . . . Umm, I'll skip ahead here . . . Haji was born into a wealthy Punjabi Muslim family but is not known to practice Islam, blah, blah, *blah* . . . family moved to New York City in 1994, became American citizens in April 1995, Haji studied at— buncha stuff there about all the private schools—attended Columbia then transferred to Harvard, PhD in Economics, MBA, Phi Beta Kappa, blah blah blah, became a junior executive in the investments division of Crossworld International in August of 2012 and then there's a lot of stuff about how you're a whiz kid, a golden boy, how you're nicknamed 'The Prince' by the Big Biz insiders . . . says, Haji worked his way up to Chief Executive Officer in under twelve years, company consistently showing gains under his leadership and so on. . . . Ummm, Crossworld is a multinational plastics manufacturing corporation diversified into food synthesis, automobile manufacturing, aircraft manufacturing, extensive weapons development defense contracts, banking, real estate development, especially reclamation of 'urban deterioration zones' aided by tax incentives. Ummm, Haji known for his emphasis on real estate and quick turn-over of properties, blah blah *blah* . . . Haji is unmarried, his psychological profile suggests—"

"Fine, you memorized my bio," Haji interrupted.

"Jerome has a chip implant," Dana said. "Lots of information files."

"So you know something about me, you think that's good for a ransom? My company has standing orders to pay no ransoms—"

"Mr. Haji," Carson broke in, his voice shaky, "don't be hasty. What I heard, they make secret deals with people sometimes. We'd better look at all the options, you know?"

"We are not holding you for ransom, Mr. Haji," Dana said. "You can't take the plane, but you're free to go. Jerome will show you where to get out and where our only public online booth is."

"Right this way, my man," Jerome said, gap-toothed grinning.

The crowd started to drift away, heading for storefronts or for the frozen escalator. One man hesitated, staring at Haji. Someone Haji hadn't noticed before. Now, here was real hostility. He was gaunt, with yellow sunglasses, a greasy T-shirt, and his hair tied back in a braid. Saying: "Lemme talk to the guy. I can't believe we got this guy here and we're going to just—"

"Forget it, Pringle," Dana said. Dana put his big hand on Pringle's bladelike shoulder and herded him away. "Jerome's briefed. We agreed this was the way. Come on . . ." Pringle walked away with the crowd, glancing venomously over his shoulder.

Haji stared after them. That was really *it*? They weren't

prisoners? Watched by just this one guy?

From somewhere not far outside the mall, came a dull *thud* and a long architectural shudder. The vast interior spaces thrummed subtly with it, and then it was gone. "They're moving in," Jerome-X said. "That's the outer barricade going down. We better go, Mr. Haji."

But Haji found himself watching a little Hispanic girl who came out of one of the storefronts, carrying a plastic bucket. She went to the fountain, dunked the bucket, and carried it awkwardly back to the squat, her shoulders hunched under its weight. Haji had an impulse to help her carry it. But he stayed where he was, and asked Jerome, "They're drinking from the fountain? Is it potable?"

"For sure. It better be, it's our only source of water, man. We, like, had to set up a pump down the waterline for it. Your boys cut off the other clean water mains, they missed this one. It's the only one left that's not toxified."

"How many people here?"

"In the mall, in shelters out back, in the car wash, the discount tires place . . . maybe five hundred total decided to go shut-in. Lot of em would change their minds now, if Starger'd let 'em. We're running out of food, and the barricades are coming down. . . . Come on, man, let's show you that online. You can see about getting a message out. See how it goes. . . ."

Haji looked at Carson, who shrugged, with an expression mixing relief and amazement. They followed Jerome-X past the reclaimed storefronts, down an unevenly lit hallway. Haji was surprised at how clean and organized the place was. He'd always pictured squats as trash heaps, occupied by people the way rats occupy the city dump. It didn't even smell bad.

Your boys, Jerome-X had said. And he'd mentioned Starger by name. And they were just north of Ventura. The pieces fell together. This was the Santa Clara development, Crossworld Development Enterprises Project CAL43. A Reclamation Project. Haji had scanned the report: Crossworld Development had bought the property, the squatters refused to leave, the ACLU had defended the squatters, getting an injunction stopping the police from moving them out, but Crossworld had lobbied in the state capitol for the right to use its own security force. Crossworld had the clout; Crossworld won. Last he'd heard, the place was under some sort of siege.

"Look," Haji said, trotting to catch up to Jerome-X, "I don't have the power to give you this place to live in—I'm the CEO, but I have to answer to the board of directors and the stockholders. I couldn't do it if I wanted to." Not true, but chances were good Jerome-X didn't know that.

Jerome-X glanced at him. "So you figured out part of it. You got a long ways to go."

"You have some kind of political brainwashing in mind?"

Jerome-X laughed. "What'dya think, this is a reeducation camp? No, man. Most of 'em here, they're pretty ordinary Americans. They don't know ideology from gynecology. We're organized into a kinda co-op because that's the only way to survive here, not because we're Communists." He turned and they paused in the hall as Jerome-X looked at Haji with weary amusement. "Indoctrination! Shit, man, you don't know Dana. Most of the people who escorted you in and, you know, helped him set this thing up—even Chancey, the hacker that brought you down—they're part of a *congregation*. Dana's flock. Not me—I'm just kind of helping him out. I like the guy. But see, Dana was a priest. He split with the church—I guess he figured their stand on birth control was really stupid—but he's still a kind of priest. Keeps the faith, you know? And he says violence is unChristian."

"I saw people patrolling with guns. . . ."

"Right. Some of 'em are for real and some are a bluff. See, when they organized things here, it broke up into two factions. The ones willing to use violence and Dana's people. Dana brought you here to show 'em there's another way. You got to understand this: you lucked out, man. If Dana wasn't here, there are some other people around this place that'd hang you up by the balls."

"They'd kill me over a housing disagreement?"

"It's more than that. Come on, check it out for yourself. In here." He led them through an open door, into a smell of antiseptics and urine. "This is the infirmary."

It was a long, curved room that used to be a Chinese restaurant. There were still fake-Chinese lamps and a sign on the wall that said, "Our guarantee—No MSG!" In place of the tables were beds; none of them hospital beds, irregular sizes and shapes. They were all occupied. A black man in a white doctor's jacket and a young Hispanic woman in cutoff jeans tended the sick. Haji steeled himself against all this: it was a ploy. They were going to try to play on his pity, this way. He couldn't abide being manipulated.

He felt spavined here, now that the fear was gone. Impotent. He'd grown up with a rather businesslike nanny and aloof parents, who fought constantly and finally moved into separate wings of the house; he'd been culturally displaced as a boy and later found himself one of the few Pakistanis in the Ivy League institutions they sent him to. A persistent sense of rootlessness and loss had been a powerful motivator for career security; for acquisition of power and control. Now someone had taken control from him as easily as a parent takes a dangerous utensil from the hands of a toddler. An infantile frustration seethed in him. He wanted to hate these people.

But the patients in the infirmary were not easy to hate:

they were mostly children. This little boy with his left arm missing: his left side, visible now as the "nurse" changed the dressing, was a blotchy, multicolored welter of blisters and open sores. He shivered but he seemed too exhausted to cry out as she poured antiseptic and water over him. "We out of painkiller?" Jerome-X asked her.

"Yeah. Also down to the last bandages, maybe two hundred cc's general antibiotics, one package of burn dressings."

"See if we can get somebody out."

"You do, they'll probably just end up in here, make things worse."

"Let's see what we can do." They went on, two other children, also with burns; a little girl, maybe three years old, with broken limbs, her gaze lost in the brush patterns of the ceiling plaster. Lost for good, Haji felt. There were two men, one conscious and the other unconscious and feverish, thrashing under improvised restraints. Other adults with broken limbs, one with a shotgun wound. More children. Several of them were sallow, sunken, profoundly sick but not burned or broken-limbed. What was wrong with them?

A listless twelve-year-old boy, withered to the size of a five-year-old, lay curled up in a broken-down sofabed. Jerome-X asked the black man, "How they doing? Toxicity down?"

"We haven't got any testing kits left, so I don't know for sure, but I don't think they're processing it out very well." He said it softly so the kids wouldn't hear.

Carson stared at the emaciated child. "What's he got?"

"Liver cancer," the black man said, not looking up as he took the boy's blood pressure from a limp arm. "We got four kids down with it. There used to be more. There's a for-real cancer cluster here from waste toxins over to the

Oxnard plant. Came up through the water table."

The Oxnard plant. A plastics plant the EPA had been trying to close, claiming steady leaks into the local water and
air. ChemGro International: a Crossworld Subsidiary. Was
this for real? Were the children really victims of his wreck-
ing crew, his factory toxins? Or was this being staged somehow? He looked at the child, the child didn't look back.
The boy's eyes were open; he breathed; but he didn't look
back.

Haji turned away. He was determined not to fall into any
emotional traps. Still he was relieved when they left the
infirmary, and, walking down a concrete utility corridor at
the back of the mall, he heard himself ask, "Either of those
people—are they doctors? Those kids need professional
treatment."

"James, he's a paramedic. Beryl had three years' medical
school, dropped out to help us, just before the shut-in.
We'd get 'em to professional treatment, but we can't get
anybody to come in and we can't get out. . . ."

"Those kids," Carson asked. "Something collapse on
them? You guys shouldn't be living in these old buildings,
they fall in on people—"

"Somebody *knocked* the building down on top of 'em,
man," Jerome-X snapped. "Some of 'em run out, got themselves caught in a microwave beam. Nobody shut down the
demolition for 'em. The cocksuckers didn't even slow
down. That kid with his arm burned off—that's Pringle's
kid. You notice Pringle? If it wasn't for Dana he'd kill you
for sure. . . ."

"Where'd this happen?" Carson asked. "These kids getting hurt?"

"Row of old houses up the street. Five A.M., everybody
asleep. Wasn't an accident, you know? What you see are the
survivors. Three other kids died. Seven adults. Couple of

'em took a few days to die. . . . The barricade was weak there—we managed to get the survivors back behind the second barricade. Lost two of our guys just pulling 'em out. Fried."

Haji snorted. "This is the groundwork for indoctrination, and I don't believe it. Any demolition crew would be arrested for knowingly knocking a house down on people."

Jerome-X chuckled. "Where you been, man? You think we didn't try the cops already ten times? I'm telling you, your people have got this sewn up. Housing crisis just goes on and on and on, you know? People protesting for a decade now. The public gets callous after a while. Your people in Sacramento, pal, they got a court order saying that if the squatters don't move out, it's their own responsibility. The Crossworld security chief is a tough motherfucker. Your man Starger. He's making examples."

Haji thought, Starger's tough but incompetent. Because here I stand.

Jerome went on, "The Crossworld lobby is tough too. Tough and big. One of your lobbyists camped in every state senator's waiting room every day it's open. Publicity campaigns about how reclamation means new housing, less crime, you know the drill. Leave out that it's new housing only for the rich. And the rich are the minority. They haven't got a housing problem."

"We lobby for the freedom to do business in a productive way," Haji said. "We don't lobby for murder."

"They don't call it murder. If there's any publicity, they make it look like the people were hanging out in the buildings secretly, defying the law, crazy on drugs, bunch of dangerous lunatics. No one knew otherwise. But mostly there isn't any publicity. Your people pull the strings on the press. Who's the major stockholder in North American Media? Crossworld."

Haji ground his teeth. Don't let yourself be baited, he thought. But the maddening thing about this Jerome-X was his casualness. He talked of these things as he walked along, with no self-righteous indignation. He might have been commenting on the weather.

Another distant thud; another shudder around them.

"What was that?" Carson asked.

"They're breaking through the barricades," Jerome-X said. He chewed a lip, some of his composure gone. "Busting shit down. They're closing in . . . Here's the online."

They'd come to a row of phone stations, each with a TV phone cable and a PC monitor. The phone companies had taken out the TV phones when the area was abandoned, but the IBM people hadn't done a thorough job on the computer links. "Only one of 'em hooked up," Jerome-X said. He led them to a station. "Dana thought you'd want to see where you stand. Go ahead, see if you can get through, Mr. Haji."

Haji stared at him. Were they really going to let him contact his people? Maybe the police? He could send for a helicopter. . . .

Haji's hands shook as he drew out his card and slotted it into the online. The screen lit up.

WELCOME TO IBM'S ONLINE SERVICES. PLEASE INDICATE PERSONAL CODE NUMBER. He typed in his PIN and waited. NO ACCOUNT LISTING. PLEASE TRY AGAIN. He did. And again. He tried requesting a balance statement; he tried everything. "You tampered with this machine," he said, his voice taut.

"Naw, uh-uh," Jerome-X said. "It works for me. I got an account. Not much of one but I got one." He took out his card and demonstrated.

"Then use your card to put me through to my people. I'll make it worth your while."

"Sure. But you won't get through. They're screening them all out. Our hacker set it up so they think you're off taking care of personal biz. Meanwhile Chancey broke into the system, blotted you out. For now, you got no account. Now you can try to contact your people, but we got the underground sending fake calls in from you, all over the country. They think it's a hacker hoax."

"When I get to San Francisco, I can get reinstated," Haji said. "There's really no point in all this. You might as well be holding me by force. You could have saved yourself the computer work with a gun. Like any other criminal."

"No, man. You don't get the idea. The idea is for you to have it like us. Be subject to the same conditions, you know? I mean, what'dya think, these people are criminals? I got to point out the gap between the rich and the poor lately, man? It's like pointing out the Grand Canyon. You can't miss it. These are desperate people. Good people that had no work, ran out of food, lost their homes—all they're trying to do is protect their kids. We're living on scavenged food, and even that's almost gone. So I'll tell you, my heart's not bleeding over your fucking computer bank account. Sure, you'll get the account, your position, every-thing reinstated. Dana wouldn't want it any other way. But you'll have to get out of the shut-in first. Easier said than done. See, man, you might not survive being one of us."

"THEY'RE NOT GOING TO push my buttons, Carson," Haji said through heat-cracked lips. "And they're not going to make us panic." They were walking along with their jackets over their heads, stripped down to T-shirts beneath.

"No sir. But how the hell we going to get out of here?"

The heat shimmered off the trash-strewn parking lot, vis-ible even through their goggles, and their sweat ran like grease on grilled sausage. Behind them was the mall, partly collapsed, the string of department stores long since caved in. The section Jerome-X had shown them was reasonably stable; but Haji knew what the microwave beams and the maxidozers would do to it. Ahead were the houses, the barricades, the way out, and Jerome-X, walking ahead of them, in a hurry to be out of the direct sunlight. The greenhouse effect and heightened UV from ozone depletion had made hurry a reflex for people who lived outside the smog shields.

If you want to know how to get out of a thing, you have to consider how you got into it. So Haji ran it down in his mind: how had it all come about?

Maybe it came down to the smog shields. *"Smog shields" is a misnomer, of course,* Haji had said, ten years before, writing a report for the Crossworld execs. Written back when the shields were just beginning to be erected. The shields were designed for "outdoor" temperature control and UV reduction; as a side benefit they filtered smog. They were great porous bubbles of transparent organometallics, and people living outside them had soon found the living nearly unbearable. If they had no place else to go, they improvised their own shieldings, or simply stayed indoors. Which was all right, except that there wasn't enough housing—and every so often, with the truculent randomness of bad luck, the killer smogs came, synthesized from the synergistic reactions of pollutants under the catalyst of high UVs. Waves of aerosol death.

The devastation had come to the area six years before. Greenhouse heat and cruel UVs were the arms that swung the sickle: the Black Wind. It came like a harvesting blade cutting down and sweeping away. The survivors fled to an area that was funded for smog shields. Ventura County was abandoned.

But Crossworld knew it was prime real estate, if it was

properly protected. There was water from the desalinization project on the coast. There was room for golf courses, once smog-shields were erected. Haji—almost as an afterthought, a minor concern in the course of a day involving a score of deals—bought up the land for a few cents a foot and sent in the developers. The developers looked it over, saw the potential for up-scale development, once Crossworld bankrolled the shield, and scheduled demolition. Only, the place wasn't empty; the squatters were there, the new recession's crop of homeless and unemployed. Although most of them had actually rented, till the place was sold out from under them.

Haji couldn't see an easy answer in any of it. All he could do was follow Jerome-X. Who was going to show him a certain alley, "a place you can maybe get out, maybe not. It's the best we got right now. It ain't gonna be easy. . . ."

They'd reached the end of the tarmac, come to the barricades. There were three rings of barricades, mostly built out of old cars, fused with stolen concrete. The crumpled junk cars were like great fossil carcasses in limestone. The third, outermost barricade was already fallen, and the houses that had stood inside it were crushed now to untidy hills of scrap looming like prehistoric grave barrows in the distance. Just this side of the second barricade men from the other squatter faction patrolled with guns to keep Starger's thugs from overrunning them. The siegers had opted to stay behind the armored demolition machinery. Let the metal do the work. And just then, with a chill, Haji saw the demolition machinery moving toward the barricades. The yellow metal humps of the maxidozers and the big snouts of the microwave guns.

The Occupational Safety and Health Administration had tried to block deployment of microwave demolition units. Too high a risk of a worker stepping in front of a unit, maybe getting boiled from the inside out. It had happened a few times. But Crossworld had lobbied hard, and won again. The units cut demolition time by seventy-five percent. Point one at the wall, throw the switch. Nothing seems to happen. Then turn the gun off, send in your maxi-dozer—and the wall collapses with one swipe. It's been softened inside, like a tree with a rotten core, it crumbles to gravel and dust. They had a short range, forty feet, and they were used only on highly resistant structures.

So why were there two of them pointed right down the middle of the alley at him?

Jerome-X was waiting in the ramshackle shelter built on this side of the second barricade, just to the right of the alley mouth. The houses to either side of the alley had been flattened, plowed together into helter-skelter cones of debris; parts of them broken to moraines of powder and gravel. Drinking water from a plastic jug, Jerome stood in the shade of four overlapping chrome car hoods on a frame of fenders and foil-covered wood—the whole a crude UV reflector. He passed the jug to Haji and said, "Can't even try it. They've got microwave guns in the alley. They'll fry you. Last time it was blocked off but there was a chance—they must've figured we were getting through that way."

"Why would they want to stop you from getting out?" Haji asked, passing the jug to Carson.

"Because they know that's not the end of us. We'll sabotage their equipment from the outside, do anything we can, and they know it. We've talked to them, see. To Starger, your security guy. We understand each other. He knows we're not here to squat anymore—we're here because they can't go on with this shit. We're making a stand. And they're making an example. The word won't get into the papers, but it'll get around on the street. They know what they're doing."

Haji noted that Jerome-X consistently said "they" instead of "you." Trying to nudge Haji into identifying with the squatters. But Haji wavered between empathy and resentment.

"I don't believe any of this," he said, letting the resentment carry him. In the heat, it was easily the victor. "The guns are there as a warning, or for storage or something. They wouldn't use them on people."

"Starger's hired thugs for this. Kind of guys you pay them enough, they don't give a fuck," Jerome-X said.

"Crossworld doesn't hire people like that," Haji said.

"You're right, Mr. Haji," Carson said, squinting through a crack in the sheller at the alley. "I can't believe they'd fry us. That's bullshit. They'd recognize Mr. Haji."

Jerome-X laughed. "Sure. Right. They really expect him here. They'll see some dark-skinned little guy coming at them and think he's another 'woggie' squatter—if you'll excuse the expression, man. He won't get a *chance* to make 'em see—"

"Bull*shit!*" Carson barked. The heat was getting to him. He turned savagely to Haji. "Fuck this. I'm going. You coming . . . sir?"

Jerome-X said quickly, "Look, I thought it'd be tough—bad enough for you to see how it was, but not impossible. The guns weren't—"

He broke off, staring after Carson, as he stalked out of the shelter and down the alley. Haji ran after him, "Hold up, Carson! Let me go first, they'll recognize me!"

"I got Mr. Haji here!" Carson yelled hoarsely. "The head of the company! We work for the company! Hey, listen we—"

But Haji was only a yard behind Carson when the air began to drum and the chrome radar-scoop snouts of the microwave units began to whine, and the virulent heat of the day seemed to gather itself up into a tornado of unseen fire and Carson screamed. . . .

A bubble was growing out of Carson's right side. A bubble of flesh, a blister bigger than his head that burst and sprayed boiling blood and yellow steam as other bubbles sprouted and he fell whimpering into the dust in a puddle of himself—

Haji, just out of range, saw it over his shoulder as he ran. And then turned away, gagging. Running and gagging.

THEY HAD BEGUN TO MOVE half an hour after Carson went down, the maxidozers and the microwave caissons rumbling up to the barricade, methodically trading off, microwave and then dozer, metal grinding out a dull protest as they shouldered through the dike of dead cars and concrete. The microwaves didn't work well on the car metal. But the demolition proceeded, inexorable as old age and much faster. They were coming.

They, Haji thought. Them and us. Was he that far along?

He didn't have time to think about it much. He was too busy. He was shoring up the walls around the infirmary, using quick-set cement and diagonally-planted metal girders. The work was physical and mental, you had to think out the engineering of it, work out the support angles, so the beams couldn't fall over on the kids. Haji was working with Dana and the wiry blond hacker, Chancey, and the black paramedic. And it gave him a feeling he had forgotten about: a kinship of toil, of mutual concentration and dependency. A freedom from the pressures, the feverishly whispering urgencies of the self. The relief of being, at least partly, someone else for a while.

In the early days he'd felt something like it at Crossworld. There was corporate loyalty, some sense of belonging. But the higher you went in the company, the falser the camaraderie became, and the more you knew that what

217

appeared to be cooperation was ambition, was a kind of competition.

Feeling a girder cinch securely into place, he smiled.

"How come you're smiling?" the boy asked him.

Haji glanced down at the boy lying in the bed beside the wall he was working on. A boy of about six with dirty brown hair, a face that was a welter of bruises, and a broken forearm in a splint. Haji and the boy had been talking, on and off, for an hour. "I feel good about putting the girder up," Haji answered. "It's going to protect you."

"So we'll be okay here, right?"

"For a while. Then we'll get you out of here. We'll all be okay."

Listen to me, he thought suddenly. What an ass. You think they put you on this infirmary detail by accident? Same as Iraq, every time the war flared up again, sent us the TV images of kids hurt by the Iranian shellings. We were supposed to feel sorry for the kids and back the Iraqis. Don't be pushed, Haji, he told himself.

But when the boy said, "Can you get me some water?" Haji ran for it.

He was cradling the boy in his arms, giving him the water, conscious that what the boy really wanted was the contact, when Jerome-X finally showed up. Haji could see by his expression that he'd failed.

"It wasn't supposed to work out like this," Jerome-X said. "And I didn't think they'd find that last online cable. But they did or they busted it accidentally, because we ain't getting a thing. I tried the other possibility, do a transer linkup, that's where I've been, but there's just too much microwave activity now." After a pause, he added, "I'm sorry about Carson. We just wanted you to see what it was like here, maybe scare you, then we'd get Chancey to set you up again on that line, hope you called off the Crossworld dogs.

Didn't see it turning out this way."

"Okay." Haji felt leaden. "What about the plane?"

"That's still a possibility. They saw it come down but we checked their frequency, they think it's some kind of Communist sympathizer airlift or something. We can't get through to them to tell 'em different so we got to try to get you out to that plane. But they're busting through the barricades, moving in on it. Not much time. We'll set up the computer so it'll fly you out—"

"I didn't mean for me. I meant for him," Haji heard himself say, nodding toward the boy. "And the rest of the people in here, whoever else you can get on board." After a moment he added, with some effort, "Me as well, of course."

"Of course," Jerome-X said, shrugging. He looked blankly at Haji. Carefully expressionless. "We got to get out there now, get the kids that aren't going on the plane into the infirmary—hey, Dana!"

After that it was all bustle and shouting and carrying and sweat, improvising stretchers, using the few available wheelchairs, covering the sick against the UVs, moving them out under what looked like an armed guard. Haji toted the back end of the boy's stretcher through the dull pressure of the late afternoon sun; his feet sucking at the hot tarmac with each step, his arms aching, the heat bleaching the strength out of him. Jerome-X had the front of the stretcher, his back to Haji. "I don't understand not using guns at this point," Haji muttered. He was hot and tired and scared and angry at everyone; angry enough to shoot someone. "They're ready to kill you."

"Yeah, I know what you mean but—Dana's a persuasive guy. The way he sees it, we do it without violence even if it means getting shot down. He says that if we use our teeth on their ankles, then they're right about us—that we're just a bunch of rats in the ruins."

*   *   *

THERE WERE STILL THREE to get aboard the plane when the
maxidozers broke through the barricade and came across
the abandoned freeway. Like dusty yellow tanks, paint-
scored and dented, with six enormous metal-toothed
wheels each; with serrated crystallized-steel wedges at the
front that could pull back and then ram; with faceless men
in mirrored helmets just glimpsed through the louvered
cabs. Gouting blue smoke and coming on like crawling rhi-
nos, now grinding across the far lanes, the first of them
smashing through the steel fence at the median. Hardly
slowing for it.

The plane was ready, the computer reprogrammed for
takeoff; the jet engines warming up, building to a roar that
seemed to shout machine defiance, as if deliberately
drowning out the rattle and grind of the approaching
maxidozers. Haji was peripherally aware of all this as he carried the boy up the aluminum stairs, passed him in to his
mother, then turned to help lift an unconscious young
woman with a gangrenous hand, her body a limp weight.

He glanced up, seeing the maxidozers jouncing down
onto this side of the freeway, swerving toward the tail of the
plane, their intention clear. And on the far side of the
chain link fence across the parking lot and the breached
barricades, four other maxidozers moved like enormous
metal slugs toward the monolithic hulk of the abandoned
mall. Five hundred people hunkered inside, counting the
seconds to artificial earthquake. To an Armageddon that
was just another real estate deal.

Something lurched in Haji, and he felt the horror of
profound disorientation: the displacement of the pillars of
personal truth. And then the nearer maxidozers had
crossed the freeway and were bulling at the tail of the

plane, smashing at the rear wheels; another gunning up to the stairway as Jerome-X pushed Haji toward the door and dived free. The stairway buckled under Haji; he jumped for the door. Someone caught him, and pulled him inside. The plane was moving; erratically but moving. The maxidozers ground at it, crushing the detached stairs under their wheels, digging long, sparking rifts in the sides of the plane; the squeal of metal meshing with the scream of terrified people inside.

The plane shuddered. Not so far away, a corner of the mall began to crack apart.

And then the door slammed shut, the plane moved away from the demolition crew, the vertical, harrier-type thrusters added their lift to the jet suction, and they rose into the sky.

Haji shoved through to the pilot's cabin. Chancey was at the radio. "We're above the microwave interference," Chancey said.

"Then take down these call numbers, link with the phone lines—there's someone we can call who knows my voice."

It took about three minutes that stretched into a pitiless forever, until Haji heard Buford say, "Mr. Haji—that you?"

"It is. Buford, we got a demolition team in Ventura County—shut it down. Now. Get through and shut it down, pull 'em out of there. Not tomorrow, not when you get time. This second."

"You got it."

"IT'S BRILLIANT, MR. HAJI," Buford told him, his voice unctuous with admiration. Buford was a pale red-cheeked man with a round face; endlessly dieting, endlessly primping his suit, adjusting his jeweled choker.

Haji and Buford were in Haji's penthouse office; Haji

seated on the edge of his desk, as usual ignoring the chair. Oblivious now to the quality of the light. Buford shifting his weight from foot to foot, holding the data-tab for the grant they'd worked out, brown-nosing with the expertise of a lifetime. "Setting up the low-income development, the housing for these squatters, free smog shield, environmental purification systems—the timing is perfect! Exactly when we needed a *massive* tax break!" He shook his head in grave appreciation and went to the door, paused to wink at Haji. "Smart PR, smart tax sense, smart timing. It's good to see you haven't lost your killer instinct, sir!"

"Yeah," Haji said. Almost laughing; almost crying. "Get Starger on the line."

"Certainly." Buford left, and Haji wished he hadn't. He'd never much liked Buford, but he was afraid to be alone, just now. He wasn't sure why. He remembered the sallow, sunken face of the boy with liver cancer. He'd shut down the Ventura plant, but there was no way he could stop the momentum, shut down plants all over the country, completely redesign all of them. No way he could do the other thing that Dana said he ought to do: admit publicly what Starger had done.

Christ—he had seen them murder Carson. Cook him alive. Outright murder. He hadn't known how they'd been carrying out his orders; he was insulated from the lower echelons. But he might well be prosecuted anyway, if it came out. And it would, perhaps, undermine Crossworld for good.

He couldn't do it. Maybe the squatters would try to get convictions. He wouldn't try to stop them. He ought to help them. But . . .

He just wasn't capable of going that far, and it made him feel lonely. He yearned for the feel of the girder under his hand; the boy cradled in his arms, drinking water from a

222

red plastic thermos cup.

His control here was an illusion. Crossworld was its own entity, a shambling behemoth that Haji could only nudge a bit this way or that, could never fully control.

Maybe that was a lie. Maybe it was more denial. Maybe it was cowardice. But he was who he was. He couldn't go any farther.

Buford's voice from the desk speaker. "Red Starger's on hold, sir."

"Put him on voice, no picture."

Starger's voice rasped the room. "Starger here."

"I ought to prosecute you, Starger. In the end, if I did, I'd be prosecuting myself. That'd be the right thing to do. I'm just not capable of doing it. So you're not going to get busted, that way. Some other way, if I can think of one."

The screen of the TV phone was blank. He couldn't even look at Starger now.

"You're talking about prosecuting *me?*" The outrage in Starger's voice was palpable. "I was doing what I was told! Anybody ought to be prosecuted, it's those people hijacked you, attacked you. You're telling me that's nonviolent? They had guns, my people saw 'em! Don't tell me those assholes don't have no weapons!"

"Just shut up, Starger, okay? Just don't dig it any deeper." Haji hung up. Somehow, he would see to it that Starger paid for the murders. Starger was a sadistic asshole. But Starger's last comment still hung in the air. Yeah, Starger was right about one thing: They'd used their weapons and they'd won a victory. Weapons? Remembering the boy with the dirty brown hair and the little girl carrying a bucket . . .

Yeah. They had weapons.

He went to the window and turned off the tint. Light flooded into the room. It burned his eyes, but he didn't look away.

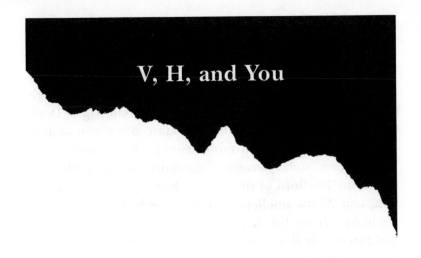

V, H, and You

THE WORLD SUCKS. Children suffer hugely and nobody gives a fuck. The planet has a grudge against children. We're all a lot of children, stumbling in the dark, always; but small children suffer more deeply than the adult sort.

This is an inverted horror story, recently published in a literary magazine called *Zyzzyva*. In most horror stories, the "horror" element is supernatural, and real life, so-called, is the refuge of reassurance. In this story, real life is the horror—and the supernatural world is the refuge. This story is my reaction to the world itself, no matter who's in charge. The vignettes incorporated into the story are based on real incidents. Some people love this story, some people can't stand it and find its devices annoying. I really don't give a fuck.

This is also, to some extent, a pastiche of Dickens. We live in a Dickensian age. Many of the events described in it really happened to people. The kids in the beginning are, sadly, real (their parents are now in jail).

Take it off the CD player if you don't like it. But it'll still be playing.

IN A PLACE CURRENTLY CALLED San Francisco, in the slow energy of winter, Tammy and Glenn Stollard, sister and brother, stood on the street corner. They were sticking out their hands, trying to look hungry. Tammy, though, didn't feel very hungry. She usually didn't feel much in her middle parts, and anyway they'd had a big honkin bag of Doritos and a couple of Pepsis for breakfast. But if you looked hungry, people gave you more money. She wanted to get lots of money today because if she didn't, Jenna might give her to the landlord of the Ellis St. Hotel, Zitgut she called him, and Zitgut smelled really fucking bad and when he made her sit on his dick he always held onto her elbows and forced her down on it and that made her po-po bleed and cramp and his teeth were green and he was all sticky. "You got a nice butt for a nine year old," Zitgut'd say, every time. "Nice round girly butt." It didn't hurt quite as much when he did it to her in the butt lately, but it made her want to stab him with a kitchen knife and she didn't like feeling that way because she knew she couldn't do it. Because of the things that would happen if she did.

"We ain't gettin shit," Glenn said.

With some difficulty, because the wind was hobbling her lips, Tammy said: "Fuck if I don't know it. They gone be pissed." She looked at Glenn's red hair; at the cigarette burn inside the hairline; that was Jenna's favorite trick. But Tammy could see the burn because the wind was messing his hair. "It's this fucking cold wind," Tammy said. "Nobody want to take they hands out of they pockets." Glenn's blue eyes were red around the edges from being out in the wind so much. If they just piled up ten bucks—

DISEMBODIED BUT VERY REAL, Mr. H and Mr. V are floating about streetlight-height above the blackened curbs, invisible to all but one another, watching the boy and the girl from within and without; one of these watchful spirits chuckling to himself cynically: that's V; the other shivering in every skein of his etheriplasm: that's H. He's not shivering from the cold; he's not "there" in the same physical sense as the children he observes. He's shivering in the moral vacuum.

"What is it, H?" V asks. "You look ill-taken."

"I am disposed well enough, sir," H replies. "I am simply dismayed by this brutishness. And I cannot but doubt your purpose in bringing me to witness this. . . ."

"This world? It is the same world, but farther along in their time-stream. You asked to see it farther along and—"

"We left the Age of Dickens, as you called it, because of its brutishness; now you show me another age equally brutish."

"Time does not improve it, sir. Here is the Age of Dickens in polyester drag. . . ." He inhales a bit of the prevailing zeitgeist and goes on, "It's fucked-up all the way down the line. What'd you *think,* man?"

"Don't be so fucking smug, V," H replies. "You steered me to this world's worst. It isn't fair."

"Hey—you think this is as bad as it gets? You must be kidding. Look—you want to reincarnate here, right? Let me read off the prescription from your seraph: You're selecting a venue for incarnation, because you want spiritual enrichment through direct suffering. Well, you picked this world, so take what you get. Find a host and incarnate."

—JUST A TENNER, they could give it to Jenna and take a break and go over to the Woolworth's on Market to get warm and steal some candy bars.

Tammy saw a policeman cruise by, and she dropped her hand back into her thin coat pocket, and pretended to skip around, like she was playing with Glenn, the way Jenna had taught her; Glenn caught the cue instantly and pretended to horse with her, until the cop cruised on. Tammy was afraid of the police: Jenna had said that they'd take Glenn and put him in a foster home or some place and she'd never see him again. He was only seven and she had to take care of Glenn herself, she had to keep him close to her. He never complained anymore, or cried or anything, so she knew she'd better keep him close to her or he'd do something that would make Buddy lock him in a closet for a few days. Right now she was starting to get scared because she didn't have any money yet. Glenn wasn't getting any money. They weren't getting any and it was fucking cold outside and what was going to happen was, Jenna or Buddy was going to burn her with cigarettes again. Jenna would do the cigarettes but Buddy he liked to slap her. *Jenna and Buddy;* she didn't like to say Mama and Dad and anyway they didn't care whether or not she called them Mama or Daddy unless they went to the welfare office. She and Glenn knew all the things they were supposed to say and not say at the Welfare office, though sometimes it was confusing; it used to be they were supposed to say, yes, the twins Elma and Sandy were their sisters but now they were supposed to pretend that Elma and Sandy didn't exist because Sandy died when Buddy locked her on the roof and Elma died when Buddy beat her up for screaming about Sandy and now of course they had to pretend they had never had any twin sisters. Never had any, didn't exist. Never saw through the hole in the closet door how Buddy put the twins in those big garbage bags so he could take them down to the wharf.

Maybe she could get a drink from the stinky man in the long coat, he'd give them a drink if she looked at his dick, he only liked to show it, she didn't have to touch it, and the sweet wine always made her feel warmer and if she got enough she didn't feel the burns or the razor much when Jenna got mad. She was going to try the cocaine if Jenna fell down asleep again; after one of Jenna's four-day runs, sometimes she'd just collapse, and then maybe Tammy could get a little of that cocaine rock and that might make the landlord better or else she'd have to stick something in him, maybe that little kitchen knife or one of Buddy's razors but if she could get Glenn sometime and go to Disneyworld they could hide there in the rides, Disneyworld was on the TV in the burrito place sometimes, when Jenna and Buddy got their burritos, and it looked like there were places to hide in Disneyworld—

"Don't be sittin down, Glenn, shit."

She tried to pull him to his feet.

"Fuck off. Just a second."

"Glenn—Jenna's coming, and she's smokin a ciggie right now. She gone burn you, Glenn, *get up*—"

"GET US THE FUCKING HELL OUT, V, and fast," H says. They drift away from the girlchild and the boychild and their mother, who's pulling the children into the doorway to hurt them again, and H has to convulse and shed to feel clean. "Feel better?" V asks after a moment, when they have the false objectivity of relative height, the two of them hovering invisibly near the rooftops of the Tenderloin's weary buildings.

H responds with a qualified assent, and then asks, "Where's the reverence for innocence, in these people? I mean—is this isolated, what was going down, or what?"

"No way. Far from it. But let's check out a more peaceful surround. . . . It's down in San Jose. . . ."

IT WAS RELATIVELY QUIET in Agnew's Facility for the Impaired that morning. Maybe because the cartoons were on. Felch put the cartoons on when he could, even though Jansen thought they were too violent, because the strap-downs just

sat there mesmerized and they even seemed to shit themselves less. There were seventeen strap-downs in the chairs
lined up in front of the big-screen TV, most of them pasty-
faced adults in diapers, the particularly brain-damaged ones
howling and snapping their heads around, but for them
that was quiet. The Dog Boy was chewing on his straps and
Snaggletooth was trying to chew through his shoulder, but
the straps kept him from getting much of it. Time to check
out the children's ward—he hoped nobody was eating feces
today, because if Jansen found out she made Felch brush
their teeth and if they bit you with shit on their teeth you
could get a *nasty* infection, worse'n usual. Hey maybe the fat
girl with the big tits was quiet today, he could slip it to her if
he gave her a little more medication, fuck her fast before—

"I'M GETTING OUT of this asshole's head *now,*" H snapped. In
a second they were floating above the ward, drifting back
toward San Francisco. "Come on, man, you've gotta be
prejudicing things in your choice of specimens. In most of
the world—"

"In this world, homey, in this dimension, it's just a matter of whatever form it chooses to take; some are just more
out front than others."

BEN WAS SURE THE NURSE was going to come soon, because
his bedsores were burning, which meant he'd peed himself
again, and that meant that it was mid-afternoon, which was
when the fluid from the IV built up enough to require
elimination, and the nurse usually came about then. He
couldn't feel very much down in some parts of his body, but
that numbness was just another malicious irony, considering how much he could feel in the rest of him. The demen-
tia wasn't too bad today. He could think. He could antici-
pate the nurse. The nurse was good: the nurse would give

him a shot. They didn't give the shots to him often enough
—he'd gotten AIDS from shooting drugs so they didn't
trust him to tell them how much pain he was in—but each
shot was a little vacation, for an hour or two. A vacation
from the waiting place he was in. There were ways to get
through the waiting; if he was waiting for the burning and
the itching and the stink of rot in his throat to subside—
waiting for the rapacious carpet of fungi to recede a bit on
the latest wave of medication—he could focus his attention
on his swollen joints; or the great oily, oceanic rollers of
fever; or the viciously painful spasms in his bowels; or the
corkscrewing pain in his swollen liver; or when the lesions
on the inside of his nose and lips and rectum got bad
enough he tried to imagine the sensation as pinwheels of
different colors. He could focus on the leaden burning of
the returning pneumonia in his lungs; or he could try to
move the little sticks of his arms in some sort of pattern in
the air, till the effort of a minute or two made him exhausted, or he could focus on the smells of things rotting in him
and try to work out from the smell alone just which part was
decaying. If his mind was clear that day, he could try to
compose letters asking for more funding for research,
more humane treatment, more anesthesia. Or for the right
to kill himself. He had an impassioned letter mentally composed down to the last comma and period, for that one.

Was that the cymbal racket of the nurse's cart? Oh
please. Oh yes. Come on, bitch. Come on.

"HEY, V, SERIOUSLY—that wasn't fair either."

"He's not in such bad shape. We could wander through
the ward, check out some others. Let me take you down to
the children's cancer ward. That's a good one."

"Hey. Come on. We're going where *I* want to go."

"Suit yourself."

*   *   *

"IT'S YOUR CHOICE," the chief of security told Herrera, in Spanish. "You can use the saw or we kill her now."

"The children are watching," Herrera said. In Spanish. "What have they got to do with this?"

"It's funny how often you terrorists ask that question. Big terrorists make little terrorists. Chickens make chickens, dogs make dogs. We hope to educate them."

"I am not a terrorist; I am a coffee farmer."

For that, they did what he knew they would do: They put the wires into his nose again, up into the sinuses, and let the electricity flow through it; then they held his head under the shit-water for a while. He had deliberately provoked them so as to put off the decision about Carmen. His wife. He tried to keep his mind busy, wondering how long it would be, before he was like his brother Angel, who, after a time, gave them suggestions as to how to torture him.

He wished they would simply kill them, his beautiful children. He knew that the girl was being raped every night. He wished he could kill her himself, to free her. He wished too he *had* been a terrorist, so that this might mean something.

As they finished near-drowning him in the shit-water, he wondered if perhaps they were bluffing about the saw. As they had been about the executions. Three times they told him they were going to execute him. They took him to the wall, pointed guns at him, and pulled the triggers on hollow clicks. "Next time," they'd said. So maybe with the saw . . .

"I'll do it," he said.

So they gave him the old, dull saw and showed him where they wanted him to saw off his wife's arm, as the children watched, as his wife—who had not spoken in a month—looked blankly at him and waited. Herrera knew they wouldn't just kill her, if he refused. They'd . . .

But when they began to strangle his little girl, he found himself obediently sawing on his wife's arm—

V AND H MOVE ON TO RIO. Mistake. They watch as death squads murder children because they are homeless. H decides to try Africa. Mistake. The suffering is as vast as the veldt. He goes north, to the Middle East. There is a war going on. The bombs are sent with great deliberation, but seem, in some places, to fall at random; seem to choose people to dismember and crush with grim whimsicality.

V and H go farther east, to India. Mistake. North to China; stop off at a place that seems very orderly and quiet and turns out to be a sort of concentration camp for freethinkers. Mistake.

H finds his way to Western Europe. He dips into some viewpoints. At first it seems a relief. Then he begins to see that with the relatively healthy and comfortable, the suffering is more attenuated and prolonged; it is a breaking on the wheel of isolation and self-doubt and ambition. It is a slower meat grinder.

They drift west to New York. H dips his mind into a woman working in a textile sweatshop; she's working for minimum wage and it's not enough to shelter her family and she's locked into endless days and the short nights and another succession of endless days of pain and ironclad drear, and she'd like to get out of it before she's used up completely but she can't because of her children so it'll never end until she's too old to . . .

H gets out. He finds someone in deep euphoria—at last!—but discovers it is very short-lived. Very. About two minutes. Then the euphoria is replaced by a profound depression: echoingly deep, cold as subterranean granite, when the crack wears off and the dried-out husk of the man's brain collapses into itself. The man in question later sells his daughter at a nearby bar for $20 to get more crack, knowing that he'll only pitch himself deeper into the pit.

H tries three middle-class children in the suburbs: one of them is being molested by his uncle; another's mind is now indistinguishable from television; the third is relatively happy—but H senses a cancer growing in her brain.

JANICE THOUGHT, yes, the attendant would be coming soon. She was fairly sure of it. She could feel the telltale burning on her bedsores that meant she had peed on herself, and that usually happened in the late afternoon, right before the nurse came with her medication. She didn't mind the bedsores or the soiled linen or her swollen joints so much; but the smell of herself rotting, *that* tormented her.

She was hungry but the food made her sick, here; she wanted to get up but it hurt a great deal just to go sit outside and she couldn't see much anyway because of the film over her eyes and the place was nearly underneath a great freeway that sent out a cloud of fumes that started her emphysema up and then the coughing started and they'd get angry at her—it was funny how they got angry when her suffering rose clearly into view and sometimes they'd pretend that she'd gotten "unmanageable" so they'd strap her into bed and pretend to forget her for a day or so just to punish her. No one would speak to her and since no one ever visited her—her children found it too depressing—she would go days at a time speaking only to the attendants and she found herself saying things that annoyed them, asking them to kill her, especially after a few days without any real sleep because the pain of—

* * *

"YOU TRICKED ME SOMEHOW, V. That one was strangely like the one dying of AIDS. You're playing some kind of game with me."

"Bullshit. You picked that one on your own. The suffering most people go through in old age parallels AIDS. The pattern of neglect is similar, too. Tell you something else—you know how long people on this dimensional world live? On average, about seventy-five of their years if they're lucky. I use the word 'lucky' fully cognizant of its irony."

"Seventy—? But they only seem to get a handle on their lives when they're in their forties or fifties—at the earliest! And then their bodies are already badly deteriorating. Everything slowing down. Just when they start to get it together—"

"Hey. Tell me about it."

"Look, I know I can find somebody young who's on top of the world. . . . I sense one on that freeway. . . ."

IT WAS A GOOD TIME for black filmmakers. And yeah, coming home from the meeting with his agent, Garrison was feeling good. They were going to let him direct a property he believed in. Make a statement that would maybe raise some consciousness. He and Julia would be able to have that baby now. God, thank you—

That's when a drunk lost control of his TransAm and spun into Garrison's ten-year-old Toyota. The Toyota rolled like dice, cracking its gas tank, stopping with four wheels in the air. Two more cars couldn't slow in time and hit it. Gasoline puddled; flame engulfed the Toyota. Garrison couldn't work his broken arm; the door on his other side was crumpled in and he couldn't get his feet up to kick out a window. The car got oven-hot. There were bubbles in his skin like the bubbles on the paint of the car; his insides were oozing out his mouth.

* * *

H GETS OUT. Finds himself dipping into a CHP cop help-lessly watching the man in the burning car.

SPRAGUE HAD USED UP his fire extinguisher trying to put out the fire in the old Toyota. The driver would be dead—which was just as well, considering—long before the fire trucks got there so there was no reason he should watch the man screaming for someone to kill him, please kill him, while his face dripped off its bone. He was frustrated, because he couldn't kill the man to put him out of his misery: they'd take away his pension, his wife would leave him—she just might anyway, he was pretty sure she was fucking his brother and—

H GETS OUT OF THE COP. Drifts up, in a relative way, above the burning wreckage. The suffering muted to a distant whistle, like the sound of the teapot forgotten on the stove of a 19th-century Englishwoman they'd observed, in an ear-lier visit, the prostitute who hung herself with her tea water still boiling. And H asks V, "There's no good biological rea-son they should be able to feel so much pain—is there?"

"No. It's just bad design. Or malicious. Of course, shock sets in, but by that time they've suffered just incred-ibly. For some people, the world is, for short periods, more benign. But then comes old age. You've seen how that comes out . . . So, all this considered, do you still want to incarnate into this world for your own spiritual improvement?"

"No fucking way. This is way too extreme. Let's get the hell out of here."

"Sure, sure, we're going. I was just taking a last look. I will say that this world is sort of interesting as a study piece, if you don't get too close."

"You're a *student* of this world? But why? What's the attraction? That seems kind of . . . sick."

"Maybe. I've always had a thing for horror."

WITH THAT, THEY LEFT. Like a man on his first visit to a slaughterhouse, eager to get out. They left by the first exit. They simply left.

You can't. Not that way.

Where It's Safe

PERSONALLY, I THINK YOU CAN kiss civilization as we know it now goodbye, about the year 2040.

Written for the anthology *The Earth Strikes Back*. Tales of Ecological Horror, and none of them, in my opinion, far fetched. I predict most of what happens in this story will happen—particularly the famine as a result of UV overkill.

The punk element should be obvious.

NEPHILIM SET THE CHARGE and stood back. Crowel chuckled, with his tongue caught between his teeth in that yokel way he had, and said, "Don't need to worry about blast. It don't work that way."

"I know," Nephilim said. "It's—I'm used to non-directional explosives."

"Me'n Crispin, we lucked onto some beauties at th' armory raid—"

A muffled *whump* as the explosion, directed precisely from the blast plate they'd attached to the airlock of the smog shield, punched out the locking mechanism. The mechanism fell away with the slight reverberation of the controlled blast, leaving a perfect oval cut through the six-inch door around the lock, the cut's edges giving out only wisps of gray smoke.

"Very nice indeed," Nephilim said. He reached through the gap with the battery-charged alligator clamps, and sparked the electronic tumblers. The door hummed, and gave a click. For Nephilim that sound was an affirmation of life; it was a tiny little sound that was all hope and meaning. It was an affirmation of death, too.

Crowel pushed the airlock open as Nephilim turned and signaled the Pack.

THE DOW JONES INDUSTRIAL had dropped two and a half. Secondary and Tertiary markets were suffering a –3.1. But AkInc's own Montana Chemicals was up. That cheered Akwiss a little.

He looked up from the morning financial print-outs, squinting through the glass roof of the breakfast room to try to see past the gray smog shield. He couldn't make out the clouds. The shield was too smudgy. Better have it cleaned.

He was planning to copter to New York that afternoon, if the weather permitted. They got some vicious crosswinds in July, and it might be safer to take a tunnel shuttle, though it was a longer trip.

Akwiss decided on the shuttle, and went back to his stewed prunes and print-out. The prunes were execrable. Sometimes he thought the doctor was giving him this pain-in-the-ass diet out of personal animosity. He had only the doctor's word; for all knew he could be eating eggs and bacon with abandon. Hell, he could always take a choles-terol sweeper.

Lunch was the one meal he was permitted to enjoy a lit-tle. A lean-meat sandwich, a piece of Jorge's very realistic apple pie—it was something to look forward to.

He scowled at the prunes and cereal and orange juice. A man could starve on this diet.

Akwiss looked around in annoyance, hearing the whine of the MadeMaid rolling into the room, its electric engine complaining for lubrication. The robot was a metal box with complicatedly jointed hydraulic arms and whirring graspers and a rotating camera. It reached up clumsily to clear the dishes onto its tray and promptly swept them onto the floor instead. "Whoops!" said the female voice from its speakers. Its voice was the thing that worked best about it. He ought to have it answering phones instead of cleaning up. Normally he didn't use it at all.

Akwiss thumbed the intercom button. "Murieta! Get in here!"

His Mexican butler came in with startling immediacy, smiling. Irritatingly chummy, Akwiss thought. "Murieta— what the hell is this? Where's Dunket? This clunker is supposed to be in a closet somewhere. It never did work and I find these things offensive. People should be served by people. This company is all about providing good work for good people, Murieta. We make an example, here."

Murieta smiled and nodded just as if he bought into Akwiss's reflexive company-slogan populism. "I know, I know that, I told Dunket we need you, he say chure he come back this afternoon, until then we use the ma-cheen, he said—"

"Come back this afternoon? I didn't give him any time off."

"He said you give him time to go to the doctor. Chure."

"Well. I don't remember it. I suppose if he needs to see a doctor . . . well. Well, uh—clean up this mess, this damn thing can't manage it."

"Chure."

Akwiss exhaled windily through his nose. Dunket should have called for a temporary from Chicago Central. The damn fool should have known better, anyway. He'd served Akwiss for years.

He hit the intercom again. "Finch? Yo, Finch!" He looked expectantly at the video monitor flush with the table top, expecting to see his Security Supervisor appear. The screen stayed blank.

Murieta was busily picking up chunks of crockery with his bare hands. The MadeMaid was whirring confusedly back and forth at his side, getting in the way. Akwiss watched Murietta for a moment, then quietly asked, "Murieta—did Finch have a doctor's appointment too?"

"I don't know, Mr Atch-wiss." He didn't look up from the dish fragments. "I deedn't see him."

THAT ONE, NEPHILIM THOUGHT, is probably Finch. Lean guy with receding blond hair. Definite ID or not, he had to go down: he had a gun on his hip.

Finch was just rounding the corner, coming down the Eastern corridor to check on the breach in the mansion's Eastern airlock. Looking bored, probably expecting to find it was another false alarm triggered by acid corrosion. Then he saw the Pack and froze in his tracks. Nephilim expected him to go for the gun but he just gaped in surprise. He'd never had anything to do here but scare off salesmen.

Crowel was raising his gun, but it was Nephilim's practice to take responsibility for these things when he could. If the Feds pulled off a swoop some of the Pack might get off with twenty years if they weren't tied to killings. He pushed Crowel's gun-muzzle down and said, "Mine." His autopistol hissed as he swept a four-shot burst across Finch's chest and the guy went spinning down. Finch had been pretty complacent, as expected: He hadn't bothered with armor.

*　　*　　*

Akwiss was waiting for the elevator. It was taking too long. Another glitch. The whole estate needed a tightening-up from top to bottom. Maybe one of the girls he'd brought over last night was monopolizing the elevator, on her way home. He certainly hoped Finch had sent them back to town. They got on his nerves when they hung around.

He glanced at the out-conditions indicator, for something to do as he waited. Air Quality for the morning of July 18, 2014, was pretty good outside. One could walk about freely.

It wasn't as bad as people made it out, any time, of course. Only when the rare Black Wind came along was a respirator necessary. Most of the time, the smog shield's importance was security and not bad air. He'd explained that pretty handily to the reporter from UNO, last week. The media ate out of his hand; always had.

He could hear the elevator moving now. It was about time. Maybe he ought to have a new elevator put in. But most of the time he was the only one who used them—

The doors opened and the elevator was filled with strangers.

Nephilim didn't bother to chase the fat guy down the glass hall. He knew he wouldn't get past the breakfast room.

Crowel laughed, watching Akwiss wheezing along.

"So that's Akwiss," Holovitz said, coming out of the elevator behind Nephilim. "Well anyway it's his butt. Fat as his cred-account."

Nephilim said, "Holovitz, wait here for the others. Bring 'em straight along this tube after us. Crowel, Crispin— come along."

In no particular hurry, Nephilim strode along after Akwiss. Crispin, who carried the tools and the bags, gave a yellow, snaggly grin, and fell into step beside him.

THE NEAREST GENERAL ALARM BUTTON was in the breakfast room. Akwiss thought his heart would hammer its way out of his chest before he got there. It was stupid, fucking stupid. There should be an alarm every forty feet or so. Where the bloody hell was Finch?

Maybe they were a work crew or something. Maybe that had been a lube gun in his hand. . . .

Murieta was standing over the console on the breakfast table, working busily with a cutting torch. Akwiss skidded to a stop in front of him, wheezing, sweat tickling his neck, staring.

Murieta was humming to himself as he melted away the inside of the console. A few sparks spat through the crater in the plastic hull, smoke curled up. No alarms went off. He'd burned through the alarm circuits first. He switched off the cutting tool and smiled up at Akwiss. "You're back surprisingly early, boss. Surely you didn't forget your briefcase."

Akwiss tried to swallow, but his throat was too dry. It felt like there was something obstructing it. He could just barely breathe. "You . . . you're not . . ."

"My accent? Oh chure. I forgot." His eyes were as bright as the flame of his cutting torch.

"You fucking traitor." Akwiss was thinking about trying to run past Murieta. But the way the man was tensed . . . the way he held that torch . . . "How'd you get through the screening?"

"Your personnel-screening database is more porous than you think, boss."

Akwiss heard the others coming up behind them. He

tried to compose himself as he turned to face them. Thinking, *Anything can be negotiated. Just stay cool.*

The short, stocky one with the dark eyes and the cryptic symbols cut into the black hair on the side of his head: That would be their leader. The other two were most definitely followers, Akwiss thought, but they were hungry looking men who seemed hardly in check. All three of them wore fatigues tucked into military boots, iridescent anti-UV ponchos, respirators slung around their necks. They were all a bit grimy, unshaven. Thin, ravenous men. Those weren't lube guns in their hands. And one of them was training a videocam on him.

"Oliver Akwiss," the dark-eyed man said, "CEO, president and owner of Akwiss Incorporated, a multinational corporation also known as AkInc, I arrest you for the Citizen's Reclamation Troop on a charge of mass murder."

"'Citizen's Reclamation Troop'! You're a *Pack*, is what you are," Akwiss snorted. "You can dress it up any way you want." Careful, he told himself: *You should be pacifying them. They have the guns.* But his pride demanded some rebuke to this outrage.

"We are, yes, what you call a 'Pack'," the man said, shrugging. He went on smoothly, with a characteristic glibness that Akwiss found increasingly irritating. "And a Citizen's Reclamation Troop. Your Congressional lobbyists push the buttons on the official laws so the public's own justice has to be enforced by a pack of outlaws. It's a damn shame but there it is. You can call me Nephilim, Mr Akwiss."

Akwiss thought, *Stall them.* He glanced past Nephilim through the glass of the corridor, hoping to see a security team moving up, outside it. No one yet.

Nephilim read Akwiss' glance. "The outdoor guards are all getting loaded on Hot Morph at the South gate, Mr. Akwiss. We've been selling it to them on the cheap for weeks. They've been using more and more heavily. Not Finch, of course. Him we had to kill."

Akwiss decided to fake admiration. He glanced at Murieta. "And this one you planted inside. Ingenious."

"No it's not. You and your security got sloppy and complacent. The price of living so long where it's 'safe'." Four more of the Pack were trotting up behind Nephilim. Well armed.

There would be no escape. It was all up to negotiation now, Akwiss thought. Well. That was his strength, after all.

Nephilim nodded toward the corridor leading into the living room. "Let's go in there."

Akwiss licked his lips. Have to calm down. He was dangerously close to hyperventilation, maybe heart attack. He nodded, and made himself breathe slowly, as he turned and walked between the man who called himself Murieta, and Nephilim, to the barn-sized living room of the main house.

"Whew!" the skinny one said, looking around. Adding mockingly: "This is, like, so tasteful. And yet so elegant."

The others laughed. Akwiss felt his face go hot.

"You got the disc, Crowel?" Nephilim said, to the skinny one.

Crowel took a sealed videodisc from a pouch on his flak vest, and went to the player. Murieta was smiling mysteriously up at the big beams thirty feet overhead; they were genuine wood, retrofitted from a 20th century yacht. Near the fake-log fireplace was a big grand piano that had once belonged to Leonard Bernstein. The other furnishings were expensive designer antiques, which Akwiss had once thought a contradiction in terms. But his decorator had insisted it was all a matter of style, not materials or chronology. And Akwiss had to agree: Surfaces are all.

Some of the men seemed a little in awe of the vast room, the *faux* antique furniture, the gently segueing videopaintings, the yellowing impressionist oils, the platinum lamps.

Prompted by Crowel, the video screen rose from the floor: Ten feet by fifteen, high-rez and state of the art. "Have a seat, Mr Akwiss," Nephilim said, gesturing at the blue velvet sofa.

"Thanks, I prefer to stand," Akwiss said, trying to create an atmosphere of equality.

"I said sit the fuck down," Nephilim said quietly, as Crowel handed Nephilim the video remote control.

Akwiss sank onto the sofa.

Crowel went about setting up a small video camera on a thin aluminum tripod, and a recording deck. It was trained on Akwiss, Nephilim and Akwiss's video screen.

"What's the camera for?" Akwiss asked. "Proof to my company for the hostage money?"

Nephilim shook his head grimly. "For the trial. We're making a whole set of them to mail out to select media. Last week we videotaped your good friend George Pourneven. The video deck belonged to him, in fact."

"George? There was no report of anything unusual with—"

"You didn't look at anything but the financial news today, evidently." He stepped a little closer to the small microphone attached to the videocam. "Now. I'm going to have to hold forth a bit on certain subjects—things you know about but the public doesn't. You and your cronies having done very well at keeping the public in the dark. . . ." He tapped the remote, and the disc began play. "You're on trial, Akwiss. Kindly review the evidence with us."

Akwiss looked at the images rezzing up on the videoscreen. It was as he'd expected. Pictures of starving children. The bleeding hearts were always trying to intimidate him with starving children. As if he were one of the parents, the people really responsible for those kids.

"This is today," Nephilim was saying. "The Great American Famine. Ten to twenty thousand children die every week in our America the Beautiful, of famine or famine-related disease. It's going to get worse before it gets better. . . ."

Akwiss blew out his cheeks and looked at his shoes. They needed a shine, he decided.

He felt a small cold circle pressing into his left temple: A gun muzzle. Akwiss looked at Crowel from the corners of his eyes; Crowel, his cheek twitching, was saying, *"Look at the fucking screen."*

Akwiss looked at the screen. The gun muzzle was withdrawn. But he thought he could feel it watching him.

On the screen: Rows of emaciated children lying on cots in some school gymnasium. Small children of every color. But there were lots of white ones in particular. It must be around Des Moines or Salt Lake City. Children who couldn't hold their heads up on their shrunken necks; whose skin seemed shrink-wrapped over their bones. Whose bellies were horribly distended from famine bloat. Their bugging eyes listless, wandering. Only a few of them with strength to cry. Most of them would die, of course.

"In 1990," Nephilim was saying, "children were dying in the so-called Third World at a rate of about 40,000 a day, from hunger."

"'Or hunger-related disease,'" Akwiss heard himself say, dryly. *Don't sneer at them.* he warned himself. Suppress your pride. He went on hastily, "Oh, I know! And AkInc gave a fortune to famine relief for Ethiopia in the 90s."

"Actually you gave exactly as much as you needed for the tax break you required, and not a penny more," Nephilim said, casually. He was maddeningly casual about it all. At first. "Anyway—40,000 children dying every day globally was acceptable to people in the U.S. because it wasn't their kids. They didn't feel responsible. Now the famine is *here*, in the USA, and people at last are looking at some of the causes, at least the causes in this country. Let's rewind a little. . . ." The disc zipped back to its beginning. Shots of AkInc factories and similar outfits—Dow, Union Carbide, Exxon, Arco, Georgia Pacific, others. Chemicals plants, oil refineries, paper mills, heavy industry of all kinds.

But they kept coming back to AkInc plants: AkInc sluicing toxic fluids into rivers, gouting toxic waste into the sky, burying cheap barrels of toxins; dumping barrels of toxins into the sea. "It started even before the CFCs began to chew away at the ozone. You are a chemicals octopus, Akwiss. You have a tentacle in every chemicals product. Foam packaging. Plastics of all kinds. Pesticides and herbicides particularly, in the early years. Between the years 1960 and 1990 the rate of stomach cancer quadrupled; the rate of brain cancer increased five hundred per cent. A lot of people think it was pesticides in our foods." Footage now of children and old people dying in cancer wards. Sickening stuff. Akwiss tried to let his eyes go out of focus.

Nephilim went on: "Pesticides in the air, too. They evaporate from fields and lawns, so eventually we even inhale them. Some pesticides run off into the streams, into the oceans. We eat pesticide-tainted fish, pesticide-poisoned produce. It builds up and up in us—and in the environment. Dolphins and seals begin to wash up dead from obscure viruses because the toxins undermine their immune systems. The dead dolphins were just a symptom of what was coming: *all* the fish dying, sea creatures of every kind."

"And all this from my pesticides? I hardly think you can pin it all on me, personally," Akwiss said, as politely as he could manage.

"You and a few hundred others at the top of the pyramids of big business—you are the most culpable. But the rest of us too. We didn't vote out the Congressmen who buckled under to your lobbies and campaign-contribution bribes. . . ."

The bathroom, Akwiss thought. If I could get into the bathroom. There's a phone there, one they may not notice in the cabinet by the toilet. Let them burn off a little of their self righteousness with the lecture and then if I can talk Nephilim into letting me use the toilet . . .

"The pesticides contributed to the great famine in half a dozen ways," Nephilim went on, his professorial tone weirdly incongruous with the gun and fatigues. "They destroyed beneficial bacteria and threw the ecological balance in the insect world completely out of whack. The side effects got worse and worse. The airborne pesticides merged into the clouds of toxins altered by UV light—and synergistically combined with the other factory toxins to make the Black Winds."

"You've obviously had the opportunity to memorize your accusations," Akwiss pointed out. "I haven't had a chance to memorize a defense."

"You've made your excuses and your defenses for years," Nephilim said calmly. "You defended yourself with your PR firms, your congressional lobbies, your doctored environmental impact studies. It's our turn now."

Akwiss licked his dry lips, and nodded. *Let him get through it. Then . . .*

Nephilim picked up his rote speech where he'd left off. "The killer clouds they call Black Winds kill not only people—also wheat and orchards and cattle and sheep and chickens. And of course the UV burn was worse than ever because of the CFCs that companies like AkInc were mass producing. Chlorofluorocarbons that nibbled endlessly at the ozone layer—the huge growth in the incidence of skin cancer was the least of it. In 2002 . . . where's that shot . . . Here it is . . ." He'd fast forwarded to a long sweeping shot of a dust bowl field. "Looks like Oklahoma in the early 20th century. But it's good old Iowa. Here's another in Kansas. This one is Oregon: The Willamette Valley, one big dust bowl. . . . The unchecked ultraviolets killed the plants and small organisms that held the topsoil down. They killed crops and they—"

"Now really, CFCs—they were used by virtually everyone," Akwiss protested coolly. He glanced toward the door to the bathroom. Should he try for it now? Not quite yet, he decided. Damn, he wanted a drink. "Probably you used them yourself when you were young. Spray cans and such."

"Your company—at your instigation—spent millions suppressing the evidence, paying off research scientists, giving campaign contributions to Congressmen in exchange for slowing the ban on CFCs."

Startled by the range of Nephilim's inside information, Akwiss blurted automatically, "Nonsense, we did no such thing—!"

"We have all the documentation, Akwiss. You weren't picked arbitrarily. We don't go about executing innocent people, you know."

Akwiss's throat constricted. *Executing.*

Get to the bathroom. The phone. Fast. "Listen I need to—"

Nephilim over-rode him, going on, "I almost admire the subtlety of your favorite strategies. Your industry-sponsored 'environmental initiatives'—which did nothing but cancel out the real initiatives, if you read the fine print. And your bunk 'studies.' You—and the other big companies did the same, of course—you'd fund 'independent' researchers, push them into churning out studies that seemed to show that pesticides were safe for consumption, that CFCs weren't necessarily the agent in depleting the ozone layer, that low-level radiation from nuclear power plants was no danger, that the toxins you were spewing by the thousands of tons into the air wouldn't cause cancer and birth defects. And so on. There were always contradictory studies by responsible people, but a great many of the newspapers—usually owned by one of your conglomerates—cited only *your* studies, strangely enough. . . ." The men around him laughed.

"Look—the country needed jobs—"

"Dead men are unemployable, Akwiss," Nephilim went on relentlessly. "And it's not as if you couldn't have had your factories without polluting—that whole line is a lie. *You could have!* The technology to clean all emissions and convert waste—*it exists*. Has for decades. But it was costly. And you didn't want to spend the money, you and your cronies. You were too greedy. And that's what this is all about. *Greed.* Greed is the reason for this. . . ." He gestured at the screen. "Here we have a lovely shot of some birth defects traceable to emissions from your chemicals factories—this child born with his brain hanging outside his head died, of course, but his brother, the imbecile with the flippers and the missing jaw you see now, survived to crawl through his own shit the rest of his life. . . ."

Akwiss had to look away. Crowel started toward him but then Akwiss turned desperately to Nephilim. "Please—I have to go to the bathroom." The others laughed. Controlling his resentment, Akwiss went on, "You're trying to conduct this in a civilized way, aren't you?"

"Yes yes, we don't want to have to clean up after you *again,*" Nephilim said with heavy sarcasm.

It took Akwiss a moment to get it. Then he smiled weakly. "Yes. Well. The bathroom's just over there. . . ."

"Take the man to the bathroom, Crowel. But look around in there for alarms or telephones."

AKWISS THOUGHT HE WAS close to a heart attack as Crowel searched the bathroom. But Crowel didn't find the phone. He evidently expected to see it attached to the wall. It was a cellular phone, in a drawer.

Left alone in the bathroom, Akwiss did his best to use the toilet; Crowel was just outside the door. Akwiss didn't want him to get suspicious. But his bowels didn't want to work, at first.

At last, as the toilet flushed, Akwiss tapped the code into the little touchtone keyboard on the cellular phone. He didn't dare use the phone vocally. Crowel would hear him. But the code should set up a buzzing in the guard house, at the checkpoint, and in their jeeps. The alarm buzzing meant, *Come to the main house at once.*

A thumping on the door made him nearly fall off the toilet. "Get out *now* or I'm comin' in!" Crowel yelled.

Hands shaking, trying to make no sound at it, Akwiss replaced the phone in the drawer and closed it.

"THE ... THE OTHER MEN ... ?" Akwiss asked, looking around as he and Crowel returned to the main room. Only Nephilim, Crowel, and this odd, eager fellow Crispin remained. Murieta had gone too. That might make things easier for Akwiss. . . .

"The other men aren't here as soldiers, in particular," Nephilim said distractedly, fast forwarding through the video disc. He seemed tense and impatient. Soon, it'd be over, one way or another. "They came along to move out your food supplies and anything that'll help us buy more food on the black market." He stopped the disc and turned a cold, onyx glare at Akwiss. "Your people—your class, if

253

that's what they are—monopolize the available food, of course. After destroying most of North America's capacity to grow food, they hoard what's left. A lot of real charmers, you and your cartel buddies. My own kid died of diarrhea, Akwiss. My boy Derrick. Diarrhea's the leading cause of death for children, globally. Has been for decades. Did you know that . . . Akwiss?"

"Yes. Yes I—I'd heard that." Try to show them you care, that you know about these things. "The, ah, hunger weakens their immunity, so they get a diarrhea which dehydrates them and they die of, ah—"

"My wife and I," Nephilim interrupted, looking abstractedly at his gun, "got stuck out in the new dust bowl, looking for water, and the car ran out of charge . . ." Hardly audible, he finished: "And I couldn't get Derrick to water in time . . ."

He turned to gaze emptily at Akwiss. And Akwiss thought Nephilim was going to shoot him on the spot. He held his breath.

And then let it out slowly when Nephilim visibly regained control and turned to gesture at the video screen. "Cancer patients downstream from AkInc factories in Louisiana. The link between your dioxin and their cancer was very clear but the whole thing was suppressed—"

"Now wait a moment," Akwiss broke in. Thinking, now's the time to really stall them till my men get here. "Honestly—if that's what happened I really did not know about it. I mean—maybe some of what you were saying is true. But like every man in a high position, I'm surrounded by yes-men." He tried not to look at the archway behind Crowel, through which his outdoor security men would be coming. "My subordinates tell me what they think I want to hear. About the environment. About our . . . our impact on it. I'm sure no one told me about the Dioxin link to cancer in Louisiana and I doubt I ever got honest information from my people about CFCs and the dangers of famine—"

"First of all, yes you did," Nephilim snapped. "Your attorneys gave you an extensive briefing about all these issues when they were trying to protect you from lawsuits. We have a tape of that briefing, from *fourteen years ago*. You understood, all right. Second—even if you hadn't been briefed, the information was out there. You were responsible for finding out on your own, Akwiss, what your company was doing to the world. But that's a red herring—you ordered the suppression of the truth. 'Smokescreen it' you said, on one occasion. You had a lot to do with weakening the various Clean Air Acts, you and your lobbies—and you knew exactly what you were doing." He looked into Akwiss' eyes, and spoke with a certain formal finality: *"You knew people were dying because of what you'd done."*

"No, truly, I—"

"You knew!" Nephilim roared, leaning over Akwiss, who shrank back on the sofa, glancing at the archway. *Where were they? Stoned or not they had to come.* Nephilim turned away, pacing now, shouting, "You knew damn well! And you didn't give one rat's ass about the children dying of cancer, about the birth defects, about the emphysema, about the destruction of the sea, the destruction of the farmlands, the famines that would have to come. The *millions of Americans* dying from famine! You son of a bitch, you're the biggest mass murderer since Hitler!" He stopped pacing, his back turned, his voice breaking, sounding far away as he admitted, "But we all practiced denial. And none of us wanted to admit that criminals were running the country. We just didn't want to believe that it was murder. That it was mass homicide. Just a kind of carelessness, we thought. Or ignorance. When it was

nothing of the kind. . . ."

Crowel nodded, put in hoarsely, "It was murder. Pre-fuckin'-meditated."

And then Brightson and Margolis stepped into the arch-way, guns in hand. Brightson a young, heavy-set black guard with an elaborate silvery coif, and Margolis the potbellied, gray haired white guard. Where were the others? Were these all that would come? The drugs, the damn drugs!

Crowel and Crispin vaulted over the sofa and crouched back of Akwiss; Crowel looped his wiry arm around Akwiss's throat, nearly crushing his windpipe, holding him in place where he sat.

Nephilim stepped behind the piano, loosing a sloppy burst of autofire at Margolis. Missing. Nephilim's rounds traced a crooked line of holes across the walls of the corri-dor as Margolis and Brightson jumped back beyond the edge of the archway, out of the line of fire. "Jesus fucking Christ!" Brightson muttered.

"You men stand firm!" Akwiss yelled hoarsely. "Get the police! Get the other men!"

"We can't find the others!" Margolis yelled. "Outside phone lines are down!"

"Mr Akwiss!" Brightson shouted, from around the cor-ner of the archway. "We'd better go and try to get help, these fellas got us outgunned!"

"No! No, don't leave—"

Crowel tightened his choke-hold around Akwiss' throat. "Shut up, asshole."

Nephilim yelled out, "You men out there—you want some Hot Morph? It's pharmaceutical! We got it on a pharm-industry raid and it's the same good stuff you been getting! I'll give you an ounce if you go away and forget about this! Just tell em we got past ol' Finch and there was nothing you could do!"

Hesitation. Then Margolis yelled, "Hell yeah! Toss it over and I'm gone!"

They could hear Brightson hissing at Margolis. "God damn it that ain't no way to treat the man, he employed you ten years!"

"He underpaid everybody ever worked for him, Brighty! Fuck him and fuck you too!"

Another traitorous bastard, Akwiss thought.

Nephilim tossed over a sandwich bag full of yellow powder. It slid past the archway, into the corridor. They could hear Margolis scoop it up and run. His bootsteps receding down the hall. Gone.

Nephilim shouted, "Throw down your gun, 'Brighty,' cause I'm coming over there and if you're armed—"

Brightson, bless him, responded with two gunshots that rang out dissonant, hysterical notes as the bullets struck the piano. Nephilim ducked back, cursing under his breath. There was a burst from another automatic weapon, out of sight in the hallway. A cry of pain. The sound of someone falling. Footsteps. "Hold your fire!" Murieta called, as he stepped into view. He was grinning, carrying a small machine pistol. "Brighty's gone down, Nephilim. Let's get back to the trial."

Crowel released Akwiss. Gagging, trying his best to look pitiful, Akwiss turned to Nephilim. "Look, let's negotiate this. I can offer you a fortune. You—you have to give me a chance to—"

"You had your chance." Nephilim moved out from behind the piano, and pointed to the video screen. The image was frozen on the face of a starving child. "He had none. Your guilt is clear. The penalty . . ."

"You're not going to torture me," Akwiss broke in, losing control. "You're not that kind of person. I know that. You're not!"

"Torture you? You mean force you to die slowly—of cancer? Of starvation? No. We're not barbarians, Akwiss."

THEY AREN'T REALLY GOING TO DO IT. Akwiss thought. He was standing on a chair, with a neatly-tied hangman's noose around his neck, the knot behind his left ear. The rope running up to loop over his beautiful real-wood rafters. *They're trying to scare me into signing over my money.*

"I can sign over a great deal of money to you," Akwiss said.

"You could stop it getting to us, too," Nephilim said. "If you were alive. You've given us your account numbers, that'll help. We'll feed a lot of kids before your Swiss banks figure it out. You got any last words?"

Now even Akwiss' knees threatened to betray him. They were going gelatinous. "Please . . . I didn't know . . ."

"You keep saying that," Nephilim said. "But I keep saying: Oh but you most certainly *did* know. Akwiss—haven't you wondered why I know so much about the inner workings of your outfit?" His voice broke, but he went on. "I worked for you, Akwiss. We never met—but I was one of the two hundred some lawyers AkInc employed. That's how I got my hands on the tapes of your briefing. And that's when I resigned. I could hear it on the tape: *You just didn't care.* I have a theory, Akwiss—that you have to be a real sociopath to get to the top of American Industry. And a sociopath feels nothing for anyone but himself. So it didn't matter that you knew your company was helping launch a famine in which millions would die. You felt nothing. *You* were living where it was safe, after all. . . ."

They were both crying now: Akwiss and Nephilim. Nephilim said hoarsely: "I was a damn good lawyer. I defended you people—I ought to be up there with you, with a rope around my neck. And someday I will be, when all this is done. Now. This is for Derrick."

And then he kicked over the chair.

This time, and for the last time, Akwiss' bowels worked very well.

THE OTHERS WERE BACK; the trucks were loaded with tons of stashed food. No sign of Federal troops or police. It was going smoothly. Just one thing left to attend to, Nephilim thought: the very last of the liberated food.

That was nearly ready, too. Nephilim saw that Crispin was almost done cutting the meat off Akwiss's body, and putting it in the bags.

The kids wouldn't know the difference. It might save a life or two.

"What kind of meat you going to tell them it is?" Crowel asked, smiling. "Pig?"

"No," Nephilim said. "No if I told them that, they might guess what it really is."

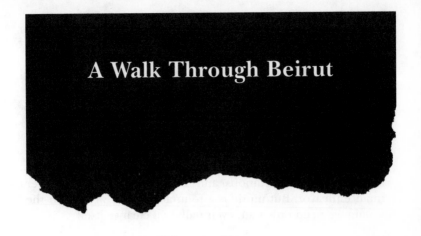

A Walk Through Beirut

I WAS FUCKING A GIRL who wore long black dresses and boots and no underwear on the roof in the driving rain during a lightning storm. This is a fact. Lightning smashed around us as we fucked; rain lashed us; to us it was like listening to music as we fucked. It was my only experience with PCP—and that by accident. Some cab driver had sold us a joint, and we smoked it and it turned out to be a dust joint. I'm scared of spiders but I was so fucked up that I had my foot shoved in a spider's web and *knew it* and, for that single time in my life, didn't even care. Later I discovered I was bitten and the bite became so badly infected I had to have IV antibiotics.

My spouse of the time was screaming at me because I went to band rehearsal without telling her about it and anyway I spend too much time and money on the band and not enough of either on her and it's destroying our marriage and why don't I fucking grow up and choose . . . choose . . .

I was in bands, I was recording, I was writing books. But it's even tougher making it in bands. Eventually you have to make a choice. The world is chaos. Robert Anton Wilson said that there is no *one* conspiracy running the world—if there was, the world would make sense. There are dozens of conspiracies vying for control. And we're caught in the crossfire.

This fusillade in prose appeared in an anthology called *Newer*

York. New York City, in my little fiction, has balkanized like Beirut, and it's the symbolic stage for the hero's self-exploration. It's about maturity, yes, but it's also about renewal of youthful purpose and idealism against all odds; it's about cynicism's "hideous strength." The punk element will need no adumbration.

The story is also related, in terms of my trajectory, to the journey my life has been so far, to "What He Wanted" and *City Come A-Walkin'* . . .

Rock'n'roll is as ruinous and disillusioning as any other human endeavor. But music is a fountain, and if we poison the fountain we need only wait, eventually it'll cleanse itself. . . .

BLACKOUT.

All through Lower Manhattan, blackout.

The street wasn't completely dark. Stretching between buildings was a diffuse web of light from the lit part of the city, north of Fourteenth Street, where the affluent had a backup power system. Rusty light fluttered from the fires someone had set in the stores, two blocks up, at Delancey, and a yellower flame guttered in the broken windows of the graffiti-tattooed elementary school across the street. The Children's Christian Militia were bivouacked in the school gymnasium. Dexy could see the desultory beaming of flashlights through the gym's open doors.

The summer of 2022 had been a hot one, was oozing like molten wax into fall. It was still a warm evening, but Dexy knew it'd get colder, about one A.M., so he'd worn his wild-dog jacket. He ran his hand down the stiff, short-furred pit-bull hide and cocked his head, like a dog himself, listening to the whoops and feverish shouts from Delancey; the perverse ringing of breaking glass. A gunshot. Another.

"Oh, totally THRASHIN'," Marilyn yelled, clattering clumsily down the chipped stone steps of the tenement on her high heels. "A *black*-oouuuuuut!" Skateboard under her arm. She was going to skateboard with her heels on? No, she took the shoes off, stuck their spike heels in the waistband of her skin-tight neoprene skirt, so the pumps hung like gunfighter holsters. She jumped on the skateboard, pumped it, its gear system translating the kinetic energy of her leg pump into forward motion, and she shot down the sidewalk. "Come on, Dexyyyyyyyy!" She had all her animatoos going, the animated images on her skin looping through their horror-story comic-book sequences; her short, translucent jacket was TV-receptive, randomly displaying whatever transmission was passing through her: just now, across her back, it was collaging a CNN image of an astronautics construction worker riding a maneuverer through the unfinished skeleton of the L5 colony, with a PBS shot of a medieval painting of Christ Ascending to Heaven. A spark of synchronicity.

As Marilyn receded down the street, her animated tattoos and the luminous blond of her Monroe wig and the shifting pictures on the TV jacket all ran together, blurred into one figure, a Pierrot made of restless media.

She's a McLuhan cut-out, Dexy thought, all reflective surface and no fucking character.

Marilyn did a wheelie, a pivot, pumped back up the street to him. "Come onnnnnn, Dexy!" Using her soft, husky Monroe voice. He was glad Zizz had run off; when Marilyn and Zizz got together, best buddies in giggling affection, it could ill you out.

Coming at him now, her image-squirming outline resolved once more into tattoos and jacket TV reception. On one side of her open jacket a frontal shot of the Boy Ayatollah preaching gravely into the camera; on the other, beyond the DMZ of her bare skin and her upturned, unnaturally perfect breasts, an animated political cartoon from the anarchist pirate radio transmissions showing two car-toonish infants—the Boy Ayatollah and the Reverend Baer, the Christian Fun General, reduced to sadistic infants, the two of them pulling the wings off of a screaming pigeon whose body was stenciled: NYC.

As she spun out to stop, Marilyn squeezed a tab on her belt, switching on the speakers miniaturized into the bikini under her skirt. The music was another kind of collage, a shaped-static band house-mixed with an old world-beat disco tune. The music boomed from the form-fitting speak-ers at her crotch. She made rhythmic thrusts with her hips into the crotch box's sonic vibrations. The way she did it, that kind of penetrating thrust, seemed male, to Dexy; that, and a wideness in her shoulders, the knobbiness of her knees, made Dexy wonder again if Marilyn used to be a boy. She was always a little exaggeratedly girlish in her pouti-ness, adorned with media imagery that might be a kind of stage magic distraction technique—all things Dexy associ-ated with queens. But if she was a transsexual, she was a damn good one. Must've had her Adam's apple reduced, face expertly reconstructed. Lots of hormone pills, too, for softness. He was never quite sure.

If he really wanted to know, he should bop her once. Having sex with her ought to clear up the issue. Not be-cause she wouldn't have a vagina—she might, by now—but because she'd have to use artificial lube, and her clitoris wouldn't look quite right. Unless maybe she could afford a clitoral transplant, like his Uncle Ernie had: the old fag had a clit transplanted into his throat.

"You want to scope the riot or what?" she asked him, tilt-ing her head just to make her glowing hair droop over an eye.

"You don't know there's a riot," Dexy said.

"There's always a riot when there's a blackout. Especially

over in Little Beirut."

"That's another thing, Marilyn. They don't call it Little Beirut because they've got maybe some Lebanese living there. You know? It's because of the fighting."

"I don' wanna go alone."

"I'm waiting for the *Surprise* to come on. I don't want to be in the middle of that kinda mess and have it hit me. I wanna get used to it."

"You took *Surprise*? Can I have some? I'll give you some speed."

"I only had one hit."

"Buhshit."

"It's true."

"Where'd you get it?"

"Fu."

"Fu? I'll bet he'll be at the riot. I'm stoked. Let's cruise. It'll hit you before we get there."

He looked at her. Wondering if he should tell her why he'd taken the stuff. What he was doing.

But even a brainjammer like Marilyn would probably take time out to lecture him. Give him the same shit his video therapist had come out with. How a decision about self-euthanasia is maybe not something that should be made under the influence of a drug. Suicide is serious, take your time before applying for that SSEU (his therapist stupidly not realizing Dexy would never use a State Self-Euthanasia Unit, he'd do it himself someway that, at least, had some *statement* about it). And how suicide's usually inadvisable anyway. Blah blah blah. Stating the obvious. Ignoring the fact that he couldn't find another way to make the decision. He'd tried for months. *Surprise* was all that remained. The only thing that could make up his mind. Or so Fu said. And Fu was the neighborhood shaman.

Surprise. The drug was supposed to talk to you. Tell you

things about yourself. Something like ibogaine or ketamine but more . . . cinematic. Less psychedelic. And the hallucinations didn't have a preceding buzz to warn you they were coming. They just slid themselves in with your ordinary perceptions. Hence the name.

"Who did the blackout this time?" he asked absently.

She shrugged, jumping the board up onto the curb and off again. "I heard on my battery box a buncha different claims. The Holy Islam seps took credit—"

"Fucking separatists are lunatics if they think they're going to have an independent Islamic state in the middle of New York—"

"—and the A-Team took credit—"

"Fucking anarchists—"

"—and the skinhead seps took credit."

"Fucking skinhead racist morons."

"I think it probably was the skinheads, they ain't scared of nothing. Too stupid to be."

He said, "Fuck it." And set off beside Marilyn, who was pumping the decal-patchy skateboard just enough to skate a few yards ahead of him, coasting to a stop, striking a pose, waiting till he passed her, pumping again, her movements synced to the world beat emanating from her crotch. . . .

He wondered vaguely if she were here at all. Maybe the *Surprise* had set in, he was hallucinating her and didn't know it. It could be like that, they said.

He'd heard stories about people taking *Surprise* and having no spectacular hallucinations at all. They hallucinate an old lady pushing a shopping cart in the supermall. A bit of trash in the gutter that wasn't really there: just an ordinary scrap of paper. Irrelevant, boring hallucinations. It depended on who you were, and what was significant in your subconscious, and how perceptive and imaginative you were. That's what Fu said.

So maybe she was a hallucination, he thought gloomily. I'm probably vapid enough to hallucinate my damn neighbor down the hall.

As she went by on the skateboard, he reached out and poked her—poked a cop firing a laser gun, in distorted TV image on her shoulder—and she weaved a bit on the board. "Hey!"

"Just wanted to see if I was hallucinating you."

She grinned, pleased. Misunderstanding. "Really? Jenny was saying my look was unreal today, too."

Dexy stopped, staring up the darkened street, listening, as sirens howled a few blocks west, then more sirens from the east and north.

Sounded like they were converging on something. Maybe on the riot in Little Beirut, maybe on some other blackout action. There'd be trigger-happy police and snipers, up ahead. . . .

What do I care about cops and snipers? he asked himself. I'm gonna be dead soon. Aren't I?

He looked around, expecting the *Surprise* to answer him with a vision. Nothing. Not yet, anyway.

Marilyn used her long, luminous yellow nails to pluck a drug patch from her skirt pocket, peeled the stickum paper off with her teeth, spat it out; the round, slick white paper curled on the street like something curling up to die. She stuck the drug patch up under her skirt, onto a thigh, and shivered as the DMSO carried amphetamine into her. Started chattering. "You feel stoned on that *Surprise* stuff?"

"Nope."

"Thas whus eerie about it, I heard, that you don't feel stoned an' you don't hallucinate for, like, twenty minutes at a time and then all of a sudden something hits you like a spiked dildo . . . and then it's just gone and for a while there's nothin'; and then . . . and then . . ." Her voice trailed off into a staccato chant that went with the crotch box's rhythm. "And then and then and *then.* And then and then and *then.* And then and then and *then.* And then and—" So forth.

The box was grinding out a groove, the singer was Johnny Paranoid, the lyrics were:

There's a truth you can't avoid
Listen to Johnny Paranoid
Life will end in the burning void
Shakin' shakin' shakin' like a
rock'n'roll chord . . .

Maybe that's a sign, Dexy thought. Maybe it's an aural hallucination. Life will end in the burning void. Go ahead and kill yourself.

Maybe the drug was making him more sensitive to synchronicity messages, too. Either way it was the same message: *"Do it."*

But he was a long way from being sure. He looked around at the street and murmured to the drug, "Show me."

Still nothing out of the ordinary. There were other people out now, talking in clusters, some with flashlights, some with rifles. Or heading in small groups toward the riot, the looting, the action they could all feel, somehow, calling from over there. . . .

Now the crotch box was playing another tune, "Six Kinds of Darkness," and Dexy thought he could feel the kinds of darkness draped around them, could feel the penumbral layers parting like spiderwebs across him as he strode down the sidewalk in his imitation-snakeskin cowboy boots. Six kinds of darkness and more. Darkness diffused by starlight and the squared-off galaxy of skyline glowing from uptown;

the inky darkness in the empty doorways; the striated darkness of the sewer grate; the pooling gray-black darkness as the street narrowed ahead; the raggedy darkness where the school burned with intermittent fires back down the street. The darkness of uncertainty.

Another gunshot from Delancey. And then two more.

He thought, Is this the kind of suicide I want? Hit by a stray bullet? He'd had something like a comfortable overdose in mind, or maybe blow himself up on the stage of some cheap club. Make it a performance-art piece. He'd fantasized about ripping off a car, hiring some of the Palestinian guys he knew over on Houston Street to rig it for him so he could drive a car bomb into some mob fascist's limo. Like the Yakuza/mafia scumbag who'd taken over Hard Disc CDs and dumped half the label's bands. Including Dexy's band. Blow that sucker up. Take him along to hell.

Just a fantasy. He knew that. Knew it was adolescent too. That's what happens when you're a thirty-nine-year-old rocker, you're an emotional adolescent in a middle-aged body. Embarrassing. No way he was ever going to get past it, either.

They reached a corner, turned left. Marilyn circling him now, looking him up and down. "You got a nice butt," she said.

"Shut up."

"Those Astaire pants are too loose, you should show your butt off with some tighter pants, Dexy. Did you kill that jacket yourself?"

"Oh, right, you bet. Like I'm going to go and hang out in Central Park with a rifle waiting to be eaten alive by a pack of wild dogs. I ain't that fucking desperate."

"You desperate about something, though, huh?"

"That's just an expression. Stop circling me like that, it's making me nervous."

"I'm not circling you . . . *Uh*-oh."

He looked at her, saw her smirk. "Very funny. Don't play with my head, pretend I'm hallucinating when I'm not. It's fucking dangerous."

She said something he couldn't make out under the boom of the crotch box. "What?"

"I said I'm sorry. Are you mad at me?"

"No." Like he even knew her well enough to get mad at her. They were just run-into-each-other-at-clubs acquaintances. See-each-other-in-the-hall-and-bitch-about-the-landlord acquaintances.

"You going to give up getting your band back together? I noticed you grew your hair out natural color. You should get a scalp-up, a dude like you, in his thirties . . ."

He winced. She went on, obliviously.

". . . a guy like you looks younger with a scalp-up."

"I don't care if I look younger or not." He didn't sound convincing, even to himself.

"No?" Marilyn looked away. Her luminous wig swinging a little off-center as she looked around. "Let's go this way." She picked up her board and added, "I think I can get us past the police blockade." She led him through a brick-strewn vacant lot. They risked an alley, walked up north a half block, turned left—the noise of the blackout riot growing like excitement in a boy watching his first porn video— and then they had to sidle through a trash-gummy space between two old tenements. And then . . .

Then they were in a party. Or a riot.

It was both. First the shouting, crashing sounds. Voices distorted by the cavelike echo of smashed-open store-fronts. They stepped out onto the sidewalk, saw the shadows that filled the shop-lined street boiling with action. The street was crowded and the crowd was street. Dexy made out the scene in flashbulb flashes from light sources that came and went. An erratic comet, zigzagging, was someone with a chem lantern running by, carrying a ripped-off virtual-reality set under his arm, running past a bunch of teenagers tug-of-warring back and forth, fighting over something he couldn't see.

A storefront window disgorged something rectangular and bulky: a sofa being pushed out a window. Flamelight from other storefronts. Fistfights, over there—and there. A chunky Hispanic mother scrambled after her three grade-school kids, shouting at them in Spanish, her eyes bright with fear, but no fear on the wide-open faces of the kids as they ran helter-skelter through the riot in unfettered delight.

The air was scratchy with smells of smoke, cigarettes, spilled beer, an acrid smell that might have been some kind of gunpowder. There was a stuttering series of detonations: strings of firecrackers going off, whoops and laughter from the people who'd set them; a small skyrocket arced up, trailing a confetti of fire. A group of people in a smashed-open adult-video store passed a hashpipe; someone threw a bottle at a window, *bonk;* it bounced off, but they tried again with a brick, *crash,* tinkle of shattered glass hitting the sidewalk; an angry shout, more firecracker bangs, louder than the first, in a storefront to the right . . .

. . . as Marilyn squealed happily, "This is so THRASHIN'! Let's STEAL something!"

. . . and Dexy realized that the detonations in the storefront weren't firecrackers, they were gunshots, maybe some underinsured shop proprietor was trying to protect his goods, and someone screamed and there was a string of muzzle flashes. Dexy backed away from the curb, feeling suddenly agoraphobic. Snipers turned up at these things, all manner of lunatics, and at some point the cops would get it together and move in, shooting first and not necessarily rubber bullets.

Dexy backed till he stopped against a brick wall. Looked around, trying to get a handle on this thing. Was it a faction riot? Christians rioting through Islamic holdings? Muslims looting the Christians? Maybe the Sikhs looting the Hindus . . .

But the crowd was mixed and so were the storefronts. Pizzerias, discount dives, a shop that dealt in luminous tattoos and bone-implant radios. The DEA's licensed recreational drugs kiosk—untouched because everyone knew there was no stock in it at night. A hairdresser's, a manicurist, and a scalp-up place offering: *New Scalp-Ups—Scalps painlessly remolded! The new Shaps are Hear!* A group of angstrockers stood with a black hooker in a doorway, passing a stem around, getting some serious Bic-thumb from smoking synthetic rock, arguing about whether or not they really got a hit that time. One of them, a short girl in Harley boots and a stained wild-dog skirt, her knees bruised and scarred from skateboard fighting, reached up into her scalp-up, fingered out a "bottle" with a couple more rocks of synthetic crack. Her scalp-up was molded on her hairless scalp—of transplanted cartilage and collagen and skin—into a three-dee sculpture of a really nasty car accident.

Just the usual neighborhood stuff.

The street was barricaded off at the corners, way down by the smashed Citibank ATM station on one side, and by the uptown R subway station on the other. Cars turned sideways, trash cans piled up, old oil barrels, heaped furniture, burning boxes. Police lights whirled beyond the barricade. Some sort of ominously brisk activity there. But not much. They were waiting for backup, Dexy guessed—there was too much going on, all over downtown. This was probably just one of half a dozen outbreaks. Maybe some shelling, too: He thought he heard the distant *CRUMP* of mortar fire.

In the middle of the street, in front of him, the crowd was thickening like a bee swarm, and most of them were dancing, a kind of rollicky, improvised carnival dance to a beat box. . . .

Marilyn's beat box. She was pumping in the thick of the riot, slamming to the beat box's thud. She's gonna get hurt out there.

A Hispanic guy with a sweat-sheened face, wearing a ripped spangled-paper jumpsuit, ran by on bare and bleeding feet, giggling, "Awright awright awright *noche partida.*" His testicles waggling like a dog's tongue out a rip in his jumpsuit. Guy looked happy as a fag priest french-kissing Jesus, Dexy thought.

Was the guy even there? Dexy wondered. Maybe there was only five people in the street and the rest was the *Surprise.*

No. This was real. So far.

He spotted Marilyn again. The crowd was clumping around her. Around the music booming from her crotch. Marilyn dancing, shaking libido in their faces, wallowing in the attention. Someone bringing out a steel drum, someone else a conga, adding salsa to the beat box's drumming, Hispanics and blacks salsa-dancing and skanking, sharing bottles and dust joints; someone rolling an oil barrel up, setting it on end, cramming it with crushed boxes and wood, squirting charcoal-lighter fluid, tossing in a match— WHUF! of flames blossoming over the rusty old can . . . And Marilyn was pressed by the crowd in toward the burning can—the dancers began to circle her—Marilyn dancing giddily on, a creature made of TV and moving tattoos overlapping indistinguishably in jittering firelight . . .

Stupid bitch is going to get hurt, Dexy thought.

And for some reason she was his responsibility. Or maybe she was his point of orientation. Whatever, he was

getting scared for her. It was as if she were some crystallization of his crisis, and it didn't matter at all that she was really no one to him.

He took a deep breath and started toward her, preparing
to plunge into the crowd. And saw Bunny García, Dexy's
old guitar player. That fuck-head. Bunny popping up out of
the crowd, in his open guerrilla jacket and black rubber
pants, Brazilian-made high-top skates, grinning, going,
"Hey, *qué pasa*, Ugly?" Doing some kind of new complicat-
ed handshake on Dexy's palm so fast he couldn't even feel
it. Bunny with his Marshall-Amp-with-a-screaming-skull-for-
a-speaker scalp-up, expensive animated tattoo on his chest
showing an eighteenth-century pirate crew looting and raping on a twenty-first-century yacht. He'd had the animatoo
for a year, though, and it was getting old fast; the anima-
tions beginning to flicker and fade. Couldn't afford to
change it now. Must've been cut off by his parents—his dad
was the biggest bookie in Spanish Harlem, owned this huge
kitschy house with gold wallpaper in Brooklyn Heights.
Bunny used to brag about his mob connections, which
turned out to be bullshit when the band needed them:
when they were hassled for payoff money so they could go
onstage at a mob-owned place called the Cat Club, and suddenly Bunny was whining, "Hey, I got to use those mob
favors for something important sometime, you know?"

So here was Bunny, now Bunny, the prima donna who
burned through solos faster than everyone else and
bragged about the pickups on his fingertips that were
installed at the guitar-surgery clinic like no one had ever
done that before; Bunny, who'd ditched him to join some
dweeb hip-hop rockoreography band. Here was Bunny, all
of a sudden acting like a deep comrade. "I don't have any
money and I don't have any drugs, Bunny," Dexy said.

"I don't want shit from you, man, except to say it's good

to see you, we oughta get a rage on sometime." Still grinning, doing that junkie rub with the back of his hand on his nose, the other hand in the pocket of his green Brazilian-guerrilla-fighter jacket—that jacket, an affectation if ever there was one, since Bunny'd shoot a hole in his foot if he ever picked up a gun.

"Yeah, right," Dexy said. twitching as somebody smashed a bottle on the street not far behind him. Someone else shot out an unlit street lamp. He looked around. "This shit's getting out of hand."

"Don't worry about it," Bunny said as the tumult went into third gear, the crowd noises beginning to really roar. Flames licking out from a third-story window across the street; red light rippling across a very short Asian guy humping a tall black woman in a doorway; she was squatting some so he could thrust up under her African skirt. Her bare breasts glittering with bead insets. The man's face straining with concentration, not wanting to miss out on this opportunity; the woman laughing hysterically. A group of children dragging a mattress, while another child, following them, tossed matches on it. The matches went out, but he kept trying. An old Italian woman in widow black with a looted fake-Tiffany lamp under one arm and a holo-set under the other, hurrying bent-backed through the thickening smoke. A couple of Iranian-looking dudes, submachine guns under their arms, on the other side of the crowd, just looking around. Marilyn still bobbing in the party midst, by the fire. People still crowding her, but she was keeping her head up, like she was treading water.

Sirens warbling from three or four directions, but no direct action from the cops here yet. How long could it last?

"Those Iranian guys, or Arabs or whatever they are, you see 'em, Bunny? Maybe that means they're gonna use this

275

opp, do a push. They start by shelling, mortars and RPGs and shit. I'm gonna get Marilyn, get the fuck out of here."

"Hey, I'm telling you, don't worry about it, man. You was always getting worried about shit—"

"That's the only reason we ever had a rehearsal or got a gig together, because I worried," Dexy snapped. "I hadn't, we'd never have done shit. You and Lunk'd sit around and play TV themes and smoke dope all day if I didn't worry and hassle you. We got two gold records, the only reason is because I worried. Those sessions were all worry, Bunny, and I was the only one who ever did any."

"That's mostly right, man, but that was because you was the one who loved the worrying, loved chewing your nails and pushing and nagging like a daddy. You fell into that role, see."

Dexy stared at him. It was amazing how well he could hear Bunny with all this noise going on. It was as if they were in a bell of glass, with the riot raging on around them but not touching them. The noise and bustle of it was there, but muted, distant.

"Hey, Bunny, you like playing in that rockoreo shit? doing those disco moves in that bourgeois uptown club? Those implants makin' you jump like that? I couldn't stand to be puppeted around by some fucking dance computer fucking with my nervous system. The music's already robot shit—"

"Of course I don' like it, man, what you think?" He scratched his crotch. "But Hemo wasn't happenin'. The band just wasn't happenin'."

"And you had a habit to support."

"Oh, yeah. Everybody's got something to support, Dexy. Or what? Everybody. You too. You got to pump up that big lead-singer ego of yours with lotta clothes you can't really afford. Parties. Where's your royalties money? You got into

276

some drugs too. Blue Mesc. You and Rickenharp used to get together, do Blue Mesc for two days and nights straight, then whine about it when you had to crash. Where's your money from those gold records, Dexy? Where's the money from that endorsement you did for that Soviet Microphone Company? What happened to that slick loft you used to have in Chelsea? You living in a dump down the hall from that hustler Marilyn, with roaches for roommates now." Smiling with an uncharacteristic gentleness all the time, as he said this. "Truth is, Dexy, we all stumbling around trying to get by the best we can. I was hurting and someone offered me a way out of the pain, that's all. To you it was disloyalty, or some shit. To me it was survival. For a while. My parents cut me off, wouldn't give me any more money after I got busted for dope. I got kicked out of that apartment I had in the old World Trade Center—did you see that place, after they made it into apartments? Huge honkin' old skyscrapers turned into apartments, I thought it was gonna be great, but I moved in and it was just another big shitty tenement, kept up as bad as any place in the Bronx. A slum in the sky. And pretty soon, I didn't even have that. I was just trying to get by, man."

Dexy shook his head in amazement. "You must be getting some good dope. I never heard this kinda speech from you."

"I talked to you, my way, but you never listened. You were too busy bitching. You got to stop blaming people for stuff. Your old man, for instance, how he never understood what an *artiste* you are; your girlfriend, who was supposed to stick with you even when you brought home a drippy dick from half the groupies in United Europe. She was supposed to just understand. And you get into diddly little fights with Kevin Keys about the band's musical direction. . . . Shit, Dex, you could've compromised, the man only wanted two tunes out of each set. Now you're getting some gray hair, you're slow coming out with lyric ideas, the record company drops you when sales nosedown, and you want to blame everybody else and take it out on us. Going to kill yourself to punish us. Get yourself on the cover of a magazine one last time. Shit."

"You killing yourself for years with dope, you should talk." Wondering, How did Bunny know about the suicide thing? Maybe Bunny had come over when he wasn't home, maybe he still had the key. Maybe he'd gotten nosy, played back Dexy's video therapy program. But, no, Dexy'd deliberately scrambled up the shrink program because he'd gotten pissed off about its advice; got drunk and programmed a rat's head onto the animated shrink and made everything it said come out in rodent squeaks.

"I *did* kill myself with dope, in fact," Bunny said offhandedly. "About two A.M., this morning. They haven't found my body yet. It was an accidental OD—I'm not a wimp like you."

Dexy's mouth dropped open. "You're—"

"*Surprise!*" Bunny said.

"—a hallucination. Or a ghost."

"A hallucination. But I did die. Or anyway, Bunny died."

Dexy felt a chill that seemed to shiver even in his hair and teeth and the tip of his tongue. "You're talking to me from the Other Side? I mean, there is life after death?"

"Oh, no. Well, I don't know. Bunny's talking to you from inside your own head. Bunny's a hallucination. But you're on the frequency where you can pick up on some things, is how you know that Bunny is dead." The hallucination talking about Bunny in the third person now.

The Bunny thing turned and looked at the place the Muslim guys had stood. They were gone. "They've decided to do a push through here, use the riot crowd for cover.

They going to expand territory."

"Oh, shit."

"Works out good. You stay here, Dex, you get killed. Go down in a riot: shot dead by militia, or by cops, pretty good rock'n'roll death, wouldn't you say?" The Bunny thing's face was changing. Sucking into itself. Skull pushing out through the skin, eyes becoming little glints in sunken sockets. Gums shriveling back, teeth exposed. The scalp-up sinking into itself, rotting off, ragged sections of yellow cranium showing through in patches. But he kept talking. More or less in the tone of voice Dexy's video-shrink used. "Remember that time, before the city was Balkanized, you lived in Chelsea? And you walked down to Houston one night and blundered right into the first Islamic Fun uprising. You couldn't believe it, your little downtown art and rock scene just irrelevant, silly-looking because these guys in cheap paramilitary outfits come running down the sidewalk like kids playing army, busting caps with those Kuwaiti carbines. They take part of the East Village and the whole of Soho hostage, all those pink-boy Soho art galleries and, like, neo-neoexpressionists an' shit, all of 'em suddenly under the gun? I remember an anarchist friend of mine laughing about it saying Yeah, now *that* is art! It was kind of cool, the Soho artists and the deputy mayor, all of 'em held hostage by the Islamic Funs—"

Dexy nodded. At the time, not so long ago, it had seemed outlandish, outrageous, bizarre, and scary as hell. They'd thought it would blow over any day. It just couldn't go on. But then the Islamic Funs started making demands, the Boy Ayatollah took over that little TV station, the choppers come in from the artificial islands where the Libyans were building up all that arsenal—it had just started unfolding like something totally out of control and it wasn't so funny anymore.

Thinking about this, Dexy watched the Bunny thing

becoming shorter, as if his legs were melting. His eyes had vanished completely now. His neck shrink-wrapped his upper spine; his clothes hung on him like his bones were a hanger. Dexy watched in horrified fascination. It was as if his metamorphosis was some anthropomorphic parody of the city's own transformation into Little Beirut.

The Christian Funs had come out of Queens, down from Upstate and Maine, with their private red-neck militia; the mayor looked the other way, even told the National Guard to let the ChrisFuns through the blockade. And then the sniping started, the mortar shelling. It was weird how fast you got used to seeing people killed. How some mindless social inertia could keep you in the crossfire while Christian Fundamentalists shoot at Islamic Fundamentalists and the MosFuns shoot back at the ChrisFuns. Photos on the front page of the *Post* showing a Black Muslim grade-school classroom after it was hit by a mortar shell. . . .

"Yeah, that was a key moment, that picture on the *Post,*" the hallucination was saying, reading his mind because it was his mind. "Remember that one? Those burst-open kids? Art my fucking ass. That's what turned people against the ChrisFuns, so they had to dig in, in their own part of town. Just when you think it can't get worse, *bang*. That's when there was all that serious shelling back and forth and the hostage thing gets worse and both sides block evacuation moves and backers airdrop supplies and ammo and nobody can get up the nerve to take responsibility for the political risk of sending in the National Guard or the marines or whoever . . ." Now his flesh was puffing out again, blowing up into a different person, a smaller person with a different face entirely. Fast-forward animation.

And the riot went on in the background, someone dumping a garbage can off a roof so it tumbled end over end, fell onto a group of people who screamed as it struck them; a bottle arced and smashed nearby. Flying bricks. Marilyn struggling now, trying to get out of the crowd, panicking. The music warping as some punk in the crowd ripped her crotch box from her. All of this some distant backdrop as the metamorphosing thing jabbered on, ". . . because if they did that, sent the army in here, there'd be a huge bloodbath, all this innocent bloodshed, so they spend months in negotiations, and the JDL gets involved in the fighting and the kid militias spring up and it gets worse, shooting on the street every day, everybody starts to get used to it, the black marketing spreads out, gangs like the Crips make deals with the factions and use the faction territories for hideouts. And here's Dexy, now, stuck in the middle of all this, because you can't afford to move. Partly because about the same time you lost your record deal. That's when it happens, right? So your cash flow dries up and here you are on the edge of the fighting. But, hell, that fits your rock'n'roll feelings about things, right, Dex, you *like* that action, right? Oh, sure. You're ready to rock till you're dead anyway because you're an *artiste,* you're *chosen* to incarnate That Energy, that's what you always believed—" There's nothing worse than a sarcastic hallucination.

The Bunny García thing was gone; the hallucination had become a boy. A fourteen-year-old brown-skinned boy in a turban. The Boy Ayatollah, the child Imam, looking both stern and cherubic. Both a familiar media figure and something exotic, in his black-and-red robe. "So, then, my friend," the Boy Ayatollah said. "What are you scared of? My people are coming here tonight, and many will die, and you can go down among them, in some kind of glory—what kind of glory is uncertain. But some kind. What are you, then, afraid of?"

Dexy's mouth was dry. He had trouble talking. But the kid was so earnest, he was talking right to the heart of him.

Dexy had to answer him. You couldn't lie to this kid. Finally, he said thickly, "I'm afraid of dying. But I'm afraid to go on the way I have been and just sort of shrivel up into just another shuffling old geezer, too. I feel like . . . like I'm not alive anymore because I can't do the thing, you know, the thing that . . . I don't know how to say it . . . The thing that made me feel like being alive meant something."

"Have a look around with me, won't you?"

The boy put his hand through the crook of Dexy's arm, strolled with him down the street along the edges of the crowd. It had thinned out some.

Dexy could no longer hear Marilyn's crotch box booming. They'd taken it. Maybe hurt her.

Then, *crunch, squeal.* As a police armored car with an earthmover-blade for a battering ram smashed through the barricade by the Citibank, whirling the watery-neon shine of its cherrytop beacon over the lizard-skin asphalt, cops in armor and heavy riot gear running behind it booming out unintelligible warnings with bullhorns, firing tear gas, the rioters scattering . . .

The Islamic Funs choosing the same moment to come pouring out of the subway station and the old burned-out Tad's Steakhouse from the other direction, probably not seeing the cops' push till too late, firing at anyone handy. Going for an expansion of territory in the Holy Name of Allah and in the glory of the Sacred Martyrdom of the Boy Ayatollah's precocious New Fundamentalism . . .

. . . Triggering the Christian Funs, who were financed and armed by the Birchers and the KKK, to open fire from the rooftops, chickenshit snipers, as usual, so that a few of the onrushing Fathers of the New Islamic American State went down, writhing. . . .

(Dexy wondering at his own fearlessness, here. It wasn't suicidal fearlessness—it was a sense that he was protected, surfing the Luck Plane. . . .)

"Now see them again," the Boy Ayatollah said, his voice, through the screaming and gun-shooting and sirening, coming with eerie lucidity. He waved his hand, and Dexy saw the gunmen and the rioters were not men and women any longer.

They were small children.

All of them: the Skinheads, Brownshirts for the Chris-Funs, dropping into the fray, now, from the fire escapes; the Islamic Funs darting down the street; the rioters and looters; the police coming from another direction. All of them were transformed—or revealed: they were children. The cops' battering vehicle was a toy thing of cheap plastic in bright primary colors, and there was a jolly clown's face painted on its earthmover-blade. The children who had been Christian Funs and Islamic Funs militia weren't playing army; they were frightened kids in costumes, running through a maze that wasn't quite there. Their play with guns was hysteria, crying and laughing at the same time, seven-year-olds with toy guns that killed like real guns. Children, all of them, children with a searching in their faces— all of them weeping, mouthing Mama, Daddy, all of them running someplace. . . . You could see they were running to some hypothetical shelter, trying to get past the other kids, driven through them as if they were running from something—yes, Dexy saw them clearly now: The children ran from flying apparitions of translucent violet plasma, etheric fiends screaming at them in hot pursuit; creatures that were all mouth and no eyes . . . the children trying to get away from the apparitions, firing at one another as they went . . . as the scene got darker, and darker and darker . . . the apparitions flowing down into the shadows . . . until the children alone remained, their guns vanished, just children blinded by darkness, flailing about, colliding sightlessly, stumbling at random this way and that.

The apparitions had melted down into long, attenuated cables of ectoplasm that interlinked the various groups, a network of the stuff, linking the children who were Christian Funs, other skeins linking children who were Islamic Funs; other nets linking the cops . . . The nets tangling, the tangles violence . . . The children mouthing something else now . . .

All of them saying the same thing, though they made no sound at all. Saying, Where are they? When will they come?

The Boy Ayatollah remarked, "They're waiting for the adults to find them, Dexy, to bring them out of the darkness, the permanent blackout of uncertainty." The Boy Ayatollah looked at him earnestly. "But, Dexy, *the adults never come. The adults never will come, my friend. The children are on their own forever."

"Oh, man. Don't say that." Dexy near tears.

"It's nothing to you, though. You're a rock star. A performer. A rock'n'roll hero. 'You're all just fucking peasants as far as I can see,' John Lennon said, long ago. You want to live fast, and die young, no? What is all this suffering to you?"

"Shut up. That's pure crap. Just shut up."

"You prefer one voice to two? It happens mine is fading anyway. . . ."

Surprise: the hallucination passed. The Boy Ayatollah was gone; the darkness eased, the full noise of the street roared down on Dexy like a runaway bus. And the children were transformed, magically matured, once more adult rioters, cops wrestling with them; other cops firing suppressive rounds at adult gunmen. Looters flattened on the street, crawling to avoid the gunfire. A couple dozen were fallen and wounded. Some of them dead.

But some were still quite active. Dexy saw two pasty-white

skinheads dragging Marilyn into a looted storefront.

Dexy told himself, You should run and help her.

A bullet spat asphalt near his foot, and he jumped back, the back of his head feeling soft. He ducked into the shelter of a darkened concrete doorway. The fear finally hitting him, now that the hallucination had passed, adrenaline whiplashing through him. Run. Cops hunkered behind the armored vehicle, moving past him, shouting warnings at the Islamic Funs who were backing off; the bullets still flying; the crack of another sniper rifle on the roof. Run. Get out of here. Back the way you came.

But the two guys were out of sight, now, in that storefront, hidden in there with Marilyn, doing something to her . . .

Shit.

Run, man, nothing you can do to help her.

But . . .

Forget it. Maybe you wouldn't get killed—maybe just suffer. Maybe a bullet to the spine, quadriplegia or something . . .

But, shit. Marilyn.

He grabbed a ten-inch piece of broken pipe from the sidewalk, ran across the street, behind the cops, sprinting toward the storefront. A bullet whined past, close enough he nearly wet his pants.

The storefront. A Korean grocery-import store. In the shifting red light from the cop car and the fires, the buttress sections of old grime-gray brick walls to either side of the storefront looked like squared-off pillars at the entrance to some ancient temple. The graffiti spray-painted over the buttresses seemed cryptic as the pagan glyphs of the temple's forgotten race. . . .

The drug hadn't completely worn off. He was just reaching the curb in front of the Korean storefront, hearing

Marilyn screaming something, when the second-story window above the storefront erupted outward, showering broken glass past the rusty fire escape. Dexy looked up and saw a cloud of spinning glass fragments falling toward him, glittering red in the hellish light. *Surprise:* the cloud of glass slowing, stopping in midair, floating there, was now a cloud of moths whose softly beating wings were of broken glass and whose faces belonged to demented angels. Showers of glass shards: silicon grace. He gaped at the hallucination . . . and the broken glass fell on his face.

He shrieked, *"Fuu-*ucccck," and dropped the pipe, clawed at his eyes. Felt splinters of glass like pin feathers on his cheeks. He thought, My eyes!

But he blinked . . . looked around. The glass had missed his eyes. He let out a long breath and, stomach quaking, plucked shards from his face. Too freaked to feel any pain yet. And again remembered Marilyn. (As behind him were screams, cracks and rattles of weapons, more sirens, laughter, someone pleading.)

He reached down to the pipe lying in the broken glass. Saw fragmented reflections of himself in the glass, jigsaw mirrors, lying around the pipe. Picked up the pipe. Saw the glass move by itself, the jigsaw parts coming together, fusing the pieces of his reflection. A kid. A lost kid. But someone was standing behind the kid. Himself: as an adult. Who put his hand on the kid's shoulder. The kid was Dexy at seven. The adult had come, after all.

Dexy was running into the Korean store then, flagrantly proud of himself for coming to Marilyn's rescue. Looking for the men who would be raping her.

There—in the light from a chem lantern, over in the corner, beyond overturned shelves tumbled with Korean ideogrammed packaged foods. There they were.

Dexy stopped, staring.

Marilyn was bending over the two men who'd dragged her in. Both guys were out cold, bleeding from head wounds. She still had the spike heels she'd used on them in her hands. She dropped the shoes, squatted beside them, legs awkwardly apart, barefoot still, like a little girl toying with a mud pie, singing something tunelessly as she poked through their pockets. All she came up with was a half-empty pack of THC syntharettes. She stuck them into the band of her skirt. Dexy noticed a half dozen synthetic-crack drug patches, the street-made kind shaped like iron cross-es, on her arms. "You shouldn't mix coke with meth," he heard himself say. "You shouldn't be taking any of that shit, anyway."

He stared at her as she turned, smiled loopily up at him. He felt foolishly disappointed when he realized he didn't need the pipe bludgeon. Odd, because he didn't really like fights. He tossed the pipe aside. Turned and looked out the broken storefront.

Looking at the fighting. Rioters running from cops, yelling they were ready to surrender but getting their heads busted in anyway. Skinheads and Christian militia fighting with Islamic Funs. He thought about what had nudged the Islamic Funs into taking over their sector: per-secution from city administration and landlords who wanted the immigrants moved out for real estate develop-ment—jingoistic legislation, too, restrictions on Muslim rights to build mosques that had come from an increas-ingly conservative government controlled by Christian Fun bigots. The Christians feeling pressured by a growing Islamic community; the Muslims threatened by the Christian reaction. This wasn't Little Beirut—this was the whole planet. This was Jews and Arabs, Sikhs and Hindus, Serbs, Croats and Bosnians, Communists and Capitalists. This was the way they all were.

In the face of that suffering, the pain of that societal autism, his petty priorities, the primacy of his career, seemed irrelevant. Pathetic, insignificant. So much self-indulgence. Particularly, suicide.

Dexy seeing again, for a flash moment, the confused children—children caught up, he saw now, in a desperate effort to find their way home by superimposing a purely arbitrary order on the chaos of an overwhelming uncertainty. Arbitrary ideological nets tangling, children strangled in the mesh.

Any mesh. Anything you artificially attached importance to. Some mesh of meaningless priorities that tangled you, choked you. Some arbitrary identity . . .

Like being a rock star. Just for example.

He went to Marilyn, reached out, grabbed her hand, pulled her to her feet. Squeezed her hand. She was real. Probably not a real girl, not originally, but he didn't care.

"You checkin' to see am I a hallucination again?"

He nodded. Realizing that a bubble had burst, somehow, a membrane had split: the drug had worn off. But it had spoken to him. Something, anyway, had spoken to him.

The gunshots were diminishing outside. People coughing from tear gas. Lights wheeling in his peripheral vision. Curls of smoke.

"I feel like I'm gonna be real, real sick," Marilyn said, slumping, clutching herself.

"I know where there's an anarchist clinic, they'll give you a shot to take you down. After that, you better stay away from drugs. They fuck up your priorities."

She bent over and threw up. He waited. Finally, she straightened up, spat a few times, and croaked, "Can we get outta here through the back?"

"I think so. Come on." He picked up the chem lantern, helped her clamber past the overturned shelves and

Korean produce. She was shaky, now. There was blood trickling from under her wig. They paused, and he peeled the wig off her and looked. It wasn't bad, just a scalp cut.

As they went out the back way, into the narrow walk space that led to the quiet of the next street over, she said, "This was a hot date. What you doing tomorrow night?"

"Resting up. So I can apply for a job with my head screwed on right. I was offered an A-and-R gig at Roadkill CDs. . . ."

"You giving up partying? Going to go real serious?"

He hesitated, then said, "Not really. I'm gonna have spare time. There's something we could do, just for fun, if you want. You know how to play an instrument?"

"No. But I can sing. Real good."

"Can you?" He smiled. "I can play bass. Good enough. Fuck it, then. Let's start a band. In my spare time. And *you* be the lead singer."

As they stepped out onto the sidewalk of an empty street he peeled the drug patches off her and tossed them away. The drug patches fell into the gutter and curled up like dead things.

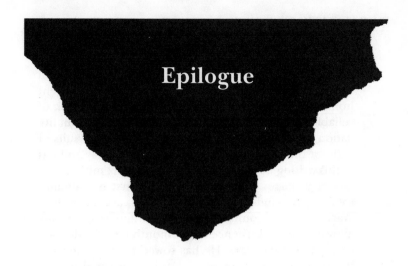

Epilogue

Youth is wholly experimental.
—ROBERT LOUIS STEVENSON

THE OTHER STORIES ARE IN chronological order. This one is out of order because . . .

Read it and you'll see. It's closure.

But I'm still recording. I was recently in a metal band called Children of the Night; it broke up. My band, now, is called The Panther Moderns. I can't seem to help myself.

While editing these stories and writing these intros I was listening to the following music: Metallica, Nine Inch Nails, The Cure, The Sisters of Mercy, The Charlatans UK, Iggy Pop (early to recent stuff), Blue Öyster Cult (early to recent), Mike Chocholak, The Call, Nitzer Ebb, Big Black, My Life With the Thrill Kill Kult, Radiohead, Rage Against the Machine, Pantera, Jesus and Mary Chain, The Young Gods, Henry Rollins, Terminal Power Company, Sixteen Horsepower, Lou Reed, Zappa, King Crimson, Thomas de Hartmann, Marilyn Manson, L7, Hole, Nick Cave, Coil, and The Panther Moderns.

EXCERPT FROM *Hustler—Madman or Missionary? The Strange Events at Mojave Stadium:*

"... shortly after being released on his own recognizance, one month after his admission to the minimum security prison in Sacramento, all charges of negligent homicide and manslaughter were dropped for lack of reliable evidence. This did not secure Dunbar from litigation, however. He did not try to fight the lawsuits of eight of the families of those who died that day and has at this writing been ordered to pay some six million dollars in damages. His profits from his first two albums, totalling two-and-a-half million dollars, according to a Warner Bros accountant, have gone almost entirely—allowing only subsistence wages monthly to Hustler—to help pay the damages. He has vowed to continue touring till he's paid them all ... And has learned to take over the lead 'guitar' role himself, after guitarist Jimmy Williamson was found dead of an overdose two months after the incident at the stadium. Hustler's first bass player has not turned up since the incident. Scientists to date are still trying to explain. . ."

THE CAVERNOUS AUDITORIUM blazed with lights, sizzled with crowd-energy, jewels surgically inset into fifty thousand living skulls glowed throughout the crowd—the jewels were emotion-indicators, translating feeling into intricately codified colors beaming faceted fury from between each pair of concealed eyes. Everyone in the agonyrock audience had a passion jewel . . . just as most members of that audience wore a chrome mirror-mask. Each face reflecting thousands of other masked faces, thousands of passion jewels, jewels within jewels and facets within facets, facial expressions jailed within mirrors . . .

EXCERPT FROM "The Hustler Cult" an article by Jerome-X:

"... Self-expression through electronic means became fashionable in the summer of 1998, when Oslo Barth perfected his 'Brain readout pulser' which he alleges

'Communicates, through my visual flash-code both
gross and simplistic emotions and subtle ones—for
those who know how to read the equipment properly—
and is also capable of expressing mundane desires and
business dealings. We have access to a special privacy
vital in this age of electronic surveillance and over-
crowding. We have the choice of expressing emotions or
not, and when we do express them we can learn,
through this medium, how to express them without the
chance of misinterpretation and misunderstanding . . .'
The mirror-masked pulsers utilized by Hustler fans are
said to symbolize the mirror-surface of the great bubble
over the stadium . . ."

STROBING GOLD FOR EXPECTANCY and anticipation, the thousands of jewels replicating, concert in a fly's eye. . . . The
holographs overhead, big as a building, seeming solid, fulsome in three-dee realism. Just now, the image was a come-
dy-holo, designed to curry the crowd's amused docility as it
waited for The Hustler. The crowd was a monstrous multi-
scaly creature, moody and irritable, a sleeping dragon of
fifty thousand limbs just waiting for an excuse to erupt into
riot—it crackled, as pleasure-bursts spangled its hide, elec-
trotitillation stoning the crowd into one-mind. . . . The
comedy holo was a moving, mammoth image of a man attempting to seduce a woman into taking off her mirror-
mask during sex—she slapped him, cracking his mirror so
that shards at its polarized eye-level drove into his eyes,
making him caper and pratfall: a scattering of the audience's passion jewels embered flashing blue for laughter,
the ends of their upraised metalmeshed fingers sparked for
applause.

But more and more passion jewels, like a demented
neon constellation flashing rudely for attention, burned
red for impatience and demand. The mood caught and
built into a frenzy, until fifty thousand mouths chanted into

fifty thousand personal audio amplifiers: HUSTLER PLAY NOW HUSTLER PLAY NOW HUSTLER PLAY NOW

And the stage went black.

Silence fell, a silence as ringingly profound as a suicide's horror when he realizes what he's done—

Hustler hit the stage. He bounced, thanks to a nulgravity field, somersaulted backwards, landed on his feet squarely and savagely, arms outspread and challenging. He was nearly nude, his genitalia seen clearly floating in a bubble of silvery oil.

His shoulders showed their veins, his neck pulsed with life. The audience raised its fifty thousand pairs of hands, applause-gauntlets shedding red and blue sparks into the air. Hustler wore a death's-head signet on either cheek of his mirror mask, above which were the black opaques concealing his eyes. The audience waited for the signatory moment . . .

. . . he reached up, put his fingers to his eyes . . .

. . . and as his passion jewel flared white for sexual triumph he tore the shields from his eyes, exposing them to everyone, anyone not too embarrassed to look. The holo, a gigantic re-creation of the Hustler moving second by second, showed his grey eyes vividly, luridly—naked *physical emotion* poured from them. An involuntary moan hissed from the crowd's personal amplifiers, They could scarcely believe it. He had done it for two nights in a row: exposed his eyes for everyone to *look* at. His real, *fleshly* eyes. An innovative performer indeed.

Couples, excited by The Hustler's emotional exhibitionism, began to copulate indiscriminately in the front rows, passion jewels flaring white, white and whiter.

Hustler waited as cybernetic attendants on hushed wheels rolled to and fro about him, affixing the long wire leads on his body. When the hemostatic pickups had been positioned, the machines rolled away; the audience waited in goldenflashing anticipation.

Hustler began: his music began as the geologic activity in the earth's infancy must have begun: with a volcanic roar.

Walker's drumming was there, joyfully timely.

Pained, exquisitely agonized, the audience clapped its gauntlets to its thousands of ears, writhing as the hurtfully loud roar resolved into an irresistible beat, the beat of the concealed biologic clock within us all, and The Hustler twitched out the first screaming leads . . .

. . . For you see, muscles make signals when they flex. These signals are very much like those registered by a guitar's amplifying pickups. Via a computer and a synthesizer each motion of the body (each organic secretion, tissue pulsation and fibrous straining) can be translated into sound. And Hustler knew how to make his body move into melodies . . .

He danced savagely, he moved spasmodically—his music was savage and spasmodic. Somehow, too, it was compelling, driving, viscerally seductive—somehow it captured every man and woman of the fifty thousand fixedly watching him and his holo . . . the holo portrait moving in rolling, thunderous turmoil overhead like a gathering of stormclouds shown in time-lapse. He moved with bullwhip elasticity, he moved like the needles on the Richter scales during the 'quake that took Los Angeles in '83. And the music came on like a palpable thing, like an army of rock'n'roll roar on the attack, bearing down on the white-light/white-heat center of consciousness that burns in secret fission within us all— Soundwaves move air, powerful-enough soundwaves can disintegrate concrete buildings. And they can shimmy human flesh and resonate the bone within that flesh like a cock roiling within its chosen orifice.

Passion jewels pulsed brighter and harsher, the glare nearly blinding the holo operator hidden in the auditorium's high metal rafters, near its shadow-shrouded ceiling. The Hustler, eyes flashing like twin passion jewels with raw biologic roar, danced like a battle flag snapping in a windstorm: the music literally pouring out of him, his hips the source of the drumbeat, his torso the bass, his facial expressions the keyboard sounds, his limbs thrashing out the lead—

Abruptly, there was a disturbance in the audience. The fifty thousand uniformly bouncing dancers were astonished by a discrepancy, an anomaly in their deliciously agonized midst. The group mind was united by regular pleasure-bursts and obsessive fixation on mounting rock'n'roll, the music a second-to-second matrix of energy linking mind-to-mind—so that each mind instantly became aware of what every other mind knew, and all knew of the anomaly in the instant when the nearest few discovered it. The anomaly was *one man*, a man who later became known as the open-faced dancer.

The open-faced dancer spun, leapt, winged, bounding impossibly high without the aid of a nulgrav field, his arms flailing in time with The Hustler's everpresent pounding bodybeat. The dancer was like a living manifestation of The Hustler's musical message—he was the avatar of The Hustler's charisma, And he was there, right there in the cyclone's eye of the great rippling Force that was the audience.

The Hustler watched the dancer, excited by the man's dynamic articulations of the Music. Hustler watched and danced and the agonyrock poured out to make the great Beast of fifty thousand thrash in the wake of its rhythmic passage, marking the timed compositions in the person of the open-faced dancer. The crowd had pulled back, itself still bounding, awed by the possessed dancer, giving him room for his glissandos, his twists and elemental self-wrackings. The Hustler and the open-faced dancer became more perfectly of one-mind, like two lasers fusing into one cutting beam.

And as everyone watched, entranced by the energy crackling, now viciously visible in blue-white arcs between the dancing performer and the performing dancer—

—the mysterious dancer, frenzied, smashed his fists into his shards over his limbs like a suit of lights. And now the only mask on his face, rawboned features very much like The Hustler's own, was a mask of blood streaming from wounds inflicted by the shards. The audience moaned at this exposed visage, and rampant coupling spread like a joyful disease through the great Organism that was the crowd.

And, something else—

The man, the open-faced dancer, began to ascend.

The attention of every man and woman of the fifty thousand was fixed on him, psychically welded in a great mental circuitry that somehow used The Hustler as a generator and the dancer as a transformer. Fifty thousand minds linked telekinetically to fix on The Hustler and the dancer. Both ascended into the air, apotheosized by levitation, with arms writhing like still-living pinioned dragonflies, glittering with mirror and blood. Hustler rose, trailing wires; the dancer lifted, streaming blood, both of them moving in strict descant, in loving counterpoint to one another and to the music that The Hustler's gyrations generated.

Greater the crowd's enthusiasm, hands sprang into the air and seemed to buoy the two levitators higher on an uplifting cloud of blue sparks from the applause gauntlets. Two sweatgleaming, mirror-blood-flickering writhers encompassed by The Hustler's own godsized translucent holograph, through which they were still dimly visible so that they became like manshaped organs in the giant's imaged body. Up and up ascending, in tandem spurts, each one seeming to compete to outdo the other in sheer height, in frenetic activity, the crowd suffused with wonder and hypnotized by racing sound. The Fifty Thousand urging the Two. Willing the Two higher, one and then the other, The Hustler overtopping the dancer, the dancer bobbing over The Hustler, until they were almost lost in the lofty shadows of the whalebelly auditorium's rafters—and then as the music achieved a shattering climax the open-faced dancer made a whimper—a whimper that was somehow amplified into a *bang*—and a final desperate effort:

He was rocketed straight up, carried on a furious wave of his own psychic determination and the crowd's willed sympathetic telekinesis, lifted straight and hard—

To smash into the ceiling with a forcefulness that pulverized him utterly, raining shreds of his flesh and a shower of blood onto the eager audience beneath.

The Hustler drifted gently, like a falling leaf, down to the stage, and retired to his dressing room.

Later, reflecting on the incident, he was quoted as saying: "I'm still alive because I never get high without knowing just how far the ceiling is above me."

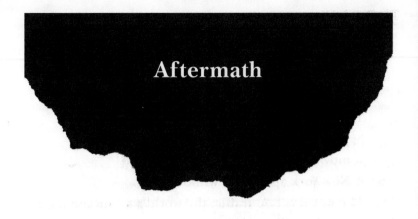

Aftermath

RIGHT AFTER I WROTE *The Exploded Heart,* I wrote *City Come A-Walkin'.* About that time in my life I was briefly locked in a small jail cell with thirteen shrieking transsexual junkie prostitutes and a stuffed toilet, and the transsexuals were all going cold turkey. They were all in disheveled drag, screeching at one another, and clutching themselves, and smearing their makeup, and accusing one another of trying to steal their bracelets, and—this is no shit—I heard one of them talk with icy satisfaction about having used a razor blade to kill a trick who tried to take his money back and I had been in there with them for about twenty-five hours and hadn't slept a wink and they were getting sicker and sicker from withdrawal and louder and shriller and meaner. They were white and black and Puerto Rican. They had all been hauled in at once because SFPD was doing some kind of sweep of the streets where they sold their muscular little asses. Never mind why *I* was in there too. It was bedlam, it was like being in one of those medieval torture scenes, where they sew you into a leather bag with live roosters and pigs and dogs and cats and then drop you in the river . . .

Next morning the cops let me out. I had the scene in the original version of *City Come A-Walkin'*—but the editor didn't believe it.

. . . got some spare pages, here're a few song lyrics I wrote for Blue Öyster Cult and The Panther Moderns . . .

You're the Reason

The world is like a thresher
Separating chaff from the wheat
A movie about slashers
A New York apartment without heat
The world is L.A. traffic; the world's a Chicago train
You never will outlast it;
   the world takes your name in vain
You're the only reason
To put up with this scene
Yo' the stroke of color, turns grey back into green
Yo' the vindication for the human world . . .
The world's a casting director;
   the world is in my face
My set is not erector
And we're soon gone without a trace
The world's a veg-o-matic
Slicin'-dicin' all our plans
The world is automatic
Its software is pure chance
You're the only reason to put up with this world
It's all on you, my girl
The world's a sink disposal
Any second they'll flip the switch
The world is too emotional
The world keeps losing all its pitch
You're the only reason
To put up with this world . . .

Found You in the Dark

It was late when I left the bar
Streetlight moths my roving stars
I was wondering about the women I met
Is it even worth getting what you get?
And then the blackout rolled over the town
A wave of darkness
Without a sound
I put out my hands, felt my way
Touched something sweet, and I heard you say
Found you, found you, stumbling in the dark
Nothing to see is nothing apart
Found you, found you, falling in the dark
Darkness in the world, glow in my heart
Found you, stumbling in the dark . . .

And the blackout set free their rage
A million people stormed to the stage
Breaking windows, breaking hidden chains
Blood in the streets, blood in the drains
In cement arteries we found our way
The valley of the shadow for those who need to pray
Stumbling in the darkness, arm in trembling arm
Find in our blindness, the secret urban charm . . .

(lyric fragment)

pretend I'm gone
It'll help you stay sane
pretend you're alone
in your lonely li'l brain
or admit that no matter
what you do, where you go
the one who left his mark on you
will be right along too
o look for me
in the light on broken glass
o look for me
in the stain on the sky
o look for me
in the gutterin' rain
in the gasoline rainbow
that's spinnin' the drain
look for me
in the blur aftermath
of some idiot auntie's
camera flash
look for me

I'm lookin' back
I'm lookin' back . . .

I'd Like to See You in Black

I'd like to see you in black
It makes me feel like your husband's dead
I'd like to see you in black
We could make him suffer instead
I'd like to see you in black
Love to see you in black

You can't lie to me, Ann
You can't pretend he isn't beating you up
I saw the marks of his hands
I saw your blood on your coffee cup
I'd like to see you in black
Love to see you in black

The wind plucks your black lace gown
You're standing calmly beside his grave
I see you there in black
Gently smiling and oh so brave
I'd like to see you in black
Love to see you in black

We'll run away to Greece
We'll walk in the ruins of the Parthenon
We'll drink ouzo in our coffee
Watch the dust billow till the light is gone
Like to see you in black
Love to see you in black
I'd *love* to see you in black

Nightmare Epiphany
(recorded by Blue Öyster Cult)

Dahlia floated
like chimney ash
up into
a shredded sky
it was raining
acidic trash
on the moon
there crawled a fly
Burning Pintos
were driving by
at their wheels
were drunken mimes
and from the darkness
there came a howling
and somehow
it called her down

    our nightmare
    our nightmare epiphany
    our bad dreams
    a nightmare epiphany
    nightmare epiphany

And she saw him
howling fury
as he struggled
with elastic chains
and his parents
smiled coldly
as they shackled
him down again
There were leeches
that were spiders
and spiders
that were flies
the very stones
who were his teachers
simply laughed
in mockery
Then sweet Dahlia
reached out to him
and she tried
to pull him free
but fallen angels
who ran the place
enfolded him
with monstrous glee

our nightmare
our nightmare epiphany
our bad dreams
a nightmare epiphany
nightmare epiphany

Then Dahlia woke
in clinging sheets
her fever broke
but the dream remained
she couldn't forget it
though a season passed
she wouldn't let it
slip away
and then she met him
down in the mall
on the edge
of the parking lot
it seems that
he went to her school
she was popular
and he was not
I remember
(he told her then)

I'll never forget
the dream of chains
you tried to help me
tried to descend
offered me something
besides my pain
now I've found you
in this concrete world
that only fools
believe is real
see, I knew that
you belonged to me
in my nightmare
epiphany

    our nightmare
    our nightmare epiphany
    our bad dreams
    a nightmare epiphany
    nightmare epiphany

The Horsemen Arrive
(recorded by Blue Öyster Cult)

Forgive me if
my laughter sounds cracked
Forgive me if
I smile bitterly
It's only that
I've run off the track
derailed by irony

All the false prophets
point at the horizon
dreaming of profits
in their vanity
and all around us
the pain and famine
a growing franchise
on insanity

    Can you hear the hooves
    Can you hear the riders coming?
    On Presidential roofs
    listen to their sinister drumming

They warn us of
Armageddon
They warn us of
Apocalypse

The future as
a fool's invention
of choking skies
and computer chips

The four horsemen
have already arrived
I see them above us, already here
the horsemen
with hooves like knives
I say again: *already here!*

(their names . . .)
This nightmare, civilization
This monster, industry
This devil, human corruption
This vampire, human greed

Can you hear the hooves
Can you hear the riders coming?
On Presidential roofs
listen to their sinister drumming

This nightmare, civilization
This monster, industry
This devil, human corruption
This vampire, human greed